"Just when you think there's nothing new to be done
with the serial-killer novel ..."
—**Ed Gorman,** *Mystery Scene*

The *Instinct* novels of Robert W. Walker

Killer Instinct

*The stunning debut of Dr. Jessica Coran, an FBI pathologist
tracking the blood-drinking "Vampire Killer" ...*

"Chilling and unflinching ... technical without being
heavy-handed, and brutal without glorifying violence or
murder."   —*Fort Lauderdale Sun-Sentinel*

Fatal Instinct

*Jessica Coran is summoned to New York City to find a
cunning, modern-day Jack the Ripper nicknamed
"The Claw" ...*

"A taut, dense thriller. An immensely entertaining novel
filled with surprises, clever twists, and wonderfully drawn
characters."   —*Daytona Beach News-Journal*

Primal Instinct

*No killer in Jessica Coran's past can compare to
Hawaii's relentless, psychotic "Trade Winds Killer" ...*

"A bone-chilling page-turner ... Every bit as exciting as
the chase is Coran's rigorous examination of the evidence."
—*Publishers Weekly*

"*Fatal Instinct* and *Killer Instinct* showed Walker at the
top of his form. With *Primal Instinct*, he has arrived. [It is]
a multilevel novel packed with detective work and an interesting look at the Hawaii that exists beyond beachfront
hotels."   —*Daytona Beach News-Journal*

Pure Instinct
The "Queen of Hearts" killer is stalking New Orleans. And the police commissioner has requested—by name— Dr. Jessica Coran...

"Walker takes you into a world of suspense, thrills, and psychological gamesmanship."
—Daytona Beach News-Journal

Darkest Instinct
In Florida, they call him the "Night Crawler." But when similar murders surface in London, Jessica Coran faces double jeopardy. One killer? Or two...?

And don't miss Robert W. Walker's new series of thrillers starring Native American police detective Lucas Stonecoat...

Cutting Edge
An on-line computer role-playing game leads Stonecoat and psychiatrist Meredyth Sanger into a literal Web of intrigue, murder, and mutilation...

EXTREME INSTINCT

ROBERT W. WALKER

JOVE BOOKS, NEW YORK

EXTREME INSTINCT

A Jove Book / published by arrangement with
the author

PRINTING HISTORY
Jove edition / January 1998

The Putnam Berkley World Wide Web site address is
http://www.berkley.com

ISBN: 0-515-12195-9

A JOVE BOOK®
Jove Books are published by The Berkley Publishing Group,
a member of Penguin Putnam Inc.,
200 Madison Avenue, New York, New York 10016.
JOVE and the "J" design are trademarks
belonging to Jove Publications, Inc.

PRINTED IN THE UNITED STATES OF AMERICA

10 9 8 7 6 5 4 3 2 1

Going to extremes in fiction isn't nearly so fearsome or exciting as doing so in real life. This novel of "extremes" is sincerely dedicated to my two beautiful sons, Stephen Robert Walker and Devlin Alexander Nigel Walker, both of whom are extreme only in the best possible meaning of the word. . . . And both of whom I sincerely love.

Acknowledgments

The author would like to thank the editors of *National Parks: The Magazine of the National Parks and Conservation Association.* I would also like to offer my gratitude for the *History of Hell*, by Alice K. Turner, and for the remarkable collection called *Death in Yellowstone: Accidents and Foolhardiness in the First National Park*, by historian and author Lee H. Whittlesey. A final thanks to authors Dominick J. DiMaio and Vincent J. M. DiMaio for *Forensic Pathology*. And of course a big thanks to Dante Alighieri.

EXTREME INSTINCT

· PROLOGUE ·

Yet when I hoped for good, evil came;
when I looked for light, then came darkness.
The changing inside me never stops.
                                        —Job 30:26, 27

June 11, 1997
Las Vegas at Dusk...

"You will ensnare her. Bring her to me." The Antichrist's voice kept repeating in Feydor Dorphmann's head.

Feydor imagined doing it, imagined trapping his victim, tying her on the bed, making the phone call, and igniting the victim's body with the gasoline and torch.

As crazy as it had all sounded when he had first heard the scheme, he knew now that it could be accomplished.

He also knew this was the time and the place.

With a convention of medical examiners in attendance here at the Grand Flamingo Hilton hotel, the challenge Satan posed for criminal investigators, and one in particular, meant that Evil would triumph as Evil always did in this world. Nothing Feydor could do now would stop cosmic forces beyond his ken.

Feydor had robbed a man at knifepoint two nights before. With the money he'd stolen, he had bought some clothes and had cleaned himself up to where he didn't recognize himself. He had also purchased all the necessary items, everything that his god had told him he would need.

With the Dark One whispering in his ear, Feydor had

his courage bolstered and engaged the young woman in small talk at the bar—talk of the weather, the hotel trappings, the news reports coming in over the TV at the back of the bar. When she left, he shadowed her out to the underground parking lot where she had bags to carry in. He pretended their meeting in the lot this second time was purely coincidental, and while she didn't believe it, she nodded when he offered to help with her bags.

She seemed most suspicious of him, yet she allowed him near her. Then he realized that with her keys outstretched, she meant to threaten him with a small canister of Mace attached to her car keys.

"Stay back," she warned. "I know that my father has sent you."

Feydor wondered if she meant that her father was Satan himself.

"Put your hands where I can see them," she commanded.

Instead, Feydor struck her with a sudden, vicious jab of a hypodermic needle into her shoulder, while simultaneously grabbing the hand holding the Mace, the stream going astray. She dropped to her knees, slumped against the car, her key ring with the tear gas attachment rattling against the concrete. She had buckled instantly when he jabbed the hypodermic—filled with a strong sedative—into her soft flesh. She yielded with a mere yelp, like a pinched dog. Her blood quickly absorbed the drug and sent it through her body, dizzying her brain.

Feydor felt an instant charge of power course through his body. He'd felt the same high when he had killed Dr. Stuart Wetherbine some months earlier back in San Francisco. Feydor's intentions were suddenly being realized. *Driven*, he told himself. *I am driven to carry through with this.*

Next he snatched all her bags from the trunk and replaced them with her now inert body. He stopped to stare at her pretty young face, the tender lines and contours, momentarily wondering who she belonged to, who she might be, but Satan yelled, "Stop that instantly!"

"Feydor! What are you doing here? What in God's name?" It was Dr. Wetherbine's voice, somehow here, all the way from the grave, Wetherbine's new home since the institute in California.

"What in God's name, indeed, Doctor," Feydor barked in reply. "I'm obeying my master." The gaunt Dorphmann spat out his words, "Satan is my god now, not you, Doctor."

"You are a fool. Satan will betray you. He betrays all of us, everyone. Give it up!"

"No! No, I give *you* up, Dr. Wetherbine. You!"

Feydor recalled how Wetherbine, with his owl eyes framed in horn-rimmed glasses and his face covered in gray beard, had followed him from his office that day, spying on him, interested in seeing if Feydor had stopped taking his medications. Wetherbine made a lousy detective, and Feydor knew he was being trailed. He led the doctor into an alleyway where Satan screamed in a fit of rage for Wetherbine's blood. Satan had gotten his wish when Feydor lifted the knife and brought it down sixteen times into Wetherbine's heart.

Ever since, however, Dr. Wetherbine continued to interfere, as now.

"You can go to Hell, Wetherbine," Feydor suggested, a slight grin finding its way to his sad countenance. "But I've got a way out . . . a way out. . . ." He pointed to the moaning, shaking figure of the girl in the trunk.

Feydor came back to himself, to this place and time, finding himself staring down at the girl's angelic face, framed as it was in short-cropped blond hair, her cream-colored complexion and freckles inviting to the touch. He reached down, caught a tear on his fingers, and tasted of its saltiness. She had wide, almond-shaped blue eyes held open by the sudden rush of the drug, seeing yet unseeing.

He closed out all light when he shut the trunk on her.

He then scooped up her keys, unlocked her car door, and tossed her baggage into the backseat, where he began searching through it all, scavenging.

He could hear her moaning through the car cushions.

Looking around, he saw no one; and no one saw him.

She had said that she was staying at the hotel, and he had located the room key in her purse. He would wait until dusk to get her up to her room, there to begin Satan's work.

Feydor lifted the dehydrated and drugged woman from the trunk of her car where he'd deposited her earlier. The heat of the Las Vegas sun had done much to debilitate the woman. Easily led, she felt like putty in his hands. Satan had been right. Feydor got the young woman to her feet. She represented nothing to him but a means to an end, a sacrifice to all the traitors who ever strode the earth. He knew little or nothing about his victim personally; and he hadn't learned much about her from her purse and luggage, only that she was staying at the hotel tonight with plans for leaving on a bus tour the following morning.

For six long years Feydor Dorphmann, now twenty-nine years of age, had tried to get help from any quarter; he told everyone who would listen all about the shadow people he saw in the irises of his eyes whenever he stared long into a mirror. He admitted to seeing drowning people in fire pots of seraphim wax or white mud that spat, spewed, and bubbled; he saw great, fanning fire pits vomiting forth cloud after continuous cloud of choking, eye-irritating sulfuric smoke: Acid smoke, his mind had named it.

Spectral as it all was, he nearly asphyxiated on the sulfur. His eyes burned and his ears bled with the silent screams the shadow people emitted. It was all so obvious to Feydor, but apparently invisible to everyone else. For he could see into the spectral world, and he could see the gaping, widening mouths pull apart with flames licking, turning their visages into molten wax.

There was a certain fascination about it all. In fact, he'd grown so accustomed to the spectral burnings of the wretched and damned that he felt certain he could carry through with Satan's wishes.

He certainly didn't want Satan pissed off at him.

At one time he readily told people about the visits from creatures not of this earth—grisly little beasts with human features and limbs that stuck like pitchforks from their gnarled, gnomelike bodies. Some a melding of human, animal, insect, and plant life, but all of these ugly little fellows came on their all-fours for only one reason: to keep an eye on Feydor, to keep track of his comings and goings, and to report back. And when Dorphmann told the doctors all about these insect and animal succubi—Satan's familiars, Hell's agents—the doctors had simply placed him into an earthly inferno, locking him away in an insane asylum where they pumped him full of drugs to dull the phantoms and the *phantasma-gloriosa*, as one young medical man had kiddingly termed his complex mental problem.

They had so enjoyed his case. They'd enjoyed experimenting with various psychoactive drugs on him in an attempt to cure his so-called severe hallucinatory and schizophrenic tendencies and problems—his fantastic fantasies and overwhelming fear of the Antichrist. But there'd only been one way to overcome his fear of the Dark One, and that was to agree with him.

The doctors had claimed he had fixated on the Antichrist, Satan himself, and that he had fixated on helping to combat Satan's enemies. Satan, known also as the Ruler of Wind, feared any assault on his godlike powers. In an attempt to protect himself and his rule, Satan used weak men, men like Feydor, or so Feydor had surmised around the psychobabble of his therapy.

Dr. Stuart Wetherbine had understood, up to a point.

He'd once told Feydor, "Yes . . . we know that people are sheep, that we are all such fools."

"Precisely," agreed Feydor.

Wetherbine had continued, "People in general haven't the slightest idea that should the Antichrist select any one of them, that they, too, could become Satan's tool, his instrument or plaything."

Feydor nodded vigorously, adding, "Satan's slave."

"So many naive among us who fail to understand that Satan is capable of overwhelming anyone he may choose, that 'there for the grace of God go I. . . .' "

It was then that Feydor's eyes grew to saucer size and he revealed, for the first time, the red brain thoughts firing his insides and coursing through his very being. He'd pronounced his truth in calm understatement, so as not to frighten Wetherbine, because at the time, Feydor had believed that perhaps he had finally found another human soul who might possibly understand. It was a requiem he repeated to Wetherbine three times before he realized that Stuart Wetherbine was just like all the others.

He'd told Wetherbine, "Satan feeds me filthy, crawly things to eat, and I become those things I consume, the things I eat. Satan scalds my mind, brands my brain, and while I am screaming, he . . . he adjusts me, rewires the circuitry so that I am now his puppet on a synaptic string. . . ."

Feydor had once been a practicing psychiatrist, before the Evil Wind began to whisper in his ear.

When the bastards at the mental institute weren't treating him like a highly interesting case or a piece of cardboard, they had treated him like a child. All the while they were pumping him with more drugs—and getting his drugged consent to go farther—until one day, suddenly, he was told to go home, to have a nice life . . . that he was cured so long as he remained on his medications. But this came only after long years of learning precisely how Feydor's doctors *wanted* him to behave, to duplicate the exact mannerisms and beliefs the white-coated army expected. His newfound behavior had worked, for when he began to do as they wanted, when he shut up about the horrors he saw behind his eyelids, they finally released him to a halfway house. Following this, he continued in Pavlovian fashion to tell them what they wanted to hear.

He learned to deny his own reality, learned to deny Satan and Satan's enormous revelations to him. The doctors wanted lies . . . that he knew neither Satan nor the ways of the Antichrist . . . so, he had given them lies that bespoke his healing.

Still, none of the pull and draw of Satan's grim gravity had ever truly been reduced, not a whit of it, which he learned for sure after taking his last pill for what his doctors called religious-linked psychosis nervosa. They said it was a psychotic condition that engendered hallucinations—in Feydor's case, hallucinations surrounding religious icons and beliefs—but that his condition also caused strong allergiclike reactions in the skin and orifices. This was their explanation for the red scaling of his skin, the purple-red palate, the red eyes, the pounding, pumping, burning blood in his ears.

Feydor Dorphmann and Dr. Wetherbine alone knew the true cause of the red. Where it came from, how it came to be, who and what brought it about, and that no amount of medical attention would ever, or could ever, eradicate the red.

The red filled his brain.

The red fed on his soul.

The red was forever with him, unless he made a deal with the Devil.

When he said yes to Satan, the scaly, itchy redness subsided, the heat below his skin, and the puffiness about his eyes, and the fire in his mouth scaled down to an acceptable, tolerable level. A kind of green glow engulfed his mind and staved off the red. And now he found it—the red—getting better since having abducted the girl, since doping her up and arranging for her cremation. . . .

What relief from his demons came, however little it might be, was welcomed, and he'd spread the green relief over his body like a balm. This relief was promised him if he'd follow his instinctual need to rid this world of what Satan considered necessary, and how better to do so than to do his bidding.

Satan talked to him in many voices, many tongues, acid and green, creamy and white, buttery and yellow, putrid and rancorous and bile-tasting in his mouth, burning pokers in his ears whenever the Antichrist became angry with him. Still, no matter how many voices there were, no matter how many disguises, still Feydor knew that all their voices and inflections and dialects channeled through one voice: the voice of his god, the voice of the Dark Angel, the ruler of storm and calamity.

No end to him. No end to his being. . . . Certainly no end to his being in Feydor Dorphmann's head, unless Feydor obeyed, faced the tests, conquered in the name of the Prince. Satan. Satan was without end. . . . No end to his pattering about the coiled recesses of Feydor's mind and intestines, playing havoc with Feydor's sanity and bodily functions down to his sexual requirements and ejaculations. No end to the wailing, the tolling of the bells, the cacophony of animal and bird and jungle bug noises in the inner ear, noises that were constantly nibbling away at his strength, sapping him of any resolve. He hadn't told Wetherbine or any of the other doctors the half of it.

He had attempted suicide, several times, but the Beast within wouldn't let him die. Suicide was not an option. The Beast needed him . . . or rather, needed Feydor's limbs, his eyes, his mouth, his body to go about in this realm of reality, on this plane of material existence. And so Feydor's body was chosen, and for a time Feydor had felt a surge of elation at having been a *chosen one*, an outpouring of pleasure in knowing that some supernatural being had selected Feydor Dorphmann to do its bidding.

After killing Stuart Wetherbine and finding Wetherbine's notebook in his breast pocket, Feydor realized that the doctor had understood more than any other man alive. Satan read Wetherbine's words over Feydor's shoulder that night. Then Feydor's headaches came, the nausea and vomiting, the sick, empty feeling in the gut and the tug to earth, as if all of the entire force of gravity was being focused on Feydor. Soon Feydor learned to detest his fate, detesting his lot in life, detesting the things that now lived inside him, but more importantly and beyond all detestation, he feared. He lived in constant fear. He feared when the Devil of devils, when Satan himself, came calling. And lately, he came often.

Wetherbine knew this much, but his counsel and his medications were no match for such supernatural powers.

In the end, the institute had put Feydor back on the street. Only Dr. Wetherbine had held out against approving his release, but the good doctor's objections held up matters for a mere month.

Feydor had seen a lot of television at the institute, particularly CNN, which he enjoyed. He enjoyed seeing the clear mark of Satan the world over, and what better place than on CNN—live? Disasters both natural and man-made abounded, murder was rampant, Satan was afoot.

The tube said it was so every day.

It was on the tube that he caught his first glimpse of the target Satan had set for him. Her name was appended to a degree, a medical degree: Dr. Jessica Coran, praised by the reporter interviewing her as the FBI's number one serial-killer catcher.

Feydor was no serial killer, nor would he ever be—not in the strictest sense of the word, he told himself—but now Feydor saw his mission clearly. And this felt good and right and correct; it felt like Satan's hand at work. That all these years of badgering Feydor had been for a reason, this reason had to do with Dr. Jessica Coran, for she, like

Wetherbine, knew too much about Satan's comings and goings, knew too much about his business.

For Feydor a whole new hope opened up. He now had a plan; finally, a way to end his misery, a way to leave this world on the even keel he had begun, a way to ante up and bow out with grace and dignity and perhaps escape Hades in the bargain. It was a plan posited in his brain by no mere hellion emissary this time, but by Satan himself; it was a plan Feydor had at once agreed upon, and it had brought him to Las Vegas to kill a young blond woman he didn't even know.

God must be forgiving of me, he thought, not daring say "God" aloud, *for if He understands that Satan is, after all, the breeder of all serial killers walking this world, that I am nothing, a mere vessel, a helpless conduit through which the master killer of all time has chosen to continue his awful work on Earth, then God must save a place for the likes of me. . . .*

Satan had come to Feydor, had selected him specifically to fulfill a task. It was Satan, and not Feydor Dorphmann, who had become fixated on this path of pending destruction of life, this murderous romp, and nothing and no one could dissuade Satan from his plans for the woman Satan most hated of all women in this dimension. How better to destroy her than through Feydor Dorphmann, Satan had said, whispering a coiling message that slithered through Feydor's brain and being.

Sometimes Satan took the form of a dense black shadow that lay over Feydor like a heavy blanket; other times Satan existed as a mere milky cloud, sometimes a mad, slavering hound, sometimes a horned goat, an eyeless bat, an enormous spider larger than Dorphmann himself, sitting in the corner of a ceiling. More often of late, he came as a hunched-over, horned gargoyle sitting squarely atop Feydor's chest whenever he tried to sleep, sucking in Feydor's breath while the helpless mortal lay there exhaling.

Still other times, the Devil came as a solid black cube

turning on an axis directly between Dorphmann's eyes, square in the middle of his forehead, boring into his brain, a black inkblot, threatening to turn his mind to ink and infinite pain as well. The Beast would churn up the headaches, the ringing in Feydor's ears, making it a constant, hateful, debilitating irritation, threatening to explode inside Feydor's brain.

Then came the red. Satan turned his skin red—the redness and fire bubbling with boils just below the epidermis, staining his skin a poker-hot crimson. The Monster added scales and hair and itchiness—the itchiness of invisible roaches or locusts crawling the length and breadth of Feydor's tortured body—but then, it wasn't completely Feydor's body anymore, now, was it?

Wetherbine had understood that much. . . .

Satan sometimes came in the form of small insects or animals, staying outside Dorphmann's body, surrounding him like an army before a citadel. The siege might last for hours, a day, two days, their million beady eyes all trained on him, all like hissing black marbles, hissing a warning, all just watching him, studying him and his movements.

When he left his place, stepped out onto the sidewalk and walked down the street, there in San Francisco, going among other people, the insect army crawling over his body clung to him, shadowed him, but their spectral nature made them invisible to all others, so that when he lashed out at the insects, just to brush them from his brow, eyelashes, and mouth, people stared at him as if he were the Hunchback of Notre Dame. It was the constant vigilance of Satan's army of insect eyes that had broken Feydor. The way they moved everywhere with him, riding on him, in the folds of his skin, his pockets, in the cuffs of his pants. But now that had all changed since the moment Feydor had accepted Satan, the moment he had agreed to become Satan's hammer and breath in this world, the moment he had killed Wetherbine.

Feydor recalled it vividly, how Wetherbine pleaded,

saying, "No, Feydor! You can't succumb!"

That was when Feydor's hidden knife came flashing down, driven by the force of Satan.

Sometimes the Devil came in the form of wind—sometimes a subtle wind that whispered through Dorphmann's soul; other times an angry storm—and sometimes in the form of an old hag in the middle of the night, and the old crone would wave a wand, and at the end of this wand trailing silver glitter, Feydor could see the souls of the damned, dangling as if on the head of a pin, all blazing in the inferno, all filled with excruciating, everlasting scalding, never-ending pain, swishing about in a soupy fire there at the end of the witch's wand. Then one of the old woman's eyes would literally leave its socket, wrench free of her head, and come straight down into his throat, her huge eye becoming his, so that he could see into his own frail insides, into Satan's invisible world of the dead, into the spirits of the everlasting cauldron called Hell, which was depicted as a cosmic stomach down through which they must journey.

It was a place he did not want to see or to visit, but the witch took him there often, and without speaking a word. The place made him tremble; he knew that this was his fate unless he could deliver up to Satan a far more suitable subject, one that Satan himself had made a worthwhile, chosen substitute. A woman named Coran, Dr. Jessica Coran. . . .

"But I gave you Wetherbine," he'd pleaded.

"I don't care about Wetherbine. I want Coran," Satan declared.

The moment Feydor pushed open the door to room 1713, he felt a sudden surge of control. He was now in control. It was a feeling that had eluded him now for so many years.

It was the right time, the right place.

· ONE ·

Scream like the devil's baby.
—ANONYMOUS

"Says here Nevada's the seventh-largest state in the union," John Thorpe told Jessica Coran, reading from his guidebook in an attempt to bring her from her doldrums. "Yet it has one of the smallest populations."

The cab they were in almost hit another, their driver shouting an obscenity and blowing his horn, all for naught. Jessica imagined that half an hour from the clutter and clatter of downtown Vegas, all she might hear would be a desert wind howling across the uninhabited red earth, playing the sagebrush like so many lilting harps. She was wishing to be there, maybe in a Jeep, exploring the vast and strange and otherworldly wasteland of the arid West. Such a lark had to beat hell out of the casinos and the proposed series of dull talks on forensic medicine. If she wanted to return home with any lasting memories—she'd been told by those in the know that the real Nevada had nothing to do with the unreal surreal called Vegas—she'd take Warren Bishop up on his offer, and she'd escape Vegas for the surrounding mountains. However, ditching J. T. could prove hard, and she didn't want her friend's feelings hurt when she did it to him. So she'd told J. T. nothing and decided to bide her time; when the time was right . . . maybe . . .

Warren Bishop knew the terrain, and she had always felt secure and safe in their friendship, which had, off and on, flirted with something more serious than just friends. Warren had been one of her training officers at Quantico when she'd first become an agent. He was a man who subtly got his way by making a recruit believe she was doing precisely what she, not he, wanted. He had a gift as a teacher, and no one knew firearms like Warren Bishop. Four years ago, he'd been offered any branch field office in the country, and he had chosen Vegas for reasons still unclear to her. He wasn't a big gambler, but he had fallen in love with the area, and he kept a wide collection of Wild West and American Indian paraphernalia, including old guns. She'd been looking forward to seeing Warren and rekindling their friendship. But a quick call from the airport to the Vegas FBI branch office told her that Bishop had been unexpectedly called out of town, so she was now nursing a funk that poor J. T. hadn't a clue about.

"Population 1,201,800, it says here," J. T. continued, "but they say Vegas is growing by leaps and bounds, the fastest-growing city in America, a Mecca for jobs. Capital is—"

"Carson City, I know. Minimum age for casino gambling is twenty-one, driving sixteen."

The cab ride was hot and jostling and bone-jarring, the machine obviously in need of new shocks, and the Nevada heat created an ovenlike atmosphere, making Jessica Coran wish that she had the natural protection God gave an armadillo. With her natural defenses up, she actually felt armored and apart from all that was going on around her, felt like an armored knight in woolen underwear riding a cantankerous horse, in fact. It had been a long and difficult flight on the Delta jetliner, due in large part to the scarcity of legroom. They'd booked late, failing any chance at first class, both she and J. T. not sure until the last minute that they wanted to attend this year's function.

"Las Vegas, Nevada, of all the damned places on the

continent. Why is the most prestigious forensic medical group in the country meeting here?'' Jessica grumbled to hear herself, adding for the driver's benefit, ''You ever hear of air-conditioning? Crank that thing up.''

''I am so sorry, ma'am,'' the man replied in his most polite, most condescending tone, ''but it needs repair, and I'm putting three *niños* through school, and my wife . . . she is on disability.''

This made Jessica frown and close her eyes. Beside her, J. T., whose lopsided, boyish grin leaped ahead of his reply, said, ''If you'll just temper that cool, critical eye with a bit of patience, Jess, we're almost there. After a change, you're going to love Vegas. Wait'll you get a look at the Luxor and the Excalibur and the MGM Grand hotels. You'll see Vegas is more than a collection of casinos along a strip, believe me.''

Although J. T. was in his early forties, his dark hair, smooth skin, and energetic step, along with a quick, alert eye and a great sense of humor as well as a questioning, probing mind, were all qualities that made him seem younger; Jessica liked these qualities in her friend and colleague. Together, they had made a ''mean team'' for the FBI over the years. J. T. was her ever-faithful friend and collaborator against some of America's most horrific criminals. As a result, they had shared information, experience, and sometimes nightmares regarding such killers as Mad Matthew Matisak, Robert Kowona, the Hawaiian maniac, the Florida Night Crawler, the Claw of New York, and the New Orleans Queen of Hearts killer.

It had been at J. T.'s insistence that she had agreed to accompany him to the annual Forensic Science Association of America convention, ostensibly to seek out some much-needed R and R for both of them. J. T. had been ecstatic at the idea of seeing Las Vegas again, having visited a few years before with his then wife, whom he'd since divorced.

''Some of my best memories are of this city,'' he'd confided earlier on the plane as they circled the city in search of clearance from the tower. "My dad used to fly us out here at least once every few years."

She had replied that her best memories were of Greece and Rome. The recent separation from her lover, James Parry, still felt like a barrage to her soul; she'd been unable to get him from her mind. Her depression over her and Jim's situation hovered over every thought like an albatross, for when Jim had once again left her for his homeland of Hawaii and his duties there, she had vowed to find a way for them to be together, but the way had not materialized. . . .

Here in the limo, J. T. reached over, took her hand in his, and squeezed it; he gave her hand a firm little shake and pointed out the back window at a cowboy on a horse riding down one of the main thoroughfares, adding to the congestion of bumper-to-bumper traffic. "There's one cowboy's got the right idea," he chimed, his voice firing off sparkles of enthusiasm for this Mecca on the desert floor.

Outside, in the blistering heat, construction sites all around them sent up strange, ghostlike clouds rising with the gusting, late-afternoon wind, each creating whirling dervishes of candy wrappers and discarded plastic bags and other debris. This would be trailed after by another, less encumbered, yellow dustbowl-like apparition made of sand and wind, yet the wind had no effect on the heat, except to slam it about.

"Come on, Jess. You'll have fun; maybe it'll get your mind off Parry and—"

"Leave Parry out of this," she sternly scolded, her eyes dimming.

"—and your other problems," he weakly finished. "Hell, cut loose a little, seize the moment, look around you! This place is a glitter dome at night! That's your problem. You haven't really experienced Vegas till you've experienced it by night, dinner clubs, shows, Broadway-

style revues, dancing. You've got to give it a chance . . .
loosen up. . . ."

"Maybe I'll do that," she challenged, staring out at the
dust-laden streets of Las Vegas, across which desert sand
continued to sweep from the multiple construction sites of
this modern desert boomtown.

Odd, Jessica thought, how this place was growing both
upward and outward: newer, taller, grander, gaudier casinos, show houses, hotels, and circuses being built in a city
already overcrowded with so many casinos and lavish ex-
travaganzas of one sort or another. There seemed no possible space nor need for another in this mechanized,
industrialized contrivance of a holy temple to which the
human race paid homage in the form of coin.

But Jessica's primary thoughts wafted across her own
shabby life. She was sick to death at having had to part
from James Parry again. Their time together in the Medi-
terranean had been exquisite, but far too brief. They had
talked for days about how they could work out the thorny
problems of their long-distance love affair, but very little
had been resolved. Rather, they were more deeply in love
than ever and just as far apart as ever—he in Hawaii, she
in D.C.

Two people couldn't get much farther apart than that,
and Jessica, of late, had come reluctantly, onerously to the
conclusion that she would never marry; and more sadly,
more impaling to her heart, she had come around to accepting the fact that life, and whatever forces attended her
fate, had never intended her to ever have children.

It was a conclusion that, though necessary to reach, to
put behind her, remained no less painful for its finality. It
was what her friend and favorite psychiatrist, Dr. Donna
Lemonte, would term a not atypical female reaction to an
expected and even instinctive event—having children. Almost every woman's inner soul and drive allowed for that
tugging refrain of the womb, a refrain that had come down
through the ages, paradoxically or not, genetic predispo-

sition or not, that told a woman she was incomplete until
she fulfilled the circle of life that she—created as she was,
with the requisite equipment—was so much a part of. Jessica knew such thoughts were offensive to some women
who proclaimed they need not have children to be whole,
but for her and she imagined most, these thoughts were as
natural as tears. You're born to give birth, from life comes
birth; you can't dispute the fact that it's in you to do so,
that you are equipped to conceive, incubate, nurture, and
feed a growing life within you. You're ''bred'' to believe
it's part of your identity to have children, you're raised on
the belief. So, naturally, most if not all women either had
to have children or confront the phantom child they failed
to bring from within: face down the guilt and remorse and
move on in an atmosphere of acceptance or be eaten alive
by the penitence of regret.

Religious leaders and theologians claimed that while it
was a powerful and painful process, guilt was a good, natural instinct, without which mankind would have nothing
to clutch on to in times of darkness and loss. There was
the belief that it was one's own fault somehow when a
loved one committed suicide, or that the loss of a family
member to a fire or cancer or to some other disease was
due to a punishment meted out by a god one had somehow
wronged over a lifetime. It all seemed somewhat foolish
to Jessica, knowing as she did that disease and suicidal
tendencies and fire had scientific causes, that they were
actually more natural in nature and in the species than was
guilt. But in a larger, social sense, maybe the theologians
were right.

Sure, science and technology outstripped human evo-
lution, human growth potential, the brain, socialization, education, racism, prejudice, leaving cavemen with
cave-dwelling beliefs and notions while allowing them
easy access to automatic weapons, drugs and poisons, the
information to make a bomb from items below his kitchen
cabinet; but hey, so long as there remained guilt and re-

morse, what did it matter? Perhaps the theologians did know more about the heart and the soul of mankind than science could ever know. Without feelings of sin and remorse and guilt, we'd all be killers, she thought. And maybe if some of the serial killers she'd trapped and put away and destroyed over the years had harbored any sense of guilt whatsoever, they'd have controlled their psychotic fantasies and ended their mind-made killings before acting on such murderous desires.

Perhaps if such sociopaths could be injected with a hormone called guilt, they couldn't play the psychological games they played with authorities to please their blood-thirsty demons and gods. The worst kind of killer, a sociopath, lived without remorse and without guilt or guile or empathy or conscience. What manner of being was this to be created in God's image? Would science come to the answer somewhere along the DNA double helix before theology found an answer? Would there come a day when science could be tapped into to supply the guiltless with a dose of guilt, remorse, grief, caring, love?

Here in the bumpy cab—which the driver dared call a Vegas limo service—Jessica wondered about the old phrase, ''Religion is the opiate of the people.'' But certainly not all people; some appeared to require a more potent opiate. Men like Tauman, the Night Crawler of Florida. Men who relished torturing their victims required serious behavior modification if they were ever to feel the pain of their victims. Religion hardly amounted to a conscience. . . . In fact, some of the thrill-seeking, feel-something-anything murderers she had known claimed to have killed in the name of religion, usually a religion with a following of one. And, of course, Jesus Christ remained the number one cause of death among the dying who'd left this world ''in the name of Christianity. . . .''

Jessica was brought back to her present discomfort by a news report over the limo's scratchy radio, something about the recessing U.S. Senate. No surprise, she thought.

The Senate was always out to lunch or recess. It took great reserves of talented men and women to catch elusive serial killers, to bring such monsters into the light of justice; but try to tell that to a Senate investigation committee looking into slashing the FBI's budget.

When their airport curbside limo came to a stop at the light, J. T. pointed out the famous Luxor Hotel and extravaganza. The lingering Nevada sun sent shards of light against its black glass surface, only to create an impenetrable image. Fascinating, more so than any of the steel and glass temples erected to the sky and the almighty dollar, its unusual size and pyramidal shape made it a marvel of human accomplishment and construction. It was the pyramid at Giza replanted here in the American desert. It was a stunning modern-day answer to the Egyptian pyramids, this answer to any of Hollywood's infamous, big-screen Babylons.

Like Vegas itself, it made for a stifling whore, this symbol of how far wealth and power were willing to go for the sake of more wealth and power. Audacious, grand beyond scale, and as gaudy and garish as all of convention-central Las Vegas's megacasinos combined. Like all of Vegas, the Luxor combined gargantuan themes and dreams of "epic" proportion with a crude commercialism possible only in America, a place where one casino's take in nickels alone on any given day might feed some Third World countries for a year.

But all J. T. saw was the grandeur of this architectural marvel, and all he could say was, "See what I mean? The city's desperate for a new image as a family-friendly place."

She cynically nodded and replied, "Yeah ... sure ... And what kind of conference can we have, J. T., surrounded as we are on all sides by ... by so much ... temptation?"

"You, tempted?"

"No, not me ... everyone else."

"Oh, I see . . . everyone else. You're worried about everyone else . . . everyone but you." He laughed and ran a hand through his thick mat of dark hair.

She frowned at his response. "What's so funny?"

"Jess, do you really think you're immune to gambling?"

"I do and I am. . . ."

"So, you're just worried about everyone else in the forensic science community being able to abstain?"

"Think about it, John," she quickly replied. She only called him John when she felt annoyed. "Adewah, Repasi, MacEachern . . . Sloan, Slaughter, Oleander, for that matter . . ."

He pictured each of these infamous medical examiners in turn.

She continued, "They take out bets on which one will find the most unusual and unique stomach contents on a victim in six different categories, E-mailing each other weekly to compare findings, so just imagine them surrounded by slot machines."

Again J. T. laughed. "So, big deal. We do the same to ease tensions in the lab . . . which wound on a stabbing victim will be the first fatal blow, whether a time of death will or will not turn an acquittal into a guilty verdict. Whether a young attending female student will find me attractive or not. . . ."

"Big wooooo!" Now she laughed in response. "Still, if everyone's at the gambling tables and the bandit boxes, how're the brightest minds in the forensic world ever to come to any consensus about our bylaws, current issues with regard to the witness box, the latest in DNA findings, serious matters of ethics, legislative issues, and—"

"That's your problem, Doctor."

She halted, her eyebrows lifting like birds on the wing. "What's my problem, Dr. Thorpe?"

"Too damned serious for your own damned good at

times, Jessica Coran. Life's short. When do you intend to find time to enjoy yourself, your life?''

''Hey, I had a great time in Athens and Rome with Jim, and now I'm back. I have plenty of fun . . . plenty . . .''

''And if Parry hadn't flown down to the Caymans to find you with those two tickets in his fist?''

Her eyes widened. ''I'll be damned. You put him up to it, didn't you?''

''No, no . . . no,'' he denied, his eyes darting, searching for someplace to light, a pair of confused birds let out of a cage. He wondered how he'd gotten himself into this cage.

''And here I thought it was all Jim's idea. Didn't I tell you not to go playing Cupid? You're not that cute . . . although since putting on a few, you do have a cherubic quality about you.''

J. T., pleased he was only mildly scolded, instantly defended his weight, saying, ''For a man my age, thirty-nine next month''—he lied about his age—''it's not so bad, or so I'm told by my trainer. Axel always says—''

''Axel?'' She stifled a laugh.

''Yeah. Axel always says, 'It's good to have a little to *burn*. . . .' ''

''I'll just bet good ol' Axel says that. And just what burner are you working on?'' she continued to tease.

He was glad that she had been pleased down in the Caymans when she had reached out and found Jim Parry appearing from nowhere while she, like some real-life Perilous Pauline, had hung suspended over a bevy of hungry, blood-sniffing sharks. Parry had literally saved her from death in the waters off Grand Cayman, a surprise that had been totally unexpected. Then he whisked her off to Athens, where they remained for a week, followed by a second week, in Rome. And for a time, J. T. believed Jessica Coran would never return to D.C., and sometimes he still wondered why she had.

''As for me, when it comes to a gamble,'' she was say-

ing now, uselessly pointing in the direction of the Flamingo Hilton, fearing the driver was taking a circuitous
route, "I can take it or leave it."

"Who's a bigger gambler than you? You gambled and
won against Matisak in New Orleans, and you did the same
with Tauman in the Caymans. Take it or leave what?"
Then he wondered if she had meant Parry and paradise,
feeling a bit awkward at putting his foot in it.

"Gambling, gambling, and this Mecca for gamblers and
people who crave to throw their fortunes, big and small,
down the most extravagant 'come on' toilet the world and
history has ever seen—that's what I'm talking about."

"Ahhh, come on, Jess. There's got to be some redeem-
ing factor about Vegas. Every city has some . . . upside."

"Well, there is plenty of—"

"Neon?"

"Parking," she finished.

Jessica was well aware that the low-lying metropolis,
nestled as it was on the desert floor, represented the fastest-
growing city in America and that its growth had changed
its character over the years. However, she firmly believed
that all character began with a bedrock that remained in-
transigent and unchangeable. A city openly spawned on
corruption and greed could not deny its roots or heritage
by raising temples to the sky, even if they held "family"
attractions within. The central root upon which it all flourished remained human fallibility, greed, and feeding off
that greed. Sure, the limbs of the tree had sprawled far and
wide from its core—downtown Vegas being the hub from
which architects and city planners worked—but there was
scarcely a household on the desert floor left untouched by
money had from gambling in one fashion or another.

Absolutely, Vegas brimmed full with good and decent
people—families eking out a living, children struggling in
schools at all levels, playhouses, cultural events, museums,
and small pleasures that on the surface appeared to have
nothing whatever to do with downtown Vegas or gam-

bling, but then, no place in the city was immune. The entire tax base rested on gambling, and every 7-Eleven, every gas station, Laundromat, Chinese restaurant, and grocery store, as well as the airport, had slot machines for casual ''play.'' She imagined it must be an extremely confusing place to grow from childhood to man- or womanhood.

The limo pulled into the Flamingo Hilton drive, flanked by O'Shea's on one side, the Barbary Coast Casino on the other. The Hilton hadn't escaped the towering tackiness of the place any more than the more modern ''erections'' here, she thought.

''I'll get the bags, you get the tip,'' suggested J. T.

The weather was searing, a torrid 101°F in the shade, and while a wildly gusting wind blew a thin, near-invisible desert veil over everything, it did nothing to cool but rather irritated the skin. They'd been sweating since leaving the comfort of the airport, the driver obviously no good with controls, or perhaps he was saving on gas, or simply had no understanding of air-conditioning. He wouldn't receive a full tip, not from her, despite his familiar woes.

After helping J. T. with the bags, the cabbie said to Jessica, ''Wel-come to Los Veegas, pree-ty la-dy. . . .'' His accent, jet-black, sweat-saturated hair, broken-toothed grin, and swarthy skin gave him away as a Hispanic immigrant, possibly an illegal. A once-broken nose and a serious, healed-over scar also marked him as a former brawler; perhaps a man who had fought in the ring—either amateur or lightweight division—or in a back alley, if not simply for money. He seemed a bit punchy, his shirt half in, half out of his waistband. She handed him several folded dollar bills, despite the awful conditions of the so-called limo, when suddenly the cabbie began to thank her profusely, saying, ''Ju know, dis's dee only tip I've got all de day long? God bless ju, and—''

''The only tip you've gotten all day long?'' asked J. T., astounded. It was nearly six in the afternoon.

"It has been dis way lately. No one comes. Too many cabs"—he pointed to the long line of cabs lined in a row in front of and behind them like sentinels, all awaiting another fare.

"So, t'ank you, *amigos*, and have a nice day." It was a practiced line. "And my shill-dren and my wife, dey, too, bless you." He smiled and started for the other side of the cab, waving and leaving her feeling guilty. She and J. T. exchanged a look before she snatched open the passenger-side door and tossed in an extra ten to the man.

When she straightened up, J. T. instantly pulled her aside and asked, "What's the matter with you, Jess?"

"Whataya mean?"

"That was a scam. You just fell flat-assed for that limo driver's scam, Jess."

"You think so?"

"I know so. All that God bless 'ju,' business. He dropped his guard, said 'you' twice in that last remark to 'ju,' pree-ty la-dy."

"Damn." She stared at the limo, which had remained static, the driver waiting his turn for another fare. She considered going to his window, flashing her badge, and perhaps giving him a taste of what it was like to be hassled by a federal agent. "I'm going to do something about that," she muttered, the oppressive heat bearing down like some mighty entropy.

J. T. firmly shook his head, saying, "It's too late. He took you, fair and square."

"What's that? Vegas rules?"

"Don't forget where you are. You're out your money, kiddo, and somewhat out of your element. . . ."

"Shit," she angrily muttered, feeling like a large member of the cat family just cheated out of a meal.

"Forget it, Jess. It's only a tenner. Don't sweat the small stuff. If ju don't lose it here, ju lose it in the slots inside. So, big deal."

She frowned, accepting her moment of naïveté, a moment when she let her guard down and was burned for the privilege.

J. T. called for a bellman for the bags. Jessica knew her friend and colleague was itching to get into the casino to lose his money in a game of chance, and this consoled her to some degree. At least she hadn't knowingly, consciously thrown her money down a toilet, as John intended. In fact, it appeared J. T. meant to binge on gambling, and this worried her.

But for the moment, glad to be getting out of the oppressive desert heat, anxious for a shower, maybe even a swim at the pool, she hurried ahead of J. T. and the bellhop to locate the registration desk. Signs greeted them in the lobby, signs reading WELCOME FORENSIC SCIENCE ASSOCIATION OF AMERICA—EAST PAVILION. And despite Jessica's frown, J. T. insisted on getting a photo of himself where he now stood, alongside one of the huge, expensively framed and gaudily lettered signs. Then, to her consternation, he insisted that the bellboy take a snapshot of the two of them together beside the welcome sign.

"For my album," he said in her ear, hugging her as the photo was snapped.

So far Vegas sucked. *Get me to my room!* she mentally screamed.

· TWO ·

*Startling, like the first handful of mould
cast on the coffined dead.*

—P.J. BAILEY

Feydor Dorphmann had kept the woman sedated enough
so that she was no trouble. She tossed and blubbered and
talked to herself, but this did not bother him, so long as
she did not scream.

Still, Feydor was upset. Things were not going as well
as planned, nothing as neat and tidy as imagination.

"Might've expected as much," he muttered to himself.
Why had Dr. Coran delayed her flight to Vegas? Was she
coming at all, or had she postponed altogether? He replayed the events of the day in his head, wondering what
he might tell an angry Satan when next they met.

The newspaper account of the day before had told him
where Satan's target would be, at the Flamingo Hilton.
Satan told him how to position himself. What to do, precisely what tools and instruments he required, each step of
the way, each step to take, every detail, down to making
a list, and precisely how to make contact with Dr. Jessica
Coran. It had been Satan who'd revealed to Feydor whom
he must destroy, and that in the destroying, he must kill
six of lesser importance to get to the seventh most important of Satan's chosen.

Feydor, of course, like many Americans, knew of Dr.
Coran. He'd read widely the accounts in newspapers across

the country of her battles with such notorious serial killers as Mad Matthew Matisak and that freak on a boat in Florida they'd called the Night Crawler. He knew of how she'd dispatched a ruthless killer in Hawaii and another in New Orleans. Who didn't know the name of Dr. Jessica Coran, the FBI's most valued forensic detective? It just never in a million years would have occurred to him that one day he would be directed by the potentate of Hades to pursue and destroy this woman.

Feydor also knew that men whom society termed "monsters" were in fact extensions of Satan on earth, that Jessica Coran prided herself on hunting down and destroying such monsters, and that now he himself was the next such extension, but that he was being given a special opportunity, unlike all those who came before him, to free himself of Satan's terrible grip, the inviolable hold over his mind and body.

"If I cooperate," he said again and again in a mantra to himself, "if I cooperate with Lucifer, then later . . . later, after Satan satisfies himself over Coran, then Feydor Dorphmann—after all these years of being afflicted by Satan—can go back to being an ordinary man to lead an ordinary, healthy life and find redemption in Christ and the church."

It made sense. It made perfectly sound sense.

The young woman tied to the bed squirmed on hearing the mad rantings of her abductor. He saw her discomfort and shook his head wildly, trying to explain, saying, "It's true. It's the deal we struck . . . the deal I struck with the Evil One."

He could hardly afford the hotel room, but the girl was different. Her purse was stuffed full with hundred-dollar bills and credit cards. She had already covered the cost of the Hilton. Oddly, however, according to papers she had folded and pushed into her purse, she had registered under an assumed name, or at least one that read differently from her credit card. While her credit card name was Chris Lorentian, she was traveling under an alias, Chris Dunlap, a fact that caused some mild curiosity in him but not so much as to dissuade his actions. And with previous arrangements made at the hotel using the name Chris Dunlap, he'd had no problem getting the room card key.

After tying the woman's hands and feet, he'd gone down to the desk to be seen and recognized, although the makeup and wig he wore would keep the game interesting. He told the desk clerk that Chris Dunlap was his wife, and that she was already at the slot machines, unable to control her gambling fever, so he needed a second key. The desk clerk, seeing that he already had one card key to 1713, didn't question him but simply handed over a second key. He had smiled and laughed with the cute little clerk behind the counter over the fact his wife had discovered that she had gambling fever. Meanwhile, Feydor gave the clerk ample time to eyeball his rash, a bad one having cropped up on his neck and chest.

"She also likes her sex rough and tumble," he said with a boyish grin, a proud little shrug of the shoulders.

The clerk remarked on how interesting that all was, when in fact she felt nothing but revulsion. The clerk stared at his hair and remarked, "It's the brightest red I've ever seen except maybe for the actor David Caruso."

She was lying. She didn't like his hair any more than she liked his rash or his crude comments, but that was okay. She would remember him, and he wanted her to remember the "fireman" and his red hair and his red rash, because he wanted to be noticed.

He meant to sprinkle seeds of bait for Coran to come to him, just as he'd read about in her famous case involving Mad Matthew Matisak in his failed quest to kill her. Satan had a real liking for this Dr. Coran.

The red rash was real, but Feydor's true hair color was actually a mahogany brown.

"I'll call a bellhop for your bags, then, sir," the desk clerk had said.

"No, not necessary," he said, putting up a hand to her,

and with the other hand he displayed his only bag, a brief-case, Samsonite with large clasps on either side. "Wife's bags are still in the car, and I can pick them up later," he had quickly added.

The clerk again smiled, but she seemed a bit perplexed with him by this point.

Later, he'd gone out to the car in the lot, hustled the girl named Lorentian, alias Dunlap, from the trunk of her car, and ushered her through a back entryway he'd located. Anyone seeing them might think her drunk but otherwise okay. The drug had kept her still and silent, and the oven-like conditions in the trunk had done the rest, wilting her and her hair. She had perspired so badly in the trunk that she now smelled like a pig.

Satan had said to him, "How she smells matters little, not where she's going." Then the thunderous roar of his insane laughter filled Feydor's brain like an inky black splotch.

After securing her to the bed, Feydor had returned for her baggage. In the backseat of the car he had rifled through her carry-on and found a bus ticket made out to Chris Dunlap. Nothing else of consequence or use was found in the carry-on, so he decided to leave it and simply hold on to the big suitcase. There might be some other treasures in these he could use later.

Satan had called Feydor to the desert, away from home in San Francisco, called him here to Vegas and had told him to wait here until he should be called on to do the Devil's bidding. Satan told him that eventually he would end the game at the Devil's Well, that he would see both Feydor and Dr. Jessica Coran at the Devil's Well, but that he must be patient to get to this place, which Feydor had seen once as a child. And so he had waited with intermit-tent visits from Satan's army of familiars, ranging in age and form and ability to deliver pain, all coming just to tell him to wait longer.

It had been nearly three months now, living out of

Dumpsters, panhandling for coffee and bread until finally the time had come. He knew it a few days before when he'd picked up the Vegas paper that carried the story of the gathering of the Forensic Science Association of America and the Medical Examiners Association meeting at the Flamingo Hilton. It carried only a line or two about Dr. Jessica Coran, singling her out due to her reputation earned through a series of daring FBI cases she had cracked. He, of course, remembered her from previous newspapers, TV interviews, and nationwide manhunts, and this sudden revelation filled his brain to overflowing. The image of her on the spoiled page he'd held up that day was enough! It clearly told Feydor who it was that Satan had left him sitting around here and starving here and waiting here for.

Only after having stripped Chris where she lay on the bed, hands and feet tied, her eyes fixed and dilated, a gag in her mouth, her clothes stuffed in around her there on the bed, his privates aroused, did he telephone down to the front desk and politely ask after Jessica Coran.

"I'm calling about a colleague, a Dr. Jessica Coran. Has she checked in yet?"

"One moment, sir, and I'll see if I can verify that for you. . . ."

Even the brief wait was damnably long after so long a delay getting this close to a closure for Feydor, and the Lorentian woman was moaning like a drugged Siamese cat now, a bit loudly. Someone walking by might hear her. He checked the gag, tugged on her bindings at hands and feet, to be prudent. He'd tied her with a cheap belt and tie he'd brought for the purpose. He wore surgical gloves, not wishing to leave any prints.

"Sorry, sir . . ." muttered the clerk into the phone. "I'm afraid that Dr. Coran has not yet arrived, but our records show that she has made reservations and is expected."

"Expected when?"

"We can't precisely say, sir, but her room has been guaranteed for late arrival."

A glance at the clock radio on the bedside table told Feydor it was nearing six thirty-five. Again, the woman on the bed painfully, mournfully moaned, her legs kicking out as if a bad dream were chasing her.

The clerk, hearing the moan, asked, "Is everything else all right, sir?"

"Yes, yes . . . thank you," he told the clerk and hung up.

He removed the handkerchief gag from the woman's mouth to allow her to breathe easily. The gag no doubt had his prints on it from earlier touching, but this mattered not. The fire would obliterate any hint of it.

He had earlier laid open the Samsonite bag he'd carried to the room, and he began preparations, laying out all the tools he'd brought in his case. Lifting a Polaroid Instamatic camera, he took a before shot and mumbled, "The right tool for the right job."

The sight through the camera lens gave him a slight rise in the heat of his body, the red returning, a volcanic, liquid fire below the epidermis. His penis hardened but little, semen stirring slightly, sluggishly with his blood, but that part must await the burning flesh as promised by Satan, his reward.

It was a feeling he had not had in many, many years, not since childhood. He knew now that the Antichrist had likely spawned him, fed a fiery liquid mush to him as a child, coddled and nurtured him. That it had been Satan in his head all those times he'd burned things both inanimate and animate. A bit of fear along with anticipation and remorse rose in him along with his sexual organ.

After having been caught and punished many times, young Feydor had simply stopped burning things when he became older. The consequences were too great, the suffering at the hand of his earthly father too much. He'd become interested in psychology and psychiatry largely to understand himself. In college and graduate school, he'd excelled and had come out a practicing psychiatrist, believing he now could control the fire that raged within. He'd practiced medicine for only three years when the voices inside him began. It was the voices of the phantoms behind the irises of his eyes. Next came the years of hospitalization and treatments, all amounting to nothing. No one could help him. Not even Wetherbine.

No one until now . . .

Satan would be angry with him if Coran was a no-show.

He tried to shake off the fear that Satan would punish him, but a sense of dread overwhelmed as he pictured the spread of the red rash to all parts of his body and brain.

It wouldn't matter to Satan that it wasn't his fault that Coran hadn't arrived. Wouldn't matter if she canceled and was a no-show. The punishment would be the same. It didn't matter that it wasn't his fault.

He busied himself with the materials he'd brought for the occasion. Wasting no more time, he dug around for the screwdriver, located it, and laid it on the dresser alongside the pint-sized can of petroleum he'd brought, and beside this, the small canister of butane with its praying mantis–like wand. The torch would set off the fire instantly and quickly, and it would be over, and Feydor would once again feel some relief from his demons, and he'd be a step closer on the journey, saving his soul from the everlasting tortures already assaulting him.

As for the girl . . . he truly didn't want to think about the girl, but Satan had selected her, not him; and he had said she was a traitor, and so punishment must be meted out. And if not her, it would be Feydor branded as a traitor and someone would come after him with petrol and butane and a plan that would return him to the Devil's Well. . . .

The hotel was jam-packed with not only forensics experts but also two other conventions going on simultaneously. The hallways were littered with men in hats and name tags. On the elevator going up, Jessica gave a thought to the Forensic Science Association of America, the FSAA. She'd been a member for nearly twenty years and had never actively participated as a board member, nor did she wish to now. She wondered how people as busy as she could possibly find the time to be treasurer or secretary or to steer such a cumbersome organization down a direct path to such a thing as a successful convention. She believed there was no more cursed a thing on earth than the possibility that someone would ask her to direct a committee of forensic people to organize such an extravaganza. Obviously, now, she had gotten what she deserved. Some committee of her peers had decided that Vegas, of all places, would make for a great place to hold their annual convention. Like complaining over an election when she hadn't voted, she had no right; she had gotten precisely what she and the other hands-off members deserved, because she had not gotten involved.

But now that she was here, she *would* make the best of it, she scolded herself.

When she settled into her room atop the Flamingo Hilton, Jessica did as always when entering a hotel room. She immediately turned on the air-conditioning unit, flooding the place with as much cool air as possible, and she tore back the drapes over the window to take in the full view of the city from atop the skyscraper. She felt as if she were a mile above the city, overlooking the busy, frenetic world that money and gambling had built, this modern-day Sodom and Gomorrah.

The entire city paid homage to P. T. Barnum's famous line ''There's a sucker born every minute.'' Watching the comings and goings of the air traffic, Jessica said aloud to the now winking lights of the city, ''And the airline industry would add, 'a sucker flown in every minute. . . . ' ''

Barnum would be on his knees at this altar, his eyes welling with tears, his wildest schemes eclipsed by this town. It was a city where Mafia gambling was not only tolerated but also how the city got its payroll. It gave her pause, recalling poor little Grand Cayman and its graft problems, so inconsequential to this.

Vegas was gambling's greatest temple, the world's largest roulette wheel, and perhaps that was its greatest appeal—the fact that it imitated life as most people felt it, knew it, believed it to be: a boundlessly huge, universal gamble.

The gamble might one day pay off; in the meantime, you kept coming back to drink of it, always hoping that one day your "luck" would change before life simply crushed you. The gamble might be fun in and of itself, but no one was getting out of the game alive. Consequently, the more dangerous, the higher the stakes, the more the payoff in feeling for those otherwise dead nerve endings; the higher the stakes, the deeper the fall, the pain, the suffering when you lost your gamble with relationships, with life.

Cars, trucks, moving vans, trains on tracks—industry was moving far below her now where she stood, all those working machines and people twenty stories below her. She wondered how many, at the end of the day, blew their hard-earned cash at the massive casino downstairs, which filled a football-field-sized lobby with wildly flashing Christmas tree colored lights, slots, and gambling tables.

Jessica turned from the window, inspected the place where she intended living for two nights. She'd best unpack, hang out her things, especially what she intended to wear tonight, and ready herself for a shower. As she did so, she found her thoughts returning to life's ever-changing game of chance.

In her line of work, gambling often meant taunting death itself, and while she had been lucky on many occasions, Jessica believed in luck only insofar as she could control it, make it work for her, create it by action and deed. In her worldview, there was no such thing as some entity called Luck sitting out there like a Rumpelstiltskin to be tapped into, or to fall in debt to. Chance, coincidence, the roll of the dice all occurred independent of personality and action, just as one molecule chanced into another. But when a person put faith and self-reliance and confidence on the line to assert herself, she became lucky—lucky even to be around.

It wasn't luck that befell any hapless one. This regardless of the housewife who steps into a 7-Eleven, purchases a ticket, and wins the lottery. There was no luck involved, only random chance. Jessica believed luck to be a conscious lifestyle, a choice.

She finished her unpacking and checked the time: six-forty. Still a good hour remaining before the registration and reception downstairs. She returned to the window and stared out beyond the Strip to the gorgeous, fire-red mountains in the distance.

On the plane and on their way in from the airport, she and J. T. had seen how the city sprawled and crept like an octopus from this central crown, how an entire world of schools, hospitals, malls, neighborhoods, housing developments, and suburban areas now filtering into neighboring valleys and snuggling amid the outlying mountain ranges had grown up around Bugsy Segal's Flamingo Club. Here, as in any city in the United States, there were buildings given over to governmental affairs and offices, politicians, judges, lawyers, doctors, teachers, and "normal" people leading "straight" lives but whose jobs, while on the surface independent of both the casino trade and the tourism industry, were inextricably entwined with these trades. For underlying every brick of public improvement, every referendum, every move made, if you were a Vegas homeowner, franchise owner, doughnut salesman, or car mechanic, *gambling* was not only in your face, it also represented the elixir—as important as water—that kept this town alive amid a desert. Gambling purchased and brought in more electrical power and water than any city in the United States, and here, in the midst of one of the driest deserts on earth, every man, woman, and child had more water to waste on their lawns, cars, and themselves than any other place on the planet—all due to the mighty dollar and the thing that brought it here, greed and a healthy dislike for laws that attempted to legislate against human nature and addiction.

Jessica's mind's eye took in the cityscape, the shapes and the florid lights, and it said to her, "This is a city created on the premise that if you are artful and a dodger, if you can play exquisitely well on the weaknesses of the human animal, then you can become rich beyond all reason, and if you can convince those you are fleecing that they are having a good time in the bargain, then all the better. It is a city where the hotelier puts you up for a price, allows you to gamble within his walls, to shovel over any funds you'd like for the privilege, feeds you at a price then and there, and finally offers you a grand Broadway-style musical or revue, again for a hefty sum, all under one roof. A thing of beauty for those in control, and the house never loses, for even when it might lose, like some pagan god, it wins on. . . ."

In fact, there was nothing in Vegas that didn't carry a price tag, but millions of Americans a year were convinced that anything in Vegas was worth its price, including the fun of losing.

Cabbies depended on the good graces of those whom they carted between gaming tables and big-ticket shows. And gambling table people depended equally on tips. No one working in Vegas at such jobs was making a killing; most were barely eking out a living, in fact. Neither showgirls nor hotel clerks, hairdressers nor prostitutes, were paid well. It was a right-to-work state—no unions; those who lived and worked in Vegas did so at the mercy of employers, and there was always someone waiting in the wings, anxious for your job.

Jessica kicked away her shoes. She continued to undress, trying to get the dust of this evolving city off of her, and trying to get its problems out of her head. But even as she tried, her concerns beat an anthem in her brain.

Beneath the surface of the blinding neon rivers over which she again looked, of light-fed mosaics and facades, she saw the poverty-stricken and the homeless out there, while inside this hotel everyone else fed the slots. This fantasy-world denial of so much misery even beneath the flood of light and golden crowns, silver columns, rainbow arches, pink pinnacles, and onyx pyramids simply bothered Jessica to no end.

And it was to no end that she worried about such matters. Nothing short of a new species of *Homo erectus* would ever change people, and any attempt to legislate smoking, drinking, or gambling or drugs—what people loved—was doomed to failure, even in the face of facts such as those telling people about the connection between heart disease and cigarettes, about black lung, or that more than half of all vehicular fatalities came about by drugs or drinking and driving. Gambling, even if it was with their children's lives at stake, in one form or another, existed in every state, in every household, in every life. People gambled with the rent money in D.C., with their brains on drugs in Chicago, with the last vestige of clothing on their backs in Seattle.

The U.S. government couldn't do a damn thing about such people, and had in fact sanctioned preying on the weak, the deluded, and the poor with its own brand of gambling. State governments had long since bought into lotteries to raise revenues, doing exactly what Bugsy Segal and every gangster since him had done, preying on weakness. What man or government could stand in the way of progress? And who or what could stem the tide of human ignorance, with its underlying cousin, avarice, and sister, poverty, and brother, powerlessness?

Like pornography, it all fell under that umbrella catch-phrase that Jessica saw as a ridiculous oxymoron, adult entertainment. Yet here was an entire, brazen city dependent on all of this. If it existed anywhere else in the world,

Americans would scream out for an air strike against the immorality of it all. But here it was king, and it was proud; the most famous monument to gambling, greed, and so-called adult entertainment ever known to man, sprawled across the desert landscape like some giant Babylonian whore.

Maybe she was getting too moralistic in her old age, she gibed herself. Maybe J. T. was right; maybe she should lighten up, if only she could.

It still seemed an odd place for a scientific gathering of the minds, with or without her moralizing. Certainly it was the last place on earth she would have placed a convention of her peers, but the Forensic Science Association of America wasn't always gifted with precognition or simple foresight, and like any cross section of America, it was not without its share of gamblers, drinkers, druggies, and womanizers.

She now located and unlocked the dry bar and sampled a wee bottle of wine, which she sipped from a plastic cup. She then returned to the window again, standing there in her bra, her alone time fleeting. She again located her best evening gown, which she intended to wear tonight at the reception, and upset with the fold lines still clinging to it, she took it into the bathroom and hung it on the door. A hot shower would do both her and the dress some good, she reasoned. Half undressed for her shower, she was startled by her ringing telephone.

Jim, she wondered, hoped, her heart leaping.

Who else knows I'm here? she silently asked on the second ring, making her way toward the phone. Or was it J. T. already calling her to go downstairs? She'd asked for a little time, some privacy. On the third ring, she lifted the receiver.

"Yes?"

"Is . . . is'sis Doc-tor . . . Doctor Jess-i-ca Cccor-Coran?"

"Yes, it is. Can I help you?" She didn't know the strident, panting female voice on the other end. The caller sounded tearful, as if she must choke out every word.

"Doctor . . . I . . . I'm suppose' to tell you . . . tell you . . ." The woman sounded as if she were on something, every word labored.

"Yes?" *Damn it, girl,* Jessica thought, *spit it out.*

". . . my name."

"Please do." Was she dealing with a child?

"It's . . . it's . . . C-Chris . . ."

"Chris? Chris who?" She didn't know anyone by the name.

Gasping as if unable to breathe, whimpering as if hurt, the girl's voice replied, "Lor-en-tian."

"I'm sorry, but I—"

"Gotta help me. . . . Stinks like hell. . . ."

"I don't know you or anyone named Lor . . . Lorentian?" It sounded like a stage name. "Are you hurt? In some sort of trouble? Are you trying to reach your parents?" Jessica wondered how this Chris person had gotten her name and number, what the stranger wanted, even as she wondered at the girl's age, if she were a runaway. But why had she dialed Jessica? She'd asked for Jessica by name, and now Jessica grew impatient at the silence on the other end, unhappy that she was getting no answers to her questions.

"He's taken my clothes off . . . going to . . . to kill me."

"Who, Chris? Give me a name. Who're you talking—"

"Tied me . . . to the bed. . . ."

"Where are you? Tell me where!"

"Doused gasoline all over me . . . go . . . go . . . going to burn me!"

Suddenly there was no more.

"Hello, hello?" Jessica asked.

But she got no answer. All that Jessica heard now on the other end was a garbled, keening sound, the noise of a wholly frightened animal. Then came a scream, which was immediately followed by a sudden violent *whoosh* of what sounded like forced air, a soft explosion, intermingled with a strangled cry of excruciating pain; then followed the crackling roar of what sounded like a raging fire. The fiery sound was mixed with female screams, and simultaneously a cackling laugh, deep and throaty, seemingly male.

"What the hell's going on there?" she shouted into the receiver.

And the line went dead. The dial tone like a death knell.

Jessica stared at the receiver for a moment, wondering what in hell it had all been for, wondering if some of the raunchier forensics men in the "club" might not have gotten together to pull a prank call on her, thinking her an easy target, gullible. Oleander, Mac, any one of them could easily have gotten her number simply by checking with the desk. Some of those old whiskered grunts were not above it, scientific standing and professional bearing notwithstanding.

Hell, her mind raced, the lot of them were always anxious to break the tedium of their profession with anything that might relieve stress, anything that smacked of fun, and by far, the worst of the bunch was Karl Repasi, but he had his cronies, too, and he was quite the persuasive bastard, easily convincing younger colleagues into participating in such pranks.

He'd obviously gotten help from a woman, too. One of Jessica's own female colleagues, of whom there were a surprising number, or had he roped some poor room attendant or barmaid into his little hoax? Great sound effects, though, she concluded.

She'd find out soon enough, she reasoned, imagining their smirks when she entered the reception downstairs. For now, a quick shower was called for. Maybe the steam would clear her mind and relieve some of her pent-up hostilities, and it might help to uncrease the wrinkles in her gown.

But only now did she realize that she still clutched the

receiver so tightly in her hand as to make her knuckles white. Gasping, she placed the receiver in its cradle.

She wondered if she'd be as angry with Las Vegas if Jim were here beside her.

Still, the call, the genuine nature of the horrid cries of the voice calling itself Chris . . . it all seemed so real and unrehearsed. Then again, if an actress had been hired, then why not? she told herself. But suppose it had been real? her mind nagged.

She dialed the desk operator, identified herself as an M.E. with the convention and as a guest of the house, giving her room number, 2017, and adding, "Did the phone call I just received—did it originate from outside or inside the hotel?"

"It was from a house phone, Dr. Coran."

She smiled. "Repasi," she muttered.

"Pardon?" asked the desk clerk.

"Never mind."

The clerk then interrupted her, saying, "I'm sorry, that call originated from another room, Dr. Coran."

"What room?"

"Seventeen thirteen, Dr. Coran. Below you. Would you like me to call them back?"

"Yes, please." She decided to cut short Repasi's little fun.

But the number continued to ring, unattended. An automatic tumbler clicked in and a too-pleasant, syrupy female voice asked, "If you would care to leave a message for the current occupant, please do so at the sound of the tone."

The tone came and she felt foolish. What sort of message should she leave? She wasn't even sure it was Karl Repasi. There were plenty of others who might have cooked up this little scenario. "This is Jessica Coran," she finally said, "and I just want you to know that your joke's as little as your penile extremities, gentlemen!"

The moment she hung up, she regretted stooping to their

level, becoming the thing she hated. Still, it felt good to jab back, and she was, after all, only human.

What did they expect her response to be? To telephone the Las Vegas Police Department? There a desk sergeant would take her complaint, and one of the boys would contact the sergeant for a copy of the complaint, which would be read at one of the sessions to a screaming, howling bunch of sawbones. Jessica would bear the brunt of the joke, along with the FBI, and her description of the "crime" her ears had witnessed would be recounted. This followed by colleagues, wiping tears from their eyes, staggering to her table to thank her for all the laughs while politely, civilly enjoying their stress-reducing weekend.

They'd get the biggest laugh when Karl Repasi role-played the sergeant at the desk, saying, "Okay, so what do you want us to do about it?"

"Trace the call. Determine its origin. Something of that nature might be in order," another would respond, playing Jessica's part.

"We'll look into it, Dr. Coran. Enjoy your stay in Vegas. . . . Don't drop too much at the tables," Karl would finish with a flurry.

"Well, to hell with that," she told herself, pleased now that she had put the kibosh on the hoax. She now urgently sought out the refuge of a hot shower, anticipating the relaxing spray.

When she stepped from the shower not ten minutes later, she heard an assortment of noises outside her door and up and down the hallway. The circus was in town. It sounded like conventioneer central. One of the other conventions in conference here was a rowdy bunch of Michelin Tire Corporation reps from all over the country. Whoever these characters were rampaging about in the hallway, they sounded like they meant to get their party's worth.

Still, in the thick terry-cloth robe she'd bought while in Hawaii some years before, Jessica was startled when someone banged bearlike on her door, screaming something unintelligible from the other side. She wondered if it were Karl and his crew, disappointed at her earlier lack of response, but a look through the peephole revealed a stranger mouthing the words, ''Fire! Fire in the building! Get out!''

· THREE ·

Some say the world will end in fire.
—ROBERT FROST

Still in her robe, Jessica threw open the door. She could smell the faint odor of smoke as it wafted through the hallway. Somewhere, overhead sprinklers had gone into service, while her room and the hallway remained dry. Instantly, she recalled the bizarre phone call and the room number the desk had given her when she'd asked to be patched through to the mystery caller.

She instantly returned to her phone and again dialed the desk, shouting, "There's a fire up here somewhere, and I believe its origin is room seventeen thirteen. Get the fire department up here, now!"

As she held the receiver in one hand, she worked a pair of panties beneath the robe and up her legs. She then thought of J. T., who was on the floor above. She dialed his room, telling him to get out, that there was a fire on the seventeenth floor. He thought she was pulling his leg until she screamed, "Goddamn it, J. T., move!" With that, she slammed down the receiver.

She looked about for something to throw on, grabbed a pair of Guess? jeans, a pullover T-shirt with a Magic basketball logo on it, her card key to the room, and she then rushed barefoot toward the elevator, where she found the stairwell. Along with others in various stages of dress and undress, she moved along in an attempt to get below the fire, telling others she suspected it to be three or four floors below them. One or two of her traveling companions were curious how she knew this fact.

"The odor is quite pungent," she explained, "and that means it's rising toward us, or at least that'd be my guess," she told others within earshot.

Once on the fifteenth floor, they first heard and then saw firemen storming up the stairwell. Other firefighters were unloading from the elevators and spilling into the hallways above, or so it sounded, some shouting like commandos at the civilians, moving them out and down. Jessica lingered on the stairwell above the fifteenth floor, waiting while others, in various stages of panic, passed her by, some assuring her that the only safe place was the lobby below. Firemen called out to her, telling her she could take the elevator on fifteen for the lobby below.

A crowd too large for the limited number of elevators had emerged by now, and J. T. found Jessica on the stairs, where she'd remained a flight below seventeen. "Hell of a welcome to the Hilton, huh?" J. T. said.

"Yeah, I'd just gotten my shower, and now I'm going to smell like fire," she replied. "Look, I've got to go up there, have a look at the room where the blaze started."

"Funny no alarms or waterspouts went off," he replied. "You suppose all the fire detectors and sprays in all the rooms may be, you know, inoperable or something?"

This high up in a building, she little wondered at J. T.'s distress. A skyscraper could quickly turn into a death trap for those reposing inside.

"Do you have your ID on you? I just grabbed my key and left everything in the room," she confessed.

"Yeah, I have mine with me, but Jess, why do you want to go chasing a fire?"

"I have a grave feeling someone has died in this fire."

J. T. stared a moment. "You getting spooky on me, like that psychic detective Dr. Desinor or something, Jess?"

"No . . . I *heard* her death. . . ."

"Heard?"

"Over the phone. She called just before the fire reached her—said something about gasoline, about someone's wanting to kill her. Said her name was Chris Lorentian." Despite the fact that Jessica spoke her remembered thoughts to J. T., she believed her own thoughts sounded too insane to utter.

He shook his head. "Are you sure you didn't just dream this up?" he replied. "Jess, it's just a fire right now. We don't know that anyone's died in it."

"But I'm telling you someone has, and that I spoke to her."

J. T. looked away, his expression saying, Come on, Jess, the reception's already under way downstairs, and those gambling tables are waiting for us, too. But thankfully, he did not say it. Instead he asked, "But why'd she call you? How'd she know about you?"

"How the hell . . ." she burst out but slowed down, taking a deep breath. "I don't know the whyfors or the how-tos here, J. T. I'm in the dark. I mean, victims usually talk to me, but normally they're dead when they do their talking," she added. "This . . . this is just weird. This victim, I think, I fear, spoke aloud and directly at me. I don't know how or why . . . or what to make of it, John."

"Easy, Jess," he offered.

"Let's just get up there and have a look."

John Thorpe could only stare, his mind racing to put the incomplete details together as they climbed toward the seventeenth floor, where they were met with resistance from firefighters who blocked their way until J. T. flashed his FBI identification and announced who they were.

"FBI?" asked the fireman loud enough for the fire marshal inside to hear him. "How did you guys get this one so soon?"

The fire marshal came to the door and introduced himself as Fire Detective Charles Fairfax, a tall, firm-looking man in an untoggled fire coat and flopping, loosely pulled-on fire boots. "I was downstairs in the casino myself when my beeper went off," he explained. "Dr. Repasi had me paged."

Jessica hardly looked the part of an FBI medical examiner at the moment, but Fairfax, a tall, gaunt man with deep-cut wrinkles and leathery, perhaps fire-retardant skin, she mused, took her appearance in stride. She was barefoot, her hair wet, her T-shirt inappropriate. Fortunately, J. T. had his ID and was dressed in a suit for the reception downstairs. The building was full of forensics people, and apparently the fire marshal was also in attendance for the conference.

"Have you come to any conclusions, Detective Fairfax?" Jessica asked.

"Flat out murder by fire. No surprises, really, except for the mirror."

"Mirror?"

"You'll see it inside. Anyway, there's an accelerant pattern that shows up under blue light clearly enough that tells us she was doused with what we believe to be ordinary gasoline, which was ignited by an unknown source. No book of matches for this guy. Some of our guys think the fire was ignited by a torch wand, which would give the killer some distance from the blaze."

"How do you know it was a torch wand?"

"A second accelerant pattern, a bit distinct from the first. Appears he may have fired up a butane torch and sprayed the gasoline with the butane flame. But this is all guesswork until we can get the lab analysis work done, of course."

"Understood."

"I mean we've got a lot of experience standing in the room. Myself alone, I've seen more than two thousand suspicious fires."

J. T. whistled in response.

"You know fire's the third—"

"Greatest cause of death in the country, yes," finished Jessica.

"Some six thousand Americans a year die by fire, and fifty percent of 'em come up suspicious, requiring the fire marshals. So we see a lot, and nowadays, what with modern science to back us up, we can put quite a case together before it's over."

"Let's have a look-see," suggested Jessica.

"Dr. Repasi's already inside with our fire investigation team," Fairfax explained.

"We just want a look," replied Jessica.

"You got reason to believe it's an FBI matter, then be my guests."

Sure enough, Karl Repasi was inside, leaning in over the bed where an unidentifiable body lay scorched beyond recognition, curled into the familiar, fetal-like position of those suddenly caught in an inferno, as if warding off Hades with merely hands and feet and flesh were defensively possible. The wrists appeared broken, but Jessica had seen victims of fire death many times before, and she recognized the wilted limbs as bones cracked due to the intensity of the heat the body had suffered. Later, during autopsy, X-ray examination would reveal many more broken bones in the body, in legs, arms, and possibly elsewhere.

The entire mattress had gone up, along with a stash of clothing tucked on either side of the victim's body. This added some less than volatile materials in the mix, since most all clothing was fire retardant nowadays. The killer, no doubt, wanted to leave more smoke than flame and to keep the fire localized over the bed. He obviously knew something of the nature of fire and how to control it. Two of the fire marshals were discussing this feature as they entered the room.

"Bastard was in control from the moment he planned the fire to the moment he stepped away from it," one of Fairfax's men concluded.

A scorched black roof mocked from overhead; the

nearby wall remained untouched save for peeling, blistering paint, and soot.

Fairfax said to Jessica, "The scene looks like a spontaneous combustion in some regards. I think this guy wants us to think so, too, but we're not stupid."

Jessica saw that the intense source of the fire was localized over the bed, and it did give the appearance that at one moment the victim lay sleeping peacefully in her bed and in the next instant was consumed by fire. Still, much of the room was painted in black soot and creosote, from floor to ceiling; it had been fire alarms in the rooms above and below the fire that had alerted neighbors to the danger. The alarm and sprinkler system in 1713 had been disconnected, presumably by the killer. Atop the ugliness of the fire soot and grease came the sopping, soapy, drenched-in-water layer, creating a moist patina overall, thanks to a snakelike hose meandering through the room.

Jessica gave a quick glance to the awful body lying balled up on the bed. Her mind, almost independent of her, ticked off the results of what to her meant obvious murder: massive tissue damage, burning and charring, the limbs swollen and split open from the superheated air, like so many grilled hot dogs. Fried nerves, cooked brains, instant cataracts, ruptured and bleeding eardrums, but the blood was seared to a black oil. The heat on the bed not only sizzled and blackened the woman's skin, distorting all features, but had broken bones beneath the skin.

"A lightning strike of a hundred million volts of direct current, reaching fifty thousand degrees Fahrenheit, would've been preferable to this death," Karl Repasi was telling the firemen. Jessica surmised that Karl was right the instant she glimpsed the tortured features of the victim.

"Is that right?" asked one of the fire marshals.

Repasi replied, "When struck by lightning and the current passes through the brain, a person immediately loses consciousness with the crack of the bolt: All breathing halts, you see, and one giant spasm ceases the rhythm of the heart, leaving it in one tight contraction from which it generally cannot recover.''

''So there's less suffering than the usual fire death, I see,'' said the fire investigator, whose hand unconsciously gripped his gun for something solid to hold on to. The combination of the stench and the sight of the grilled and blackened young woman on the bed was enough to over-power anyone, even seasoned veterans such as Fairfax and his men.

Repasi seemed now to be holding court. He continued on the relative merits of being hit by lightning rather than dying in the fashion that their present victim had, saying, ''After a short duration, the heart muscle relaxes and may or may not resume a normal, spontaneous beat. Recovery is only possible if the damage to the brain is minimal, but in the case of considerable burn damage to brain tissues, death is absolutely certain. But for every fatal victim of a lightning strike, there are three hit by nonlethal, stray current charges splintering off from the main bolt itself. Such questionably 'lucky' folk are merely stunned and have stiff, sore muscles and small burns where the current exited their bodies. But here, now, the body on the bed represents a gruesome difference from the painless, quick death of a lightning strike.''

For Jessica, the burned-out eyes and the grotesque mask left little doubt that Chris Lorentian, if this were she, had suffered an excruciatingly painful death at the hands of her attacker, proving that fire was not as forgiving as lightning.

The body and facial mask, painted with the sickening and odorous creosote of superheated body fluids and fat, resembled the look of an ancient, cave-dwelling man dug out of a glacier, a fellow whom Jessica had met once at the Smithsonian Institution one Sunday afternoon when she and other FBI employees were given a private tour. The mummified remains were as scorched and blackened as this body before them, but his tissuelike body and rag-ged cloth remnants had had a hundred thousand genera-

tions or more to become blackened and crumbly, not from
fire but from ice. Yet the results appeared the same.

Jessica turned away to find J. T. staring with equal fascination at the bureau mirror, which reflected the seared
body back at her. Superimposed over the image of the
body was a smeared message written in black soot and
grease—perhaps the grease of the burning victim—across
the gleaming surface of the mirror. The killer's message
read:

#1 is #9—Traitors

"He's obviously trying to open a dialogue with us,"
J. T. was saying in her ear, but she didn't want to hear
this, didn't want a dialogue with the Devil. She didn't want
to deal with another Matisak, not now, not ever, but it
appeared another was being foisted upon her nonetheless.
Still, she didn't want to believe that this madman had singled her out for a dialogue.

Just the same, even as she heard the voices, the boots
and rustle of fire hoses and paraphernalia, even as she
heard the words of the men in the room, Jessica was off
in another place, staring at the strange message on the
looking glass, the shape of the killer's handwriting, making
mental note of its eccentricities as she'd learned to do from
Eriq Santiva, wondering at the message's hidden meaning.
The bizarre equation, one equals nine, made no more sense
than the single word "traitors," yet the cryptic message
beat an anthem in her head. Who was the traitor here? The
killer or his victim? Someone who had betrayed the killer,
someone he meant to kill over and over? Were there other
traitors waiting to be burned alive? Perhaps the traitor
wasn't the victim at all; perhaps someone close to the victim whom the killer wanted to see suffer? Was Jessica
herself seen as some sort of traitor in this perverted,
twisted mind? And what did he mean to imply with the

numbers? What kind of reasoning was this? That the number 1 represents the number 9?

"What is that?" asked J. T., equally confused.

Jessica stepped closer to the mirror. "Fairfax, have you found any prints in the room?"

"No, nothing. This guy was extremely careful. Likely wore gloves."

Jessica knew that fire investigation had come into its own with modern, computer-enhanced gas chromatography and lasers. "Do you have a blue light with you?" she asked.

"Right here."

"Shine it on the message in the mirror."

Fairfax, impressed, came close to the glass with his handheld laser. One of his junior partners turned off the portable lights they'd brought into the room. Everyone's eyes were riveted to the strange grease marks across the mirror, now highlighted beneath the blue light.

"Do you see what I see?" she asked.

Fairfax gasped. There were multiple print marks in the grease.

"What kind of grease marker is this guy using?" asked J. T.

"We'll need lab analysis, but it appears to be hot grease from the flaming victim. It dries hard and waxy on the mirror's surface, and he took his gloves off to write in it," Jessica explained. "Unless someone in here touched the grease?"

She and Fairfax scanned the room for anyone who might confess to having touched the lettering and numbers on the mirror. There were no volunteers. "Just the same," said Fairfax, "everyone here not on my team, leave a set of prints with Dennis, here."

Dennis had been doing the fingerprint search. He gave out with a "Yo" for all to identify him.

"We should also scrape the message for a sample of the grease he used to smear out this message with, to con-

firm my suspicion,'' Jessica told Fairfax. ''Also, see to it
clear laser photos and the usual photos are made from
every angle on this mirror, before anything is removed.''

"Not to worry, Dr. Coran,'' Fairfax assured her.

The blue light disappeared when someone turned on the
portable lights the fire investigation team had brought into
the room. The electricity in the room had long since departed.

Karl Repasi now stepped over to where she stood before
the mirror. ''Impressive, Doctor, but you can be assured
that I have everything here well in hand. So, you and Dr.
Thorpe ought really to go back to the convention, enjoy
yourselves. This is hardly an FBI matter.''

Jessica did not release Repasi from her glare. ''Karl, I
want a copy of every photo shot here,'' she replied. ''And
if you autopsy her, I want a copy of the protocol.''

"We'll have to get a laser camera from the lab,'' complained Fairfax, who sent one of his men out with the
chore.

In the meantime, Repasi gave Jessica a hard stare, as if
to say, *Who's in charge here?,* but he kept silent counsel
while the flash, flash, flash of the 35mm Kodak camera
and the repeated whining of its automatic forward gave
positive response to Jessica's request. The noise of the
camera also came as a welcome relief to Jessica's thoughts.
Other noises and voices now filtered in from the hallway,
where people were gathering and being held back by uniformed policemen.

"Here's the answer to your earlier question, Dr. Repasi,'' declared Charles Fairfax, who also vied for control
of the crime scene. Fairfax's hair was light and wispy,
making him look like a candidate for baldness within a
few years. His stony eyes and grim demeanor were in
keeping with both the scene and his job. He presented the
picture of confidence and knowledge. ''Whoever doused
her with the gasoline and set her aflame, first went to work
on the overhead sprinklers and the alarm.'' He pointed to

the melted alarm box, its wires exposed and singed like
dead and hardened worms.

For Jessica the crime scene took on a surreal nature, as
if time stood still.

Repasi was still defending his position with Jessica, saying, "I was only a few doors down. I stumbled into this,
just as you have, but now that I'm here, I'm obligated to
see it through."

Jessica nodded in response, knowing Repasi to be an
ambitious man by nature, and that M.E.s as a rule were
ambitious and tenacious. Good attributes for the profession. He surely saw the media attention such a case meant.
Jessica, like Repasi, had known in her bones, the moment
she'd stepped into the room, that it had to be murder and
no mere fire suicide.

Jessica, ignoring the others, now stared at the body and
the bed upon which the woman had died, the bed that had
been turned into an inferno, the remnants now black and
dripping a mucky residue all about the carpet around the
fire hole in the bed, the body on the bed sagging through
to the blackened carpet beneath. The body looked like a
martyr upon a cross, its hands and feet stuck together as
if soldered that way, the remnants of whatever binding that
held the victim in place now turned to black snakes coiled
about her wrists and ankles.

Jessica's eyes, as if fitful and resisting her stare, blinked
again and again over the sight like two small cameras re-
cording the indigestible truth, while the photographer with
the fire department continued to snap photos from where
he stood on the opposite side of the bed.

Everyone was going about his or her duties, doing what
must be done while Jessica felt impaled in thin air, unable
to make a decision, unable to think clearly, feeling a helpless fool, just in the way here, as Repasi believed, while
her mind replayed the telephone call again and again in its
every detail. She must recall every word, every nuance, for

every utterance, every sound, could be important. The one sound—that rush of fire—she would never forget; it had been like death's angel whispering in her ear.

She felt J. T. tugging at her to come away from the body and the room; she felt all eyes upon her. But the photographer, Repasi, the firemen, none of them had spoken with the dead woman only moments before. They could afford to be nonchalant about the murder; they didn't have an emotional stake in the circumstances surrounding the killing. Nor could they possibly know what was going through her mind, how she felt, the overwhelming remorse and helplessness she now endured.

"Jesus, the odor . . . damn, look at it. . . ." said J. T. with a moan at Jessica's side, the sight of the charred corpse getting to him now, too.

Jessica's mind retreated, wanting to shout at Karl or any other easy target: *This isn't really happening, is it?* Some sort of gag, an elaborate hoax put together for the convention, a fun "whodunit" for the weekend get-together of forensics champions, to keep everyone occupied? M.E.s liked healthy competition with one another, and Repasi was beating hell out of her. Her instincts had been right on. The fire, Fairfax, and the firemen added a nice touch, along with the body via a Hollywood prop specialist. It all made for a fun-filled mystery weekend game engineered by Karl and his pals, and, J. T., the double-crossing, scrawny traitor, was in on the joke as well. . . . If only it were true.

Jessica felt J. T. pushing a handkerchief into her hands. He'd already placed one over his own nose to ward off the sickly sweet and sour odor of charred flesh, which she knew only too well to be real—no moviemaking magic could capture such a stench. Handling burn victims was never easy.

J. T. was saying, "Gives me the heebie-jeebies just lookin' at her."

"Yeah, right," agreed Repasi. "Makes my skin crawl,

too. Thorpe, this is a real body, a real crime scene. If you ever got out of that laboratory of yours in Quantico, you'd know this is the rush we live for, right, Jess?'' he suddenly asked her, making her feel even more responsible for this young woman's death than she already did, if that were possible.

When Jessica failed to agree with him or meet his eyes, Repasi shook his head and stared back at the dead woman, muttering, ''Hell of a way to go out, but maybe she was dead when he did her. Only an autopsy'll tell us so.''

''Any ID on the victim?'' Jessica asked, drawing Fairfax's attention.

''Nothing found so far. No purse or wallet, no, but a front desk check says the room's registered in the name of a Chris Dunlap. We might assume this is Chris.''

''If the room is registered to the victim here, it should be a Chris Lorentian,'' she muttered in response. ''Maybe Dunlap's a maiden name.''

J. T. put an arm about her.

The fire investigator's eyes widened as he asked, ''You knew her?''

Repasi jumped into her face. ''How do you know the victim, Jessica? Cops are going to want to talk to you. Is she with the convention, in the club?''

''Only briefly met by . . . by phone, and no, she's not with the convention, so far as I know. I only spoke briefly to her. Damn . . . damn,'' Jessica further muttered as if to herself, the men in the room all staring now at her.

''Whoever killed her, he or she held the room for some time before doing the deed then,'' J. T. pointed out unnecessarily, likely needing to hear himself speak in the face of such horror. Jessica realized that he seldom got out of the lab and that he was hardly used to such awful crime scenes as this. She instinctively grasped the protecting hand he'd placed on her shoulder, giving it a squeeze.

''You okay?'' she near-whispered to him.

''Don't worry about me, Jess.''

"You look a little pale."

He stepped away from her, closer to the body, giving it his full attention, holding himself in, and lying without saying a word.

Jessica began barking orders, saying, "Contact the desk again. Find out for certain who the room was registered to. See if it's ahhh . . . ahhh . . . see who signed for the room."

"Yeah, like the bastard's going to leave his name at the desk," mocked Karl Repasi. "Maybe toss his business card into the jackpot drawing beside the clerk?"

"Karl," she said, looking at the man's light Polish features, "did you place a call from this room earlier?"

"What? What in hell are you implying, Dr. Coran?"

"No way," said the fire investigator. "Phone line was seared through and the electrical in here is out. I had to go next door to call the desk."

"Damn it. Well, don't anyone touch the phone again. It may have the killer's prints on it." She then again turned to Repasi and asked, "Then you didn't at any time use the phone?"

His frown was answer enough, but he muttered in agreement, "Yes, beneath all that grime on the phone, there's likely to be some prints we might salvage. No, I haven't touched the phone, dear, believe me."

The use of the word "dear" for her was condescension enough, but then Karl asked, "You look as pale as your pal Thorpe, Dr. Coran. Can I get you a glass of water?"

The stench of charred flesh had its dizzying effect on her, but more so was the realization that she had spoken on the phone with the victim, at the killer's arrangement, less than an hour before. "Oh, God . . ." She felt a bit light-headed, the room and the still-smoldering flesh conspiring to create of her a nauseous and useless bundle of nerves.

"Why don't you Quantico folks let me take care of this bit of nasty business," continued Repasi, a stout, squat, yet powerfully built man whose ego was also stout. "Go on along now, the two of you. The Vegas coroner's been called. There's nothing more you can do here."

It was obvious Repasi wanted the case, or at least to be a large part of it; he no doubt had decided on entering and seeing the sooty writing smeared across the mirror that this would be a high-profile case, one that might bring him some notoriety. Part of Jessica told her to do as Repasi wished—step away and leave it for others to clean up. She didn't need this. Another part of her recalled the screams of the young woman lying now like so much petrified wood on the burned bed.

J. T. half-whispered to Jessica, "Then it was her on the phone."

Jessica was slow to agree. There seemed something indecent in the circumstances, something vile in having just spoken to the dead woman, and despite the fact that Jessica hadn't played a voluntary part in Chris Lorentian's brutal murder, she somehow felt responsible. But these feelings must be kept capped; it wasn't something she wanted to open and examine here and now.

But Karl Repasi remained keenly curious. "Are you telling us that the victim telephoned you just before the murder?" he pressed.

"That'd be impossible," countered Fairfax. "Her hands and feet were tied. The ropes are burned into her flesh."

"Then the killer dialed for her," replied Repasi, "telephoning you, Dr. Coran. Why? What does that mean?"

"Yeah, whataya make of that?" chorused Fire Detective Fairfax.

"The killer . . . the man who did this . . . telephoned Jessica," J. T. admitted. "Moments before the murder, to tell her what he planned. Isn't that right, Jessica?"

"Not quite. He never spoke a word. He just wanted me to hear her shrieking death as she burned to death, the unholy bastard."

Repasi's mouth fell open, but he managed to say, "He

called you? From here? From the crime scene? And you asked if I used the phone?'' His twitching mustache combined with his doughy, round-faced features to fill the bowl of consternation looking back at her.

Jessica's simple reply held an elegance of its own. ''There's a record of the call with the desk, yes.''

''Then he called you before the fire?'' pressed Repasi, fascinated now. ''He actually spoke to you? Told you what he planned?''

''I spoke with *her*, not him, never him.'' She pointed to the dead woman as she corrected Repasi. ''She asked for me, for my help.''

''By . . . by name?'' asked Fire Detective Fairfax, amazed.

''And the killer? What did he say?'' Repasi again pressed.

''Nothing, not a word.''

''He said nothing to you?''

''Nothing and everything,'' she countered.

''What's that supposed to mean?''

''Bastard just wanted me to hear her die, and I did. I heard it all. . . .''

The men in the room, including her friend and partner John Thorpe, stared in blank astonishment at her words.

''He wanted to make sure I knew what he did to her; wanted me to hear her suffer, wanted me to hear her pleas to him, and her pain when he turned her into a ball of flame. And he got exactly what he wanted. . . .''

''What exactly did she''—Fairfax pointed to the body with the pen he'd been waving around—''say to you?''

''She—what I take as our victim here—she asked if it was me, asked by name . . . told me her name, Chris Lorentian, she said.''

Fairfax's face scrunched up as if trying to decipher the information.

Jessica continued, ''She was crying, blubbering, terrified.''

"Told you her name?"

"Chris, she said . . . Chris Lorentian."

"Sounds familiar," Fairfax replied, setting his hat back on his head, contemplating this.

Jessica lifted a fist and added, "She said something about gasoline, that he doused her with gasoline. I heard the whoosh of flame, heard her scream . . . heard him—"

"Her attacker?" asked Repasi.

"Heard him laughing, cackling, at the sight of her tied to this bed and burning atop it."

"My God . . ." J. T. tried to find a pocket of breathable air.

Jessica, too, felt faint. She tried to think of pleasant places, blue skies, green meadows, Hawaii, James Parry, anything but this reality before her.

"She wasn't tied to the bed," Repasi corrected Jessica.

"What?"

"She was bound, hand and foot, face up and watching when he put the torch to her. Fairfax believes he had to've used an easily controlled and focused flame, as with a wand and torch, say a butane torch, right, Fairfax? Fairfax says he concentrated the burn at the eyes, but that he did a pretty good job of frying her altogether, since he doused her body and clothes with gasoline."

Jessica went for the door, where she held tight to the moldings, her emotions intermingling with the recent memory of hearing Chris Lorentian's agonized screams, the thought now overpowering her emotions. She glanced out into the hallway over her shoulder where people were being gently assured that they might return to their rooms, that there had been a false alarm, no fire. In the crowd of faces, she saw that morbid curiosity that comes with the smell or the sight of death. In the hallway, she thought that perhaps she might find some semblance of clean air, perhaps escape this nightmare. Instead, she found the drooling crowd and wondered if the killer himself might not be here, watching . . . overseeing his handiwork. . . .

J. T. agreeably joined her, himself anxious to leave the death room odors and sights.

"Good idea," she heard J. T. say.

Repasi joined them in the doorway and muttered, "Yes, good thinking. I'll take care of things from here, Doctors."

"Be my guest," J. T. told him, wrapping an arm about her, and while he attempted to lead her from the death room, Jessica stood her ground, a sooty carpet. With his failed attempt to get Jessica away from room 1713, J. T. tried dark levity. "This is going to put a hell of a crimp into the convention, huh?"

"It is so odd, Jessica," began Repasi again. "You say you don't know her, yet she calls you for help." A big man who might've played linebacker in college, Karl instantly dropped his stare, realizing how crude he was being, or perhaps he had gotten a glimpse of himself, his reflection, in her hazel eyes; she was unsure which. Karl's eyes now fixed on her bare feet, and indicating the soot all around, he suggested, "You might want to bag your feet, if you're staying." His own shoes were covered with polyethylene bags, and the carpet was scorched in irregular patches, mostly about the bed, where the fire had scattered like so many sprites and unthinking fairies at play.

Jessica wasn't answering Karl, nor did she notice the stares garnered by her from Fairfax and the photographer who'd obviously overheard enough to make him stop shooting pictures. Jessica stepped away from Repasi and located a box of polyethylene bags near the door and placed them onto her feet, securing them with rubber bands.

"I want a closer look," she announced and stepped back into the charred ruins of the room.

· FOUR ·

Swift as fear.
—THOMAS PARNELL

Fire Detective Charles Fairfax described the condition of the room when firemen first arrived, relating what others had told him. The body was already burned to a crisp, and smoke plumed out the door. The door was left ajar by the killer. He wanted her found just as she lay as quickly as possible after writing out his message. But if he used her body creosote and his hand to write his message, then he must exist on carbon monoxide, unless—''

''Unless he wore a gas mask of some sort.''

''An oxygen mask, like a firefighter,'' Jessica guessed.

''Even so, with all the smoke he created, he'd have to get out extremely fast before becoming disoriented and unable to see.''

''Another minute or so,'' explained Fairfax, ''and a flashover would've occurred here. Everything in the room, including the mirror, would've melted. But this guy somehow controlled the fire he set.''

''Looks like murder, pure and ugly,'' Karl now said, stepping in a bit closer to the god-awful remains. ''Some creep, for whatever perverted reason, douses her with gasoline, ignites her with a butane torch, if Fairfax is right, reaches out and touches you, Jessica, and he leaves his nasty little message on the mirror for us to ponder before simply walking out amid the confusion of a fire alarm while the victim is turned into so much toast on the bed.''

"She went up like a marshmallow," Fairfax indelicately added. "Room is adjacent to a stairwell. My guess is he used it to escape unseen."

"Are you sure, Jessica, that you do not know the victim?" asked Repasi.

"I'm sure. Besides, even if I had known her at some time in the past, she's certainly unrecognizable now."

"All right, then you didn't know her, and perhaps she didn't know you. . . . Then . . ."

"What, Karl?"

"This isn't Chris Lorentian, this Chris person wants us to believe it is she, so she can make a clean escape from whatever or whomever she's running from. So she arranges for a stand-in, and *voilà*—one crispy-fried body."

"That's some leap," protested J. T.

"If not, then there is only one other conclusion."

All eyes turned to Repasi, and he liked the attention he was getting. Finally J. T. asked, "And what might that be, Karl?"

"The *killer* knows you, Jessica."

"We don't know that," defended J. T. "I mean, he may know *of* her, but there's little chance he actually knows Dr. Coran."

Repasi's impish eyes threw out sparks. "Maybe it's Matisak, back from the grave. Just kidding, of course. . . ."

J. T. instantly shouted, "That's not funny, Karl!"

"I told you, Karl," Jessica differed. "She was alive when he did her. I spoke to her, goddamn it!"

"You don't know for sure, not one hundred percent, Jessica," Repasi countered.

"I know what I heard."

"The ears can deceive. Whoever set up this elaborate game may've wanted you to believe exactly as you do. Let's say this Chris Lorentian person was trying to hide from, from whatever. What better way than to fake her own death? Another possibility is that the sounds you heard were prerecorded."

She swallowed hard. "I hope you're right, but I rather doubt your theory will pan out, Karl."

"For all we know, this person here may've been dead when she was put to the torch," Repasi added. "The killer or killers could've taped the screams earlier, played her screams into the receiver for your benefit, and—"

"I held a conversation with her."

"The kind of technology that's available these days, that, too, can be explained away."

"No, it was a conversation. She responded to my words. That couldn't have been arranged for my benefit. God," she said with a moan. "For my benefit. You hear what that implies?"

Repasi put up a consoling hand to her and said, "He or they might've fired up the bed, maybe . . . but just to burn her alive? We best not assume anything, Jess. He or they could've put her out with an injection, a ball peen hammer, any number of—"

"You've no way of knowing that until an autopsy is performed, not in the condition she's in," countered J. T.

"Not a mark on her other than the catastrophic results of . . . the flames?" Repasi theatrically asked. "Impossible to say here and now, correct."

"Are you taking charge here, Karl?" asked J. T.

"Not likely. I hear Lester's someplace in the hotel, probably at the gambling tables." Lester Osborne had been the Las Vegas City coroner for the past ten years, and he'd been most instrumental in getting them all here to Las Vegas, or so Jessica understood. Osborne was on the steering committee that had chosen the Flamingo Hilton as their rendezvous point.

"Come on, Jess," suggested J. T. "Let's leave this mess for Karl and Lester, then."

"I want photos of the mirror, the message, the body all sent to . . . to Quantico, to Eriq Santiva, Karl. You understand?'' she asked, finding the steel she needed for a graceful exit.

Repasi nodded reassuringly, saying, "Consider it done. I think Thorpe's right. You're too personally involved in this one, and you look like a ghost, Jess. Better get out of here, now.''

''Let me know what you and Osborne learn at autopsy,'' she countered, getting in the last word.

Jessica, feeling emotionally overcome, now willingly allowed J. T. to guide her from the death room and down the hallway, where she removed the plastic coverings from her feet. There, suddenly the elevator doors opened and a grinning Dr. Lester Osborne, his round head speckled with freckles, appeared like a hefty ostrich in a plumed baby blue tuxedo that screamed eccentricity and bad taste, a lethal fashion dose.

A small, potbellied man in bow tie and ruffles, Lester stepped high and energetically off the elevator with his black bag in hand, and now he stood before them, his eyes instantly going to Jessica's bare feet. "Cute," he muttered, "but I would've imagined you did your nails in red or black.''

"Dr. Lester," replied J. T., "you've got a handful down the hall."

"So I hear. Well, Doctors, hello and welcome to Las Vegas just the same, and how was your flight out from D.C.?''

"They've got a badly burned murder victim inside, Lester," replied J. T. "I think you're needed by the fire marshal. Repasi's in there with the fire team now.''

While Lester balked mentally at learning about Repasi's interest, he kept silent about it and nonchalantly replied, "No one's going anywhere, besides . . . what with all of you here and Repasi on the inside, who needs an old fart like me in the way?'' He looked down the hallway to where Karl Repasi stood shaking his head, a curl of smoke issuing from the death room crowning the man, creating an aura about him, making him look more devilish than usual. "Look at that bastard," Osborne finally noted, sending Jessica's eyes back toward Repasi. "I guess I can't let Karl beat me in my own hometown, now can I?"

"I want you to know, Lester," began Jessica, "that the victim was alive when the killer put the torch to her. I heard the sudden rush of fire, obviously, when he ignited the body with the torch."

"She? The victim? Torched? And you heard it all?"

"Burned alive, Lester."

"And you can tell that at a single glance, can you, Jessica? What a miraculous pair of eyes you've developed over the past few years. Have you become psychic as well, Jessica? Your old man would be proud, but I think he would also be cautioning you—"

Jessica didn't want to give Repasi the pleasure of repeating her story to Lester Osborne. If he must hear it, he'd hear it from her.

J. T. tried to usher her onto the elevator, but she pulled free from his grasp and continued. "The victim was speaking to me on the phone *when* he killed her, Lester. He obviously planned it that way. He arranged to murder her for me to . . . to—"

"For you?"

"For my benefit. For some twisted purpose I can't begin to—"

"Then he—whoever this vile person is—intended for you to be involved in the autopsy, no doubt," J. T. suddenly realized. "He killed her because . . ." He brought himself up short.

"To test me," she replied. "To test my abilities against his, to test my reputation? To make a reputation for himself?"

"Dear God," added Osborne. "How utterly—"

"Insane," supplied J. T.

"Ruthless," finished Osborne.

Repasi had joined them, and overhearing, he added,

"Your reputation always did precede you, Jessica."

J. T. instantly reacted. "Not funny, Karl."

Jessica muttered in soft response, "He has killed some-one simply to . . . God forbid . . . to test me. It's too much . . . too damned much to deal with."

"Come on, Jessica," urged J. T. "I'm taking you to your room."

"Yes, okay . . . I've got to find my shoes and change."

"What you've got to do is lie down, Jess."

"No, we have an autopsy to perform, J. T."

"Let Repasi and Osborne handle it."

"You think so?" She looked at the other two M.E.s—Osborne, the Las Vegas M.E., and Repasi, whose home base these days was Phoenix, Arizona.

"If you get involved in the autopsy, you'll be playing right into this madman's hands, Jess," suggested Lester Osborne.

J. T. instantly agreed, adding, "You want another Matisak in your life?"

Repasi and Osborne stared at her, sizing her up, in their own way testing her mettle, all of them familiar with her history of dealing with madmen. She felt so horribly and irrevocably awful about what had happened to Chris Lorentian. Finally Repasi said, "I think Osborne and Thorpe are right, Coran." Between the lines he had clearly challenged her. "Go . . . go." He indicated the elevator with a little shrug. "Do as your friends advise. No one will think any less of you. Osborne and I have everything well in hand. We'll take care of the remains."

She hesitated only long enough to consider J. T.'s admonition. "I'll want a full accounting," she replied when suddenly the fire investigator came storming toward them.

"Lorentian . . . I just remembered. She's . . . that is, she could be related to Frank Lorentian."

"Owner of one of the largest casinos in Vegas," finished Lester Osborne with a whistle.

Repasi stared a hole through Osborne's chest. "Lester,

you think it could be Mob-related? You know, a professional job, a contract killing?"

Osborne hesitated answering, went to the door and peeked inside, turned, and replied, "Too messy to be Mob-related."

"Besides, if that were the case, why'd the killer dial Jessica's number?" added J. T.

Repasi defended his notion, saying, "Lot of those guys are eccentric types. Maybe he likes fire, likes to watch and wanted to, as she says, taunt her, test her, see if she's as good as the papers say. After all, she has a reputation as the best the FBI has to offer, and guys who travel in Frank Lorentian's circles, well . . ."

"Then you know who Lorentian is?" asked Osborne.

"I've heard of him, sure."

Jessica stared hard into Karl Repasi's eyes, angry at the suggestion and all the assumptions that went with his earlier remarks. He'd said nothing of this earlier when he had heard the name Lorentian. But she kept her counsel.

Osborne said with a moan, "Damn . . . damn . . . Frank Lorentian."

"Can't be sure till we contact him," cautioned Fairfax. "Ask him if he's got a Chris in the family and if she's missing. We need some estimate on her age, height, weight, all that. . . ."

Scratching his near-bald head, Osborne asked, "You found no ID, purse, anything with her?"

"*Nada,* zip, and the room was registered to a Chris Dunlap."

"We'll get her vital stats just as soon as you can release the body to the ambulance guys and get it down to my morgue," assured Osborne, his nose twitching from the stench.

Jessica tried taking deep breaths, but the fire odors were harsh and not to be deeply swallowed. She found the hold button on the elevator, released it, and with J. T. at her side, they floated up three flights to return to the relative safety of her room, but she now wondered at its false security. Once back at her room, she fumbled with the key, her hand shaking, until J. T. grabbed it and steadied her. The god-awful dialogue she'd had with Chris Lorentian moments before the girl was put to the torch kept replaying like a macabre script in her head, and she feared it would ever be there to haunt her, no matter what else came of the crime committed in 1713 tonight.

Inside the room, J. T. solicitously asked if she'd be okay, adding, "Can I get you a glass of water, twist of lemon?"

"Yes, thanks, and I'll be fine," she said, trying to sound brave.

"Vodka might be better for me," he suggested, knowing that Jessica had fought and won a battle with alcohol during the long manhunt for Matthew Matisak.

Misunderstanding him, she quickly replied, "Not for me, but help yourself to the bar, if you like. Key's on top."

J. T. found some ice, orange juice, and a dwarf bottle of vodka. He quickly made himself a drink and downed it, and made another. Jessica had already fallen into a chair beside the window, where neon lights reflected up at them.

"Can't see any stars even from way up here," she mused, staring out at the gray-black sky.

"This lunatic could call you again," suggested J. T.

"They say. . . . well, Warren Bishop says you've got to go out to the desert to get the full effect of the blanket of stars in the western sky. I spoke to Warren on the phone before we flew out."

"Maybe you should check out of here, or at least get another room," J. T. suggested, his thin hand tightly wrapped about the vodka glass.

"He's miles from here by now," she replied, realizing that moments before she'd been wondering if he might not be in the crowd milling about 1713. "Besides, I'm exhausted and I'm going to bed, so I want you out."

J. T. found a seat opposite hers. "Sure you don't want

to go downstairs for a while, be among friends, Jess? The reception's just getting under way, by my calculation.''

"I believe I have to agree with Karl Repasi on that one.''

"Say again?''

"I've already had my macabre reception.''

He groaned in response.

"Go on, enjoy! You can tell me how you made out at the gaming tables tomorrow.''

J. T. smiled, downed his drink, and stood up. "Yeah, sure. You're probably right about this creep. They're usually cowards in the end, aren't they?''

"They—how can *they* keep coming and coming?'' she asked.

J. T. had no answer for her. He placed a brotherly hand on her shoulder and squeezed. "I'll look for you in the morning.''

"Meantime, I have this,'' she replied, lifting her hefty Browning automatic, the gun that she'd used against Mad Matthew Matisak.

Feydor was pleased with himself, pleased with the work he'd accomplished, pleased that Satan, too, was pleased. Killing number one is nine had given him a great sense of closure. It had also given him a great sense of power, and so had making fools of the authorities.

It had also reduced the redness and swelling of his red rash. Satan appeared to be a being of his word, despite Wetherbine's continued warnings. "He'll take you down with him. He's the consummate liar.''

While they searched the usual escape routes out of the city, he had slept comfortably in a bed on the fourth floor, one he'd registered for under his own name, paying cash. While Feydor had waited for Jessica Coran's arrival at the hotel, he'd rifled through Chris Lorentian's bags and purse, and he'd found her wallet stuffed with large bills, as well as a ticket made out to a Chris Dunlap out of Vegas.

Just as he had told Feydor what materials and instruments would be needed for the work, Satan had said he would provide for Feydor's safety, and he had. Dr. Wetherbine had been wrong about everything. A man could align himself with Satan, strike a bargain, and walk away free of any lesions or permanent scars and pain.

Feydor had merely to bide his time. At dawn, he found himself waiting about the lobby and the casino, no red hair now, for the tour bus that would slip from the city beginning at 6:00 A.M. He had a ticket to ride. . . .

Feydor felt comforted now that he had taken the first step in his long journey, a journey laid out before him by the most supreme supernatural being of them all, the creature of pure evil, Satan. And happily, Feydor's first contact with Dr. Coran had been precisely as Satan had planned; it had gone so flawlessly well.

He knew, for he had stood in the crowd who watched outside room 1713. He'd seen the FBI woman's distress. He'd been questioned among others about what he might have seen or heard. He'd remained calm, assured, strong in the faith.

Seven more such victims, and Coran would make the true ninth and final victim.

Then Feydor's obligations, his pact with the Devil, would have been performed, finalized. . . .

He would make a wish at the well, and all would, in the end, be well. Feydor would be well and whole again.

Feydor handed the ticket over to the tour guide, who smiled widely and with a quick glance, said, "Welcome aboard, Chris. Why don't you check those bags with your driver, Dave."

Returning the woman's smile, Feydor did as instructed, handing the tall, lanky bus driver two bags that had belonged to Chris Lorentian, while he held firmly to a small black briefcase that held his torch, wand, gasoline, mask, and tools. After checking Chris Dunlap's suitcases, Feydor climbed aboard, clutching his own quite crucial briefcase.

He located a seat at the rear, and then Feydor leaned back into the cushions of the luxury tour bus, the one that Chris Lorentian would have been sitting on had she lived. He gave a momentary thought to who Chris Lorentian had been and why she'd been traveling under an assumed name. But it mattered little to him, so he dropped the thought for more important thoughts.

Satan was wise. Satan said he would provide, and he had. He provided Feydor with the perfect escape route and in plain view. There must be a dozen tour buses waiting for passengers to board this morning.

The tour bus would take him safely out of harm's way. What could be simpler?

Feydor had gone to the rear of the bus, from there he could keep a vigilant eye on anyone and everyone else aboard. Here, at the rear, if there weren't too many passengers, he might stretch out across two seats and finally relax as the coach rocked him to sleep. He felt now he could sleep peacefully, if everyone left him alone.

He trundled down the aisle, making eye contact with no one. When he got to the seat he picked out, he popped the overhead compartment door. He kept his tools and torch in the briefcase and he placed this in the overhead compartment, close at hand. Satan would soon give him a sign, and he would again heed the call and would again need the fire.

An exhaustive manhunt for the killer of Chris Lorentian was massed in Las Vegas. The local FBI office swung immediately into action, using what they knew of victim and killer profiling to make a guesstimate about the killer. The bulletin went out among police officials statewide, saying the killer might be a white male living in the Vegas area, either alone or with his parents, that he was likely in his late twenties or early thirties, but with an emotional age of a late teen, that he likely lived or worked close to the crime scene, had recently acquired a butane torch and other incendiary devices and had shown these items to acquaintances, was likely a "spontaneous" person with a quick temper, most likely taking great pride in his vehicle—probably a van or pickup.

More specifically, the report said that the killer may have been in the underground parking lot at the Flamingo Hilton between 3:00 and 6:00 P.M. on the day of the killing. The description went on to characterize the actions of the killer since his heinous crime, saying that his eating and drinking habits would suddenly become erratic, along with personal hygiene. He would show an inappropriate interest in the crime and reports about the crime, frequently initiating conversations about the case or fire deaths in general. He might show signs of burns, seared hair on hands, arms, face, and head. He likely worked with fire or with fire equipment; he had a knowledge of fire. He might suddenly and unexpectedly leave the area, the report warned.

Warren Bishop had gotten back to Las Vegas to find his office knee-deep in an investigation centering around Dr. Jessica Coran. He immediately sought her out, calling her at her hotel room and meeting her for breakfast. The hotel was filled to capacity with tourists and conventioneers, coming and going, and this meant a long wait for a table in the coffee shop. Limos, cabs, buses lined the streets outside. The tourist trade was in full summer swing.

While they waited for a seat in the coffee shop, Jessica repeated her bizarre story to Warren, whose reaction was one of amazement.

When they finally got a seat, Warren looked intently into her eyes and promised, "I'll see you have carte blanche with my field office, Jess. Whatever support you need, just ask. Meantime, I'll have my best techs wire your phone here, just in case."

This remark made her look up from her toast and coffee and into Warren's big brown eyes. "You don't think he'll actually call me here again, do you?"

"We'll take no chances." He reached across the table

and took her hands protectively into his own. "To date, Jess, you've been extremely lucky. I'm not going to sit idly by and see you get hurt on my watch."

Jessica gave a thought to their fleeting romance of years gone by when she was first recruited by the FBI, Warren always throwing a protective mantle about her. It was comforting, usually, but she also recalled feeling constrained and sometimes smothered by his constant attention.

"I appreciate all you and your team can do for me, Warren. And I guess you're right about the tap. Better safe than sorry."

"Getting a voiceprint on the guy could help tremendously later if we ever get him before a jury."

True enough, she realized. "Only thing is, Warren, he— the killer—didn't speak a word to me. He forced his victim to call me, and he fooled me into listening to a murder over the wire."

"He'll have to talk, sometime."

"It appears he prefers to write." She explained about the message left on the mirror. "Any ideas what 'one is nine' could mean?" she ended with a question.

He thought about the strange message, but shaking his head, replied, "Not in the least."

After that, they reminisced about earlier days, and each brought the other up on their current life outside the agency.

Warren stirred his coffee and sifted through his thoughts before saying, "I returned to the single life about two years ago, when my divorce came through; got a fourteen-year-old son and a twelve-year-old daughter whom I see whenever possible, which isn't often enough."

She informed him of her ongoing relationship with James Parry in such a way as to make it clear that she was not interested in renewing any former flame between them.

"Well, I'd best get your room upstairs set up." He stood up, his six-four frame as muscular and as attractive as ever, only his thinning and graying hair giving any hint that time had touched him. "I've got my best electronics man standing by. And Jess, don't worry. At least if this creep does call back, you won't be entirely alone with him. Your line'll be monitored at all times."

"Monitor this guy Charles Fairfax, too."

"Fairfax?"

"He's seeing to getting some laser-lifting fingerprint tests performed. Seems the killer wrote his message in the fried grease of his victim on the mirror. Stuck his hand in it. He either has a high tolerance for heat or blackened fingers."

"Grease from the burning victim? God . . . what a sicko."

The waitress, overhearing their conversation, grimaced, thought better of asking after them, and eased off.

"I'll keep after Fairfax," Warren promised. "Soon as we have the prints, we'll run a nationwide search on them."

"Thanks, Warren, for everything. You're a true friend."

"I'd still like to show you the desert sky at night."

"I'd like that, really."

"Plan on it. I'll pick you up at, say, eight?"

He was a hard man to say no to. "All right," she finally said, "see you then."

He said his good-byes and left Jessica to her day.

· FIVE ·

Silent as the sheeted dead.
—ANONYMOUS

Hours later, Jessica felt an overwhelming despondency regarding the lack of progress in the Chris Lorentian case. Despite all the FBI input and the heat put on the investigation into the heinous murder, nothing had come of all the time put in. Pictures of the young woman remained hard to obtain. Witnesses were nonexistent, and people who knew and saw Chris in the hours before her death were similarly hard to find. Her father, a wealthy hotelier with something of a shady reputation, had gone into a terrible depression on learning of his daughter's fate and was placed on medication.

Still, the newspapers and TV newscasts carried her photo and an artist's sketch of a red-haired man with whom she supposedly had been staying at the hotel. Her car and a rifled bag were located in the underground lot, but this discovery netted zero clues.

A reward for the capture and conviction of the man responsible for the horrid death of Chris Lorentian came from the family. Meanwhile, Jessica located John Thorpe, and together they decided to catch a cab to Lester Osborne's office to determine what, if anything, the autopsy had revealed.

The city crime lab and morgue occupied space with the

largest police precinct in Las Vegas, taking up an entire city block, but getting to it would take time, as it was across town.

They talked in the cab as the city that never slept seemed to be yawning in the morning sunlight, street cleaners running up and down.

"So, how did you sleep last night after all the excitement, Jess?" J. T. asked.

"About as well's could be expected. How about you?"

"Well, I admit, I was up pretty late," he replied, seeing a glint of deprecation in her sparkling eyes. "I mean, after I left you to rest in your room, I joined some of the other revelers at the reception for the convention, but . . . got to admit . . . I had little fun without you, dear."

"It's okay, honey," she shot back with a smile.

"Tell you what, though: News of what happened on the seventeenth floor spread like wildfire through our little community of forensics experts."

"Is that so? And how much did you blow on the fire?"

He tried his best to look offended. "Hey, I didn't have to say a word."

"But you did?"

He shook his head and added, "Those guys were putting the pieces together as if playing a whodunit puzzle, for the sport of it all, and by the time I got downstairs, everyone— and I mean everyone with an M.E. at the end of his or her name—had heard about your involvement—you know, the phone call—and that Lester Osborne and Karl Repasi were principal M.E.s on the case, and the poor victim, this Chris Lorentian, she'd been painted as some kind of shadowy figure somehow connected to Vegas's equally shadowy underworld."

"All that, huh? Damn it, I'd hoped to keep my involvement—my tenuous connection with the killer—to ourselves, J. T. Now look what you've done."

He held up his hands. "I swear to you, Jess. Everybody

in the community had already heard before I got down-stairs, really, honestly.''

''You're sure of that?''

''I swear, Jess. I wouldn't lie to you about that. Most everyone I talked to had the story already.''

''Repasi, you suppose? You suppose he spread it?''

''All it would've taken was a call to one of his pals. As for Chris Lorentian, most are chalking her death up to some sort of Mob-related revenge hit, not so much on young Chris as her father, whose business contacts are said to be serpentine. Oddsmakers are making book on it.''

''Jesus, is there anything in this town they don't bet on?''

''No, no, there isn't.''

The cab pulled around a line and double-parked along-side the civic center and city government building they had come in search of. J. T. and Jessica climbed from the cab and stood in the desert sun as it reflected from the blinding mirrored glass here.

Deep inside the building's multileveled basement, Jessica and J. T. found Osborne and Repasi working dili-gently over the dead girl's cranial cavity, where they'd cut her open to reveal the brain. ''Fluids completely gone . . .''

''Dehydrated,'' they confirmed for the tape-recorded autopsy report.

Both Repasi and Osborne looked as if they'd gotten even less sleep than had J. T. Each man was tired and exasperated, perhaps as much with one another as with the body, from the sound of things. A third man, a young assistant to Osborne, tried to stay out of the cross fire.

Osborne, his bow tie dangling like a dead bird below his open collar, fired a fresh volley at Repasi. ''Do you really, honestly, think cutting open her chest and snatching out her rack of vital organs is necessary, Dr. Repasi, when we know for a fact she was alive when she was put to the torch?''

''Thoroughness is my watchword, Doctor,'' replied Re-

pasi, whose wild shock of hair hung in his face. He'd long
since dispensed with his hairnet.

J. T. understood the tension, knowing its creator was in
fact the mummified corpse itself, black and clothlike to the
touch.

Osborne gritted his teeth, released pent-up air, and replied, "We have corroboration now. It's no longer just Dr.
Coran's word. We have hard evidence she died of her
burns! There's the killer's message, left in his own
hand . . ."

Repasi coolly replied, a touch of his Polish-Romanian
accent creeping in. He'd worked to control it over the
years, but his obvious weariness now got the better of him.
"What about the blow to the temple that I found? I believe
in being thorough, and if my name is to be on this autopsy
report, then—"

"Then by all means, don't put your bloody name on it.
I'll take full responsibility. It is my jurisdiction."

"And you invited my help, sir!"

"Is that what you call it when you invite yourself in on
an autopsy, Doctor?"

Jessica cleared her throat to announce her and J. T.'s
presence. They had both gowned up and wore surgical
masks and gloves, their shoes wrapped in surgical booties.
"Doctors, how are you?" she asked, not expecting an answer. "I trust all necessary information has been relayed
to FBI headquarters? I put in a call to Eriq Santiva last
night, left him a complete and detailed message about
what's going on here," she white-lied, having told Santiva
nothing yet about how the killer had contacted her. It
wasn't the sort of information one left on an answering
machine. "He's expecting crime-scene pho—"

"All done, Jessica, dear," assured Karl, his eyes narrowing in mock consternation with her. "You know I keep
my promises. And as for Dr. Osborne and me . . . well, we
are finished here, according to Osborne. What do you say,
Jessica?" asked Repasi. "Are we finished?"

"Toxicological reports?"

"Indicate sedatives, a heavy dose," replied Repasi.

"Don't suppose you could possibly tell me if there were any needle marks below the scorched skin?"

"Impossible with the equipment here," Repasi apologized, but it didn't sound apologetic. "Still, I found a bruise to the temple after noticing a slight indention."

"In all that crinkled flesh? Good work," Jessica complimented Repasi.

"Blood indicated the same high level of sedatives," added Osborne. "Some consolation in that nerve endings would've been dulled when it happened. And time of death was as indicated by the fire call."

"Her nerve endings weren't so dull she didn't scream, Lester," Jessica countered.

He curtly returned with, "You know what I mean."

"Yeah, I do, and I agree with Lester, Karl. We know what killed her. She sounded doped up when she spoke to me. I doubt the internal organs can tell us a thing more than we already know, and given the state of the body . . . well, it's already disfigured beyond recognition, wouldn't you say?"

"Not entirely," replied Osborne's quiet assistant as he put away some instruments he'd just cleaned. "Her father identified her around four this morning."

"That's what held up the autopsy," explained Repasi, speaking over the assistant. "We're given to understand that everyone and everything in Las Vegas waits on this tyrant named Frank Lorentian. As for the autopsy, I think we'd best be complete and thorough. I thought thorough was your trademark, Jessica."

She ignored this, continuing, "And I'm sure the family is anxious for Lester to release the remains to them, right, Lester?"

"As a matter of fact, yes. Mr. Lorentian's quite unhappy with us all."

J. T. added, "So, she was related to this big casino family."

"Closely, I'm afraid."

"The big man's daughter," added Repasi. "Read as much in this morning's paper."

Lester said sadly, "She'd been in the process of running away, it appears."

"How old was she?"

"Nineteen, dressed older but quite . . . immature, I'm given to understand. Frank Lorentian's known for being a doting father," Lester replied. "Lavished everything on her but what she truly needed, I suppose. . . . At any rate, she was rebellious, wanted to make a life on her own, outside Vegas, you see, away from her father's lifestyle, so she disguised herself, struck out on her own, but didn't get very far, as you see."

"How long had she been reported missing?" asked Jessica.

"Four days, according to Missing Persons."

"I'm sure Lorentian has a few enemies," suggested J. T.

"He isn't buying that theory," Repasi replied. "A kidnapping for ransom, he believes maybe, but not a hit to hurt him. He and the types he runs with, according to Lorentian, know not to mess with family, if you get my drift."

"But he could be wrong," J. T. replied.

"But there were no ransom notes, no demands?" asked Jessica.

"No, none forthcoming."

"Then it tracks back to me," she said, stepping closer now to the shriveled body of the dead woman. From the look of her, she'd been tall, about Jessica's own height. Her bone structure told Jessica that she was curvaceous, but what remained of her features left no clue as to her beauty or lack thereof. All that remained was a blackened, red- and brown-splotched mask of mottled and fire-bronzed cardboard, the epidermal layer of skin as burned away as the woman's clothes, all to feed the smoking inferno. Her eyes had, of course, been reduced to sockets, the soft tissues having sizzled away like bacon on a hot griddle, the oils easily feeding the flames. Still, somehow, the ugly, eyeless mask looked as if she were crying—impossible and quite unscientific, of course, yet very arresting. Of course, it was simply fatty tissues frozen in a moment of time—at the flash point of superheated air—intermingling with the natural bodily decay. There was no crying corpse here.

"Bring me up to date, gentlemen, please," Jessica requested.

"Well, no gunshot wounds, no contusions, abrasions, or hammer blows to the skull, nothing to indicate death before the fire reached her," answered Osborne.

"Except the single sharp blow to the temple, which I detected," corrected Repasi.

"I was getting to that, Karl," said Osborne with a moan. "The temple blow may've stunned her, but it wasn't a killing blow. That's clear."

"Fire investigation team found traces of butane, just as Fairfax had predicted, along with the gasoline." Repasi spoke in a near whisper in Jessica's ear. "Fairfax has quite a nose for such things. What do you think that might suggest?"

J. T. shrugged. "What do you mean, Fairfax's nose or a butane lighter? Neither fact is of much help."

"No, the traces of butane were at much greater concentration levels than caused by a lighter, and no lighter was recovered from the bed."

J. T. exchanged a look of confusion with Jessica before asking Repasi, "Then they're clearly saying that our killer used some sort of butane torch?"

"That's what Charles Fairfax believes," Lester Osborne replied, and believe me, Charlie's the best fire investigator in the city. He's an old friend of mine, and he was in the hotel . . . for the convention."

Repasi quickly added, "I'd seen him in the casino, so I had him paged when I saw what I . . . we had."

Lester nodded, saying, "Karl knows I don't even step into a fire-death scene until Charlie's completed his work. Saves me oodles of time and effort."

"And, last night, more time at the gambling table as luck would have it, right, Les?" Repasi teased. Repasi then turned to Jessica and said, "We told Lester here what you told us; told him about the *whooshing* sound you heard over the phone."

Jessica's eyes glazed over in thought as she pictured a butane torch with a long wand so the killer wouldn't burn his pinkies. Then he leans in over the smoldering body and sticks his fingers into the soup he's created of the victim to pen his cryptic message.

Repasi pushed her buttons further, asking, "Don't you see, Dr. Coran? You say you heard a great whoosh of air over the phone just before she screamed? Don't you see? Fairfax's instincts verify what you heard, Doctor," Repasi told her.

"That sounds about right, Karl. Now, is there anything else you two wish to share?" asked Jessica, trying to remain calm.

"Her hands were tied with a man's tie, her feet with a belt, and small remnants of a handkerchief were found amid the charred bedclothes."

"Any prints on any of these items?"

"None."

"Burned away, wiped clean, or he wore gloves."

"The phone?" she asked.

"Nada."

"All carefully planned down to the *nth* detail, and then he leaves prints in the message," Jessica said, wanting to curse the bastard responsible for this, responsible for killing Chris Lorentian for what appeared to be a random selection just to taunt Jessica Coran into giving him her undivided attention. Or did the killer know Chris? Was the charade some sort of attempt to hide the true nature of the murder?

"How did you know there'd be prints in the message?" asked Repasi.

Osborne added, "Yeah, Jess, where did that come from?"

"I smelled it, realized it was grease from fatty tissues. I just took a wild guess."

"Some wild guess," replied Osborne with a little shake of the head.

"I'd like to talk to Lorentian myself. Learn what I can about Chris. See if it helps," she suggested.

"My secretary outside has his number," replied Osborne. "Feel free."

Repasi followed her to the door and stopped her, asking, "Are you making it an FBI matter?"

"I think the killer already has, don't you?"

Both Repasi and Osborne exchanged a long stare, and they came to the same conclusion as J. T. during that moment of silence. Jessica finally spoke their fears aloud. "He may be just getting started."

Repasi instantly replied, "Yes, it's what he wants, isn't it? He'll continue to bait you this way, won't he? But what is his ultimate goal in all this?"

"He may"—she didn't want to believe it—"he may just want to outfox me."

Repasi twisted the invisible knife, adding, "He'll go on killing until someone stops him."

"And who's going to do that, Karl? You?" asked Osborne, a sheepish grin building on his face.

She drew in a deep breath of air. "It's either what he apparently wants, or it's an attempt to cover his true motive for killing Chris Lorentian."

J. T. instantly jumped on this theory. "Ingenious. Kill someone for common enough reason and mask it with a wild charade like this, calling you, Jessica, and getting the FBI chasing some mad lunatic when in fact the killer knew

Chris Lorentian and he acted coolly, calculatedly in both
the murder and in planning exactly how to throw authorities off. Could be . . . could be . . ."

"Are you going to . . ." Osborne's assistant cleared his
throat with a handful of words and tried again. "Are you going to tell Frank Lorentian that his daughter died because
some sick wacko crazy wants to play cat-and-mouse with
you, Dr. Coran?" The assistant stood, arms across his chest,
across the table from them, the younger man unable to hold
his words back. "I was there when the man identified his
daughter's remains . . . what was left of her to identify, that
is. The man crumpled."

She looked at Osborne's man. "I'm not sure what I'm
going to tell the father at this point, Doctor, and I suggest
no one speaks to the press of this until we've had time to
learn more about this psychopath."

Osborne raised a hand and began to object, but she cut
him short with, "Is that understood?" With that, she and
J. T. left the autopsy room.

"What's next, Jess?"

"We find out more about Chris Lorentian. Where she
went when she ran away, where she was staying and with
whom. Her hideouts and haunts. Apparently she didn't run
so fast and so far as she might've; perhaps if she had, she'd
be alive today; perhaps she was being given sanctuary by
a friend or friends?"

"So we find out who she hung with . . ."

"Who she knew. Where she was before this monster's
path came to cross hers. We find out where she had her
last meal, where she last bathed, where she last shopped,
and we find out what her plans were."

"Sounds logical, but shouldn't you leave it to the local
cops to talk to Lorentian?"

"I could, but I don't think the killer expects anything
less from me. I've already abdicated the autopsy to Lester.
God, I don't think I could've handled this one, knowing

what we know . . . that she died because of . . . of some twisted sicko's attachment to . . . to me, because—''

"Don't do this Jess. Don't go there."

"—because some whacked-out, wackity-wack read about me in the newspapers and came after me, and—"

"Jess, Jess . . . don't do this to yourself. There's no way this is your fault."

"You think Frank Lorentian will see it that way, J. T.? I wouldn't blame the man one bit if—"

"Stop this right now, Jess. This young woman's death is not your fault."

Jessica fell silent.

They located Osborne's secretary, a pleasant, middle-aged woman with a broad smile who quickly looked up Lorentian's number and address, asked if they'd like for her to get Mr. Lorentian on the phone or simply to type out all the information for them. She also asked if they'd like a cup of freshly brewed coffee, rattling off several names of designer brands.

Jessica declined the coffee and took the address, thanking the woman on her way out.

Jessica and J. T. went directly for the Desert Imperial Palace, owned and operated by Frank Lorentian. They were quickly across the city, despite the congestion, thanks to a cabbie who knew every byway and back road. In fact, they faced more roadblocks inside the gambling casino than outside, designed as it was to keep people in the maze. And after several thwarted efforts to get in to see Frank Lorentian, they were finally led to the man's suite.

Lorentian looked like a shriveled gnome in his bathrobe and glasses, his skin a file-cabinet gray. His eyes, sunken deep, depressed, looked like those of a tortured ghost. His eyes looked through them rather than at them, a sure sign he remained sedated. From telltale signs about the room, he also appeared to have been drinking heavily, despite the certain caution of his doctor not to mix booze and pills, and despite the early hour.

Jessica thought the room stank of cigar smoke. When Lorentian turned his sad eyes away from them, he contemplated the world outside through a slit in the heavy drapery. In silence, he peered out at the desert sun and at the expanse of concrete that was dwarfed by the mountains in the distance. He worked at bolstering himself up, to stand tall and erect, larger than his own frame and depression allowed. When finally he turned to face them again, Jessica saw a devastated, shaken, physically hollowed-out, walking corpse, a man who might easily court death himself in a mad effort to find his lost child.

Lorentian's right hand was marred, missing several fingers. She imagined that in his youth, he'd been a rough, stubborn, hard-fighting street tough in Chicago or L.A. or perhaps New York, a man who generally got what he wanted. Jessica had seen larger-than-life photos of him adorning the walls downstairs in the business office, but somehow he had become a shell, the carved-out remains, a wandering shadow of the man in the pictures. She wasn't at all sure if he'd been in ill health for some time, or if this were the cataclysmic effect of his daughter's disappearance and now her death, but she imagined the latter was at work on him. She could imagine no worse blow to an indomitable spirit than the loss of a beloved child.

Lorentian was a small man in stature, and now in his expensive robe, he wandered the room, unable to make himself clear as he indicated a place for them to sit. The room screamed from outlandishly lavish furniture and decor, the floor-length windows covered in purple and burgundy, someone's idea of royalty. The false palace—penthouse suite—had become the father's mourning room, the ornate, crystal chandeliers ostentatious and vulgar alongside the decadent furnishings, which mixed Oriental with rococo. Jessica sensed a taste of vulgarity in the man as well.

"I'm Dr. Jessica Coran and this is Dr. John Thorpe, sir," she began.

"I know who you are!" It sounded an attack, the way he put it, but then he tempered himself. "I've been expecting you. Rollo from downstairs told me you were coming up." He looked anguished, caught on an unrelenting tenterhook that had risen from the depths of Hell to enter his entrails and tug and tear and rend from him all remnants of his soul. "I know who you are, Dr. Coran, and I was told this . . . this bastard who killed Chris . . . he talked to you? Called you at your hotel room, so that . . . so that you heard her in the fire, heard her screaming?" His heartfelt anguish was unbearable. He looked into Jessica's eyes for her answer. "Well? What kind of human trash does this to an innocent child, and what connection do you have with this monster? What did he say to you?"

So much for professional silence, Jessica thought. Obviously Osborne, his assistant, or Repasi, or all three, had already spoken to Lorentian about the events of the night before in complete detail. *We're all extremely sorry for your loss, Mr. Lorentian,* she mentally ventured, instantly realizing that this kind of tiptoeing about wasn't going to suffice here. She said, "Violence, it seems, is part of our human nature, sir; and no one is immune or safe from its influence."

"Indeed," J. T. gunned his agreement. "We're going to work hard, Mr. Lorentian, to locate the killer and bring him to justice. You can count on the FBI."

"FBI!" He spat his contempt. "Justice," muttered the gray-haired, ashen-faced Lorentian. "You think there can ever be any justice after this? Just tell me one thing: What did this bastard say to you, Dr. Coran?"

She shook her head. "He didn't say anything to me. He had . . . he had your daughter do all the talking."

Lorentian's eyes welled up and he instantly wiped them with a monogrammed handkerchief. "Did she . . . did she suffer long?"

"No, not at all," Jessica half-lied, knowing that Chris

did not die instantaneously, that is, without the time it took for the dying heart, mind, nerves, and cells to shut down completely; the death process, even amid flames, took a certain amount of time. Instantaneous death came only with explosions or high-velocity impacts such as airplane crashes in which the body became fragmented in the blink of an eye, as with ValuJet Flight 592's crash in the Everglades. Fire victims, such as Chris, did not circumvent the dying process. Few people ever died instantly. The phrase, "he died instantly" was something the living consoled themselves with, but death came in stages for a trapped fire victim: Once the fire has reached you, you might pray to the fire god for the smoke to render you unconscious, for the fire itself will burst your skin after the initial blistered epidermis has been fried off; next the blood is boiled to a searing pitch, followed by shock, followed by the lethal failure of multiple organs and loss of consciousness and heartbeat. All of this takes time, even under the heat of a directed torch.

When Lorentian remained silent, Jessica again spoke, leading him to where she needed him to be in his thinking. "We want to see this bastard fry, Mr. Lorentian, fry in Nevada's electric chair, you understand?"

"We don't got the chair in this state. They do lethal injection or gas. Either way it's too good for this . . . this . . . What kind of man does this kind of thing?"

"Maybe for this creep, they'll make an exception," suggested J. T.

He stared long and hard at J. T. but only replied, "Maybe . . . maybe somebody will. . . ." The innuendo resounded clearly enough.

J. T. said nothing in reply.

"We're afraid—no, we're *sure* that this fiend will kill again, Mr. Lorentian. We need your help."

He turned to look at Jessica, some of the old man's fire churning in the sad eyes now. "My help? You want my help?" He laughed. "Government people wanting my help. And they send you, of all people. The way I hear it, this bastard was pandering to you, Coran, when he killed my little girl, that he gets his rocks off by insulting you with this phone-in murder. Some are saying you chased this pervert here, cornered him here, and this is the result, my little girl is dead.''

''No, no, sir, there's no truth to that.''

He ignored her. ''Maybe I ought to hold you responsible for this, Dr. Coran.''

The gloves had come off, and the tranquility in the old gangster's voice was more chilling than any temper tantrum.

J. T. shot to his feet and firmly said, ''Just a minute, sir. None of this is Dr. Coran's fault. She didn't drive this man to his madness. She didn't create his fixation. The storm was out there and moving toward your daughter independent of Jessica.''

Jessica stood beside J. T. now, placing a hand on his arm, the gesture telling him she preferred to fight her own battles. She now stepped closer to Lorentian. ''We knew nothing of this killer before yesterday, before his first contact, and I don't know why he chose to contact me, Mr. Lorentian. Again, I say, we need your help, sir, before the . . . before he strikes again.'' She then turned on J. T., holding up a hand to him, saying, ''It's okay, J. T. Mr. Lorentian has every right to be upset. We're all upset.''

''I don't see how I can help you, so if you please . . . leave an old man to his grief.''

''Sir,'' J. T. interjected, his hand up like a schoolboy, ''we're all shaken and upset by the events that have—''

''Upset . . . *you're* upset. *My* world has crumbled, and *you're* upset.''

''Maybe another time,'' J. T. suggested.

''We need to know where your daughter was staying, with whom she spent her last hours, sir,'' Jessica pleaded. ''We have a killer to track.''

''If I'd known where she was, I'd have dragged her

home. I didn't have no idea then, and I don't have no idea now.''

"You checked with all her friends?"

"Yeah, of course." He began pacing again, his body language telling Jessica that he meant to hide something.

"And they were all honest with you?"

"As far as I was able to tell, yeah."

"And you had no reason to doubt any of them?"

He hesitated. He stepped about the room more. He paced back toward the drapes, stared out again, and finally, he again approached the doctors. He wrapped his arms about himself like the king of Siam in *The King and I* while Jessica continued to read his body language and patiently awaited his reply.

He finally admitted, "She was being closely watched."

"Really?" Jessica was legitimately surprised. "You had her in your sights? The whole time?"

"Obviously not . . . not entirely, anyway. I . . . knew where she was . . . for the first two nights . . . of her disappearance." Talking about this was difficult for him, as if his stomach were tossing dry tennis balls into his throat, as if all the guilt and remorse were lodged in his chest and vocal chords. "She somehow . . . found out I knew . . . got angry . . . at Sharon and . . . and sneaked off from her as well."

"Sharon?"

"Sharon Pierson. Her . . . one of her best friends."

"Who was on your payroll?"

His eyebrow arched upward and darted toward Jessica, an indication he was impressed. "Sharon owed the casino. It was her way . . . of paying me back."

"This Sharon calls you up with the deal the moment Chris shows up at her place?"

"No, it was my suggestion . . . should my little girl appear. I got the distinct impression she might've been hiding out at Sharon's. Chris"—saying her name aloud was painful for him as well—"she'd run off before. I thought I'd

give her time to . . . to cool down, you know? Figured
she'd be back soon enough, but by the third day . . . and
with Sharon swearing she hadn't seen Chris, I dropped a
dime to a friend on the force to locate her.''

"Did this friend file a Missing Persons report?''

"We don't work that way, no.''

"But there was a report made out on her,'' countered
J. T.

Jessica suggested, "Her friend Sharon? When you
called Sharon, she had thought Chris had returned home,
and she told you so, right? And Sharon made the official
call to the police? Is that how it happened?''

"Close enough . . .'' He nodded and fell into a seat,
looking like a deflated balloon. "Like Shakespeare, huh?''

"Sir?'' asked J. T.

"The Comedy of Errors.''

More like the tragedy of *King Lear,* Jessica thought but
did not say.

Lorentian went on, "I thought I had it covered, where
she was staying, and I was right. But she slipped out on
Sharon, 'cause she knew Sharon owed me and would keep
me apprised. We figure she heard Sharon talking to me on
the phone. Money . . . she hated it and she loved it, sweet
kid . . . sweet Chris.'' He was overcome with grief, the
tears freely raining now.

"Do you have any idea why the killer would have written a message about your daughter's being a . . . a traitor,
sir?'' she now asked.

"A traitor?''

"Any sort of traitor, to any sort of . . . cause?''

"A rebel, maybe, but a traitor?'' He sadly shook his
head. "No . . . no. She was a bit''—he paused, swallowed
hard—"she was a bit rebellious, feisty . . . gone back to
the hippie lifestyle, the way she dressed, the damned tat-
toos, the religious icons she wore, all that, but that's natural in the young, isn't it? Traitor? No . . . no . . . the word
has nothing to do with my Chris.''

"Any former boyfriends who might've categorized her as such?" suggested J. T.

"No, nothing like that going on. I woulda known. She hadn't an enemy in the world."

"How about you?"

The lion roared, "I was her father, not her enemy!"

"I meant, sir, anyone have reason to call you a traitor?"

"None," Frank Lorentian said with a cold eye and a coy laugh, his tone implying that he had more enemies than he could count on fingers and toes.

"Can you or your secretary provide us with a list of Chris's friends, their phone numbers and addresses?"

"See Virginia downstairs. She'll arrange it." Then he turned his glassy stare on Jessica. "One thing, lady: If you don't catch this SOB, and if you don't destroy him, I'll be even more upset with you than I already am. One thing you can count on . . . a sure thing, as they say here in Vegas. Now get outta here, both of you."

The naked threat wore not so much as a veil.

Again, Jessica told the man how extremely sorry they were for his loss, but this prompted only a deeper and more dangerous silence. It was a silence that told them the interview was over. The two medical people left Frank Lorentian standing once again at the covered windows, peeking out on a world he had helped to create, a world he no longer felt at ease in, a world that had so altered him with the horrible murder of his child that Jessica wondered if he would ever fully be a part of this world again.

· SIX ·

Fear not, nor be afraid;
have I not told you from of old
and declared it?
And you are my witnesses!
                    —ISAIAH: 44:8

Outside, in the hallway, Jessica leaned against a wall and said to John Thorpe, "God, I never get used to this part of the job."

J. T. nodded. "Always tough dealing with the family, any family . . . but this guy seems a bit loopy, and dangerous."

"The man was just apprised of the situation through Lester's office, has had to ID the body of his only child. . . . I feel for him."

"He could be a real danger to us and the investigation, Jess."

She looked into J. T.'s concerned eyes, gave him a pat on the shoulder and a fleeting smile. "I don't think so. God, he looked pathetic."

"He's dangerous, Jess," warned J. T. again.

"Perhaps . . . perhaps not. Right now, all I see is a poor, shattered man."

"Just remember that I was right about the cabdriver from the airport."

Jessica pulled herself from the wall, took a deep breath, shrugged, and said, "So, we'll remain cautious of Mr. Frank Lorentian."

"You don't want to be blindsided by him."

Jessica gave J. T. a wan smile. "Let's go see the secretary."

"Virginia, yes, for tea and crumpets," he said.

"And a list of Chris's friends and associates."

After gaining Sharon Pierson's address, they found a cab and located yet another area of the sprawling metropolis in the desert valley. The older, run-down section sported broken-down cars and battered, discarded, and neglected trash cans, empty beer bottles, wide-eyed children in dirty T-shirts running shoeless across hard-scrabble lawns, as well as half-demolished buildings long since condemned by the city.

It hardly looked the place for a spoiled child to run to.

At the door of a three-story walk-up, Sharon Pierson met them as she was coming out, her purse slung over one shoulder, both hands clutching a single suitcase stuffed wide, bulging like the sides of a rhinoceros. On seeing them at her doorstep, Sharon's eyes blinked a Morse code of dread, which Jessica quickly deciphered despite the red-rimmed eyes that had been given over to a morning's worth of tears.

Jessica flashed her badge, identified herself as an M.E. for the FBI, and announced who J. T. was, while J. T. offered to give the lady a hand with her luggage. They then waltzed her back inside, J. T. placing the bag in the unlit, cavelike foyer, while Sharon Pierson bolted several latches on her well-sealed door. "Guess I know you two are safe. Read about you in the papers, Dr. Coran."

"Really?"

"Guess you're something of a big shot, huh?"

When finally Sharon Pierson turned on a light, Jessica saw that the place was small, seedy, and unkempt, papers and discarded food trays sitting about, awaiting the roaches. The sink was filled with dirty dishes, and atop the counters lay the remains of half-finished dishes, a casserole here, half a sandwich there, pizza boxes stacked to one side.

Sharon Pierson appeared drawn, haggard, her skin like leather. Certainly much older than Chris Lorentian had been, she wore what amounted to a perpetual half snarl, as if readying for attack at any moment, her hair dead and stiff-looking from too many colorings and bleachings since her teens. A cigarette in her hand represented a sixth finger, its smoke helping to punctuate her words.

"I loved that kid like she was my own kid sister. I would've done anything for her," she told them now. "Anything . . ." Tears flowed freely.

"Like turn her in to her old man?" Jessica'd had enough with the pious act. "For some trade-off, something about a debt you owed?"

The green eyes glared at Jessica, sizing her up now. "Everybody in Vegas owes a debt." Sharon's dark red hair—soggy red noodles, Jessica thought—had fallen across one eye, but rather than wisp the hair back, the woman defiantly let it lay. She'd been drinking, and from the scattered bottles and knocked-over ashtray, she'd been doing so heavily. Jessica instinctively sensed an animal fear in her.

"Tell us what you can about the last moments you saw Chris alive," Jessica said firmly.

Pierson collapsed into a collection of dirty clothes left on her sofa. "My heart feels like . . . like a pair of frozen hands have hold of it," she confided, dropping her head into her hands. "If we hadn't fought, she'd've stayed, you know? She'd've just got on that bus this morning." The cigarette was still, lifeless in her hand save for the smoke now, and now she punctuated each line with sobbing. "She'd . . . she'd've left this hellhole, and she'd be alive now, having a good time, you know?"

"Got on what bus?" asked J. T.

"She was planning a trip." Sharon's head remained buried.

"Part of her getaway?" he asked.

She looked hard up at J. T. and Jessica. "Sure, why not?

Get away from Frank, from Vegas, all the crap. I told her it was a wonderful idea, and it was. Hell, she wanted me to go with her, and for a while, you know, I thought about it, thought about taking her handouts. Not like I ain't done it before, but this . . . this would've been a lot of money, and it'd mean I'd have to go against Frank's wishes, and . . ."

She abruptly stopped herself, realizing that she'd strayed into deep waters. Jessica finished her thought for her, saying, "And maybe he'd forgive his little girl someday, but not likely he's going to forgive you, right?"

She bared her teeth at Jessica. "I told Chris I couldn't leave my job and go traipsing off with her. We argued, she left. It's as simple as that."

"Where was she planning on going after she left you?"

"See the sights. She loved nature, you know. She wanted to be by . . . with nature. Poor young thing . . . When I think of what that bastard did to her . . ."

"Her father?" asked J. T.

"No, the fire psycho!" She lifted a newspaper and tossed it toward them. It landed on the floor with the bold headline reading: PYROMANIAC BURNS LOCAL GAMBLING CZAR'S DAUGHTER TO DEATH. A subtitle read, FBI ON TRAIL OF PHANTOM TORCH KILLER.

She stared across at them, saying, "It's all my fault she was killed."

"No, Sharon," disagreed Jessica. "It's not your fault. We're dealing with a psychotic sociopath here, someone who is deadly and uncaring."

"Someone who is as predictable as . . . as an earthquake or a tornado," added J. T.

"I should've made her stay. I could've! I shoulda sat on her."

"And you're afraid that Frank's going to come around to the same conclusion," suggested Jessica.

New tears welled up from the redhead. "If he ain't already, you know, and when he does . . . I—I—I can't be here. I gotta get outta this town.'' Her eyes fell on her suitcase.

"Did Chris buy you a ticket out?''

"No, I wouldn't take it. Wish I had now . . .''

"Listen to me, Sharon,'' insisted Jessica, lifting Sharon's head and directing her eyes to her own. "No one, not even Frank Lorentian, can sensibly blame you for what's happened to his daughter. Fact of the matter is, he blames me.''

"Yeah, sure . . . and isn't that crazy?''

"Believe me, he's not blaming you,'' Jessica insisted.

"How do you know what's in Frank's head? Nobody does. Besides, since when has Frank ever been sensible where his little girl's concerned? He likely blames everybody, the whole fucking world. . . .''

"He knows it's the work of a violent killer who . . . who very likely simply took advantage of an opportunity; in a sense a . . . a random act of violence.'' Jessica knew she was not entirely certain of the killer's motives, his method of abduction, or his mind, but she meant to say anything possible to get the Pierson woman to focus off herself and onto the night of Chris's disappearance.

The frightened woman merely shook her head and said, "If you can put 'Frank Lorentian' and 'sensible' in the same sentence, Doctor, then you don't know Frank Lorentian, and when he reads the papers, he's going to be upset, not just with me, but with you.''

This made Jessica look down at the *Vegas Morning Star.* J. T. lifted it from the rug and examined it more closely. "Damn it, Jess, they've got the whole bloody story here. . . .''

"What?'' she asked.

"How the bastard contacted you . . . how you heard the murder in progress over the wire, all of it.''

"Damn that Osborne.''

"Lester wasn't the only one who heard the story.''

"Repasi?''

"And what about the firemen, the photographer? The crime scene was full when you told Repasi. And it was all around the convention floor. Could've come from any number of sources, including Frank Lorentian."

"No way. How could Frank Lorentian have known the details of the death before we told him?"

"From what I hear, Frank Lorentian pays well for information, Jess. What I'm saying is—"

"Anyone at the crime scene might've sold the information to Lorentian?"

"Or used it to pay off a debt."

Sharon Pierson looked on, a glint of pleasure spreading across her face. Jessica guessed it was the feeling of comfort that the younger woman had gained on learning that someone else shared her position on the field—that she was not the sole target of Frank Lorentian's anger and revenge. Jessica refused to give in to the Lorentian phobia, but she felt her own anger welling inside. She wanted to slap herself for having acted so unwisely the night before at the crime scene.

She turned to J. T. and muttered, "Damn it. I ought to've known better than to shoot off my mouth." Jessica paced in the tight apartment room and reproached herself. "I wanted to tell Santiva the details personally."

"I thought you called him last night."

"I did, but I had to leave a message on his machine. I couldn't go into the detail I wanted."

"Guess he's likely gotten all the details by now."

"Along with all the wire services."

J. T. began talking to himself. "A flash fire in a five-star hotel, a gambling princess burned alive, all the makings of a *Movie of the Week*. Press's having a bountiful time of it . . ."

"Stupid, stupid me. Damn, just what this phantom fire nut likely wants, too."

There came a loud, firm knock at the door.

Sharon Pierson, her print dress smudged with cigarette

and drink splotches, went for the door a bit shakily, wary, her mind filled with notions of how the powerful Frank Lorentian might wreak revenge on her for Chris's demise.

"Who . . . who is it?" she asked.

"LVPD, ma'am, Detective Sternover. Mrs. Pierson?"

"You the cops?" she asked.

"Homicide investigation, ma'am. Like a few words with you about Chris Lorentian, when you last saw her, ma'am; help us with a number of unanswered questions, ma'am."

"Why don't you guys get your act together?" she asked of Jessica and J. T., frowning before she pulled the several latches from her door. She now peeked out and insisted on seeing ID with the new intruders. Finally, she waved two men inside, this time not bothering with the locks. "Guess I ought to feel pretty safe with the cops and the FBI on my doorstep, shouldn't I, Dr. Coran?" she asked. "But I won't bank on it."

Jessica introduced herself and J. T. to the local investigators, the one calling himself Sternover nodding appreciatively, introducing himself and his partner, Ned Gaites. Sternover stood a head taller than Jessica, a giant of a man, while Gaites stood perhaps five-nine. Both men were in their mid- to late thirties, but while Sternover was graying at the temples and dressed neatly and expensively, Gaites looked like a dark-haired college kid with no regard for fashion. In fact, he wore a Hawaiian shirt, white tennis shoes, and khaki pants, completely clueless. Perhaps he was doing some undercover work, Jessica decided. Sternover was a stovepipe, Gaites the stove.

"Been reading about you, Doctor," said Sternover. "Also, Gaites and me, we were looking for Chris Lorentian as a Missing Persons case."

"Really? How long?" Jessica pretended amazement.

"Right, for the past forty-eight-odd hours," sputtered Gaites.

Sternover added, "Didn't know we'd find you here, one jump ahead of us. Guess you're as good as they say."

Gaites's lip curled just enough to tell Jessica that these men had arrived in so timely a fashion thanks only to Frank Lorentian's influence. Obviously, Sternover and Gaites had had the apartment and Sharon Pierson staked out for some time, too.

Sternover was most likely Frank's friend on the force, but Sharon Pierson obviously did not know this. She also didn't know just how right she'd been about Frank Lorentian's interest in her. Perhaps Miss Pierson was in danger. Perhaps she ought really to heed her first instinct to survival. Perhaps the only chance Frank Lorentian had at a full recovery might be through his innate nature, via a kind of global vengeance Jessica and the others could only guess at. Certainly the man's influence was being felt here, now, like some primordial octopus with multiple tentacles.

"We'd like to ask you some questions, Miss Pierson," began Sternover, his mustache twitching and feeding into a large creased wrinkle on either side of his mouth. He'd have a hell of a time as a diver, Jessica thought, for with such a smiler's wrinkle positioned as it was, no mask made could stop the leaks. She thought he resembled Glenn Ford in all the old Westerns.

"Are you here in your official capacity then, Detective?" Jessica asked.

"That's a strange question, Doctor. Just what're you implying? What other capacity would we be here in, Dr. Coran?" Sternover's thick mustache twitched.

Gaites interceded, saying, "We're here just like you, for the same reasons."

Sternover verbally shunted Gaites aside, saying, "Just seeking to stomp out the ignorance that plagues us poor working cops; just here to open ourselves to the fire of truth, so to speak."

Gaites laughed at his partner's philosophizing words. "Damn, Ted, listen to yourself sometime. Can you 'magine being next to this guy all day, Doctors? Tellin' you, it's enough to make a good man go bad." Then Gaites turned serious. "We're here because some psycho's out there with a blowtorch, and according to you, Chris Lorentian may not be his first . . ." His words made Jessica wonder where they were getting their information. Nothing had been said by fire authorities about previous fire murders in the area; nothing had indicated any sort of previous pattern. There'd been none of that in the newspaper accounts either.

". . . and it certainly, certainly won't be his last victim," finished Gaites. "So, if you Feds'll stand aside and allow us to do our job . . ."

"We're not interested in doing your job for you," countered J. T.

"There a problem here?" asked Sternover, pushing his bull weight and size forward.

"Just one," Jessica returned, holding her ground, staring long into Sternover's cold eyes, a pair of purple grapes in the dim light, no seeds at the center to reflect back light.

"And what's that?"

"How much are you in for?"

"In for?" Sternover pretended ignorance.

"How short are the strings Lorentian's got over your head?"

Gaites stared hard at his partner, either a fine actor or a man amazed. "Ted, is that true?" asked Gaites, grabbing his partner by the lapels.

"All right, all right . . . enough with this machismo crap," said J. T. in an attempt to quell the sudden animosity. He then proceeded to offer up what little they had gotten from Sharon Pierson, finally telling the detectives, "We'd hoped to get more, but Miss Pierson obviously knows very little that might help in the investigation."

"Listen," Jessica told J. T., waving the newspaper story, "I'm going to let you three men coordinate information on this, okay, J. T., and I'm going to get back to the hotel, put in a call to Eriq Santiva before he hears what's going on without my input."

"Sure, sure," agreed J. T. "We can manage here."

With that, Jessica beat a hasty retreat, glad that she had conveyed to Sternover that she knew exactly whose payroll he was on. He didn't dare rough up or harm Pierson, not now.

Jessica flagged a cab, and in the ride back to the Flamingo, she stewed about all that had happened and all that she felt must happen in the next few hours. She needed to coordinate with local law enforcement through proper channels, and this meant she needed Quantico's okay and support as well as their manpower. She also very much needed a psychological profiling team assigned to this fire phantom. Most of all, she needed Quantico's immense storehouse of knowledge, its computers, to search for like killings that might be tied to the Phantom.

And she needed to get to Eriq before the news services did, if she weren't already too late.

Jessica's phone call to Eriq Santiva at Quantico Headquarters netted a good feeling of backup. While Eriq had the physical evidence of the crime in his hands, and he had gotten bits and pieces of what had gone on in Las Vegas, at the time of Jessica's second call, Eriq had not gotten all the details of how the killer had chosen Jessica as his conduit to authorities until now, until she told him. She also told him that the newspapers had jumped on the story there in Las Vegas, calling the killer the Fire Phantom.

Eriq assured her that FBI would put all of its powerful machinery into motion at Jessica's request for assistance, and Eriq meant to personally see to the back-shelving of other important cases in the bargain. "Quantico is at your disposal, Jess. Anything you need. I'll put the red flag on the locals and the field office there. You need it, you got it."

"Thanks, Eriq." She thought, *He's now a good and tried friend and associate.*

"If you say the word, Jess, I'm on the next flight there."

"That's not necessary."

"Then you're all right?"

"Yeah, I'm dealing—"

"As usual? There's nothing usual about this business, Jess. My concern is not just for your physical safety. I'm also concerned about your emotional state. This kind of thing, the way this guy is toying with your head, Jesus, I mean how?"

"How?" she asked.

"How did this . . . this fiend behind the pyromurder of Chris Lorentian know where you would be staying?"

"Easy enough. Convention's been in the papers here and it's centered at the Hilton."

"Still, how'd he so effortlessly orchestrate this foul scheme—much less think it up?"

She sensed that Eriq's fear barometer, along with his concern, was also on the rise. And Eriq, as long-winded as he was, managed to ask all these questions in quick, fluid, Latin-accented succession. It made her think of their work together in Miami, where together they tracked the trackless Night Crawler all the way to the Cayman Islands. "You should be getting a request for a nationwide fingerprint search through the Vegas branch office, and my friend Chief Warren Bishop."

"We'll give it first priority to be sure. God"—he stopped to gasp—"I mean, it's truly sick, and the notion that this detestable monster's in a suite not three floors below yours when he contacted you, allowing the smoke and fire of his flaming victim to mask his movements. It's sheer horror."

"It gets worse."

"How so?"

"The fingerprints." She explained to him how they had obtained prints in only one place, and how the killer had written his code using the burned flesh of his victim as ink.

Eriq fell silent at the other end for some moments.

"Did you get all the photos and notes I sent you on the crime scene?" She finally broke the silence, staving off any further fits of hysteria from him.

This got him talking again. "Well, yes, I did."

"So, have you had time to analyze the handwriting?"

Eriq's forte remained handwriting analysis and documents. Being chief of a division now afforded him little time to do actual investigatory work, but he loved the work, and he liked keeping his hand in. "The fact he chooses to write out his message across a mirror rather than a wall may say something about him, but that's just conjecture at this point."

"Oh, I think he likes watching himself at work, that's for sure. Give me something I can use," she protested.

Eriq replied, "We blew up the shots immediately, and I put a team on it. Not much of a message; very few letters to deal with, you know. We didn't know that the words and letters actually consisted of . . . the victim's own creosote residue. I'll clue everyone in on that little factor. We're still studying each photo, including the crime scene photos. I have a profiling team at work on a victim and a killer profile. Have these to you, hopefully, by end of business day."

"FedEx 'em as soon as possible," she pleaded. "Going to need all the help I can get on this one. Talk to Dr. Desinor. See if she'd be willing to do the scene photos for us, okay? I have J. T. with me, and don't worry about my safety."

"Oh, sure, J. T.'s a deterrent to any maniac," he said, chuckling.

"He's been a big support; don't pick on him."

"I've taken some time to study the lettering myself," he finally confessed, "and . . ." Eriq was known for his ability at handwriting analysis. "Yes, well, it's quite revealing."

"Revealing of what, precisely?" she prompted.

"It's my educated guess that we are dealing with some sort of schizoid fanatic type, almost . . . well, like a terrorist mentality."

"A split personality, you mean? Like someone listening to voices in his head, telling him what to do? What do you mean, 'like a terrorist mentality'?"

"A fanatic, possibly a religious fanatic. Could be that he hallucinates, yes, or follows the dictates of a second, stronger personality. Or worse yet . . ."

"What worse yet?"

"Like I said, a religious fanatic, with the zeal of a righteous religious nut, maybe."

"Religion, you mean like burning at the stake in the name of the Inquisition, all that?"

"In the name of the Holy or unholy."

"What makes you think so?"

"The guy's scrawl is large, no center line to speak of, stiff and erect on the lines but erratic. Again, there's too little here to go on, but that's my best estimate."

"I would've liked to have forwarded the original, but it weighed eighty pounds and measured six by four feet, and FedEx isn't good with mirrors."

"Do you want me out there with you, Jess?" he again asked in a tone making it clear that he was prepared to take a jet the moment he got off the phone, if she so much as hinted her wish for him to do so.

"No, Eriq. I know you've got your hands quite full enough as it is with that awful child molester/killer where you are."

"Yes, well, that's true enough. He's causing havoc, all right, in the shadow of the White House. Where do you think our energies and resources and priorities ought to be spent, Jess? All the same, Jess, if you need me or anyone on the team, give a shout."

Jessica, like everyone in the country now, knew of the brutal, sadistic killer calling himself the Capital Punisher. This monster took precedence, for it had a penchant for child victims, and it was wreaking havoc in D.C., the nation's capital, and while Jessica had worked on some of the forensics and the profiling of the killer there, she was not herself a principal player on the case.

Jessica understood the media attention being given the creep in Washington. He was, after all, a pedophile of the worst order. He not only seduced and raped children, but also came out of the experience feeling extreme guilt and hatred of himself and what he'd done, but rather than cut his own throat or another appropriate appendage, the maniac turned his rage outward to the very objects of his perverted desire, the children, and in his uncontrollable rages, he murdered.

"I'm sure you'll catch this guy soon. The profile has him pegged. Meanwhile, don't worry about us out here in the Wild West. We're chugging along, plugging at our man."

"This creep we're after, Jess. He knows every back alley, open courtyard, basement window, and dark corner in D.C., and every schoolyard."

"As our profile says, he's a killer of opportunity, a difficult monster to stop. He wanders the streets by van and on foot, spends long hours simply moving around, a predator of the first order, waiting to pounce if given the slightest opportunity. Makes me wonder . . ."

"Wonder?"

"If our two killers aren't somehow . . . connected, related, Eriq."

"How's that?"

"Oh, I don't mean in the sense they know one another or are blood brothers or anything. . . . Just that sometimes you've got to wonder from what cloth these so-called men are cut."

"Yeah, yeah . . . maybe." Eriq spoke now as if to himself. "A child of eleven is ignored by his older sister and wanders through a gate, into a courtyard behind a fence, never to be seen again, his body never recovered. A little girl of twelve follows a bouncing ball into a shadow, and *he* is there. Only the ball is found. Later, her body is discovered stuffed in a drain pipe off Old Plymouth where it bisects Jackson Boulevard.''

"Has Dr. Desinor been helpful?'' Jessica asked, knowing that FBI psychic detective Kim Desinor had been called in on the Punisher case.

"She's made some impressive hits, particularly locating the bodies after their disappearances, but so far little headway on the preventative side.''

Jessica gave some thought to Dr. Kim Desinor. When last Jessica had spoken with Kim, the psychic detective had confided that the Punisher case had eroded any faith in herself and her power to do anything for the victims and their families.

Jessica finally asked, "So how's Kim really doing with the Punisher case, Eriq?''

"Are you reading minds nowadays, too?''

"Not good, I take it?''

"True.''

"You're not thinking of pulling her off the case, are you?''

"If she doesn't pull herself together, I don't have much choice, now do I, Jess?''

"It's your call, Eriq, but there's always a choice, and just remember what she did for us in New Orleans.''

"Not likely anyone's forgetting that, Jess . . . but we're talking another day here.''

"So, it's business as usual. . . . What've you done for me lately, huh?''

"Hey, I'm crass, but I'd hoped you hadn't seen that side of me,'' he joked to lighten the moment. "So, you and Parry have a good time overseas?''

Although she'd been back from her overseas vacation with Jim for some time, and although she and Eriq had worked the Punisher case to some degree together since then, it had been at remote points, as was the Phantom case now—she in her lab, he in his office, the two of them across a conference room filled with others on the tactical profile team of the Behavioral Science Unit (BSU) at Quantico. With additions such as psychic profiling, the team was no longer the small club it had once been in the days when Otto Boutine had first nurtured the unit into existence.

She knew it best to give concerted attention to how she replied to Eriq about James Parry and her ongoing, long-distance love affair with her Hawaii friend. "Rome was splendid, Athens like a dream."

"That good, huh? Why don't you gush a little?" he continued to joke. "So, was Parry splendid, too?"

"When in Rome . . ."

"I don't see it, but if you say so, Jess, he must have something special."

"He is something special. Do you really want me to expound?"

Obviously not, for Eriq quickly changed the subject with his own question. "Jess, are you sure you and Thorpe can handle things there alone?"

"We're hardly alone, Eriq. We've got the LVPD and Warren Bishop's local bureau to reach out and touch if we need it. Thanks now to your influence?"

"You don't sound worried about this creep's having reached out and touched you personally, Jess."

Jessica wondered for half a second if Eriq could mean Frank Lorentian, but she hadn't bothered to tell him of the threat Lorentian posed to the investigation. "I'm not worried about my personal safety, Eriq."

"You sure that's being wise? And God, but you do attract the perverts, Jess."

"Thanks, but I don't deserve 'em, as for worry . . . worry? What's that? Me, worry? Eriq, he's a maniac, a killer, but remember when Matisak was stalking me? This guy's but a faint shadow of Matisak, even fainter of that

Night Crawler bastard we caught together last spring in Grand Cayman. I'm on top of it.''

"You just give a holler, then.''

"I will. So, any more initial impressions of this creep's handwriting?''

"Initial . . . clever girl, Jess. Well, he's all over the spectrum, clearly demonstrating a madness, but as I said, there's little to go on with, but the one word and the two numbers.''

"Make any sense of that, 'number one is number nine' and 'traitors'?''

"First impression? She pissed him off like a cat, nine times, nine lives maybe, and maybe the ninth time, *whammo* maybe, although she was his number one squeeze, because she was a traitor, and she didn't live past her ninth life? Who knows?''

"Good question: Who does know?''

"Besides the killer? Well, Billings and Leonard Winstone in documents and literature are having a look-see, so not to worry. Something'll come of it. Those guys are the best.''

"We need the best on this, Eriq,'' she returned. "Any rate, I need you to see to it that previous MOs are checked in the history banks, see if this boy's been bad before, okay?''

"Sure thing, Jess. As we speak, it's being done.''

"Then I'll hope to hear from you soon?''

"Very soon.''

"Thanks, Eriq, and good night.''

"You expect he'll call again?''

She hesitated answering, not wishing to voice her fears. "I've had my phone tapped. Hopefully we'll get a voiceprint, if he is that stupid.''

"Crime does that to you . . . makes you stupid. Good thinking on the tap. Then someone'll be listening in with you. You won't be alone with the Devil, as they say, if the creep contacts you again.''

"Warren Bishop's seen to it, or so I was told."

"Good man, this Bishop?"

"Tops."

"Oh?"

"Warren's a friend. I knew him when I was going through academy training. He's a great guy. He was one of my training officers."

"Good . . . good . . ."

"And good night, Eriq."

"Not so quick, Jess. I mean it. I want you to take all due precautions. Don't get careless with this 'faint shadow of Matisak,' as you call him. There really are no faint murderous maniacs."

"The Phantom's a wimp . . ."

"What?"

"The press is calling him the Phantom, even though he's only killed one we know of; someone in the fire department put out a statement that he may be linked to other fire deaths around the city and outlying areas. See what if any truth is in that."

"Is he linked to other fire deaths?"

"Nothing even closely resembling this modus operandi in the previous fires alluded to that I can see, certainly no phone calls to me, no. And no fire investigator worth his salt would call these fires connected. This fire investigator guy probably just got carried away with the press attention."

"What's your gut reaction to this guy they're calling the Phantom, Jess? Honestly, now."

She let out a long spray of air in chaotic response. "Guy just may shoot himself in the head or burn himself up before he kills again, for all we know at this point."

"How did he get your number?"

"As I said, he must've somehow found out I'd be staying at the Flamingo, where the convention is being hosted. Likely just assumed as much, called the desk, and confirmed. We got a composite from the desk clerk 'cause the killer signed in using Chris Dunlap's registration. But the damn composite looks like a clown.''

"Well, keep us apprised here, and like I said ... You need anything, give a call."

"Thanks, Eriq."

They hung up, and she paced the room. It was a bit overstated in its decor, this place, far too much pink and flowers for her taste. She had wanted to attend some of the sessions today at the conference; there were always new methods, procedures, and information to learn at such conferences, and it was part of her duty as a medical examiner to keep abreast of the latest in forensics and science in general. Still, she was torn. There was much to do with regard to the Lorentian girl's death. Her friends, school associates, other relatives ought to be interrogated. Whoever got to her seemed to have known her movements. As it happened, she'd had a previous reservation or two at the Flamingo, quite possibly as a rendezvous place for a lover or lovers. From her pictures, she'd been quite beautiful.

Still, all such information could as well be gathered by the local police, and since they were on the case, Jessica decided to take advantage of the day to make the best of what had become an awful stay.

She dressed comfortably and casually for the day's sessions, went to the ones that piqued her interest and curiosity, and got her mind off the Phantom, his victim, and Frank Lorentian's unveiled threats.

· SEVEN ·

*Sin is a sort of bog; the farther you go in,
the more swampy it gets.*

—MAXIM GORKI

Jessica was awakened in the middle of the night by an insistent phone at her bedside, where a digital clock read 3:10 A.M. She hadn't answered a telephone ring since hearing from—she wondered if she dared think it him now—the Phantom Killer. Not knowing how many rings had already come, she still hesitated answering the annoying machine, like some clawing Rumpelstiltskin at her bedside. Her hand, as if independent of her mind, halted in the air over the receiver. A fearful dread continued to blot out her resolve.

Possibly . . . probably Jim . . . calling from Hawaii. It's late there, too—1:10 A.M.—and he's thinking of her, and he wants to hear her voice. Or perhaps it's Eriq Santiva, or someone else at Quantico with an urgent message, something about the case that simply couldn't wait till daybreak. Perhaps it was Kim Desinor with some psychic words of advice . . .

She lifted the receiver. Placed it tentatively against her ear. Muttered a soft, "Hello?"

"Dockkkk." The word was chillingly choked off. "Kkk-Coran?"

The voice sounded like Chris Lorentian's; it sounded like a voice from the grave. Jessica immediately wondered if she weren't simply in the midst of a nightmare, one of those horrible replays of a true event the brain safely tucked away but the soul took out to examine more closely, always about this predawn hour. Yes, her weary mind playing tricks on her, but her blood temperature plunged at the chilling tones coming over the spectral wires, while her hands—trembling with the dreamed-up receiver—turned strangely clammy, her mouth as dry as potato dust.

Finally, she heard herself ask, "Who is this?"

A high-pitched voice replied, "Mel . . . Marrrr-tin."

"I don't know you. Who are you?" The voice sounded far away yet strident, pulled tighter than a guitar string, shaky and twangy. A quaking, older-than–Chris Lorentian female voice, she felt certain now. If it was the nightmare of the other night happening all over again, there seemed to be certain minute changes. Still drowsy, part of Jessica remained just as certain that she'd wake from this all-too-familiar nightmare any moment now to find a silent room, the receiver on its cradle, her nerves intact, her bodily control and functions returned to her. Another part of her mind screamed that this was no ephemeral event.

"He made me . . . made me call." The disembodied voice filled Jessica's ears; the shaky, cracking voice resounded with terror. Obviously in pain, obviously in tears, the caller conjured up the image of the helpless form Jessica had seen in room 1713 of the hotel, the scorched remains of Chris Lorentian.

"Who is he? Who is the bastard? Give me something, anything, any clue," Jessica pleaded.

"Any Chhh . . . Christ . . ."

Any Christ? she asked herself. Was the caller swearing? "A name!"

"Beelzebub!"

"Satan?"

"Doe . . . douwhn . . ."

"Dough?"

"Doooon't let him hurt me! Says . . . says he's doing it for . . . for you."

"Doing what for me? Who is he? A name! And what does he want from me? Ask him! Ask him! Keep him talking," Jessica pleaded.

Another voice, all male and vicious and throaty, growled into the receiver, "I . . . I kill for . . . thee, Kkkkoran. . . ."

"Who are you? What are you?"

"I am Charon!"

"Listen to me, Sharon."

"Char . . . Char-ron," he corrected. "And there's no time for Hellsmouth like the present. It's over for number three."

She only understood his threat. "No . . . no," Jessica muttered and then screamed, *"No!"* even as she heard the *slosh, slosh, slosh* of a wet substance, and she heard the baritone voice of a male shadow, the Phantom, saying something in the background that sounded like a muffled, "Burn . . . die, bastard thing, burn in the mouth of Satan for all eternity, burn in the well!"

"Mel!" Jessica shouted just as the *whoosh* of super-heated air traveled through the lines, stinging her ear. She could smell the fire and feel its singing, singeing song amid Mel Martin's single, long, contorted wail of pain until there was nothing left but the beating of the fire's wings moments before the phone line went dead.

This is it . . . I wake up screaming now, right? Jessica thought, all in the same instant that the phone line went dead. *I wake up now.* But she realized it was no dream, that she was awake, and that the weight and firmness of the receiver in her hand were corporeal, not spectral.

She choked and coughed as if the fire had somehow singed her own lungs, and gasping for water, she slammed down the receiver and grabbed the glass of water she routinely kept at her bedside, knocking it over, spilling the contents over the carpet.

"Damn, damn, damn this *mudderfreakingsonofa-bitchin'bastard* of Satan!"

Tears had come of their own volition. Jessica had seldom felt so maligned, so abused, and so helpless. She wanted desperately to reach out and touch this someone, this SOB. Then she recalled the security measures Warren's local bureau had placed on her phone. She prayed they had the fire freak on tape, and that they could place him precisely where he had called from this time without delay. She prayed the fiend had remained close by and that FBI operatives were busting in on the monster at this very moment.

She'd gotten the killer to speak to her; small comfort, but it was something. Warren's vigilant men must have gotten the killer's voice on tape, which meant a voice-print—surefire evidence against him once they apprehended the creep. Too late for poor, defenseless Mel. She was obviously gone now, the way of Chris Lorentian.

"God," she wondered aloud, "could he be in the hotel again?" Could he have remained that cool, to stay that close to her and the scene of his crime, she wondered, knowing that criminals, more often than not, enjoyed revisiting the scene of the crime in an effort to relive the moment of their having been in complete control of the murder victim's life, to feel again that sense of power over another life.

She instantly and instinctively reached for her Browning automatic, a gun that had saved her life on more than one occasion. A million questions positioned themselves all in a row for her consideration, but all of the little soldiers were tripping over one another as in a Laurel and Hardy movie, causing a havoc of confusion and wonder. But uppermost and clear in her mind was one question: *What was his reasoning?* Did he believe that he would eventually do her in the fashion of his other victims? Did this bastard believe himself born of fire, that he would die by fire, and did he want her in that fire with him? Why had he singled

her out for his sick game of flesh-burning murder? Why
was he so bent on torturing her through vividly displaying
the torment he inflicted on his victims? And again she
wondered, how close was he to her at this moment?

She wanted to yank the receiver up again, call the desk
to determine the origin of the call, but she couldn't. She
was expecting another phone call any moment from Harry
Furth, the genius who put the tap on her phone, but she
hadn't seen him actually get the job done, and she hadn't
gotten back to Warren's Las Vegas FBI branch to find out
for certain. She cursed the possibility that once again she
might be the only one privy to the killer's chilling audio
setup. She hadn't been 100 percent happy with the idea of
people listening in on her phone calls, but for the sake of
narrowing down the facts about their Phantom Killer, she
had little choice in the matter.

The phone rang.

Could it be the monster returned? She hesitated until it
rang three times.

Finally, she lifted the receiver, saying nothing.

"We got the asshole. We got 'im."

"And this is?"

"Agent Harry Furth." Harry Furth's thick voice
sounded a direct opposite of the killer's hollow tone.

"Where? Where is he?"

"Page."

"Page what?"

"Arizona."

"Arizona? Page?"

"Lake Powell."

"Lake Powell?"

"Page, Arizona."

"But . . . isn't that . . . hundreds of miles away?"

"I don't need a geography lesson, Doctor." Harry
sounded tired, brittle. No doubt like herself, feeling helpless as he listened in on this brutality he could not stop.
"But it's not really so far. It's near Bryce Canyon and

Zion National Park, actually closer to Monument Valley. By air, you can be there in under a couple of hours.''

"We got anybody there, on it, now?" she wanted to know.

"We've got local law enforcement on it. They're crashin' the place as we speak. Keep your fingers crossed.''

"Where . . . I mean, exactly how far is this place from here?''

"A day's drive. Not far. Happened at the Wahweap Lodge and Marina, on Lake Powell. Great place to vacation.''

"Not so for Mel Martin, obviously . . .''

She was relieved in one sense that this cruel, sadistic monster was not in the building, that he was not as close to her as he'd been only the night before, but she was disappointed he'd not remained in the city, that he was expanding the geography of his kill spree, in a sense creating a larger radius for them to cover. Was it part of his plan? Usually, the Behavioral Science Unit of the FBI must work diligently to narrow the geography of the crimes to a specific location, to hone in on the killer, often doing so well as to locate the street on which the killer lived. Usually, the killer lived and worked and killed within a relatively confined area, close to home and to places he felt familiar and comfortable with. The crime geography remained fairly constant with most serial killers—save the Henry Lee cross-country types—even if the killer happened to be mobile, but this pyromaniac killer had jumped to another square quite quickly and unexpectedly, enlarging the geography overnight. It made her wonder where next he might strike. No one could possibly know using the normal techniques. Not with this guy any more than they'd been able to use normal procedure in the apprehension of the Night Crawler in the Caribbean the year before.

She considered her options. Stay put; return to Quantico;

go to the second fire death scene. ''I'm getting dressed, Harry. I want to get out there to Lake Powell.''

''Whoa, wait up there, Doctor. You need to stay next to this phone, where he can reach you. We need as much tape on this creep as possible, need to study the tape in depth, and we need to get a fix on him next time. Somehow you have to keep him on the line longer.''

''That's ridiculous. He's not on the line with me, his victims are! How do I keep the victim alive and on the phone longer, long distance, when this mother's in control of her and me and the time clock?''

''I don't know, but the phone line's our only link to this crazoid.''

''Harry, if you want someone to man this phone, then get someone, but I won't be a prisoner to this madman, and I don't intend staying in the Flamingo another night. Do you understand?''

''But Dr. Coran—''

''No, no argument.''

''All right . . . all right. We'll get an actress to play you, a decoy.''

''Now, that makes a great deal more sense, Harry. My time's worth more than that of an actress.''

''Guess you ain't heard the latest contract Julia Roberts signed with Disney.''

She only snorted her reply. ''Hmmmph.''

''Meantime, we'll get a voiceprint made. This time the guy screwed up big time. We got 'im on tape, and we got 'im spoutin' off in the background, but the scatter needs cleaning up. I can do that, but it'll take twenty, maybe thirty hours, depending.''

''Do it, and let me hear of the results. As for now, can you get me to Lake Powell, to this Wahweap Lodge?''

''I'll get a chopper prepared out at the airport; go to Hangar Twenty-four. They'll be expecting you.''

''John Thorpe may be accompanying me.''

"Gotcha, and I'll let the guys in Arizona know what's going on soon as I hear back from them."

"Do you think they might've gotten in there on time?"

"Doubt it. There was only a small window, a few minutes watching her burn, and he may've gotten out before the fumes got to him, which doesn't leave our guys much time to converge."

"Then you heard the entire conversation?"

"Every word, Doctor. Made no sense. Guy's completely nuts. I don't know how you held it together as well as you did, but you did, and you got a hell of a heart—gumption, my pappy used to call it."

She didn't feel like she had any gumption, or that she'd held anything together. Still, she replied, "Thanks, Harry. Tell 'em at Powell to not disturb the body or the crime scene. Understood?"

"Will do."

"Will I see you at the airport?"

"No, I want to get right on this tape. See what comes of it. Maybe later, I'll see you in Page, you know, when I've got something."

"Damned glad you got in here and set up the tap when you did, else we'd have nothing."

"Couldn't do otherwise. My boss was roasting my chops to get this set up. He seems to think you're pretty special . . . priority one, Dr. Coran."

She smiled at this. "Tell Bishop thanks for me. And Harry, I've jotted down a couple of things the killer said that may be especially relevant to our narrowing this mystery man down. I want you to tell Bishop these could be important clues to reveal something about the killer, the words he used to refer to himself, Char-ron, he'd said, or Charon, and the unusual word Hellsmouth. Could be a place."

Furth replied, "I thought he said Char-man, that he was like this char-grill guy, char-man. Didn't catch the reference to Hellsmouth. Any event, you can tell Bishop your-self.''

''How's that?''

''Warren's got a thing for you. Why don't you give him a call? He's gonna want to know about this new wrinkle. May even want to accompany you to Page, knowing War-ren as I do.''

The innuendo was thick enough to slice with a blunt scalpel, she thought, but it was no secret how Warren Bishop felt about Jessica Coran. She'd seen Bishop at one of today's sessions, and they'd had more coffee together. He'd been understanding—sweet, even—when she spoke of the awful first phone call from the Phantom's supposed first victim, telling him in graphic detail how horrible it all was. He'd been sympathetic, suggesting that she have something a bit stronger than coffee later with him in the lounge, suggesting they have dinner together.

They'd known each other for years, since her first year in the FBI Academy. They'd been close friends and had studied together, competing with one another to be the best. He was so good in hand-to-hand that they made him an instructor on the spot, and so he'd actually become one of her trainers.

Over the years they'd stayed in contact, remaining best of friends, but when the death of Chris Lorentian had hap-pened and Jessica had been placed in danger, Bishop had been out of town on another case, which had taken him to New Mexico.

Now he and his team had gone into swift action, surfing and sifting through FBI computer files for any and all sim-ilar fire deaths that might be related. These fire deaths ranged from those ruled accidental to those intentionally set fires that engulfed whole homes, restaurants, or ware-houses, leaving someone dead in the process. They'd nar-rowed the list down to seventy-two that smacked of similarities, primarily the use of butane as an accelerant alongside the smoked remains of some poor slob, male or female. Bishop and his team were reworking and rethinking every angle on each such case, but Jessica's gut reaction was one of skepticism. She believed this guy had started with Chris Lorentian—that ''#1 is #9'' pointed to this supposition. The phone call to her, the message written in the victim's own bodily grease, all had something to do with the number 1 and the number 9.

Perhaps the killer had a preset game plan that called for nine lives. And it had something to do with the notion of traitorous behavior.

She believed the victims knew their killer, or at least had had some previous contact with him. And this assumption was a world of difference from its opposite view, that victim and killer were strangers, that these were stranger killings.

Bishop was a broad-shouldered, handsome man with a wonderful smile and a great sense of humor. His sense of duty and honor were equally honed. A Desert Storm vet, he would make any woman a great prize, but like Jessica, his work had for all these years kept him from a personal life. It was natural and easy for the two of them to share time together, reminisce about the academy, about their earlier lives and the people they had once been. In fact, Jessica rather liked being reminded of a time when she was a naïf, an innocent. Bishop made her feel good, made her laugh, as he was still capable of doing, but she was also sure that he also made her look hard at what she'd become without the slightest intention of doing so.

They'd parted at her door, all thought of their jobs and professional selves abandoned. They'd kissed, for old times' sake on her part, but somehow it had become a passionate embrace, one she felt safe within, confident with. Still, she had halted him at the door, telling Warren that her heart belonged now to James Parry, and that regardless of her strong feelings and attachment to him, she simply couldn't betray James. ''Not like this,'' she'd said, and Bishop, in his usual poise and with a grin of acceptance, thanked her for what he termed "The best evening of my life in a long, long time."

"Liar," she'd countered.

"I mean every word of it, Jess, and if Parry doesn't take care of you, I'll go looking for the bastard."

"My hero, my shining knight."

"Uughhhh! Now you're making me sick." He remained laughing all the way down the corridor and when he waved good-naturedly from the elevator. "Don't worry about a thing, Jess," he assured her then. "I've got Harry Furth, my best man, on the wiretap. If this murdering piece of filth does call you again, we're going to nail the putrid excuse for a human being. Trust me."

"Yeah, Bishop," she'd replied. "I do—trust you, that is."

"Trust me to take this elevator down and leave you in peace, you mean?"

"That, too, Warren, and thanks for understanding."

"Long as you're happy, Jess."

She had smiled then as the elevator doors closed on his strong, tall form. It would have been so easy to have invited him in. . . .

She now pushed the thought away, telephoned for a cab, and began packing an overnight bag for Page, Arizona.

Jessica's next call went to J. T., alerting him to the alarming news: Once again the Phantom had struck like a flaming shadow, and the SOB had forced his victim to contact Jessica via telephone so that Jessica might listen in on the murder. J. T. instantly reacted, coming to her room to stand in wait with her, to be with her, to console her. They ordered a pot of black coffee from the all-night room service, and between gulps she told him as much as she could recall of the ugly, bizarre, phoned-in murder of the Martin woman; then they packed, not knowing if they'd be returning to Las Vegas. John Thorpe insisted on accompanying her to Lake Powell at Glen Canyon.

"Ever hear of a name like Charon?" she asked J. T.

"We'll have it run through the FBI computers. See what kicks out, follow leads to his crooked past. We'll get this twisted bastard, Jess."

Warren Bishop met Jessica and J. T. at the airport, where a helicopter had been chartered for their early-morning flight. Bishop had come rushing to her side as soon as he'd learned of the phone call that had so rocked Jessica's night. In the dismal gloom of an airport at 5:20 A.M. of what already felt like a scorching day in this desert paradise, they stood waiting on the flight pad.

Warren, looking sleepy and fatigued, like a bear just out of hibernation, walked Jessica aside and apologetically said, "I wish I could fly up there with you, Jess, but I can't drop everything here. Too many pressing and politically charged problems, and being the guy in charge . . ."

"No need for apologies, Warren. You and your men have done quite enough."

"Furth'll get on the voice tape, see if we can learn anything from it, and there'll be Arizona–Utah branch agents there to meet you in Page.

"Jess, promise me you'll take every precaution against this guy. Obviously, for some screwball reason, he has it in for you."

"No need to worry about me, Warren, and I fully understand. I have a pretty fair idea of the scope of your responsibilities here. Don't forget, I'm in love with a field chief."

"Just the same, I may follow you on a later flight."

"We could be back in a day or two, depending."

"Then again, you might not. We've hardly had time to recapture . . . old times." For a split second, the look in his eye gave Jessica a start. She feared he might suddenly surprise her by taking her into his arms and passionately kissing her. To stave off the moment, she turned to search for where J. T. had gotten off to, and seeing that he was busy with the young chopper pilot, she said, "I'd best board before J. T. bores the pilot to death.''

"Wait, Jess," he said, giving her a bear hug and a kiss on the forehead. "A little brotherly kiss, huh?" he asked. "Just want you to know that you can count on me, Jess."

"Thanks, Warren . . . but I know that—always have."

"Have a safe flight."

"I'm sure we will."

"Some of most fantastic scenery on the continent between here and Page. You'll enjoy it. And don't forget to look up at the stars once in a while, for the soul."

"Hey, I look up plenty. Last time I came on vacation out West, I was practically a youngster. Visited Yellowstone up in Wyoming. Did some hiking, fishing, and photo hunting."

"Yeah, I can see you in Yellowstone," he replied, smiling wide. "You always did love the outdoors, nature. Time you got back to it, maybe."

"Perhaps you're right." She smiled and turned, saw that J. T. had already seen to their bags and was waving for her to board. At the helicopter, the rotors already spinning and sending up a whirlwind of dust, the young pilot—young enough to be one of Jessica's nephews—stood alongside his chopper, a sight-seeing chopper pressed into sudden service by the FBI.

"How safe is this thing?" she wondered aloud.

"We take special care of our birds at Vermilion Cliffs Tours," the bush-cut-headed pilot replied with a smile. The young man told Jessica to sit up front in the copilot's seat, having learned she had experience as a pilot herself. J. T. had nestled into the back of the helicopter.

Still, Jessica impulsively rushed back to Warren for a final word, her eyes moist with a mix of emotions. She'd been on a roller coaster of confused emotions since the first telephone call forced on her by this madman with a torch. "Warren, you be good to yourself, and you take care of yourself, too," she finally said to him, unsure if any words she might utter could possibly ease his apparent loneliness and pain. "I'm sorry this once I can't be there for you, Warren."

He smiled, laughed even, and his usual gruff voice became melancholy, sweetly tolling in a rhythmic, metered away. "Don't worry about this tough old 'gator. Hell, my hide's as thick as pine bark. It's just . . . well, you touch something in me that never fails to peel a layer or two off."

"Bishop, you're as tough as my Aunt Sarah," she joked, making him roar with laughter, and she mirthfully joined him when she caught sight of J. T., who'd been watching from the chopper, a frown signaling a groan escaping him. To spite J. T., Jessica hugged Bishop a second time, and from over Bishop's dropped shoulder, Jessica could see a deeper frown turning Thorpe's face into a large prunelike growth, ugly even from this distance. She now quickly boarded the whirlybird, and Bishop waved them off.

Jessica was soon settled into the cockpit passenger side of the helicopter. She'd learned to fly small planes and she loved flying, but she had never flown a chopper. It looked like great fun, and she talked to the pilot the entire time, even while he went through his preflight check, telling him of her love for flying.

The young pilot beamed. He shared her love of the air.

The inky sky was giving way to light the way a watercolor painting gave way from one color to another, bleeding into one another, and on their way to the Grand Canyon, the sun was meeting them. Within the hour, Jessica and J. T. were treated to an aerial view of the colossal Hoover Dam, one of America's seven modern civil engineering wonders, on beautiful Lake Mead, the dam's reservoir, which equated to the largest man-made lake in America.

Even from this height, Jessica saw that the dam dwarfed everything around it, even the mountainsides into which it nestled. Cars and trucks drove across its razorback highway, which capped the Great Pyramid scale of the dam.

The pilot obviously spent more time flying tourists than marshals of the law, and he automatically explained what they were looking at. "Construction of the dam began in 1931, and the last concrete was poured two years ahead of schedule, in '35. Power plant wings were completed in '36, and the first generator began operating in October the same year. The seventeenth and final generator went into commercial operation in 1961."

Jessica and J. T. took it all in; the place inspired awe.

Young Joseph Duncan, the pilot, continued to fill them in on the facts, as he'd long since memorized them. "Hoover Dam represents a godsend for Colorado, Arizona, Nevada, and California for electricity, domestic water needs, irrigation, generation of low-cost hydroelectric power. It was named one of America's seven modern civil engineering wonders in 1994 by the American Society of Civil Engineers."

All Jessica knew was that it shone in the morning sun like some majestic giant's stone palace. She watched a lone bald eagle soar above the dam. The combined sight was breathtaking.

The pilot spoiled the moment, informing them of the army of men and machines, and the years of toil, required to build the dam, finishing with a story about "those poor unfortunates who gave their lives in the mammoth undertaking, some having literally done so, as they are still entombed in the dam, having fallen in with the tons of concrete as it was poured . . . on various occasions."

J. T., through his headset, replied, "I heard that was all a lot of nonsense, that no one died in that fashion, and no bodies are inside that colossal accumulation of rock and mortar."

The pilot shrugged before replying, "Ahhh, who's to say? But it's what we tell the tourists."

From there they flew over the fantastic beauty of the East Rim of the Grand Canyon, a wonderland of carved rock formations, light and shadow, depth and distance through which trickled the dwarfed Colorado River. Jessica couldn't take her eyes from the sheer size of this magnificent geologic formation, doing so only when J. T. pointed out two enormous birds of prey flying low over the canyon below them.

"Buzzards?" she asked.

"California condors," replied Duncan. "They released about nine or ten in the canyon last year; trying to make a comeback from extinction. Nobody's seen a sight like this in seventy years here at the canyon. Let's go in for a closer look, shall we?"

Ignoring a new law that outlawed air traffic below the rim of the canyon, Joseph Duncan recklessly dove toward the condors, trying to mimic their natural flight, trying to keep up with them and at the same time keep from getting too near canyon outcroppings, walls, and floor. Once the condors disappeared from sight, he began to meander with the Colorado River instead.

Jessica found the flight the most exhilarating experience of her life, while J. T. began to clutch at the sides of the seat he was in and to moan fearfully. The flight reminded her of a similar one, years and years before, through the Grand Canyon of the Yellowstone in Wyoming, where she'd performed her first duty as a medical examiner in the field. It had been during the trip to the national park to get away from the stresses of her new job as assistant M.E. at Baltimore Memorial Hospital in Maryland. She was still very much the student of medicine in those days. Park authorities alerted to a death at one of the thousands of hot springs in Yellowstone, and learning of her presence, asked her to come out and have a look at the body, which was in a remote area of the park. They'd had to helicopter to the location. It had proved also to be Jessica's first encounter with a murderer.

But there was no time to tarry on memories or the beauty and grandeur of the Grand Canyon here in Arizona, and so they were soon raised again above the canyon rim, and in minutes the chopper whirred away from the beautiful sight of the great and enormous mother of all canyons.

Warren had been right about the scenery. It was a religious experience. Utterly and magnificently wild, as Yellowstone had been. Since her visit to Yellowstone, Jessica had been a member of the National Parks and Conservation Association, the organization that published *National Parks* magazine and fought to keep wilderness areas wild. It was the lone voice fighting not only to keep the national parks for the people but also to keep them wild, because there was ever a hue and cry to develop park areas or to sell off mining or lumber rights to the highest bidder. Others wanted every possible hazard of the parks eliminated by boardwalks, guardrails, fences, signs, and signposts every few feet, despite the fact that every known and unknown hazard could never be completely eliminated by structures or regulations any more than traffic hazards could be eliminated from the L.A. superhighways.

Now they were flying away from the Grand Canyon and straight over the famous Painted Desert of Arizona, where Navajo Indian hogans and circular patches of land marked the circle of the Navajo family unit, easily visible from the sky, where each isolated house stood. To Jessica's surprise, they weren't finished with the Grand Canyon just yet, for on the other side of the Painted Desert awaited the great and magnificent North Rim of the Grand Canyon.

"This here's the northernmost section of the canyon," Duncan explained, and from the air, this strange and beautiful place looked the part of a scarred alien landscape, another planet, its rainbow of hues like so many elusive patinas, each layer of the "mountains growing into the earth," as Native Americans said of the canyon walls, painted by light and shadow, ever changing with each passing moment, each passing cloud.

The sunrise here became a trumpet sound, a tolling bell, telling everyone on the ground to rush to the rim for sights

that would never come again, for tomorrow's sights here
would be different. In a sense, the Grand Canyon equaled
visible time. Looking across at the bands of sediment, one
stood staring into the earth's history of aeons ago. It was
no different from what astronomers said about looking
back through time via their most powerful telescopes, but
here the human eye had no need of any mechanical device
to see into the shadowy beginnings of Earth's turbulent
creation.

Helicoptering was nothing like jetting about, Jessica felt.
In a chopper, you floated, feeling like you were sitting on
a moving platform or flying carpet, and in fact you were
at the center of a big glass bubble from which you could
view everything. The cockpit of an airplane had an entirely
different feel. You could hardly see in all directions in a
small plane; hell, you couldn't see over the dash in front
of you in many models, and in a plane you glided down
to earth, but not so in a bobbing helicopter. In a chopper
you floated down to earth.

While Jessica worked the radio to call ahead to local
law enforcement people, the chopper now quickly de-
scended. Decreasing altitude, the pilot deftly maneuvered
the joystick, and they gently helicoptered down at Page,
Arizona, the brilliant orange and yellow earth and the az-
ure waters around Glen Canyon Dam winking up at them
in the morning sun. The waters all around the hills and
mountains here created a cerulean blue against the desert
reds, a spectacular sight. In fact, spectacular sights
abounded here. In the distance, as they'd approached, Duncan had pointed to the towering pinnacles of Monument
Valley, a backdrop to seemingly every John Wayne Western.

They had found Page's small business airport, where
commercial helicopters and small jets flew sightseers over
Lake Powell and Monument Valley for just under one hundred forty bucks. Here Jessica and J. T. were met by a
local sheriff's car, transporting them within ten minutes to

Wahweap Lodge and Marina, nestled amid Lake Powell's spiky inlets, the whole a man-made crater lake that had come into being with the building of Glen Canyon Dam.

The lodge was extraordinary, and it was instantly obvious why so many boaters and vacationers gathered here; and out over the lake all manner of pleasure craft could be counted, from pontoons to speedboats and cruisers. The huge, multifaceted lake with its hidden fissures and miles-long fingers, having once been a land of rocky slopes, mountains, and crevasses, was now a favorite playground for water enthusiasts, as the great dam built on the Colorado River had created a vast lake here that had raised the water level, flooding the valleys here, burying below the waterline many sacred Native American pictographs and wall paintings in the trade-off, much to the chagrin, annoyance, and anger of Native American activists, old-timers, and the ghosts of ancestors past.

Jessica herself questioned the trade-off, wondering why the pictographs couldn't have at least been chiseled out and removed for display in a museum on the West somewhere. But her main concern this morning at the lodge on the man-made lake was to catch a killer. Coming in view of the building where Mel Martin was murdered, she reached for her black valise and gripped it hard, girding herself for what she surely would find inside the lodge.

· EIGHT ·

*Ruthless as the old devil gods
of the world's first darkness.*
                    —SIR PHILLIPS GIBBS

As they approached the marina with its hundreds of scattered boats of various sizes—looking like so many birds perched atop the shimmering water—Jessica could see that Wahweap Lodge was of modern construction. Still, the colors and grounds were in keeping with the surroundings, making for a creamy blend of sand, brown, and earthy hues. It was a sprawling lodge, and it appeared filled to capacity, its vacationing horde of boaters and weekenders making the best of the heat by staying near the water.

The drive to the lodge from the airport was quick and simple, and when they entered the main doorway into the lavishly furnished western decor of the lobby, Jessica's eyes went instantly to the extremely beautiful and lifelike portraits of Native Americans—men, women, and children—adorning the walls. The local artist or artists who'd captured these figures had brought them into sharp focus and rendered them extremely attractive. The walls were also hung with Western lore items, from bullwhips to tastefully done Native American artifacts and art.

She and J. T. had little time to glance about, however, for the night manager, held past his normal duty hours now, shakily introduced himself as Mr. Nathan Wood. The man looked as if he'd been pummeled and dragged over rocks from behind a pickup truck, and he, alongside the local sheriff's deputy who had acted as their chauffeur, directed them to the fire room, where two uniformed Arizona State patrolmen (Jessica liked to call them "patroopers," as she did as a child) stood milling about.

Jessica noticed a small cardboard box near one of the officers' feet. She let it go, peeking inside to where the body still lay waiting for her and J. T.'s arrival, untouched and unmoved. It was 5:55 A.M., and the Arizona sun rained in through half-open drapes, blinding Jessica to the amount of fire damage before her. It seemed the bathing sunlight was fast attempting to wash the fire-blackened room clean, softening its appearance, and in an elusive, illusionary way, it succeeded.

"Protective wear," Jessica said to J. T. as she snapped open her valise and snatched out a white linen lab coat, rubber gloves, and a face mask. She dabbed a bit of Vicks VapoRub below her nose to cut the smell of death.

Stepping into the fire death room, a bump here against the bureau, a grind there against the bedpost, and Jessica knew her clothes would be painted in fire grease had she not taken precautions.

Two local FBI men and fire officials looked hard at Jessica and Thorpe; these men were expecting them and had remained, milling about, sipping coffee, curious about the new wave of FBI folk who'd been brought in, wondering why the doctors had come all the way from Vegas to be here. One of the two Arizona–Utah field agents looked to have taken charge, and he quickly stepped forward and offered J. T. his hand, explaining, "I'm Tom McEvetty. It was me and my partner, Kam—"

The partner hustled nearer and with a hand as large as a griddle, awkwardly leaned over and almost fell atop the charred body on the bed as he poked his hand out, saying, "I'm Kaminsky, Ed Kaminsky, special agent, Mac's partner. Friends call me Kam." Kam's gloved hand, dripping

with goo, was still held out to Jessica after he'd taken
J. T.'s handshake.

Jessica finally took Kam's gloved hand in hers, and they
shook with Mac looking on. "Nice to meet you both," she
assured the Arizona bureau men who'd hauled ass to get
here from Flagstaff.

Frowning at his partner, McEvetty continued, "Anyway, we responded to the call from Vegas to get up here
from Flagstaff's soon as we could, but it's a long way from
Flagstaff. We flew in, same as you. Your man in Vegas
contacted local authorities, and those two fellas outside in
uniform were the ones who rammed the door, but too late,
I'm afraid."

The one called Kam took it from there, saying, "The
patrolmen discovered the fire and the body, but no sign of
your shadow man, this Phantom guy, save a sooty footprint, which you might be interested in."

McEvetty, a large, bull of a man, shuffled his weight
past Jessica and J. T. in the crunched space, and now he
pointed to a large smudge on the light blue carpeting just
outside the threshold, where a small cardboard box had
been placed over the print, saying, "So's nobody can accidentally smudge the print before it gets placed in a cast."

Jessica went to the box, lifted it, and stared at the print
below. It was a clear, even shoeprint, as opposed to an
actual footprint impression, showing a worn, uneven pattern on the sole. A shoe expert might be able to tell them
a great deal about the man who left the print, but more
likely the expert could tell them a great deal more about
the shoe than about the man inside it. "You're sure it
wasn't made by one of the firemen, one of cops, or one
of you guys?" she asked.

The two FBI men from Flagstaff exchanged an exasperated look, taking offense. "It was the first thing Morgan
and Dawes noticed when they got to the door," said the
one called Kam.

McEvetty quickly added, "They preserved it immediately after securing the place."

"Good . . . good work," she said to the two uniformed cops who'd been standing idly by.

"We got other business," one of them said. "We'll keep our eyes open for any suspicious-looking characters in the area, on the roads, but we're outta here now, if you folks are finished with us."

She nodded, a half smile sending them on their way. "Sure, sure."

One of the two state patrolmen called back, "Just hope something comes of the shoeprint."

They all knew that without a match, it was like finding a fingerprint with no one to attach it to, completely useless. "Yeah," J. T. agreed.

"We might make something of it," Jessica added, "if . . . when we catch this freaking monster." She thought it an ironic twist on the missing glass slipper in *Cinderella*. She then turned back to the charred and blackened cave the killer had made of the once lovely room, her eyes traveling about the killer's incinerator. There were familiar indications—*tracks*—that the same killer had been at work here, the clues all pointing to the same man, all around the room in a constellation of previous activity that left its indelible mark. Jessica began enumerating these for the others to take note.

"Naked wires where the smoke alarm and sprinkler system were disconnected, the stage well set so that the killer would have ample time to walk away from his carnage before others were alerted to the fire, and a message smudged in black soot scrawled across the mirror, different this time, yet quite familiar."

J. T. and Jessica stood side by side at the mirror, reading the words scrawled across it. The familiarity of the message left on the mirror had the power to chill the spine:

#3 is #7—Violents

"What the hell's zat 'spose to mean?" barked McEvetty in Jessica's ear. "Violins? You think he means violins, maybe . . . hearts and flowers, maybe?"

Means the bastard can't spell "violence," Jessica thought but said nothing. She desperately tried to block McEvetty and the others out while J. T. watched her amazing concentration on the mirror, where her reflection—healthy skin, firm, rich in moisture, few lines, even-toned, supple and smooth brow, all framed by radiant auburn hair—congealed in a bizarre double exposure amid the smoke streaks and the body's unhealthy appearance on the bed—loose, arid, riddled maplike with lines, so uneven in color and hue as to rival the hard, brittle, rough colors of the dark earth, all hair burned away. All this superimposed by the smoke-painted, greasy letters left on the mirror. Her eyes screamed silent, closed over the images for a moment, and opened firm and determined once more.

"I don't know what the Sam Hill the message means, gentlemen, and we might never know, and perhaps it doesn't matter."

"Doesn't matter?" asked McEvetty, a note of exasperation in his voice.

"Perhaps no one but the killer will ever know what his numbers and shorthand mean."

J. T. told the two Flagstaff agents what had been left at the kill scene in Las Vegas.

"As for meaning in a madman's head," Jessica said now, "perhaps the hellion will take it to his grave with him."

Still, she found herself examining each character, each loop and dip in the madman's hand, sizing him up as she did so, using what little she had learned about handwriting analysis against the unseen enemy. But the process told her little that she didn't already know, given his telephone fetish, and his fire fetish, and his liking for turning human flesh into fire-blackened, dehydrated cardboard. So what if his damnable lettering screamed that he rationalized beyond all reason as normal human beings understood reasoning? That he held a bizarre and fantastic worldview that excused him from his actions, from meting out suffering, pain, and death on others so he might feel the power of holding their lives in his hands, so he might feel good and godlike? She already knew this much. Handwriting analysis might have helped them to understand the movements and actions of the Night Crawler in Florida waters. But this guy? She doubted that what few scraps he was leaving would be of any service, even if they found the best handwriting expert on Earth to decode it; only in deciphering the madman's code, its meaning, the numerical game, the puzzle of words he left behind might the firebrand's death notices serve her and other authorities. But suppose it had no meaning, that it was simply what it appeared to be, gibberish, nonsense?

"Filthy business," muttered Kam, who was on her right, also intently studying both the words and numbers, and her reaction to them.

From the killer's own handwritten message, Jessica's eyes moved coolly, somehow independently of her brain, to drift to the reflected image of the awful handiwork of the brutal monster and her own superimposed image standing over the body. Somehow, given the flood of sun rays, the morning mist, and the charred and still-smoldering room, no one else but Jessica Coran and the body were reflected in the mirror from the angle at which she now stood.

Like the message on the mirror, the body on the bed also looked familiar.

"I just don't get it," complained J. T. of the message in the mirror, the sound of her friend's voice shattering Jessica's reverie, almost as if shattering the mirror.

She turned on him. "Get what?"

"These damnable numbers make no sense. One is nine, three is seven? I mean, what's that?"

"Hell, if the world made sense, men would ride sidesaddle,'' Jessica automatically responded, recalling a favored feminist line, making McEvetty scratch his head while Kaminsky lightly chuckled. J. T. only frowned, causing her to continue, ''Wake up, J. T. None of it makes any damned sense whatsoever.'' She ran a hand through her thick hair. ''If it made sense, this madman wouldn't be telephoning me where to pick up the bodies; if it made sense, he wouldn't be out there.'' She waved a birdlike hand before them. ''He'd have been long ago committed, safely put away; if it made sense, he'd have committed himself or killed himself or accidentally caught fire himself.''

''Then we'll start with asylums and institutions. See if anyone in the head game can make out any of this cryptology of his,'' returned J. T. ''After all, at the first killing in Vegas, he left the number sequence one equals nine. Now he skips to three? Three equals seven? Numerically, it doesn't compute, but somebody, somewhere's got to recognize this . . . aberrant''—he searched for a word—''chronology.''

''Yeah, where's number two?'' asked McEvetty.

Jessica's eyes bored into J. T. ''What meaning can a maniac take from numbers, J. T.? Quit looking for meaning and method in this madness. Even if there were any, which I seriously doubt, you and I can only guess at such meaning and likely never fathom it, and at the moment, any speculation could lead us in an entirely wrong direction.''

''There's got to be a message in there somewhere,'' Kam insisted.

McEvetty, nodding, agreed and persisted with his inquiry intact. ''The first killing is given number one, the second number three? What happened to number two? Who knows? Maybe this guy is some sort of Zodiac killer, you know, killing by the stars, astrological crap, numerology, shit like that. . . .''

Perhaps it was the fact that they were all men, all bent on understanding one of their own, all bent on making sense of murder so foul as this, or perhaps it was simply the fact that there were three of them and one of her, but she refused to let these men have their way so easily.

"McEvetty," she replied, "at the moment, we've got our hands full with reality; let's don't get into numerology and shit like that, okay?"

"But Jess," continued J. T., "he might be telling us what his next message will be."

"How's that?" asked Kam.

J. T. turned to the other man and explained, saying, "It may be in the sequence. One equals nine, three equals seven would be followed by five equals five, you see? He skips one number on the first part of each equation and two digits on the second part."

J. T. began jotting down his notion on a notepad for the other two men to see more clearly what he meant.

Jessica feared they were all looking in the wrong place. Still, from what little of handwriting analysis she'd gleaned from Eriq Santiva, her boss at Quantico and an expert in documents and graphology, Jessica knew she had to start some recordkeeping of her own, that mentally she had already gathered much information about the killer by the killer's own confused script. She knew:

1. *He was in many ways creative, perhaps evilly imaginative, possibly well read, literate despite the error on the spelling of "violence."*
2. *He walked that fine line between genius and madness.*
3. *He showed signs of an internal war, a great struggle turned outward and dangerous now.*
4. *He liked numbers and word games, games involving a puzzle; possibly he had a mathematics or scientific background.*
5. *He liked yanking their chains, and had likely spent much time in isolation, perhaps prison, perhaps someplace closer to what J. T. be-*

> *lieved, what McEvetty would call a loony bin.*
> 6. *He held them and all other authority figures in great, abiding contempt.*
> 7. *He killed as opportunity presented itself after selecting a victim.*

Still, she kept all this speculation to herself. She'd write it up in a report, fax it off to the team of profilers working the case from remote Quantico, Virginia. She might also send it to OPS-1 in D.C., where it would be brainstormed; along the way a cross-reference would be made between what she believed she knew of the killer and VICAP's computer banks.

She believed her suppositions about the murderer to be true, for his lettering showed great, sweeping flourishes, uncontrolled loops and swirls, reminiscent of the Night Crawler's handwriting the year before. But with the Night Crawler, they had had so much more to analyze. He'd written whole letters and poems for publication to the newspaper. The Phantom, by comparison, must be far more introverted, shy of the light; his cryptic messages were meant for quick consumption by law enforcement only, with little or no concern for attention from the media. In fact, his words were darts meant for a singular target, for Dr. Jessica Coran, it appeared.

She stared longer at the handwriting, giving it her full attention. His hand revealed much anger and art, quite a mixed bag, actually.

J. T. could see that she was studying the lettering again, and he asked, "What's the handwriting telling you, Jess?"

She wisely withheld taking the deep breath her body wanted to take. She then answered J. T., saying, "His center line is nonexistent, which rules out any stability, and his letters roam freely about below the center line, indicating a powerful but twisted sexual drive, which likely means he got off on watching his victims burn, likely ejaculating in his pants if not over the victim. We're not likely to find much evidence of this given the fire, but we'll search nonetheless. It may be that he left a drop here or there of his secretions, which may or may not reveal something through DNA tests.''

''Whataya saying, Dr. Coran? That he jacked off over the victims while they burned alive?'' asked McEvetty.

''That'd be my guess. Pure speculation at this point, but yeah, such violence is often the only avenue for such a man to vent his psychosexual lust.''

Kam whistled and said, ''Even while . . . I mean while the victim was burning alive?''

''That's why it's called a psychosexual lust murder.''

McEvetty shook his head, adding, ''Even though the heat in here must've been searing his own skin?''

''Some like it hot.'' She tried a joke on the men, but this only got her a series of frowns. ''Might even find some evidence of ejaculation and the killer's DNA on the body, if it hasn't entirely burned away,'' she added louder for the others, ''the bedclothes, the carpet if we're lucky, if he didn't keep it in his pants.''

J. T. stared hard at her, biting his lip. ''He's got to be the sickest bastard I've ever dealt with.''

''To him it's apparently become normal, casual behavior. Sick is in the eye of the beholder.'' She continued, pointing to the handwriting. ''Other lines race above the center line, indicating a faith in his own superiority.''

''Yeah? Anything else?''

McEvetty and Kam had shut up on hearing about the psychosexual, lust-killing aspect of the murders as Jessica portrayed it, likely wondering how she could dismiss numerology but accept graphology and her own leap to this conclusion about the killer's masturbating over the victim's burning flesh.

It must seem a wild leap to them, but Jessica had seen and interviewed so many killers behind bars over the years whose sexual aberrations ranged from getting off via strangulation and stabbing women repeatedly to ripping out their entrails. Fire and sex seemed as easy to equate as murderous hands, knives, guns, or torture instruments and sexual gratification. More brutal and sadistic murder was committed in the name of sexual gratification than any other motivating conception. For some men and women, aberrant sexual behavior was a way of life, a bodily need, a religion, and she saw no reason to doubt that the Phantom was practicing his religion at full tilt on this, his kill spree. Most assuredly, his religion had evolved from an early age, his childhood spent in dark corners, shying from the light of others, from what society deemed normal and acceptable behavior, like a griffin or a Grendel creature, ugly and unwelcomed and unloved, kept at bay by his own proclivities and awful habits, and it likely involved small, helplessly pinned life forms, fire, and his penis.

Jessica continued to answer J. T. regarding what she saw in the lettering. "So far, I've found all the signs Santiva told me to watch for in the Phantom's hand. See the pressure he places on the ends of lines? The killer uses the clubbing common to aggressive, angry, out-of-control people in which letters are given large, bulbous endings, but remember what materials he's working with."

"The greasy fat of his victims," supplied J. T. for the other two men, who both swallowed hard at this revelation.

Jessica continued, saying, "He's testing us, J. T.; testing me, in particular. No sane person would leave so methodical and organized a crime scene, assuring no clues, only to knowingly douse his ungloved fingers in the victim's burning tissue to leave his prints on a mirrored surface."

"Leaving his voice on tape, placing his handwriting on the wall, and his prints," J. T. agreed, nodding. "Maybe he wants us to stop him."

"So far he hasn't used a single word with the lowercase letter *d* in it, so it is impossible to know if he uses the maniac *d*, which Santiva, during our hunt for the Night Crawler in Florida last year, taught me to watch for. Still, his long-stemmed letters are like black roses."

"Say again?"

"They're forced tersely ahead of one another, and like daggers, they stab toward the right, as if barbed, ripping to get at the object or end letter. There's plenty here to mark him as insane . . . and he's right-handed."

J. T. placed a firm hand on her shoulder and, reading her mind, added, "Insane, as if his actions haven't already told us as much. Always room for one more lunatic under the sun, hey, Jess?"

"Always the master of understatement and quiet imagery, J. T.," she replied, moving away, stepping closer to the body on the blackened bed.

Staring directly now at the murder victim, no longer using the mirror to soften the sight or ease her way toward it via the route of reflection, Jessica now looked straight into the desiccated features of Mel Martin outside the mirror.

Jessica now felt the blow, absorbing it with her entire body and mind as her eyes clearly conveyed the message of the real image of horrid death left her by the killer: the shriveled corpse, mummified remains, the limbs pulled inward, hardened by the temperature of the fire, which had created in the body its own instantaneous, solidified rigor mortis.

She read the familiar patterns present, seeing flashes of metal about the body. She saw that the killer had used items at hand to tie his victim, a blackened belt buckle dangling from the victim's hands, likely the victim's own; something like a western-style string tie about her feet, the string tie's metal nubs winking back at her, despite their having been blackened. Oddly, her feet were in good shape, not quite burned beyond recognition, like the rest of her. In fact, the feet were largely okay, and large and thick. Mannish, Jessica thought. The condition of the feet and ankles recalled the scourged body of a woman many years ago, in Yellowstone National Park, whom Jessica had been asked to render an opinion on. The woman was burned over 90 percent of her body, but the feet and ankles were not touched by the fiery liquid that had boiled her to death, a hot spring she'd purportedly fallen into that measured 202 degrees Fahrenheit.

In a sudden flash of realization, Jessica saw that there was something extremely different about this victim from the earlier hotel fire death victim. Mel Martin's fire-blackened, nude body clearly showed her to be a him, that "she" lacked breasts, and that he had male genitals hidden deep in the folds of his now fire-scourged body.

"Damn . . . he's a man?" she muttered.

"Excellent observation," replied an amused Kam.

"Last time I looked, yes, ma'am, ahhh, Doctor," added McEvetty, giving his partner a wink.

But Jessica was mentally adding an eighth item to her list of what she suspected was true about the Phantom, what she'd report to headquarters about the Hell-bound bastard:

> 8. *He killed indiscriminate of sex.*

Jessica felt a sudden need to sit down somewhere. Seeing her sudden loss of composure, J. T. whisked her outside and found a nearby room, where a Spanish maid was busily cleaning the bathroom. J. T. sat Jessica on the bed, slipped the maid a twenty, and flashed his credentials, telling the maid he was a doctor and that they would need the room for a half hour. "Come back then," he instructed.

The maid gave him a wink and a cynical smile, said something in Spanish, and disappeared.

"How can he be a man?" Jessica asked.

"Maybe Mel in there had an unusually high voice, and besides, fear can constrict the vocal cords, Jess. Let me get you some water."

"You don't have enough water, J. T."

· NINE ·

. . . as surely as a passion grows by indulgence
and diminishes when restrained; as surely as
a disregarded conscience becomes inert, and
one that is obeyed active; as surely as there
is any meaning on such terms as habit, custom,
practice; so surely must the human faculties be
moulded unto complete fitness for the social state;
so surely must evil and immorality disappear,
so surely must man become perfect.
— HERBERT SPENCER

When Jessica and J. T. returned to the odorous death room, they found a big-boned, stout, black-haired man in a flannel shirt and rubber gloves crawling about the floor, sniffing at things in bird-dog fashion. McEvetty shushed them on entering, saying, "Fire investigator. He was here earlier, but went out for a smoke."

The chief fire investigator, from whom a series of *hems, haws,* and *hums* now steadily flowed as he crawled about the floor and examined all sides of the room and the bed, suddenly leaped elflike to his feet, coming face-to-face with Jessica.

"Just checking my earlier findings," he told her.

McEvetty quickly introduced Jessica and J. T. as principal investigators on the case to Page's fire marshal. The fire investigator's name was Roy Brightpath, yet he looked like a man chiseled from the granite of this place, his skin the color of bronze. Jess realized immediately that he was part Native American.

"We at first thought it was just a guy fell asleep with a cigarette in his hand, but moment we come in, we could smell the accelerants. Dog couldn't place it anywhere but over the bed. Lennie, my lab guy, came over, took one whiff, and said it was a mix of gasoline and butane.

'Course, we'll verify that with analysis sometime late today, but Lennie's the best, and I'm pretty sure, pretty sure.'' He extended a gloved hand, and they shook. She saw by his bars that he was a captain, which meant some years of experience.

"I wasn't expecting the victim to be . . . male, that the victim's a man. I mean, I spoke to him on the phone moments before he died, and he . . . he sounded like a woman,'' replied Jessica, pirouetting about and staring, still shaken at this turn of events.

"Whoa up, there,'' said Brightpath. "Whataya mean, you spoke to him?''

"Just before he was murdered,'' she confessed. "J. T., will you explain?'' she asked.

J. T. brought Brightpath and the others up to date on what had occurred between the killer and Jessica thus far. When he finished, Jessica asked, pointing to Martin's body, "Who was he? Does anyone know anything about the victim?''

"An older gentleman on vacation, late sixties, alone from what the detectives can gather,'' replied Brightpath, whose skin, tinged with a red hue, made him a walking, talking ironic twist on the word "fireman.'' Jessica guessed his roots must be somewhere in the vast family of the Navajo or Hopi. He was short and stout with a wide face that, under better circumstances, appeared to enjoy a white-toothed grin. She guessed as much from the smile lines and wrinkles.

"Smoked Camels without filters,'' continued Brightpath, "carried a billfold full of pictures of his grandkids, beautiful children.''

Kam took up Brightpath's slack, adding, "Recently widowed, kids got together money to send him on this trip to see the West, the great natural resources of the national parks, or so his co-travelers have told us. So, he's on this trip, which is the dream of a lifetime, and *whammo*! This happens.''

McEvetty quickly stepped in, saying, "We heard about your case in Las Vegas, but this time the victim's male, an over-the-hill guy by all appearances. Nothing like your victim in Vegas, so—"

"But you didn't know about the writing on the mirror in Vegas, did you?" she asked. "Thought you'd have a little fun since we flew all the way to Page anyway. Is that about it, McEvetty?"

The Arizona–Utah agent took in a deep breath, released it slowly, and said, "Sorry. We thought it was, you know, unrelated."

"You thought?" she replied sarcastically.

Brightpath, ignoring them, said, "Dead guy's name was Melvin"—he checked his notes—"Melvin Bartlett Martin. That's according to both the seared wallet left on the table beside the bed and according to the agents here, who got their info from the night clerk."

McEvetty added, "Martin had the room all to himself, but he dined with another man, according to the waitress who served him last night."

"Left the lounge after purchasing that bottle of wine sitting over there unopened," Kaminsky added, pointing at the 1989 Chardonnay label.

"It didn't pop from the temperatures in here?" asked J. T.

Brightpath shook his head. "Epicenter of the fire was over the bed. Never got that hot the other side of the room. Not even to burn the wallet on the nightstand."

Jessica nodded, replying, "Just like our fire murder in Vegas."

McEvetty raised a meaty finger to his lip and said in such a tone that Jessica saw a lightbulb go on over his head, "Let's check the wine bottle for prints."

"And dust the whole room, and scan it with an infrared laser, if you can get hold of one, for signs of any human secretions," Jessica added, thinking it most likely a waste of time. Still, they must be thorough and hope that this madman would continue to make mistakes, as he had in leaving his prints in the messages and his voice on tape only a few hours earlier, and in leaving his shoeprint, laden with black soot, in the baby-blue-carpeted hallway here in Page, Arizona.

"I'm not so certain your theory about this monster's right, Jess," J. T. muttered in her ear. "I mean about him getting off sexually on burning corpses. Wouldn't that mean he'd need a woman, a female victim? And what about the time element?"

"No, he doesn't need a female victim, not necessarily," Jessica replied, "not if they're all so much kindling for his fantasy, no. As for time, he's spent quickly, perhaps even before he does them. He may get off on the anticipation alone."

"So, in essence, it appears this guy doesn't care what sex his victims are."

"You can't use your own sexual excitement barometer to gauge this guy against, John. He's obviously not interested in them in any sexual sense you and I can fathom," she replied, searching cursorily over the body for any signs of blunt-force injury, but she was unable to see much in the smoke-laden light. "I give him this much," she began. "He's intent on remaining a faceless bastard, careful and controlled, so . . ."

J. T. leaned in, for she was as much as talking to herself. "So?" he asked.

"So, I guess you're dead right, J. T."

John Thorpe's big, round brown eyes grew larger. "How's that?"

"We've got to crack this code of his." She now looked at and pointed to the message left by the killer. "It's got to make sense to someone somewhere. This guy has had to've talked to someone about himself, his fantasy, his sexual needs, his plans, his obsession-madness . . . and maybe his interest in numbers and words such as 'traitors' and 'violents.'"

"We could send it around to our university consultants, our arcane friends in academia. Who knows? Maybe one of them will recognize something. Maybe a mathematician . . ."

"I was thinking the same, but we also want to touch on medical people, mental facilities in particular. Maybe we should go public with what we know, spread it across the tube and the headlines. Somebody's got to know something about this nutcase, and we need information now, before he phones—kills—again."

"Obviously our documents guys aren't having much luck with the first message," he replied.

"But now this"—she again pointed at the new message—"may spur them on. Let's do both—send it to Quantico, as we did the other, and forward it on to our contacts at Harvard, Yale, Princeton, Stanford, all the major universities in the network, and our medical lists."

She turned now to McEvetty, a bearded, rugged-looking man who might well have been wearing buckskin and rawhide, he so looked the mountain man type, and she said to him, "Do you have a photographer on hand?"

"Jake's just waiting word. He's having a doughnut and coffee at the coffee and gift shop off the lobby. They opened early for us."

"Send for him. Get photos of everything, starting with the mirror, and have them send up some coffee. I need something pleasant to smell in here. What about that secretion search, Captain Brightpath? Do you have the wherewithal, or do we call for help?"

"On it," he responded, going for a phone.

"So, what're you waiting for, McEvetty?" she scolded.

"Yes, ma'am, ahhh . . . Doctor." McEvetty's moist eyes, very like those of a doe or an ox, seemingly saying that he much admired her show of strength in the face of such horror.

She turned once more to J. T. and asked, "Can you take care of getting the information around? The photos of the handwriting, the shoeprint cast, what we've got here, and route it all to—''

"Sure. I'll get on it; that is, unless . . ."

She studied the hesitation in his features, glad to have her confidant and familiar friend alongside her. "Unless what?"

He whispered, so the others would not hear, " 'Less you really want me to handle the body, Jess. Burn victims are tough, I know."

Drowning victims in the water for long duration aside, burn victims in which the entire body, head to toe, was covered in the creosote of superheated human tissues and fat represented the most difficult cases for the forensic medical person, no matter how toughened or jaded. The corpse repulsed the physician. And this did not make for the best of working relationships or conditions. Usually Jessica felt a sense of bonding with the victim, a close-knit relationship in which she shared secrets with the deceased, down to the pallor of the skin, the size and shape of every organ, inside and out. But how was this possible here? Here such a bonding was virtually impossible when looking into so completely annihilated a face and human form, when having to look into the mask of a creature molded of fire. All this was true, despite a generalized and sometimes overwhelming sense of empathy with the victim's pain, felt even more strongly if you had prior knowledge that the victim was alive when put to the torch.

Jessica could not deny the powerful impact on both the doctor and the forensic process such a thoroughly repugnant, desecrated body meant. It was just shy of dealing with an exhumed body, a years' old cadaver from a grave, and in some regard worse, for the odor of burned flesh was worse than the odor of decay.

Jessica dropped her gaze from J. T., sheepishly whispering in reply, "I'm fine here. Go on with Brightpath. Be sure we get all the equipment we need here."

Jessica relocated her black valise, and next she located

a scalpel, the one given to her by her father. She'd pulled down her mask earlier, and she placed it back over her nose and mouth, her white lab coat now having a patina of soot.

Jessica stepped closer to the mummylike corpse, inching closer until she stood abutting the blackened bed and the blackened east wall. She now meant to go to work gathering immediate samples for later lab work. She was all right, she told herself, but her thoughts over the ungainly thing at her fingertips continued.

The men in the room watched in a kind of rapt awe.

Most victims of complete burn such as this meant ample cause to rush through an autopsy. And in the rush, vital clues could be lost, and often were. Most certainly the coroner's usual care, precision, and thoroughness were impeded, if not breached completely. A good forensics man or woman knew this going in, so Jessica fought the overwhelming desire to be done with the body as quickly as possible, but Jessica also well understood the all-too-human response to the catastrophic annihilation of the body, its tissues and organs, to fire. She also understood J. T.'s chivalrous gesture was not without reservation, that he would prefer to make other vital arrangements and leave the autopsy to her. Despite his outward gallantry, she guessed that Thorpe was inwardly pleased that she hadn't jumped at the chance to trade places.

"Are you sure, Jess?" He was pushing his luck now.

"Damn it, J. T., I'm sure . . . I'm okay here. Now get going. You've got phone calls to make, people to wake up, and get that damned photographer out of the coffee shop and up here."

"If you want me to take charge here, Jess . . . just say the word."

She grit her teeth. "Now you're getting on my nerves."

"Whataya mean, Jess? I'm just trying to show a little sensitivity. You women always want a show of concern, but you also want to be treated like equals. Suppose I asked McEvetty or Kaminsky here about how their morning's going.'' He shrugged and frowned, a bit tired of her show of bravado in the face of a death so without integrity as this. And for a moment the others saw and heard what amounted to a married couple arguing about nothing. They had worked many cases together, elbow to elbow, but usually J. T.'s help came in the safe confines of a well-lit lab back in Virginia. ''What?'' he repeated, his voice giving way to anger.

''Go, get photos of this bastard's message. Get copies to Santiva and to the academics and the nuthouses, okay? I'll see to the body.''

J. T. nodded, folding her hands in his like they were an omelet. ''Whatever you want, Jess.''

She bit her lip and held back a curse, finally bursting with, ''What I want has very little to do with anything these days, John. This motherless . . . monster is using me, and I don't like it, not one fucking bit do I like it. Get that photographer in here and take care of that decoding angle for me, okay?''

''You didn't cause this, Jess,'' he reassured her, studying her constricted features. ''And nobody can believe you did.''

Ignoring this, she turned to the bed and the body, which in the fire had become an unrecognizable lump of extraneous waste dumped here like one might find back of a plastics factory: Body in repose, hands and arms, feet and legs arched inward in what firemen called the ''fetal fire position,'' the dead man frozen in a moment of excruciating pain, the gaping fissure of the mouth, the gaping holes where the eyes had been, all worked in tandem to create a mask of grimacing, tortured distress, the agony visible through the newly formed body armor of blackened tissue.

The mattress had created first a thick, black, choking smoke when the flame from the butane torch ignited it along with the body itself, the result discoloring the bedpost, walls, and ceiling, and then the mattress had exploded into flame due to the gases released. Again this meant the killer must also be using a mask or filter of some sort, if not a small oxygen tank. She made a mental note to follow up with an exhaustive list of professions that employed such materials and instruments.

Other units on either side of the fire room, and even those overhead, were also scorched, but only slightly, due to the fast action of the FBI having contacted local authorities, and the fire department's subsequent action to contain the fire. Still, Melvin Martin—his unopened, label-scorched bottle of wine standing upright and mocking him—now melded with the charred furniture, a part of the soaked and sopping material left in the aftermath of the fire, followed by the fire hoses. He and his mattress one object now, and not just an object of pity. . . . He had literally been soldered to his mattress and box spring. Martin's remains could not fully be separated from the chemicals and sodden materials adhering to him. This could only be done in the morgue with great care and handling and swathing and bathing, to make him as presentable as possible for burial, for his family's sake.

She left the side of the body, grabbing hold of her valise for something solid to hold on to, and she again stepped from the room to retrieve some air from the hallway. It was the worst condition she'd ever seen a human body in, and working over such a fire-desiccated body was no simple task. It would take several takes.

Everyone watched her. She even saw some pity in McEvetty's stony eyes. "Like a Pepsi, maybe?" he asked. "Or maybe a boilermaker?" he joked.

This only sent her back into the room sooner. She now placed her valise on the soupy mattress of the bed and snatched open a second pocket to pull forth a pair of fresh rubber gloves, indicating that if anyone needed a fresh pair, she had plenty to spare. She then located a notepad from deep within her valise, and on the ruled and printed pages of her autopsy report pad she began the tedious work of checking boxes for cause of death, condition of the body and premises.

It's going to be a long and difficult autopsy, she thought, and somehow she couldn't help but feel partially responsible for Melvin Martin's death, despite consoling words to the contrary from J. T. or anyone else. That in some sick, twisted gyration of logic Chris Lorentian and Melvin Martin had to die because of her, because of who she was, because of some morbid and as yet undetermined connection between the Phantom and the M.E., because this killer, in fixating on her, had somehow made *her* his accomplice, his confederate. The cruel, sadistic bastard.

She at once wondered how many other law enforcement agents and agencies across the country would soon be viewing it the same way. She wondered if perhaps she'd become a liability for the FBI since becoming the serial killer hunter celebrity that Dr. Coran had evolved into. Maybe J. T. was wrong; maybe she did cause this storm, due the publicity she'd been receiving on the sensational cases she had been involved in over the years. And if that held true . . .

"Why's this sicko fire freak calling you on the telephone, Dr. Coran?" asked McEvetty, who returned to the room with his partner beside him. The question was posed in so casual a manner, as if he might be asking after her preference in dishware, as if he actually expected her to have a full-blown, informed answer.

J. T. suddenly returned with the photographer and proceeded to give him orders to "shoot everything."

Now McEvetty stared across from where he stood on the other side of the bed and body. Beside him, his partner, Kaminsky, held an eager look on his face as well, also anxious for an answer to McEvetty's question when suddenly he seemed to realize the foolishness of both his partner's question and his expectant stare.

Kaminsky stood Abe Lincoln tall, bony, angular, lean,

a sure ad for the Marlboro man, but somehow he fit into his white shirt and suit with a quiet grace lacking in McEvetty altogether. Both men gave off the appearance and aura of native Arizonans, mostly via the ruddy complexions, averted eyes, and wrinkles cut like scars, but whereas McEvetty weighed in large and bullish, Kaminsky was—while just a hairbreadth taller—much thinner and more light-footed. In a coarse way, McEvetty appeared always to be sporting a perpetual, scowling frown, whereas Kam maintained a quiet if cynical elegance.

"No doubt you two've already exhausted any off-color remarks or dark humor you most assuredly needed to get out of your systems before my arrival? Where's the usual detectives' banter, boys?" She'd heard laughter coming from within the black hole of this place when she and J. T. had first been guided here by the night clerk and the state patrol officer.

"Kam's working hard on getting in touch with his feminine side these days," joked McEvetty. "Ain'tcha, pard?"

"Shut up, Mac." Kam turned his full attention on Jessica. "Don't mind McEvetty and his stupid questions, Dr. Coran," Kaminsky said in a conspiratorial whisper. "His feet were so big when he was born that—"

"Shut up, Kam."

"—that there just wasn't no other place to put them but in his mouth, and he's gotten so used to the condition. Well, it just comes natural to him."

Jessica smiled in return and began going over the body with a handheld magnifying glass, complaining of the poor light. Still, she easily saw what she needed to see. Like Chris Lorentian's nearly cremated, baked body, there were wounds to the head, but no bullet holes, no quick and painless death, unfortunately. Poor old Melvin had died a torturous, horrendous death as a living marshmallow, and for no other reason than to satisfy some sick bastard's idea of kicks.

It was then that Dr. Karl Repasi stepped into the room. Jessica didn't at first see him, although she heard J. T. asking someone, "How did you get here? When did you arrive?" And Jessica hoped it was Warren, but when she looked from the cadaver, she saw that it was Repasi.

"I'm here to assist in any way possible," he informed Jessica. "I got word from Bishop about the killing here and got a plane out of Vegas."

"This takes you some distance out of your way, Dr. Repasi," she replied, keeping her eyes on her work, wondering what his game was.

"Arizona's my territory. Now this bastard's come to my home state," Repasi answered and stepped closer for a professional look over her shoulder as Jessica examined the crinkled, crumpled, fire-blackened outer layers of the body, a kind of brittle-to-the-touch, breakaway armor.

Jessica and J. T. exchanged a glance, accepting Repasi's reasoning for the moment. He was the M.E. for Phoenix, Arizona. Still, Phoenix was a long way from Page.

Repasi found a question lurking in his head that he had to ask: "What do you think, Jessica? Same MO? Fingerprints in the written message? Identical scene, except this one's a man?"

"Cause of death is often hidden by fire, as you know, and as you've said many times, Doctor, we have to be sure, but on the surface, yes."

"The way I heard it from Vegas is that you heard this one's dying words on the phone? That he—"

"That he was smoked while I listened in."

"Then you know he was, like Chris Lorentian, conscious when he got it; burned alive."

"What is it you want here, Karl?" she asked point-blank.

"Just to offer my services. That's all. Everyone knows you've got your hands full with this. That you need help, more help than Thorpe can give you. So, tell me, what can I do to help?"

She glanced up at J. T., seeing that he was not pleased, and she said, "All right, Karl."

"Whatever you need, Jess," he replied.

"Witness the fact I find no puncture wounds, no blunt-object wounds, no knife or bullet wounds."

"What about track marks?" asked McEvetty. "You know, drugs?"

Kaminsky tried to soften the question by adding, "Isn't it true the one killed like this in Vegas was using?"

"That was never established, was it, Dr. Repasi?" she asked.

"As a matter of fact, there were some high concentrations of an over-the-counter sedative found in the blood, Dr. Coran. But no needle tracks or hard drugs, no."

"Well, if I'm to locate that kind of information, gentlemen, I'll need a lab, I'll need seven hundred thousand times the light and a powerful magnifying glass, an electronic comparison microscope, blood and serum samples, a gas chromatography setup. Do you see a possibility for any of that happening here in this room?" Instantly, Jessica felt apologetic for her outburst, for sounding off, and coming off, as so officious and bitchy, but the past two days and nights weighed heavily, a damnable burden and strain on her nerves, and these men seemed only to be adding to her stress.

McEvetty's unrestrained, snaking smile created a new mask of his face, and he sputtered in an infectious school-boy fashion now, saying, "But Dr. Coran, on our way up here, we heard you were some kinda—what, Mac?—miracle worker. That you could see like a cat in the dark. That the dead whisper in your ear? Isn't that right, Ed?"

Jessica laughed with them to lighten the moment, but just the same, she had had enough of the Hardy boys.

"Call in the paramedics, Jess," said Repasi. "Let's ship Mr. Martin here to the morgue, so I can do a thorough job of it. You'll have a copy of the report by nightfall."

With this request coming from Repasi, Jessica looked

up at J. T., who took her aside and said, "I don't know
what Repasi's game is, but he's way out of his jurisdiction.
He's the M.E. for Pheonix, not the state of Arizona.

"Yes, and he's built up quite a reputation there. He's
terribly anxious to help us out, isn't he?"

"Maybe he wants your job, Jess."

"He can have it."

She then tore off her gloves and tossed them atop the
mummified remains before her, the photographer snapping
a quick shot of her gloves atop the body. She grabbed her
bag and left the two area FBI men to exchange looks,
while J. T. followed her out and Karl Repasi scratched at
his head and beard, as if utterly confused by her anger.

Jessica, a bit tired of being assessed, stopped in the hallway, where she found the air less foul, and after taking in
a deep breath, barked orders down the corridor. "You can
get the medics in now; have 'em take the body to the
nearest medical facility with the best lab equipped for
morgue work, will you, fellas? And what would that be,
and will you get me there?"

"We only got one hospital in Page, ma'am," replied
the uniformed officer nearest her.

She nodded, sighed, feeling foolish. "It'll have to do
then."

Jessica was about to leave with J. T. at her side when a
distraught man in cowboy boots, string tie, and ornamented
belt, and sporting a Stetson hat, rushed into the fray, his
face beet red with anxiety. "My God, is it Mr. Martin's
room? I just learned of the fire. God, the bus'll be delayed."

"Did you know Martin?" asked Jessica.

"He was on my bus. One of my travelers."

"Your bus?"

"I'm Ronny Ropers. I'm a tour bus guide. Mr. Martin's
one of my charges. Someone's going to have to notify the
family, and since I'm captain of the ship, so to speak . . .
Nothing like this has ever happened before, not on my

watch. I mean, sure I've had some die on me; we book more over-the-hill passengers than any tour line going, but it's always been of natural causes. I heard talk of . . . of murder?''

"You have any idea who might have wanted Martin dead?''

"What're you talking about? We're all just touring the country, having a good time, all except Himmie.''

"Himmie?''

"Mr. Herndorf, Klaus Herndorf, dour guy, keeps entirely to himself at the back of the bus, doesn't participate, always a glum response, talks very little English, voted most likely to Uzi the bus.''

"Did you see Martin with Herndorf or anyone else last night?''

"I spoke to him myself last night before going into the village. He was fine.''

"Was he alone?''

"Yes, just going down to dinner.'' Ropers was visibly shaken. "He was just a sweet old man. Who'd want to murder him? I was just kidding about Himmie, of course.''

"We'll want to meet with and talk to everyone on your tour, Mr. Ropers.''

Suddenly he looked even more stricken than before. "But that will delay us for hours.''

"I'm sorry, but it will be necessary.''

Jessica and J. T. followed Ropers outside to his bus, weaving in and out through a parking lot littered with tour buses. They had to be led to the bus that belonged to Martin's group. There she began the tedious questioning of other tourists who might shed some light on the Martin case. So far, all they had in the way of an identification of the mysterious man who had dined with Martin was the shaky description of a waitress who had very poor recall.

From the look of the crowd on the bus, Jessica held out little hope of learning much more than why older people on vacation were willing to make absolute fools of themselves in what they chose to wear, and certainly not any more than they already knew about the killing.

"Martin was a loner," said one of the elderly ladies near the front. "He kept going off by himself. Didn't mingle well."

"Poor social skills," added the lady traveling with her.

"We tried to involve him more," said another gray-blue-hair across from these two, her garish green sunglasses and bonnet bobbing with her speech.

Ropers reluctantly agreed. "I found it difficult to involve him. Usually, I can get anyone involved in the time-passing games we play on the bus, but Martin was a real dour fellow, not unlike Mr. Herndorf in that regard, but at least Martin would crack a smile now and again, show he was listening in."

"He was traveling alone, recently widowed, somewhat soured on life," supplied another elderly lady.

The image made Jessica think of how lions in Africa picked out their prey from among the aged, dying, and weak who could not keep up with the herd. Had Martin died because he was lonely? Did he have absolutely no connection to Chris Lorentian? If so, then the victims were randomly selected by the killer, and the killer did not know his victims, save for what he might surmise from their body language, perhaps.

Did Chris Lorentian look like an easy target, like Mel Martin had looked like an easy target?

Jessica met with and spoke to Herndorf, who was every bit as sourpussed as Ropers had described him. He expressed in broken English his regret about Martin, but assured Jessica he had not seen or spoken to the man the night before and knew nothing of his accident, as he put it. Herndorf seethed throughout the interview, angry at the Gestapo-like treatment and the FBI's putting them off schedule.

•   •   •

Feydor Dorphmann felt an overwhelming need to catch up on his sleep as he boarded the large, comfortable, air-conditioned bus that had snaked its way through canyon passes, pulling out of Page, Arizona, at dawn along with thirty-six other passengers. He had seen the activity of fire trucks, a paramedic wagon, and local police milling about the scene of his last destruction.

He had located his usual seat at the rear and settled in, placing his hefty black briefcase in the overhead and grabbing a pillow for his head. He had loosened up with the other passengers now, saying good morning to each as he passed them, remembering some of the names, asking forgiveness from those he could not recall. He nestled into the cushions of one chair and put his feet up on the one beside him.

The other passengers had long before become curious about him. They had all become "real chums" at the inaugural dinner the night he had burned Chris Lorentian to death. They had all exchanged information about themselves to one another, all at the coaxing of Doris, the tour director, a woman whose makeup—if not her face—might crack if she smiled once more. No one on the bus knew anything about Feydor, and he knew he must come up with some answers to some inevitable questions. He wondered if he ought not revert to his German, as bad as it was, and pretend to know very little English. It could save him a lot of trouble.

Contemplating this, he had happened to glance out the window. His heart almost stopped, and then it started up in quick-beat fashion when he saw Dr. Jessica Coran emerge from the building near where the fire had broken out in the early-morning hours, disturbing everyone in the east wing of the lodge.

As others now began boarding the bus, Feydor quickly realized that the fire and the fire death fueled the talk of the morning for the tourists, and word came back to Feydor that the poor fellow who expired in the fire was a traveler on another tour with another bus line heading toward Vegas and coming from destinations ahead on their schedule.

Jessica Coran and a man with her, flashing their FBI badges, suddenly boarded another bus, Martin's tour bus. Dr. Coran's small black valise dangled at her side, firm in her strong hand. Feydor watched with great interest, wondering if the FBI people might yet board his bus, fearful they could cut short his and Satan's scheme. But Doris wasn't about to be held up. She'd been involved in what appeared a continual rivalry with yet another bus following the same route as they.

"Crank her up and get us outta here, Dave!" she ordered the driver.

Doris appeared determined not only to stay on schedule but also to defeat her nemesis by gaining time and getting ahead of schedule. Doris had explained that the earlier they got out, the better and cleaner the facilities along the way were apt to be, and the better the service and the better the food.

When the bus had shuddered into life, Feydor felt safe again.

And now, even as the tour director listed their stops today, Feydor began to nod off, and soon the killer nodded off completely, a half smile on his lips. He'd done a good night's work, and a respite from his fevered mind and future plans felt reward enough for now.

I deserve a break today, his mind kept telling him. Along with some peaceful sleep in the air-conditioned comfort of the bus. This compensation felt right. But Doris, from the front of the bus, started up another of her blasted sing-alongs, show tunes.

Feydor placed on headsets built into the seat to listen to some Bach, Handel, and Wagner rather than participate in this morning's Andrew Lloyd Webber tunes with the tour guide, a frustrated showgirl, Feydor decided. Even from behind his closed eyelids, he could feel the woman's wrath. She'd be after him to participate more; there was little doubt of this fact. He occasionally opened his eyes and found her glare.

The tour guide had said they must all rotate seats on each successive day of the tour so that everybody got a chance to be up front, and it supposedly made for friendlier relations among the travelers. Feydor hadn't changed seats, preferring the serenity and relative safety of the backseat. Besides, the view from here held all other passengers under his scrutiny.

But it had been a rough night, so he leaned the back of his chair as far as it would go, feigning a headache. He allowed the classical music to flow over him. For the moment, he felt relatively safe in sleeping. He remained pleased that Jessica Coran, like a beckoned shadow, had followed him thus far. He was equally pleased to have left her yet another surprise that would complicate her pursuit.

He thought of the well to which he intended taking Jessica Coran, the well of fire into which he intended throwing her. He recalled the area as it appeared to him as a child, recalled the first time he had ever taken a life; it had been another child's life and no one had ever known except for him and for Satan, who told him to do it.

He knew that Satan beckoned him back to the place where he'd killed that little girl, where he'd pushed her from the guardrail and into the Devil's lips. He had stood about with the rest of the crowd, watching the frantic parents as the little girl cooked to death in the superheated waters of Yellowstone National Park.

He'd been in search of redemption ever since, but God was in no mood to redeem him, and it appeared only one god could salvage his soul, the god of Hades.

He felt an overwhelming need to make contact again with the FBI woman, Jessica Coran, but when the bus finally stopped at a roadside café and gift shop, at eight thirty-five, his attempt to reach Dr. Coran at the Wahweap Lodge failed miserably. She was unreachable.

He hung up and dialed the number he had for her in Vegas at the Hilton. He'd get his message to her one way or another, he promised himself and his demon within. He'd talk to the FBI. Not necessarily Jessica Coran this time, but someone close enough to forward her the news. They were all waiting to hear from him again; someone would be there at the number in Vegas, waiting for his call, awaiting disclosures.

While others on the bus attended to nature and the gift shop and their stomachs, he placed the second call, making the call he'd been unable to make the day before for lack of time and for lack of a handy telephone.

As it worked out, it was provident he hadn't had a phone in the room at the El Tovar, where the group had stopped for a fast look at the Grand Canyon and lunch. While the others lunched, he had set fire to a malicious fraud in the name of Satan. He wanted to tell someone about it now in the worst way. Wanted to get word to Dr. Coran.

· TEN ·

Undulating to this side and that, even
as a wave receding and advancing.
                                    —DANTE

The Melvin Martin autopsy became a crowded affair, and
Jessica felt the crunch of others in the room whenever she
moved, for at every turn someone stood in the way. Repasi, a man of his word, remained with them. A local physician who acted as the hospital's pathologist also felt
compelled to be on hand, as it was his room.

Preliminary tests indicated that some over-the-counter
sedative appeared to be present in high levels, that Martin
had been sedated, just as Chris Lorentian had. Jessica
imagined that in time, it would be proven to be the exact
same medication. The fact that the old man had drugs in
his system suggested one thing to J. T., who was also present, and another to Jessica and Karl Repasi.

"Maybe it's the one soft spot the killer has," J. T. had
remarked from behind his surgical mask.

The room they were in had a constant flow of air to
reduce not only the odor but also the amount of bacteria
and decay as they worked over the incinerated flesh.

"Soft spot?" asked Jessica.

"Yeah. He drugs his victims to reduce the pain and
suffering he inflicts."

"A rosy picture, indeed, Dr. Thorpe," said Repasi.

Jessica replied, "J. T., this is the same guy who calls me up so I can listen to their screams."

Repasi stepped in, saying, "I must agree with Jessica, Thorpe. He only drugs them to control them."

Jessica, nodding, added, "So he can march them to the secondary crime scene. The first being his assault on their senses with the drug."

"Yes, the secondary crime scene, the comfort zone for him—the place where he can turn them into so much kindling for his fires," Repasi agreeably added, his head bobbing in accord.

"Yes, the place where he is in total control and can take his bloody awful time, so he can disrobe them. He doesn't burn them in their clothes, male or female, if you've noticed. Ties them without much of a fight being put up."

"I feel like a third . . . fourth wheel here," J. T. told her. "I might do better chasing down the shoeprint we saw."

Repasi instantly said, "Why don't you do that, Thorpe. Get to the *bottom* of things, so to speak." Repasi's little jest left J. T. cold.

"I'll see you later," J. T. told Jessica on his way out.

Jessica took Repasi aside, not wanting the Page people to hear any further dissension between them. She asked, "Do you want to tell me, now, Doctor, why you are here? And just why are you so bloody interested in this case?"

"It's a bloody interesting case, wouldn't you say? Besides, Arizona's my home state, Doctor," he replied coolly. "And another besides, I'm a board-certified forensic medical examiner, and Page operates under the old coroner system. The coroner here is Doctor Porter, a fine man, yes, but he's not highly trained in forensic science. He's a hospital pathologist with a number of years under his belt, but hardly qualified in forensics."

Jessica understood this language all too well. In fact, much attention had been placed on the continuing problem of the old coroner system, which still operated in most municipalities in the nation. With two general types of medicolegal investigative systems in the United States, the coroner system and the medical examiner system, there remained a great deal of confusion in the public mind about the differences in the terms "coroner," "pathologist," and "medical examiner." Twelve states had coroner systems at work that employed politicians and sometimes hospital pathologists to do the work of a medical examiner. Twenty-two states and the District of Columbia employed the medical examiner system, while sixteen states had both systems at work. The coroner system, the older of the two, dated back to a time when kings and dukes employed a man to determine cause in suspicious deaths, in an attempt to confiscate the holdings of suicide victims, who had blatantly wronged Mother Church, and murderers, who had blatantly wronged the Crown by reducing the taxable public by one or more members. To some degree, the coroner system remained a political arm of the legal system, and it was under this undue pressure and conflict of interest that the elected official with the title "coroner" performed his duties. It had for centuries now allowed barbers, butchers, and candlestick makers who ran for the office to pronounce cause of death in cases ranging from suspicious to ordinary, without the coroner having the slightest knowledge of medicine or forensics—medicine as it applied to law. The system had improved over the years, most jurisdictions now insisting that the coroner at least be a board-certified pathologist, but not even an anatomical pathologist—a generalist—had the training the medical examiner took years to acquire. The only training the coroner received for the position still ranged from absolutely none to a few hours to one or two weeks at best. This was an unforgivable sin as far as Jessica Coran was concerned, for therein lay hundreds upon hundreds of people getting away with murder every day. Jessica had heard Karl speak out against the antiquated coroner system on many occasions, and in fact he was scheduled to do so in Vegas today, back at the convention.

"I thought you were scheduled to speak at the convention today, Karl."

"There are more important things than shooting off my mouth on a subject no one in the forensics community wants to hear me fire off on again," he joked.

"You're sure there's no other reason that you are following . . . this case?" she asked again.

"As I said before, I offered my services to the FBI—Bishop, to be exact, and he encouraged me to help in any way possible. So here I am."

She pressed it further. "And you're sure there's no other motive at work here?"

"My, but you've become suspicious over the years, Jessica. Look, my office got word of a suspicious fire death here in Page, and they knew of what had happened in Vegas because I was in contact with them. They put it together and called me back. Bishop's office informed me where you were. It was either come here or remain at that dull convention. Which would you have chosen, Jessica?"

"All right, Karl. Let's have the truth now, okay?"

He squirmed, thinking her goddamned persistent. He looked down at his feet, fidgeted with the tails of his surgery gown, and finally admitted, "Phoenix is screwing around with the medical examiner system that I created there. They see it's cheaper to run a coroner's office than a medical examiner's office; they think cheaper is better, even more efficient."

"Christ," she moaned in sympathy for Karl.

"My office is being seriously challenged by a referendum on the ballot to make death investigation cheaper in the jurisdiction. Cheaper, do you believe it? You have no idea how close to the bone we run the office as is, but death investigation still doesn't come cheaply enough for the budget cutters."

It was an all-too-familiar lament among forensics experts. "I'm sorry to hear it, Karl." She sounded like a person giving condolences to a friend who'd contracted an incurable disease, but she didn't know what else to say.

Repasi shrugged and said, "There's the usual complaint about lack of money, which has led to inadequate staffing and salaries, and we struggle along with antiquated operations and equipment."

"Resistance to acquiring new technology, resistance to change," she sounded the mantra. "And a failure to appreciate, even understand, the M.E.'s mission. I got the same nonsense when I was M.E. in Washington, and when I was an assistant M.E. in Baltimore before that."

Finally, something she did understand. It made sense for Repasi to have shown up uninvited here. "How many ways do we have to show people that the coroner system produces inferior and inaccurate results?" she rhetorically asked. "Nonphysicians can't make accurate medical decisions, no matter how many weeks of training you give them."

"Nor can general pathologists in many cases. Sure, they can mull their way through most common cases, but the difficult ones, the cases they often don't even recognize as difficult. . . . Fools in Phoenix are taking the death stats to heart, you see. They say only twenty percent of our cases involve suspicious deaths, so a pathologist could handle the eighty percent that we do not *need* to investigate."

Jessica understood the enormous hole in this logic, and she nodded knowingly.

"How does a pathologist know which is the twenty percent if he isn't trained to recognize that twenty percent? What judge would take his pregnant wife to a dermatologist for obstetrical care? But the same politician will permit an individual with zero forensic training to testify in a case involving life-and-death decisions."

"Yeah, agreed," began Jessica. "A major characteristic of the unqualified expert in forensics is that rare ability to interpret a case in absolute and exquisite detail when there are no forensic details to be had in a case."

"Worse still is the practice of contract pathologists."

"Yes, the very notion sets my teeth on edge." Jessica's mind fumed at the idea of a pathologist paid by the case, so that the more cases he or she put away, the more money the pathologist made. "What about the local coroner here in Page? How does he work?"

"Modified coroner, M.E. system. Sends a lot of his cases up to Salt Lake City, others to me in Phoenix."

"Oh, so you two know each other well."

"Yes."

"So, he's okay with you taking charge, Karl?"

"We've talked at length. He's happy for the interference."

"That's a refreshing change. I usually meet with resistance with the natives. Good for you."

"Perhaps I'm better with my people skills than you, Jessica?"

She let this pass, saying, "Well then, let's get to work, shall we?" She returned to the body, what remained of Mel Martin: a greasy, soot-covered, creosoted lump of charred flesh an autopsy could do little or nothing for. This they all knew, but protocol mandated an autopsy be performed.

And so, Jessica, how do you approach a fire victim such as this? She heard Dr. Holcraft's voice, her mentor, now long dead, filling her thoughts.

She inwardly, silently answered, *The same way that any physician approaches any patient.* In medical school, Jessica was taught that to make a correct diagnosis, she must first take a history, perform an examination, and order relevant laboratory tests. They'd gotten only a smattering of Martin's history, knowing much less about the man than they had Chris Lorentian in Vegas. But there were no family members at hand, and time was fleeting. They were prepared to make their examination now and order necessary tests.

"I suppose you've seen your share of burn cases, Dr.

Coran," said Repasi, "but have you ever seen anything worse than this?"

She paused, considered his question, and replied, "Yes, I have."

"Oh, really? Explosion victims? Lightning victims?"

"A woman who was scalded to death."

Both doctors appreciated the severe nature of burns from boiling water, knowing that water heated to 158 degrees Fahrenheit caused a full-thickness burn in adult skin in one second of contact.

"Ahhh, bathroom shower injuries I've seen, but nothing approximating this."

"This was no bathroom shower accident. It was a victim of murder whose body was placed in a scalding hot spring in Yellowstone National Park, held under by her ankles as she thrashed. The scalding was uniform, not showing any burn variation, no multiple splash burns, just all-over fourth-degree burns. The killer hoped to cover up a rape-murder by completely scalding the body in a two-hundred-five-degree hot pool. She was scalded over her entire body, save her ankles and feet, which were only mildly burned by comparison. Sloppy oversight on the killer's part, but then he didn't know a medical examiner was in the park at the time. The murderer was a young park ranger who'd come up on the victim where she was hiking alone in the park. That was some ten or eleven years ago."

"Sounds like an interesting case," he granted.

"It was the first murder case I ever solved."

While Page's hospital was an adequate, modern facility, the death room and the forensic equipment in Page left a great deal to be desired; still, Jessica was glad to see that they had at least the rudiments for a pathology lab and that it was not placed in the subbasement of the hospital or the back of a funeral home, as was the case in hundreds of thousands of small towns all across America. There was just sufficient enough space along with appropriate lighting, plumbing, and cooling facilities. The instrumentation included an X-ray machine for the pathology lab and coroner's office to share, a luxury, it appeared, despite the fact that an X-ray machine was basic equipment in any autopsy suite. Page also had its own small toxicological lab capable of accurate, precise analysis for the presence of drugs.

In getting the autopsy under way, Jessica spoke into a microphone that recorded her autopsy for later transcription. Back at Quantico, nowadays, the entire autopsy was put on videotape, and Jessica had learned to choose her words with extreme care, for anything said now could come back to haunt the medical examiner. She announced the purpose of their coming together, the name of the deceased, age, height, weight, sex, race, condition of the body upon discovery. This led her to add, "On gross examination of such a victim, it is virtually impossible to distinguish antemortem from postmortem burns. Microscopic examination of the body tissue offers no help, unless the victim has survived long enough to develop an inflammatory response. Wouldn't you agree, Dr. Repasi?"

Repasi promptly agreed, saying, "Yes, lack of such a response doesn't necessarily indicate that the burn was postmortem. I have had occasion to view third-degree burns incurred by Vietnam veterans in which the patients died two and three days later. In some of these cases, there was no inflammatory reaction whatsoever."

Jessica agreed now, adding, "Due, presumably, to heat thrombosis of the dermal vessels."

"Such that inflammatory cells could not reach the area of the burn and produce a reaction to begin with," finished Repasi.

Jessica thought that perhaps J. T. ought to have remained; he might well have learned something about the irregular nature of burn pathology.

"In Mr. Martin's case, it is presumed he was alive when

he died due to witness testimony, namely Dr. Coran," said
Repasi for the record.

"It may also be of interest that the skin has split open,
revealing exposed muscle across the upper torso and upper
extremities, while skin over the back is perfectly preserved.
Where the skin is completely burned away, underlying
muscles have ruptured due to the intensity of the heat,"
added Jessica.

Burned bone shone as gray-white with a fine, superficial
network of fractures on the cortical surface. Repasi noted
this for the shoulder bone and collarbone as well as the
skull. With his gloved hand, he put slight pressure on a
section of skull thus discolored, and it crumbled at his
touch. He noted this for the record. "The outer table of
the exposed cranial vault," he said, pausing, "reveals a
network of fine, crisscrossing heat fractures."

Both examiners knew that it was extremely hard to burn
a body, due to its high water content, and that to do the
damage the Phantom had inflicted on Martin required a
superheated energy source. Portions of the abdominal wall
were burned away as well, exposing the viscera. The internal organs appeared charred, seared.

"In the autopsy on Chris Lorentian, who died from similar inflicted wounds," Jessica said, "there was evidence
of an antemortem epidural hematoma."

Repasi added, "We find a similar blow to the head before death in Martin; there is a sizable postmortem epidural
hematoma present. Not an uncommon sight in severely
burned bodies. See here, Jessica, the chocolate brown
color, crumbly, with its telltale honeycombed appearance."

"Yes, I see it. Large, fairly thick, overlying the frontal
lobe, extending toward the occipital area."

He lifted a tiny ruler to it and asked an assistant to snap
a picture, and for the record he announced, "Yes, large at
one point five centimeters."

"Good catch, Doctor." Jessica turned off the recorder

for a word with Dr. Repasi. "Karl, I didn't know your specialty was burn victims."

"One of many," he replied with a grin beneath his surgical mask. "Shall we have a look-see at the larynx and trachea? Examine for carbon monoxide intoxication?"

"I prefer the term smoke inhalation, Doctor, but yes."

"Semantics," he parried and scalpeled at the same time, opening up the charred throat and dissecting the larynx and trachea, which, while fire-blackened and fractured on the outside, remained intact.

Too many people in the scientific community, as far as Jessica was concerned, used the terms of the profession too loosely, such as making carbon monoxide poisoning synonymous with smoke inhalation. A number of important factors other than the presence of carbon monoxide in the blood might cause death by smoke inhalation, such as oxygen deprivation due to consumption of oxygen by the fire itself, cyanide, free radicals, and the old standby to fall back on, *nonspecific toxic substances*. Jessica knew that in cases of self-immolation, carbon monoxide, as a general rule, was not elevated, since it was a flash fire. In cases involving explosives or gasoline fires, carbon monoxide levels in the blood were usually found to be in the so-called normal range. This held true even if the body were severely charred. Every fire, in fact, was unique, and each created its own unique mysteries. Of course, Repasi knew this as well as she.

She spoke again into the recorder, saying, "Smoke inhalation reveals soot in the nostrils and mouth, but this alone is no indication the victim was alive when the fire began. Any further look into the breathing apparatus will not change that fact."

But Repasi, ever the perfectionist, wanted to see the results of this fire to the windpipe as well. He announced what his scalpel now sliced through and why for the record. The soot had not coated the larynx, trachea, or bronchi, but both doctors took this in stride.

"Well, clean as a whistle except for the gristle," quipped Repasi. "What do you make of that, Dr. Coran?"

"Absence of soot in these areas in a flash fire is not uncommon, and it does not necessarily mean that Martin was dead prior to the blaze."

"Quite right. I've seen numerous cases in which no soot appeared in these deeper areas, and yet analysis of blood carbon monoxide revealed lethal levels. Unfortunately, blisters or the absence thereof," continued Repasi, "do not indicate that the deceased was alive at the time the burns were incurred either, since they can be produced postmortem."

Jessica knew that many people, medical people included, coroners and pathologists and some medical examiners included, mistakenly believed that if blisters or burns were surrounded by an erythematous—red—rim, then this clearly indicated that the victim was alive at the time the burns were incurred. This was blatantly false. Blisters with such red rims had now been produced on dead bodies at the FBI's famous, or infamous, "Body Farm" in Tennessee. Both she and Repasi knew that heat applied to skin caused contraction of dermal capillaries, and this forced blood to the periphery of the blister, simulating an antemortem hyperemic inflammatory response.

An autopsy on such a body proved the worst kind of pathology. Fire did awful things to flesh, creating leathery, wood-grainlike swirls, like some mad tattoo artists had been allowed to go to work on the dead man. Jessica recognized this configuration as the result of actual contact with flame, that they were again dealing with a "flash" burn.

The extent of the burn was indicated as the percent of total surface area involved by the thermal injury, and chemical burns from the gas used caused even deeper, thicker blotches of mottled skin tissue. The percentage of total surface area burned was quickly determined using the *rule of nines*. Jessica, using the typical conventional thinking, considered the total body surface as 100 percent, meaning the head was 9 percent, as it was completely burned away to the bone, leaving no features. The arms or upper extremities represented 9 percent each. The front of the torso, also extremely badly damaged, counted for an additional 18 percent. The back, which was not burned badly at all, since it was protected by the victim's weight against the bed, also represented 18 percent. Each lower extremity totaled 18 percent apiece, while the neck amounted to 1 percent, equaling an even 100 percent. Martin's body was burned over 82 percent of its surface. His burns were the worst kind, third- and fourth-degree, or as Repasi's nomenclature had it, a combination of partial-and full-thickness burns. In third-degree burns there was coagulation necrosis of the epidermis and dermis with complete destruction to the dermal appendages. Most of Martin's lesions were brown and blackened, the result of charring and eschar formation. If he had survived the fire, the smoke inhalation, the shock, the dehydration, and the bursting blood vessels, this blackened skin would have healed as scar tissue, but at his advanced age, even if he had lived, he would likely be dead within hours or days. Other burns, fourth-degree burns, appeared as ashen white leather. There were no red blisters. The fire was too intense for the cherry-red burns usually associated with fire and skin, for Martin's burns were incinerating injuries extending deeper than the skin.

It was evident to Repasi, J. T., and Jessica that Martin's injuries were the result of a high-intensity flash burn, resulting from an explosion of gases. Jessica kept hearing the whoosh of the explosion in her ears. This explained why 90 percent of the burned areas appeared to have burned uniformly. The other 10 percent was due to the mattress and clothing burning against the body. When clothing ignited, a combination of flash and flash burn occurred. Flash burns usually resulted in only partial-thickness or second- and third-degree burns and singed hair, but this flash burn was directed by human means directly at the victim, making it third- and fourth-degree about the face, head, and upper torso, with nearly total loss of hair. What hair remained crumbled at the touch, like burned pitch pine.

The severity of the burn was increased by the careful method in which the killer loosely wrapped the clothing about the body. If wrapped tightly and snugly against the body, it would have decreased the degree of burn. But the killer knew that air surrounding the clothing would help fuel his human bonfire.

"Order up at minimum," began Jessica, "blood, vitreous, urine, and bile for toxicological analysis."

"I'll do the blood myself," suggested Repasi, quickly taking the blood from the root of the aorta with needle and syringe. Wise choice, Jessica thought, glad that Karl hadn't incised the vessels and attempted to catch the fluid as it came out.

Repasi next went about placing all body fluids he collected in glass tubes and bottles, no plastic. Once more, Jessica approved.

"Shall we open up the chest? Get liver, kidney, and muscle samples?"

"Ready when you are, Doctor."

Repasi was a sure man with a scalpel, and his incision helped the already fractured and split-apart chest open like a melon to reveal the viscera, remarkably but not surprisingly untouched by the fire. Due to its high water content, a body was one of the most difficult items on the planet to use as fuel for a fire—so much so that a body like Martin's, showing great and extreme damage and extensive charring on the outside, often showed perfect preservation of the internal organs, especially those below the rib cage. Household fires generated temperatures seldom exceeding 1,200 to 1,600 degrees Fahrenheit. It took 1,800 to 2,000 degrees Fahrenheit to cremate a body. Ordinary house fires lacked that kind of intensity and the time to incinerate a human body completely. As for a flash fire, involving gasoline and butane and a sudden flashover, the intensity was fleeting. A flash fire could not sustain such temperatures for a long enough period to fully ignite the body and all its water-laden internal organs.

"Liver, kidney, and muscle needn't be retained," Repasi suggested. "I can take samples only, and I'll see that they are kept for three or four years, if need be. I'll do the microscopic examination of the tissues, and I'll oversee the slides."

"Very thorough, Doctor," complimented Jessica. "Please be sure to also make a positive ID of the victim as well."

He saw the glint in her eye. "Yes, of course." He managed a wry smile.

"To make a positive and unmistakable identification, a chest X ray will be taken to be used for comparison with those of the deceased man. His dentures will also be kept in the effort to ID him beyond a reasonable doubt."

Jessica knew that in fact a single tooth could positively identify Martin, but the old man didn't have a single tooth of his own remaining.

"So, as it stands, we have no evidence he was alive when the flash fire killed him, none other than your word, Dr. Coran."

"It appears so," she agreed, but she didn't care for Karl's accusatory tone.

Now he cut off the recorder. "This business about the phone, about the killer's having constant contact with you, Dr. Coran. It's a bit far-fetched, wouldn't you say?"

The assistants in the room stopped what they were doing to listen to Repasi, who continued in the same vein, saying, "Why does he talk to you exclusively? Why?"

Jessica took her colleague aside. "Trust me, Dr. Repasi, if I thought giving him your number would help matters—"

Repasi's raucous laughter cut her off. "So exactly when

did he last speak with you, Jessica? What does he wish to convey to you? What is his ultimate purpose? His destination? His goal?''

"If I knew that, Karl, I'd have him surrounded with an army of law enforcement officials this moment. Believe me, if I could alter or end his madness, I would do so immediately."

"Would you really? Your record does not bear you out, Jessica. You're rather well known nowadays for rushing in where fools fear to tread, quite on your own, to grab the glory."

"The glory? There is no bloody glory in any of this!" She pointed to the petrified corpse, once again raising interest in the lab assistants.

"You garnered plenty in New Orleans, and with that madman Matisak, repeating a similar performance to your actions in Chicago, New York—"

Jessica's face grew stern as she listened to Repasi, her teeth grinding top to bottom, until she exploded, cutting him off. "Are you finished?"

"Oh, I see," he replied. "It only *appears* that you're interested in media attention as a modern-day Sherlock Holmes. I get it." A curling smile snaked about his mouth.

He enjoyed making her uneasy, making her squirm, she realized. "That's contemptible, Karl."

"Jessica, I've no doubt we have a serial killer playing deadly with fire here, but that he grants you a private audience with each killing? I have a problem with that."

"Bullshit! I didn't make it up, Karl! And I'm not smitten with the press or building an image for myself. There's no hoax here! Certainly none of my doing."

"Oh, I hope I didn't suggest that you were part of some elaborate medical hoax, Doctor. It's just that I'm having trouble with the idea that this monster serial killer feels *compelled* to contact you every step of the way. It's sheer madness even for a madman."

"As I said, if I could alter his madness in any way, this moment—"

"So, when did he last talk to you?" he wanted to know.

"I've taken proper steps to inform, on a need-to-know basis, my superiors of any contact made. That doesn't include you, Karl."

"What has he conveyed to you? What is his ultimate goal? And this business of him telephoning it in. Are you sure he's not just some mental patient from a federal facility whom you've had . . . previous contact with?"

She considered the possibility for half a second. "No, he is not, Doctor. And I'm not sure I like what you're implying here."

"I didn't mean to imply anything unsavory."

She pointed her finger at his eyes and sternly said, "This conversation is taking a strange turn, Karl. I think it's at an end, now."

"I, personally, don't believe a word of the rumors being touted about, Jessica, but you know what they say about appearances."

"Whatever are you talking about? What rumors?"

"Press rumors."

"About me?"

"You and this madman, yes, and the idea there might be some former connection; that perhaps you know him, or knew him, but have put him out of your mind, perhaps?"

"No, no . . . I have as much knowledge of him as you, Karl."

"Some people are throwing it out there, Jessica, this theory, and it has just enough basis in fact that credence is being—"

"Basis in fact? Credence? What fact?"

"It's a well-known fact that you have both access and control over any number of serial killers and homicidal psychopaths in federal care. Is that not true?"

She gritted her teeth, angry, knowing that Karl was right

about the press, particularly the tabloid press, with their unspoken motto: *We print every half-truth fit or unfit to see print.* And there was just enough half-truth in what Karl said to crop up in the rags. She took it out on Karl, saying, "You just reminded me again why I've always disliked you, Karl."

"Hey, don't shoot the messenger. I'm only telling you to watch your back, Jessica. That's all."

Like you care about my back, she thought, wondering anew about his motive in even being here. She tore off her gloves and mask and stepped away from the body. "I'm done here. You can finish up, Doctor." She stormed from the small autopsy room, angry and exhausted, her jaw clenched tight.

An hour later, Jessica was back at the resort marina, where she fell across the bed. She could hardly believe the madness of Karl Repasi, and the gall of the man. Hours of intense labor over a body that kept casting off bits and pieces of itself onto the floor, and then to have to deal with Repasi's obvious mental breakdown. She had suspected him of a fraud and a hoax when all of this began, and now he suspected her of the same. It seemed turnaround was fair game, but how could he believe that she'd be party to such cruelty? Cruelty even on a dead body, if he believed her capable of producing dead bodies for some fire maniac to set ablaze, and that she somehow had hidden the real Chris Lorentian and the real Melvin Bartlett Martin.

She must wash this day off, she told herself, climbing from the bed, feeling the absolute need for a long, hot shower.

First, however, she found a phone and called J. T., locating him still at work at the hospital she had stormed away from. He'd been right to distance himself from the odd and eccentric Repasi, but he was still working out of a lab down the hall from Repasi. She wondered if Karl had tried to feed any of his fantastic nonsense to John

Thorpe. If he suggested it in the least to J. T., John would deck him with a single blow, but from J. T.'s tone, obviously, Karl Repasi hadn't repeated his crazy allegations.

"Any luck on the shoeprint?" she asked J. T.

"Ruled out everyone else's having made the print," he replied.

"That's a *positive step*."

"Very funny. I oversaw the creation of a cast imprint of the shoeprint."

She let out a gasp of air. "I hope you got more results and conclusions than we did from the autopsy."

"From the size of the shoe imprint, it's apparent that the killer wears an eight and a half shoe size, extremely well worn, and due to the impression it made, fair estimates of the height and weight of the killer are also now known. The Phantom, as the press in Nevada and Utah are now calling him, is in the range of five-eleven to six feet tall."

"That's about what the waitress put him at."

"And he weighs in at a hundred seventy-nine to a hundred eighty-nine pounds."

"Excellent work, J. T."

"I next packaged up the imprint and shipped it to Quantico for an expert FBI imprint man named Kenyan to go over. Kenyan's already at work eliminating any and all footwear that the cast could not have been made from. Through the process of elimination and comparison, it's hoped something specific may be said about the shoes worn by the killer."

"That's good work, John, really."

"I take it the autopsy revealed nothing we didn't already know?"

"You take it right. Except for the fact of the victim's sex and age, the killings were identical, down to the use of a butane torch with a wand attachment."

"How do we know there's a wand attachment on the torch?" asked J. T. "Clear that up for me, will you?"

"According to the fire investigators, both Fairfax in Vegas and Brightpath here, the initial flames were extremely well controlled. They can tell from the controlled direction of the hot spots to the eyes, face, and chest."

J. T. softly whistled into the receiver and remarked, "You said this guy was a highly organized, controlled killer, Jess. Appears he has thought out his every instrument, his every move. Appears you were right again. Amazing ability of yours. You should be proud of it, the accuracy of your predictions."

"Proud? Hardly."

"Why not? They rank up there with Kim Desinor's psychic predictions."

"Believe me, John, knowledge doesn't begin to touch the feelings. Scientific investigation is one thing, instinct born of preparation, you might call it, but it doesn't soothe the gods of the dark night of the soul."

J. T., unable to respond to this bit of philosophy, stuttered into suggesting they meet later for a drink in the lounge at the Wahweap Lodge, where they were staying the night.

· ELEVEN ·

His eyes are bloodshot, his back near broke,
For he has been chasing a distant smoke.
                              —CHARLES SCRIBNER

Feydor had settled in at Ruby's Inn, a rustic roadside inn on Highway 63 in Bryce, Utah, within shouting distance of the fantasyland of rock formations created by nature that so dazzled hundreds of thousands of tourists each year. It was a place of sheer beauty, but Feydor had seen enough of rock formations from the bus window to last him a lifetime.

Whenever they got off the bus after the day's journey, everyone's bags were placed before the door at the hotel or motel they stopped at, and a key was pushed into each party's hands. The bus tour company made life easy for its passengers, and for Chris Dunlap in particular.

Inside his room now, alone, alongside a plethora of Polaroid photographs of burning bodies, Feydor stretched out his own body serpentine fashion, the mattress and his skin feeling fiery hot. But it was a good heat he now felt: neither rash nor burn. It was no longer the dreaded and hated redness Satan used to punish him with. No, this was more a warm glow, like the way other people described themselves feeling after what they termed "normal" sex, something Feydor had no firsthand knowledge of.

Still, for the first time in his life, Feydor Dorphmann felt whole and in control; there came a sense of accomplishment with performing the ritual that Satan had given him to do, but there also came a sense of purpose and power. He hadn't expected so much personal satisfaction. In fact, he hadn't expected any satisfaction to come of the gruesome work he had done, but in the *doing* he had discovered himself.

In fact, he had discovered some semblance of understanding that his purpose—guided as it was by Satan—must in fact be, dare he think it even, God's directive. For nothing Satan ever did came of his own volition, but as a scheme set into motion by God Himself, or so many Christian religious leaders professed.

Inscrutable as God himself, so must be God's plan to appease Satan, or to perhaps trip the Old Serpent up on some transcendent level mankind could never hope to glimpse, much less understand. Feydor knew himself to be in the presence of cosmic forces beyond himself; he felt privileged in glimpsing—although "glimpsing" was hardly the word—glimpsing the small truth he had glimpsed. He struggled for a better word than "glimpsed," angry at his limited thought patterns, the linearity and limited boundaries of the mind. A peek, an impression, a quick and momentary view beyond which his brain would fry. A subliminal image of his Satan, a force to be reckoned with, a force that, of course, must sense the whole as well as the parts of all existence, and this intense power must know that while Dorphmann was merely a pawn in this empyrean game of cat and mouse, that God would, in the end, redeem Feydor's soul because, after all, he was as much God's pawn as the Devil's.

And so, the grand and vast plan must go forward now of its own volition. . . .

Yet Feydor, on some primal level he did not himself understand, felt a need to rekindle memories of his last three kills, one of which neither Jessica Coran, nor any of the other authorities, had as yet discovered.

His limbs felt strong and powerful for the first time in

his life. Propped up now on one elbow, Feydor examined himself and the Polaroid photographs, one after the other. He'd earlier scattered what he called his "most memorable moments" about the bed, peeled his clothes off, and lay down nude beside the still memories. And from across the room he could see himself reflected in the mirror.

The others on the national parks tour bus with him had all been taken on a side tour, bused out to a copper mine somewhere nearby. In the relative peace here at the hotel, he found silence and solace, and he could here give full vent to his sexual excitement over the memories he had collected.

He clutched one of the photos and brought it to his chest, rubbing it into his nipples and down to his flat stomach. Each photo was taken at the moment the crackling fire opened up the bodies like melons.

God would forgive him his small and petty pleasures; Satan had directed him, and God had allowed it all. He was, after all, only human. . . .

So he would continue to indulge and enjoy himself now as he had then, on seeing them die amid licking, stroking flames. He hadn't known it would be so potent a sexual high that he achieved when the flames' tongues licked a victim's fat away. It recalled his excitement as a child when he had burned small things and rubbed their ashes against his body. It recalled a certain moment in the dim past when he'd killed that little girl, had watched her being swallowed up in the jaws of a searing fire, in the very mouth of Satan.

He had forgotten the thrill of it all, had denied his true nature. Now he knew that in order to feel—to feel anything—for him, there was no other way. At least not until his pact with the Devil was a *fait accompli*.

He stared into the next photo he grabbed up, imaginatively climbing into it to become the burning victim, his body catching the wavelike fire. The photos helped him to return to the moment and excite himself anew.

He brought the picture down to his crotch, rubbed it along his inner thigh with the other one in his other hand pressed against his penis. Semen stained the photos with his release, and seeing it come forth, he saw, felt, heard, smelled, and tasted it as an epiphany of memory, and a monumental memory came like a horseman from his unconscious mind.

He had once seen with his amazed little boy's eyes the evidence of Satan's own semen where it bubbled up from Hell, had seen it and had wanted to leap into it, but he had forced the event into a corner of the deepest cave within him. And so it felt natural, this sexual explosion he felt with each burning body. It was as natural as nature itself, he believed.

And so it was natural for Satan to have selected him for the work at hand.

Feydor groaned at the overwhelming sexual release he now felt, and he rolled over onto the other photos, his brain replaying the actual events in his mind so vividly that he was once again there in the room with the flaming corpse, first this one and then that and then the other, again and again, over and over, hearing the tormented cries, which only further excited his genitals.

Still, Dr. Stuart Wetherbine had somehow managed to keep a foothold somewhere in the back of Feydor's brain, and he now loudly condemned Feydor's puerile connection with Satan's semen, with fire and flaming corpses. Wetherbine's was the one small voice remaining in his brain that told Feydor he was simply rationalizing away his conduct, but a larger part of his brain said otherwise, a larger part brought to the argument the actual fact that he—Feydor Dorphmann—had, of all the billions on the planet, been *selected,* that he had been contacted by demonic powers due to his twisted birth needs, perhaps due to his DNA, his genetic makeup.

He'd spent years in self-analysis and had created a complete picture of his own needs, but for years after coming to the conclusion that only through burning himself with matches, cigarettes, and candles could he ever achieve any sexual satisfaction, only then could he control the urges. And he had successfully done so for most of his adult life, putting away "childish" things. However, the dike broke when Satan came into the picture, telling him to open himself up to Satan, to answer his own birth needs, to accept the seed placed in him at birth.

And so he had, and so others must burn so that he might rejoice. "Rejoice, ye sinners!" he said and laughed. "Rejoice, and behold the righteousness of evil."

Sated for the moment, he rolled over on his back, Polaroids sticking with semen to his body. He now stared up at the ceiling when Satan whispered anew in his ear, asking, *"Who's next? Number four is waiting."*

Feydor contemplated number four. He didn't think of them as kills, as people being burned alive; he thought of them as gifts given over to him by Satan. Satan arranged for the firewood, Feydor the fire. And God . . . God allowed it all. God allowed Satan—and Feydor by extension—his way.

Again he told himself, speaking to the room and to Satan, "I have done your bidding in good faith. I have accomplished far more than I ever realized possible in so short a time and in good fashion; I am fully one third of the way to your goal of nine victims."

"It's . . . not . . . enough," Satan disagreed, his voice spilling over with threat.

It's never fucking enough with you, Feydor thought but said, "Each victim has been sacrificed to you, each has become a prize for you, my demon god, and soon you will have your final prize: Jessica Coran. What more can I do? It can't be rushed."

We're traveling by bus, for God's sake, Feydor recklessly thought.

"I heard that," Satan replied with a hint of mirth, leav-

ing Feydor to wonder if he had heard all of his recent
thoughts.

"Buses are slow. The killing will take time."

"Don't question providence."

"I wouldn't think of it." Satan liked calling his wisdom
and his kingdom providence so as to mock God.

"You already have questioned my wisdom."

And Feydor had. His demon director had chosen an unusual mode of transportation, and it was on Chris Lorentian's ticket. The demon god, quite taken with
serendipitous fate, had said, *"What better way than this to
lure Coran across state lines and the country, away from
the safety of large cities and toward the gateway into Hell
itself?"*

"Where is this place?" he'd asked.

*"You have stood at this destination before, and you
once almost succumbed to the alluring beauty of a death
in the place where you are now leading Coran in pursuit
of you."*

Feydor vaguely recalled Satan's semen, a bubbling
white mud pissing upward from out of the earth in some
place he'd been as a child, some sort of tar pit of superheated, bubbling mud spurting up from the ground. This
strange place must be one of the many destinations on the
national parks tour. Feydor grabbed for the itinerary given
him on the bus the day he and Satan had together left
Vegas. He scanned each destination until his eyes fell on
Yellowstone National Park. He had been there once, years
and years before, a lifetime before, as a child. He'd stood
before the steaming geysers, hundreds of them it seemed,
with their steam and sulfur clouds creating huge, ghostly
veils, like the astral wanderings of the dead, over the land.
He'd become mesmerized, paralyzed even by the sight of
the cauldrons of boiling, superheated water belching up
from the center of the earth. He'd seen the bubbling, scalding mud pots that created lavalike sculptures. He had taken
steps toward the 280-degree water, preparing to leap into

Satan's saucepan when his father had suddenly grabbed him and pulled him away, scolding him and saving him from the scalding waters while loudly detesting his stupidity and idiotic expression.

A day later, while again in the park where death met life, he'd found a substitute for himself, and he had watched while his victim, the one he'd pushed into the scalding water of a geyser, literally boiled to death. It had been exquisite to watch, but he'd put the image from his mind now for years. Guilt and remorse had been so constant afterward that he finally erased all memory of the moment until now. Little wonder Satan had found him again.

"I promise you your freedom from me and all the demons that have ever controlled you in this life, if you comply now with my wishes," Satan sharply again reminded Feydor.

But Dr. Wetherbine's image pushed its way into his brain, and he heard Wetherbine's complaint, also loud and clear: "Don't go there, Feydor. It's a trick, all a trick. Satan cannot be trusted. He never could be trusted. Listen to me, son!"

"Shut up!" cried Satan, his voice filling the motel room, making passersby start, turn, and stare at Feydor's door, but now Feydor came awake, silencing the voices in his head.

Feydor now fully and clearly recalled every detail of the dying little girl he'd killed when he was himself a child. He wanted now, more than ever, to go in search of number four, to push on to numbers five, six, seven, and eight, and to finally kill number nine. He wanted to end his horrid suffering to become like other human beings, to be human, and to be free to conduct his life as he saw fit, rather than as Satan or God or Wetherbine or *any-fucking-anybody-or-anything-else-in-the-fucking-universe* saw fit. . . .

The Evil One, in a torrent of raging and unfeeling words, shouted down Feydor's concerns, his own dark

concerns flooding over Feydor with his insistent scream:
*"SO WHERE'S NUMBER FOUR-FOUR-FOUR-FOUR
COMING FROM FEYDOR?"*

In the lounge at Wahweap Lodge, overlooking the green
and cerulean blue waters of Lake Powell, boat lights winking up at them, J. T. bought himself and Jessica a round
of drinks. Jessica's limit these days was one whiskey sour.
She sipped slowly at it, stretching out her pleasure and
relaxation, giving thought to Athens and the Parthenon,
where she and James Parry had enjoyed the previous summer. In her head, she could hear the traditional Greek music and see the folk dancing at the *taverna* where she and
James had dined one evening. They had taken day trips to
Corinth and Mycenae, where they saw the Lion's Gate, the
tombs of Agamemnon and Clytemnestra.

Later they'd traveled by boat to Crete, where they found
King Minos's palace at Knossos and Heraklion, now a
modern city but once the center of Minoan civilization,
which at one time "ruled"—as youngsters of today put
it—the cultural world. It had all been so wonderful, magical, and now she felt a million light-years away from the
emotions she'd felt on that day. She questioned why she
was here in Page, Arizona's Glen Canyon, chasing a madman. She questioned her own steps, the path that had separated her from Jim so many months before. She doubted
that her life would ever be one of a settled nature, the hub
of which would be home, family, children, husband, and
wife. She doubted that she'd ever be truly happy, that happiness was a commodity meant for others, that this elusive
thing called joy, graceful happiness, would always elude
her grasp, due in great part to the decisions she'd made
early in life, due to the forces that molded her, and due
primarily to her decision to become a death investigator.
Like her father before her, she had chosen a career that
offered little opportunity for anything else, and the fact she
was a woman only added to the dilemma. Her father's life

and career were held together by invisible supports and
unheralded glue in the person of Jessica's patient, caring
mother, a woman who could wake him with lovemaking,
create a breakfast, and have the dishes put away before he
left the house for work. She would never have such support, not from Jim Parry . . . not from any man.

Jessica finished her drink on this somber thought. J. T.
meanwhile kept one eye on a blond bartender and another
on a notepad and pencil he fiddled with. He was still playing with the killer's words over and over, jotting them on
the notepad he'd snatched from his coat pocket.

"What're you doing, J. T.?" she asked, curious about
his doodling. "You know an expert graphologist can tell
a lot from your doodles." She sipped again at her drink.

"Look at this." His forehead scrunched in consternation, Thorpe displayed the two recovered messages from
the killer thus far as they appeared one atop the other. They
read:

> #1 is #9—Traitors
> #3 is #7—Violents

"It's still meaningless gibberish," Jessica complained,
tossing her hair back. "God, it's been a long day. My back
is killing—"

"Look closer, Jess."

She wanted to recall more of Greece, less of the present.
"I'm really not in any mood for the killer's games, J. T.
Truth be told, I'm no more in the mood for your puzzles
at the moment, either."

"I tell you, the killer's trying to tell us something."

"Of that I have no doubt, but—"

"Don't you see? Suppose there are two numbers missing," he suggested.

"Two missing numbers?"

"If there's a message missing from this list, what would
those numbers be?"

Jessica frowned, gave up on her memories of a faraway land, and stared again at the puzzle of words and numbers.

J. T. unnecessarily filled in the blanks, saying, "The number two and the number eight, if we follow the syllogistic wisdom—logic, if you will—"

"Okay, so two and eight," she replied, shrugging. "It still doesn't help us in the least."

J. T. jotted down the missing numbers between the two lines left by the killer. Then he pushed the notepad back under her gaze, a smug look coming across his face, his eyes darting again to the cute waitress who paraded by. Finally he said, "This makes the configuration of numbers all the more . . . complete."

Jessica looked once more at J. T.'s notepad. Now it read:

#1 is #9—Traitors
#2 is #8—   ?
#3 is #7—Violents

"So, we're missing a word," she said.

"I know that, Jess." He frowned. "Still, I already took the liberty to add the line 'number two is number eight' in my message to the FBI's mailing list of academicians and mental institutions and professionals who might be helpful in deciphering the killer's peculiar code."

"Can't hurt," she assured him, taking another sip of her drink. Silently, Jessica turned the small list of words and numbers over in her head several times. "It's Greek to me," she finally said with a half smile he did not understand.

"It's not Greek to everyone. Somebody out there knows what this means."

"He may be elusive, he may enjoy playing cute, but he's misspelled 'violence,' " Jessica replied, not knowing what else she might say to J. T.'s combinations with the numbers and ambiguous, anomalous, paradoxical, quizzical, puzzling, enigmatic, obscure, problematic, and terse messages left them by the Phantom for the sole purpose of taunting *them or her?* She wondered if they were specific taunts to her alone. But suddenly, Jessica now realized what J. T. was attempting to convey to her, that Martin was not victim number two of the Phantom, but number three, and that somewhere victim number two awaited their discovery.

The thought had been suggested by McEvetty and Kaminsky, but she had paid little heed to the notion there might be a third victim, since there had been only two phone calls. Then again, she'd shunned her telephone since the calls had begun. She well might have missed his call surrounding the killing of another victim labeled "#2 is #8." She'd have to call Bishop.

"He may've spelled it with the *T* at the end of violence to denote people," suggested J. T., breaking into her thoughts, repeating himself. "You know, that people could be termed the violent ones, hence *violents,* that people in general are violent, hence *violents,* rather than violence."

"So he's creating new words? Sorry, but I'm in no mood for Scrabble or lexicography. What we really need to do is to follow up on the all-points bulletin for areas between here and Vegas on any suspicious fire-related deaths," she replied. "Especially anything smacking of our guy. A message on the mirror would be a clear indication that it's our guy."

"I already have, and I've already heard back."

"You're holding out on me? From whom have you heard? Where?"

"Bishop's people in Vegas. They got another call from the killer, Jess, there at the Vegas Hilton, *your* room."

"My God, why didn't anyone contact me?"

"The killer's call came only today and couldn't be traced. He didn't stay on the line long enough. They tried to get word to you, but you and I haven't exactly been standing still."

"So you've been holding out on me," she repeated. "Why?"

He shrugged. "After seeing you, I thought you could use a break, so I kept silent until now."

"So, what's the bad news?"

"Grand Canyon, one of the lodges we likely flew over this morning. A place called the El Tovar Hotel, Yavapai East, right on the rim of the canyon. A place called Grand Canyon Village."

"What's been done there?"

"I'm afraid the body's already been removed, and—"

"Damn it. Damn it to hell."

"Nobody's fault, Jess. They, the locals, believed it an accidental fire, or a possible suicide. Clean-up of the room was begun. Evidence lost, but if you'd like to see it, we can double back. We have it secured now. A little late, but—"

"Jesus Christ, they've disturbed *everything*. . . ."

"—better late than never."

"How damned stupid are these backwoods people?" she exploded, her last nerve frayed, causing people at other tables to stare. "Who the hell's responsible for—"

"No one there *knew*, Jess. How could they?"

"He called it in, though? The killer?"

"That's my information, yes. But there was a delay. He only telephoned it in today."

"Today?"

"Right, he did, early this morning, about the time we arrived at the autopsy for Martin, around eight forty-five, nine, in there. That's what they're saying."

What caused the change? I wonder. Who are *they*? Bishop's people, Harry Furth?"

"It was Bishop himself I heard from, Western Union. Apparently they've had trouble reaching us. I think he thinks we're at this Grand Canyon Village on the South Rim by now."

Jessica felt somewhat relieved in that she hadn't had to hear—audibly live—the death of this third victim, at a remote hotel on the rim of the Grand Canyon. "So . . . was there a message on the mirror?" she asked, finishing her drink in a single gulp now.

J. T. gritted his teeth before replying, "Wiped clean by someone at the scene, but someone remembers numbers and the single word 'Fraud,' somebody else is saying 'Malice.' But the local guys chalked it up to the victim's own sorta suicide note, you see."

"How long have you known about this?"

"I didn't learn any of this before sending out our second crime-scene photos and message to Quantico when I asked it be duplicated and forwarded on to our contacts across the country. When I got back to the hotel, someone handed me the message at the desk. Did you check your messages?"

"No, no, I haven't."

"But at the time I got back to Santiva, my report to him went out before I learned of this news, so, well—"

"And so what do we know, J. T.? Damn little."

"Do you want to get over to the canyon? It's a few hours' drive, forty minutes or less by chopper."

"Hand me that map of the area you've been going over," she asked.

J. T. produced the tourist map he'd picked up at the hotel desk, opened it, and spread it before her, its colorful backdrop showing all the national parks and must-see points in Arizona and Utah.

"Bastard's leaving a hell of a winding trail, don't you think?" she asked, taking J. T.'s pen and marking each of the three locations on the map where murder by fire had occurred, asking J. T. to help locate the South Rim and Grand Canyon Village for her. Together, they stared at the zigzag trail of bodies left in the killer's wake.

"Tomorrow morning, by air," she told Thorpe. "Right

now, I'm exhausted. Can hardly see straight." Still, she asked, "What do we know of the victim?"

"White female, late thirties. Nothing like Chris Lorentian or Martin, I'm afraid."

"Doing a victim profile on this one appears hopeless."

"The victims are as different as night and day."

"Tell me this: Was the woman vacationing at the lodge? I suppose so. Why else be there?"

J. T. sipped his drink and shook his head. "Fact is, she was employed at the lodge, a waitress. Lived in the unit for free during peak seasons."

"Damn, but there's precious little to tie the victims to one another."

"The woman led a quiet life, only vice a pack-a-day smoking habit."

"And the locals chalked the fire up to her habit, too?"

J. T. shrugged. "Fire guys up that way didn't take as much care, not suspecting murder . . . Something about their one good investigator off to a confab someplace at the time, and they claim to have lost one of their last two fire-sniffing dogs to the canyon and the other to government cutbacks. The usual excuses for screwing up."

"Guess we can thank Newt and the new American attitude toward responsible behavior for that."

"Tell you what, Jess, let's order dinner on that boat they have cruising the lake, have a peaceful evening. Get all this off our minds for a while."

"You're on," she instantly agreed. "It's a date."

Dinner served on the lodge paddle wheeler, which went in a large circle around Lake Powell, was a delight, and with their steak and seafood dinners, they watched the sun go down in the western sky. Afterward they walked lazily back up to the lodge from the marina along a winding wharf, Jessica mentally counting the stars in the black firmament overhead.

"You look much better, Jess. Relaxed! I know I am," J. T. remarked, squeezing her hand.

"Thanks, yeah, much better. Nothing like a little R and R for the soul. Now for some sleep," Jessica agreed.

They weaved their way through a clutch of revelers reluctant to part for anyone, all crowded in the small lobby where the hotel clerk, seeing her, waved Jessica over. "You have a package that arrived earlier. I tried to locate you, but you were out."

It looked to be "business as usual" in the lodge, as if the fire of this morning had never occurred here.

"Thank you," she replied to the clerk, taking hold of the package rushed to her from Santiva in Quantico. A second sealed envelope, this one Western Union from Warren Bishop, was also handed her.

Soon she and J. T. located Jessica's room, where she said good night, but at the last J. T. voiced his concern for her. "I heard that you and Repasi had something of a showdown in the autopsy room. Told ya the man's an odd duck, a weird act."

"Did you hear that he accused me of being in collusion with the killer, that this was all prearranged as some sort of publicity stunt? That I'm rabid for tabloid press coverage and will do anything to get it? Is that crazy or what?"

"Just crazy enough to show up in the tabloids, Jess," he joked, poking her with a relaxed fist to her shoulder.

"I can't figure his game," she admitted, leaning against her doorjamb.

"Easy," he replied. "It's Karl Repasi who wants to be in the tabloids. Remember, he's always writing a book, and publicity—any publicity, good, bad, or indifferent—sells books."

"I suppose you're right. I just couldn't believe his gall, the way he attacked me. Really, John, have I become that much the . . . the celebrity that it's gotten in the way of my being capable of doing my job?"

"That's nonsense, Jess."

"Say it like you mean it, John."

"I do mean it!"

"Once more with conviction!" Now she teased him.

"I'm too exhausted to muster conviction for much, sorry, the day your professional ability is compromised by anything—anything whatsoever—Jess . . . well, I know you well enough, Dr. Coran, that that's the day you step away from this work."

She dropped her sleepy-eyed gaze, finished with having put J. T. on the spot, through with scrutinizing his reaction down to the least tick. "Thanks, J. T. You're a friend, a true friend. I have very few of you left, you know."

"Nonsense." J. T. pointed to the mail in her hands. "You're not going over that stuff tonight, are you? You're far too exhausted."

"No, nothing more tonight," she promised. "And yes, I am tired."

"How are you really doing, Jess? I mean, well, I know this maniac's got to you."

"I'm holding up," she assured him, thinking, *but barely* . . .

J. T. gritted his teeth and said, "And Karl Repasi's only making it more difficult for you."

"Leave Repasi to me, okay. I don't want to hear that you two've gotten into a fistfight behind the barn over my honor, J. T. Is that clear?"

"All clear, Doctor. . . . All clear."

"I know it sounds crazy, J. T., but you know what I fear the most tonight?"

"Your telephone, I would imagine."

She nodded. "Exactly. Crazy, isn't it? I mean, he can't possibly know I'm staying here tonight, yet."

"If it bothers you, unplug the damned thing."

"Unplug the phone? If I do that, I cut myself off from Quantico, from Bishop, everyone. No, I can't do that."

"Why the hell not?"

"It's not done in our profession."

"It's time you started thinking of yourself, Jess, and to hell with our profession."

She smiled back at J. T., saying, "Maybe you're right. Maybe I'll do just that, and thanks, John."

"What for?"

"For being a friend."

· TWELVE ·

Woman is like your shadow: Follow
her, she flies; fly from her, she follows.
—SÉBASTIEN R. N. CHAMFORT

Unable to sleep, her mind returning again to Karl Repasi's outrageous suggestions, Jessica wondered how many other less informed, less educated people in and out of her profession had begun to see things through the same distorted mirror as Repasi. Certainly, Karl had always been eccentric, an odd practitioner even for an M.E., but she could not fathom how he had arrived at such warped assumptions and conclusions. Then again, of late, anyone connected with the FBI, or the U.S. government in any way, shape, or form, had become targets for all the paranoia free-floating about American society, from UFO freaks, delusional fringe groups, and the man on the street, thanks in large measure to Hollywood's portrayal of government cover-ups, particularly in hiding UFOs and alien bodies, genetic experiments, and covert operatives working under the cloak of the U.S. flag; all this had become a battle cry for the fringe element and the fanatic alike. And why not exploit this uniquely American mass paranoia with such blockbuster, billion-dollar productions as now decorated the marquees of every movie theater in the lànd?

Jessica sadly realized that for many she'd become a scapegoat. Americans and people in general needed scapegoats and villains, people to point at and call less than holy, less than human, less than themselves, to point a finger at people capable of ignoring the rules all *good* Americans lived by.

Hollywood had lost many of its favorite villains, the threat of Russians overrunning America long gone, the German Nazis a thing of the past, now considered historical fiction by many young people, as if the Holocaust were a staged event for propaganda. Where better to place today's villain than squarely beneath the cloak of government, despite the fact that the U.S. government was made up of people just like all other citizens of the country, people who wanted white-picket fences around suburban homes in which to raise happy, healthy children? But nowadays Americans were drowning in their own paranoia, unable to see that the true villains, criminal-minded adults, were created out of Nazilike, Gestapolike upbringings, born to parents who abused children in cruel and torturous ways.

American mass paranoia had begun long before Waco, Ruby Ridge, and Oklahoma City. And to a certain extent, healthy paranoia, cynicism, and distrust of British authority had created the republic that was America. Cynicism formed the roots of democracy. Without it, there would be no America, a nation conceived in liberty, justice for all, and skepticism of authority.

Still, Jessica felt shocked to her core when an audience in a movie house applauded at the sight of the White House being blown away by alien invaders. She felt a wave of revulsion that films were now glamorizing such violent acts directed at the core of the nation and its symbols.

Jessica wondered at what juncture healthy criticism of the government became a bitter expression of futility, threatening to destroy all social fabric and the body politic. Popular fiction and movies of late had recently taken people into a chaotic landscape, displaying the American inability to sort out good from evil. Yet films and popular books only mirrored what was out there, what free-floated about in the ether of a place. The root causes of the paranoia didn't burst forth from film or the writings of horror and science fiction novelists, but from the collective soul.

Jessica knew that ill feelings toward government and government agencies were in the popular mind long before they were in the Hollywood pipeline, long before Hollywood embraced such scripts, before such incidents as Ruby Ridge—and that they'd grown to epidemic proportions, poisoning minds, especially those of the nation's youth, since Watergate.

Now Waco and Ruby Ridge had convinced thousands of thousands in the land that they lived under the rule of a government capable of blowing up a busy office building in the middle of a thriving middle-American city, a building housing men, women and children, for the sole purpose of getting an upper hand on the National Rifle Association. That the Oklahoma bombing was a "black ops" move in order that the president and "God Government" might point a finger at some unfortunate and beleaguered militia groups, members of which were being crucified in federal "monkey" courts where the evidence meant nothing; where defendants were railroaded to the gas chamber, as if everyone in America now lived under a pre–World War II Japanese military regime. And why would the U.S. government have planned and carried out the bombing of Oklahoma City's federal building? According to many a teen-on-the-street interview, the *simple* answer was as a show of force and power over those who dared question the president, his agenda or cabinet members, Congress or the House of Representatives, the CIA, FBI, FDA, ATF, FAA, NASA, the Centers for Disease Control, the U.S. Postal Service, the governors of every state, the mayors, the courts, the cops, and meter maids.

If you wore a badge of government at any level, you were suspect nowadays. And while writers and producers of paranoia-laden story lines only perpetuated the idea that everyone in government was for sale or had malicious intentions, Repasi remained right about one thing: Half-truths were good enough for the average reader who invested in a tabloid at the grocery counter.

Unable to sleep, Jessica tried to put Repasi and his specific paranoia out of her mind, and to help do so, she found herself drawn to Bishop's Western Union and the information packet that had arrived from Santiva in Quantico. She ripped open the message from Bishop, knowing what it must be, and she read:

> Phantom has left another body at El Tovar Hotel, Grand Canyon Village, Yavapai East. Killer made phone contact with your stand-in. Call was placed 6:09 A.M. this morning and was caught on tape. Urgent you contact me ASAP.
>
> Chief Warren Bishop

The message was damnably brief, saying nothing of where the phone call from the killer had originated. *One good thing*, Jessica gratefully thought, *at least the bastard still thinks I'm at the Hilton in Vegas.*

She put Warren's message aside and next took up Santiva's larger packet, spilling out its contents across the little table below the light. Santiva and the Behavioral Science Unit were as thorough as they could be with what little they had to go on, resulting in a less than detailed report on the suspect's profile. The unit had determined that the killer operated under a psychotic delusion involving a lust need for fire, that he was on some bizarre high and on an unknown quest, having a religious source, like some mythical archetype journeying deep into the belly of the beast to slay his personal demons. The report said that he was a thin, unremarkable, and unimpressive character with little to recommend him save the fact he appeared nonthreatening.

"Tell me something I don't already know," Jessica moaned in response to her reading of the profile thus far.

He likely lives alone, the report went on to say, or with one or more of his parents, if not a wife who generally leaves him alone for hours at a time and seldom if ever questions his comings and goings. He is likely a native of the Vegas area, or has lived there long enough to know it intimately. He likely works at menial jobs he considers far below his abilities and talents. He has an IQ higher than the norm, but he has major psychological complexes and psychotic episodes. He is highly organized and controlled in his dealings with victims, whom he selects randomly or due to some similarity in their dress or manner.

"All standard and par for the course," she muttered, "but it doesn't fit this guy. He hasn't remained in Vegas. He's come here, to Arizona, and his victims have nothing in common."

She realized that the Quantico unit had to feel they were working blind with the woefully insufficient information sent them. They simply didn't know enough about the Page, Arizona, killing, and they knew nothing whatsoever of the Grand Canyon murder. All they had at the time was information relative to Chris Lorentian's murder.

As a result, for the moment, the BSU profile was as much guesswork as was psychic Dr. Kim Desinor's added remarks on the killer. In longhand, she appended a note to tell Jessica her vision or version of the killer.

> Your killer is male, most certainly, and has fixated on you, Jessica, for some reason having to do with a twisted religious search on the order of a crusade. The voice or voices in his head are directing him, but he is also a willing accomplice, because he expects a great reward for what he has done, and on a primal level he is rewarded via the suffering he inflicts on his victims. On a primal plane, he enjoys both the fire and the

burning flesh. He puts his hands into the fire to feel the burning flesh. His hands will be darkened and hairless when you find him. The killer is unremarkable in and of himself, but the voices directing him have made him dangerous. He feels he has the power of gods behind him. Outwardly, he appears harmless and infinitely forgettable, while inwardly, he means to make history on the magnitude of an Oswald or a Manson.

All my best,
Kim Desinor

Jessica knew she could not ignore Kim Desinor's psychic sense. No one at the BSU group—indeed, no one at Quantico—knew that the killer was using his finger as a pen and his victims' burned bodily fluids as his ink. Desinor's psychic sense had saved Jessica's life in the past. "Fire-blackened, hairless hands," she said to herself. "Too bad we didn't have that bit of information when questioning the bus passengers this morning." But there were other buses, literally hundreds coming and going along the national parks route. Could one of them be carrying a killer? she wondered.

As for the killer's teasing messages, to date, no one had a clue about what the killer's messages, left at the scene of each crime, might possibly mean. Cryptologists in the documents department continued in their attempts to decipher the code but offered no hope at this time as to what it referred to, or where it might have come from other than the rantings of a maniac mind.

"No hope at this time," Jessica repeated to herself.

She next turned off the light and stretched out on the bed. She feared the phone at her bedside, feared it might ring at any moment, feared the sound of another fire victim raging in her ear. But the last call made by the killer was to her at the Vegas Hilton. The killer had no way of knowing she was here at Lake Powell. Just the same, she reached over and unplugged the damn thing.

J. T. had been right. Why not? The peace of mind was worth it.

She dreamily gave over her thoughts now to James Parry and Greece and their time there together. Soon she dozed and soon she fell into a deep and soul-soothing slumber.

J. T. had made arrangements for the following morning, and now he and Jessica were flying back toward the South Rim of the Grand Canyon in a Cessna twin-engine along a route that took them zigzagging back from Page, following the course of the Colorado River until once again they were over the great chasm.

The beauty of the magnificent canyon and its majestic size filled Jessica with emotions she'd thought long since lost. Something magical about the Grand Canyon created in the eye and the mind a religious feeling, a sense of wonder and awe at the spectacle created by nature and by God.

"They say it'd be a great place to commit suicide," muttered the old pilot of the plane, his whiskers white and brittle. "Say your family can get over your loss before you hit bottom, is what they say." He laughed at the old local joke.

During the flight, she and J. T. were treated to close inspection of the canyon walls when the seasoned pilot, learning who they were and what their mission was, took his light plane below the rim and deep into the canyon at Jessica's request. They now skimmed along the surface in the aged pilot's effort to please and impress Jessica with his agility and ability with the plane. Both pilot and crew knew that this sort of ride, along the river bottom, deep in the canyon, had long since been outlawed, and was against FAA regulations, but while J. T swallowed his teeth, Jessica loved every moment of the canyon up close and personal. She could almost feel the spray of the water, they were so close to the surface.

"Just imagine this place if you was one of Powell's crew, the first men to navigate the river from top to bottom," said Pete Morgan, the pilot. "Now she's full of weekend rafters, playing at what Powell and his men did, hardly risking anything."

When they began the descent over the narrow landing strip at Yavapai East, they could see the small village atop the rim. Morgan pointed out each and labeled each for them: the ranger station with exhibits, Grand Canyon Village, the El Tovar, a handful of restaurants, bus and car parking lots, a train station complete with operating train on a small-gauge track running the length of the rim, carrying tourists whose legs had given out to and from the hotels. The airstrip was some distance from this setting, and so they continued their descent.

On arrival, Jessica thanked the pilot for the wild and woolly ride, realizing that he'd been doing it most likely since he was a young man. They set down at the South Rim in a field just off Grand Canyon Village at Yavapai East, where the toot and whistle of the quaint little trolley-style railroad cars created a loop connecting the various lodges and hotels there.

A car picked them up, the local sheriff's office seeing that they would be transported to the El Tovar, a rustic, beautifully situated hotel a towel's throw to the rim of the canyon. It was at the El Tovar that they both expected and feared discovery of the third victim, chronologically the second, #2 is #8, or so J. T. had surmised the night before, as per his doodling and as per classification by the mad killer, if this killing fit the MO.

Sheriff Zack Colby, chewing tobacco as he spoke, welcomed them to the area and drove them to the end of "The Rim," as he called it, and they pulled to within inches of a grand porch leading them into the huge El Tovar Hotel.

They were guided to the room where the most recent victim had died, Jessica looking for signs of the killer, anything that fit his pattern. But the El Tovar, an enormous place with elegant dining room and gift shops, had acted quickly and had already arranged with a contractor to refurbish the room to its original beauty—to wipe clean any hint of disagreeableness. Parts of the walls were already gone. The burning bed had been replaced by another intact bed. It was as if nothing untoward had happened there.

"Why didn't the water sprinklers go off?" she asked, seeing the sprinkler was intact. "Or has it been repaired, too?"

"It was found to be faulty. Something doing with the wiring," said Sheriff Colby, raising his shoulders.

"If you all here were so sure that the death was accidental, why did you call the FBI, Sheriff?"

"I never called no FBI. FBI called us about six-forty yesterday morn."

"I see." She recalled Bishop's note, the time of the Phantom's last call, and realized the killer had directed Bishop's move.

J. T., searching about the room, announced, "Jess, there's no telephone in this room."

Jessica looked about. She had to agree. "Was there a phone in the room with the body?" asked Jessica. "Has that been removed, too?"

The sheriff grabbed at his beard and shook his head. "No, never was any phone in the room. She didn't have a telephone in her room. Cost less for her that way."

J. T. took her aside and whispered, "Must've been frustrating for him, Jess, not to be able to share with you at the time he wanted to. Couldn't put Flanders on the phone to beg for her life from you. Then he had to wait all day and all night to tell you about Flanders."

"Yeah, very inconsiderate of the victim and me, wouldn't you say?" she replied to J. T., then turned and spoke to Colby, asking, "Where was the killer's phone call to Vegas made from, then?"

"I don't know nothing about that, but there's a public phone down in the lobby, which is being dusted for prints but that's kinda crazy since it's public, but the other rooms have phones in them. The killer, if there was a killer here, coulda called from another room, his room, if he had a room here, if there was a killer, that is."

Jessica bit her tongue before saying, "Believe me, she was murdered, Sheriff. Look, tell me why didn't Flanders have a phone in here."

"It's just that folks who work here don't get 'em, you see."

"What time of day or night was the body discovered?" asked J. T.

"Just after the lunch crowd was thinning out. She complained of not feeling well, cramps, I'm told, so she was going to lie down till the evening dinner rush and come back on duty."

"Anyone see her with a man?" J. T. continued to interrogate the sheriff.

"No, just the usual customer-waitress cuttin' up, you know."

"Meaning?"

"Well, Muriel was a flirt, they tell me. Some say she was after a man, any man."

J. T. nodded at this and asked, "Were there any signs of booze in the room?"

"Couple of empty beer cans, yeah."

"And I'm sure the cans are history now, too." Jessica stepped between J. T. and Colby, asking, "Any pictures taken of the scene *before* it was broken down, Sheriff?"

"Thought you'd want to see how it looked, so I brought 'em," he replied with a mild show of pride, spreading them along the small bureau, which did not have a mirror. Jessica guessed that the mirror, too, was being replaced.

Jessica and J. T. studied the crime scene photos, taking

their time while the sheriff made comments. "We took it as accidental, you see. Had no reason to suspect murder. Firemen thought it accidental, or possibly a suicide, but nobody thought it homicide, no. Not at the time."

The photos were not up to standard, most of them too dark, making Jessica squint over each.

J. T. questioned, "Hard to tell much from these photos. Was she found nude?"

"Yes, sir." Colby's grimace was a sign of his embarrassment and hurt by the entire sordid affair. "She was. Things like this, murder and burning up a woman's body . . . things like this just don't happen around here."

"And her clothes, were they burned along with her?" pressed J. T.

"That's right." Colby's face lit with surprise at J. T.'s magical knowledge.

"Tucked on either side of her?" J. T. continued to amaze.

"Yes, sir, they were."

"Any odor of gasoline?" asked Jessica.

"None so's it was noticeable, no, but I'm no fire expert neither. . . ."

Jessica came upon a photo of the mirror in the bathroom. "The words written on the mirror were in the bathroom?"

"Across the medicine cabinet, yes."

"Hard to decipher from the photograph," she said, but the pinched lettering read: "#2 is #8—Malicious Frauds." "It's him, all right," she announced. "Look at this, J. T."

"That'd be my guess," he replied on seeing the photo.

"We'll want to interview the house staff and authorities, including fire personnel who saw the scene before the body was removed, before the clean-up when the writing on the mirror still smelled of animal fat," she informed Colby.

Colby's flexible features contorted into confusion now. He repeated her words, " 'Animal fat'?" Then he quickly added, "Yes, ma'am, ahhh, Doctor."

"And where can we find the bed and the body now?"

"Body's still at the hospital morgue, some thirty miles away, in a freezer, but the bed, well, it's six feet under."

"Six feet under?"

"Somewhere out at the landfill. No way to retrieve it."

Jessica gritted her teeth, saying, "Where there's a backhoe, there's a way."

J. T. joked, "You want to exhume a mattress and box spring?"

"Maybe that'd be a little over the top, huh?" she asked.

J. T. laughed. "Yeah, Jess, just a bit."

They were about to leave when Jessica noticed that the carpet was dirty with grime brought in on shoes. "The carpet hasn't been replaced," she said. "Let's take a section from near the bed, have it analyzed for accelerants." Jessica went to the spot she felt most likely helpful, and taking out a marker from her valise, she created a square some two by two feet where a fire burn had taken out a chunk of carpet now hidden by the new bed. Apparently the owners hadn't been able to get in new carpeting as quickly as everything else.

"Get someone with a carpet cutter to take this square out," Jessica was saying when she noticed a scorched, barely recognizable piece of paper just below the bed. "What's this?" she asked no one in particular.

The two men came closer to watch her dig out her tweezers. Using the tweezers, she lifted the crumpled fleck of blackened paper residue and gently slipped it into a plastic bag, also taken from her valise. The paper measured only a few centimeters.

"What is it?" asked Colby.

"Something overlooked by both authorities and the maids. It may've come from the killer, and it appears to be what's left of a negative."

"A negative?" asked J. T., leaning in for a closer look.

"Could be from our photo guy. He's a mite careless," suggested Colby.

"Seems everyone hereabouts is a mite careless," Jessica sarcastically added. "What kind of camera was your guy using?"

"Minolta, thirty-five millimeters."

"Then this isn't from his camera, I can assure you. It's from an Instamatic."

"You mean he—the killer—takes pictures of them as they burn?" asked J. T.

Again Colby winced. "That's disgusting."

J. T. put a hand on Jessica's shoulder and he leaned in near her, saying, "We need to do a quick check, make sure no one, including insurance agents, has been in the room for photos using a cheap Polaroid with self-developing film."

"No—don't you see, J. T.? This film was *in* the fire. Proving it was here when she died," Jessica assured her friend.

"We don't have sophisticated enough equipment here to determine what that fleck of paper means," Colby assured them.

"We'll send it back to Quantico for analysis," J. T. informed Colby, and on closer inspection, both she and J. T. felt certain that it represented a remnant of a burning negative from a Polaroid camera, likely belonging to the killer.

Jessica stared at the clue as if it could speak to her.

Outside, in the hallway, Jessica took J. T. aside and said, "It's no accident, his leaving this trail of bread crumbs, here the film, there the footprint."

"Yeah, it's as if he wants to be found and stopped, isn't it?"

"Not an unusual subconscious wish among serial killers, but this time it does appear he consciously wants to see me eye to eye."

"Jess," warned J. T. in a guttural moan, "don't you dare."

"I have no intention of having tea with this bastard."

"Is that a promise?"

"Promise."

"I'll hold you to it."

"Make sure you do."

Interviews with the firefighters, followed by questioning everyone who worked with Muriel Flanders, put together the portrait of a lonely, matronly woman, a woman not without a temper and flaring malice at times, a heavy chain-smoker, but hardly a fraud. Jessica began to realize that the killer knew next to nothing about his victims save their vulnerability.

She and J. T. discussed this aspect of the murderer while en route to the hospital where the remains of Muriel Flanders lay waiting for them. Outside the car windows, the spectacular views of the South Rim of the Grand Canyon winked and smiled at them as the sheriff's car sped along the winding road that hugged the cliffs. All along their route, tourists in cars, vans, and buses crowded in at the overlooks to experience the vistas here.

"I know now that he selects them on the way they carry themselves: troubled, shy, unfocused, confused, weak-looking, vulnerable people. And he labels them whatever his fevered mind imagines them to be by some bizarre scale known only in his fevered brain."

"And he's a poor-assed judge of character," added J. T.

"He just wants them to fit some preset notion—his agenda, if you will, this numbers game of his, this whole number one is number nine thing, calling Chris Lorentian a traitor, this one a fraud, old Martin a violent person when in fact none of them fit his bullshit."

"Agreed," replied J. T. "Hell, one was a runaway barely out of her teens and the other a worn-out waitress who was in a dead-end situation."

"The third a lonely old man."

"Just a lonely soul."

"But this psycho brands the man a violent person. You see just how screwed up this creep is?"

"Projecting."

"What?"

"What shrinks call projecting. The killer may be projecting his own deficient character traits onto his victims, you see?"

"You're getting good at this, J. T.," she replied. "Maybe you have something there."

They rode in silence for a moment, each with his or her own thoughts until Jessica said, "Back at the El Tovar, he didn't know there'd be no telephone in the room, but by the time he realized this, he was already too far along to start over. And if he did her during a lunchtime break, he didn't have a lot of time."

J. T. swallowed hard, his eyes rolling back in his head. "It's fairly obvious that he's got a time line and a quota to fill."

"Maybe . . . maybe he does. Kim Desinor called it a twisted religious quest of some sort."

"Maybe the body will tell us more," J. T. hopefully replied.

They were soon at the morgue, and the body was prepared for them. The autopsy was like déjà vu. Jessica kept wanting to say, "Didn't I just do this yesterday?"

After an exhausting four hours over the charred remains of Muriel Flanders, Jessica and J. T. learned that J. T. was right, that the second victim wasn't Mel Martin but this poor waitress at the El Tovar Hotel in whose room was scrawled—as they pieced it together—this message:

#2 is #8—Malicious Frauds

After the autopsy, J. T., his eyes like slits, asked, "What's our next move, Jess?"

"We fly back to Lake Powell."

"Glen Canyon? Why?"

She went to a map on the wall depicting the western states, including the Grand Canyon and the areas they'd been since leaving Vegas. Using her finger, she mapped out the killer's route thus far. "He took off from Vegas for here, the Grand Canyon, killed number two here, and went from here to Glen Canyon, where he did number three. There are no connections whatsoever among the victims, right?"

"Correct, none that we've found, no—"

"Then the only common thread we have is his route, the direction he is going in. He didn't double back on us to do Muriel—"

"Flanders, right," J. T. said as he followed along.

"He didn't double back; he did her just as the numbers imply, as number two. Now we need to determine where he will strike next . . . before he does number four."

"How're we going to do that?"

"I'm not sure, but I know we have to get back to Glen Canyon as our starting point."

J. T. considered her logic, staring up at the wall map. "Okay, then, I'm with you." The killer's route so far had taken them farther and farther from Las Vegas. J. T. put his hands together in the prayer position and said, "Let's do it. We've got to stay on his trail."

They taxied out to the airfield, allowing Sheriff Colby to get back to his normal routine, and at the airfield, they argued. Jessica wanted to fly back with the old Pete Morgan, who'd so thrilled them earlier, while J. T. had pointed out a pilot who looked young enough to be his son. Jessica won the argument and they flew back to Lake Powell and Glen Canyon in rip-roaring fashion, the old man giving them a little extra time in the air by flying out to Monument Valley, telling them how he'd once flown over a John Wayne set, ruining a John Ford shot in a film called *She Wore a Yellow Ribbon*. "I was just a pup kid at the time," he finished with a faraway glint in his eyes.

"God, you've got to be ancient," moaned J. T. from the backseat before he buried himself in the information they had amassed on the killer thus far. He'd rather do this than look out at the beautiful scenery at the speed they were going low over the incredible valley. Instead, he penciled in the missing words on the notepad he'd shown Jessica the day before. With this added to his notes on the killer's messages, his collection now read:

> #1 is #9—Traitors
> #2 is #8—Malicious Frauds
> #3 is #7—Violents

Where is it leading . . . Where will it end? John Thorpe wondered now as he stared at the killer's sick compilation of words and numbers. *And what does it have to do with Jessica Coran? Why is this madman fixated on her?*

· THIRTEEN ·

*He who takes a stand is often wrong, but he
who fails to take a stand is always wrong.*
— ANONYMOUS

On returning to the Wahweap Lodge on Lake Powell in
Page, Arizona, Jessica learned that a call from Warren
Bishop was waiting for her. He'd left her his direct line.
She immediately sought her room and telephone, placing
a return call to Warren. Sheriff Colby at Yavapai East had
mentioned that Bishop had left word there, too, for her to
call him, but she'd not wanted to waste any more time
there, deciding that a call from her room at the Wahweap
would be far more convenient and productive.

Bishop came right on once Jessica announced herself to
his secretary. There was a trace of desperation in his voice
when he asked, "Jessica? Jessica, how are you?"

"Fine. We just returned from investigating the incident
at the El Tovar at the canyon."

"So, you did get my message after all. I've been anxious to hear back from you. I got a cryptic message from
Repasi that you and Thorpe went to Yavapai East without
him, but otherwise I had no idea of your steps."

"Yes, well, I'm sorry I didn't call you sooner, but
you're out of range of my cellular phone, Warren, and as
you might imagine, we've been damned busy here. By the
way, what else has . . . did Repasi have to say about me?"

"What do you mean?"

Jessica told him of Repasi's allegations. She waited for a response.

Bishop was either stunned or trying to find words to reply. Finally he said, "That's the most asinine thing I've heard in my entire career with the FBI, and I've heard some pretty bizarre shit."

"So I hear the Phantom telephoned me there in Vegas again?"

"Harry Furth and the actress we hired to mimic you received a call detailing the burning death of a woman there at the El Tovar. We contacted the local sheriff's office there, and they confirmed that there had been a fire death at the El Tovar. That's when we sent separate telegrams to you and John Thorpe there."

"John got word early, but my message got held up, I'm afraid."

"So, then you've seen the body at the canyon? Is it part of the string?"

"It most definitely is, yes."

"We have the killer's own voice clearly now on tape then. We can assume it's him. He speaks to you directly."

"Bloody bastard. What does he say?"

"More than enough to nail him to the cross."

"And he thinks I'm still there, in Vegas, then."

"Ahhh, not exactly. He somehow figured out our ruse, I'm afraid. Good news is, he doesn't know *where* you are."

"That is good news." Jessica then repeated herself, asking, "What does he say on the tape?"

"Enough to hang himself many times over. Care to hear it?"

She braced herself. "Go ahead. Play it."

Bishop fiddled with the machine at the other end for a moment before the chilling voice of the killer came over the line, saying, "I'm sorry I couldn't reach you earlier, Dr. Coran. I did so want your . . . *participation*."

"What is it you want?" asked the actress playing her.

"I've taken the liberty of sending another evil soul to her reward. I'd hoped to contact you so that you could share the moment with *us*, but unfortunately, that was not to be. Fate stepped in."

"What do you mean by *us*? Who are you and who is this *us*?"

Either the actress was good, or Furth was feeding her questions to ask the killer. Either way, she sounded an exact duplicate of Jessica's voice.

"Us, me, number two, the malicious fraud bitch, my god, and you, Doctor, you," replied the monster.

"Charon . . . we know you want our help, Charon."

He laughed and said. "You think yourself clever, Doctor, but you are an ignorant creature, unaware of your own nature. Charon is no longer here with us! I am Nessus now."

"All right, then, Nessus. Why are you doing this?"

"Telephoning you?"

"Killing innocent people!"

"No one is innocent."

"Why must you call me, report to me?"

Jessica thought it the question of the hour, the same question Repasi was asking.

"I only do my lord's bidding for all of us."

"Why are you calling me? What have I ever done to you?"

"You've offended my god."

"Who is?" The actress had been coached well to keep the killer on the line as long as possible, and since she had no emotional interest invested, she was able to remain far more calm than Jessica had been capable of, Jessica believed.

"What god is that?" she urged him on and awaited an answer, but when none came, she added, "Won't you tell me?" The actress's voice was close, near identical to Jessica's own, but perhaps due to her calmness, somehow the killer detected the subterfuge.

"Wait a minute, you're not Dr. Coran. Who the fuck is this?" He slammed down the receiver.

"That's it," said Warren, coming back on the line now.

"Did Harry Furth get a fix on where the call originated from?"

"He did, and that's why I've been so frantic to get in touch with you all day."

"So, where did it come from?"

"Are you sitting down?"

"I am."

"Two hours from Page."

"Here Page?"

"Arizona, yes. Someplace called Long Valley Junction. Between Zion National Park and Bryce Canyon."

"He was only two hours ahead of J. T. and me at six this morning?"

"It would appear so, yes, but the route he's taking remains a mystery."

She gasped into the receiver.

"You okay, Jess?"

"Any leads from the call? Anybody know what the hell he means by Charon and now by calling himself Ness-it, Ness-what?"

"Nessus, and no, but we do know he paid for the call with Chris Lorentian's phone card."

"Why doesn't that surprise me?"

"I'm flying up there."

"Not on my account."

"This business began in my jurisdiction. I've got every reason to pursue it with you."

She unnecessarily shrugged. "I've never known you to do anything but what you intended. If you intend coming, come ahead. I won't argue, but it's getting a bit crowded here."

"What do you mean, 'crowded'?"

"The Arizona guys, Karl Repasi, J. T., me, and now you."

"Oh, yeah. I see what you mean."

"Repasi says he has your blessings coming here to Page . . . claims he simply wants to help us out, forensically speaking. Then he attacks me."

"Out to prove himself better than you or something? I'm sorry. I had no idea."

"J. T. warned me to be wary of him. J. T. questioned Karl's motives from the start."

"And you?"

"Right now I've got my hands full with a killer. I can't worry about what's in Karl's head."

"Just the same, I'm going to join you as soon as I can."

"As I said, you're quite welcome here."

"I've listened to every one of the tapes Harry Furth created from your phone tap, Jess, and this guy scares the hell out of me. Just listening to him . . . and me in a safe, well-lit office. . . . Well, it honestly has taken its toll on me. Harry and I have listened to the tapes at every speed, and Harry has separated out the back-scatter noises in the earlier tape."

"And?"

"Harry tells me that much of the back-scatter noise before the roar of the fire engulfs every other noise is of two distinct sounds."

"Yes, go on, Warren."

"One is of a . . . a moaning, groaning as if of a sexual nature and a click-zip, click-zip sound, a noise we've duplicated as—"

"A camera, the self-developing kind, right?"

"Yeah, but how did you know?"

"Found a scrap of processing paper at the El Tovar scene."

"Jess, this madman could be there in Page, in the lodge with you right this moment. You may want to sleep with that Browning of yours tonight, but I'm flying up first thing in the morning."

"One consolation," she said.

"What's that?"

"We're closer on his trail than I'd thought. And if he figures I'm on his trail, if he knows I'm here, perhaps he'll make the mistake of coming back this way to make contact with me again."

"You need to get that phone bugged."

"I will, as soon as possible."

When she hung up, Jessica felt her heart sink. Just moments before, she'd felt safe here at the Wahweap Lodge, subconsciously telling herself, *At least the creep won't be telephoning you anymore. He can't know where you are.*

Jessica had been feeling both relief and guilt over the fact that she would not be getting another phone call from the Phantom. If and when he did call again, someone else, the actress hired by Bishop and Furth in Vegas, would be having to deal with it, answering the phone calls of a maniacal killer. But now she didn't even have this cushion.

These thoughts flowed through her weary mind riverlike when suddenly the phone under her fingertips shrieked to life. She didn't want to answer; didn't want to chance its being the monster.

She no longer felt safe at her bedside here at Lake Powell's Wahweap Lodge.

Finally, on the third ring, she said aloud to herself, "It's got to be Eriq Santiva or someone else connected with the case."

She lifted the receiver and tentatively spoke into it, saying, "Hello, this is Dr. Coran."

"Jess?" The voice instantly put her at ease. It belonged to psychic and coagent, Dr. Kim Desinor, calling from Quantico, Virginia.

"Kim? It's so wonderful to hear from you!" Kim hadn't any idea how wonderful, she thought.

"I'm just reassuring myself you're all right out there. I'm astonished about what's going on out there, and frankly, I don't like it, not one damned bit."

"Eriq forwarded your reading of the situation. It's much appreciated."

"I have my good days; others, the well seems dry, the source gone, you know."

"In any case, it's great to hear from you. How's Ginger?" Jessica always asked after Kim's calico cat.

"Never mind Ginger. I want to caution you about what you're dealing with. Santiva's just as concerned over this madman's obsession with you. We're both very worried. How do I know Santiva's worried? Easy! He came straight to me for my input on this creep, and I've become increasingly worried, too, so look—"

"I'm all right, Kim, really."

"Listen to me. There's no worse a fanatic lunatic than a religious nut, and it feels to me as if this guy has some religious quest he's on, and you, dear, are at the heart of it all. Obviously enough."

"The hardest part is knowing that others are dying because of me," Jessica replied.

"Stop it right there, kiddo. You mustn't and cannot ever blame yourself for this screwball's actions."

Kim always knew precisely how to cut through the bullshit, Jessica thought now. "I will try not to—"

"Don't *try* anything, *just do it!*"

"All right, I'll do as the Nike ads say."

"I just had to make sure you're all right there, Jess."

"Seems you're not the only one."

"Really? Don't tell me, a new man?"

"No, nothing like that."

"Well, dear, Ginger is fine, and it is quite late this side of the Rockies, so good night."

"Night, Kim, and thanks for the support."

"Always. *Ciao.*"

Jessica decided sleep wasn't going to come until she telephoned J. T. with the latest news on the whereabouts of the killer at the time he had called in his second kill. If the killer was as close by as she feared, J. T. had as much right to know as she.

She lifted the receiver and began dialing for J. T.'s room when she realized someone else was on the line. She heard breathing. It sounded like flames being fanned.

"You can't hide from me, Dr. Coran," he said. "Nor from the truth, from this!" Jessica froze on hearing his now familiar voice, replaced now with a whining gibberish, as of someone attempting to speak through a gag—yet another fright-filled, slurred voice, the voice of a fourth victim on the other end, she surmised.

She desperately held on to her calm and resolve to learn more about the Phantom, this creature behind the awful string of fire murders. She recalled the calmness of the actress who'd played her, and grasping at straws, she pretended to be that actress.

"Are you in the lodge?"

No answer, just the gasping noise of the poor sacrifice at the other end.

Jessica shouted, "At least tell me where the hell you are! You coward!"

Taking the phone off the victim, the raspy-voiced killer replied, "I am climbing from the depths of Hell, which takes courage. I am no coward."

"We can help you out of the pit," she assured him.

"You can help me? Really?" he asked, his voice rising maniacally.

"Yes, we can get you the best doctors in the country to—"

His laugh drowned her out. "You are going down into the pit as I rise from it, Doctor. Don't you see that? Don't you feel it? You can help no one. Not even yourself."

"Where are you?"

"You must know by now. You must see."

"No, I don't see a thing. Make it clear for me."

"You're a smart woman. You can figure it out. Isn't that how you normally play out your petty games, Doctor?

I just want you to know that we are both cut of the same cloth, Dr. Coran. . . ."

"Really? How so?" *Damn this bastard, damn his soul and his body,* she thought.

"We are both concerned with the same . . . fears, phobias, you and me."

"What the hell fears are you talking about? And what's your name?" she challenged, hoping to keep him on the line for as long as possible, to somehow reason with him, to somehow save the poor victim he held hostage somewhere in the lodge, or somewhere beyond.

"Call me . . . call me Nessus."

"Ness? Ness-suss? How do you spell that?"

"Spell it how you wish."

"Is that your name?"

"It is the name my god calls me. I am his messenger and your guide."

"I see, Nessus. So you're not responsible for your actions, your having killed three people? You're just an instrument of some power you cannot control. Is that it, Mr. ahhhhhh . . . ?" *It isn't working,* she realized. *He's not giving out any names or reasons that make sense.*

"Perhaps if you'd crack a book once in a blue moon, you'd know what the fuck's happening here!" The sound of the torch and the screams of his latest victim suddenly filled Jessica's ears, along with the back-scatter noise of a clicking camera, followed by the deafening stillness after he, the man of the moment, the godhead in control, slammed down the receiver.

"Where are you, you cowardly freak bastard?!" Jessica shouted into the dead receiver. "Cowardly bastard!" Tears of frustration filled her eyes.

Jessica was left alone with the sound of the victim's screams filling her ears and her silent room. The phone was untapped. No one knew that the monster had again somehow reached out and touched her. She felt angry, confused, outraged all at once. She wanted to lash out at the

creature causing her such pain. But how? How did she
fight what she could not see?

Jessica immediately called J. T. to inform him of the
latest communiqué from the killer and her certainty that
another victim had already been sacrificed in the Phantom's unholy game. When Thorpe arrived, half dressed, at
her door, his hair wildly disheveled, he was still zipping
his fly while asking if she were all right. She pulled him
through the doorway, clinging to him, telling him verbatim
what the killer had said, ending with the fact he no longer
called himself Charon but Nessus.

"The names must mean something important, at least to
him," suggested J. T., who now watched Jessica pace ti-
gress fashion about the small room.

"More likely to his developing, his metamorphosis, perhaps. Maybe he thinks he's going to turn into some sort
of superhuman being or winged creature or god by killing
nine victims and sacrificing them to his fucking demons."

"Easy, Jess."

She continued, not hearing him. "I don't know, but
whatever we can learn from these bits and pieces he's offering, we've got to take full advantage of—now, J. T.,
before there's a number five, you understand?"

J. T., seeing she teetered on the edge, pleaded, "Calm
down, Jess."

"Calm down? I don't fucking want to calm down."

"You're on your way to a burnout, Jess, if you keep
this up," he warned.

"Burnout—just the right image, as always, with you,
John."

He knew that she seldom called him John, and when
she did, it meant she was either displaying real affection
for him or that she'd become annoyed. "You're going to
stay in my room tonight." He instantly waved his hands
to any disagreement she might have, adding, "You'll take
my bed, and I'll sleep here, in your room. And I'll take

any calls that come in for you. Okay? Understood?''

"No way. If that creep comes looking for me here in this room, finds you, and kills you, I'd never forgive you, John."

"All right, then, we'll compromise."

"Compromise? How?"

"We'll both stay in my room with you on the sofa, then. Happy?''

The following morning they learned of a fire that had gutted several rooms at Ruby's Inn the night before. Ruby's, they learned, referred to a well-known stopping-off point for people going into Bryce Canyon National Park in Utah, west of Glen Canyon.

"We've got to get out there," Jessica told J. T.

"But Bishop's arriving here this morning. Don't you want to wait for him?"

"I left word in Vegas about what happened last night," she explained. "Talked with Harry Furth. Bishop'll figure it out; he'll catch up with us at Bryce Canyon."

They arranged for a shuttle run to the airport. Along the way, J. T. asked, "Suppose we can get a helicopter pilot who doesn't think he's Buck Rogers?"

Once at the Page airport, they located a helicopter and flew toward Zion National Park and Bryce Canyon. Jessica had once traveled to the area, and she told J. T. that his eyes were in for a number of breathtaking sights; and the country, as they flew over in the whirlybird, did not disappoint either of them.

In Bryce, Utah, at the Ruby Inn, they touched down at a commercial helicopter pad just across the street from the inn, a mammoth, made-over ranch, it appeared. There a crowd of onlookers had gathered in the way of police and fire officials just winding down their investigations. Jessica and J. T. feared they would find exactly what they knew they would, a fourth body—another woman, by Jessica's reckoning and what little her ear had picked up of the victim this time around.

The murdered woman's name was Eloise Whitaker, an elderly window, and she was, like Martin before her, enjoying a vacation as a member of a bus tour group, using Colorado Bus Travel, and traveling solo. J. T. and Jessica had already discussed the fact that two of the victims now had been passengers on vacation buses that toured the national parks, a third victim had worked in one of the parks, and that this seemed the only tenuous thread connecting the various victims.

Jessica knew that large tour groups went back and forth through the national parks every day, following exacting schedules. A death like Martin's and now this one slowed that progress considerably, and so when they ran into the bus tour guide named Ronny Ropers and his group again at Ruby Inn, Jessica was not completely surprised.

But Ropers's face lit up in a wide, theatrical surprise. "You again? And another fire?" he asked Jessica. "Do you bring them about?"

Jessica gritted her teeth and asked, "Is the deceased one of your charges, Mr. Ropers?"

"No, thank God. This one belonged to Christy Applegate, with Sunshine Tours. That's her over there, the one who can't control her crying."

One of several huge buses painted with a rainbow of colors and letters proclaiming it a VisionQuest bus suddenly lurched at Jessica as she walked across the parking lot toward the blackened rooms where the fire had gotten out of control this time. Jessica was suddenly pulled from the path of the bus by an alert J. T.

"Damn bus driver," cursed J. T. for her.

Other buses began to follow suit, leaving the lodge to maintain schedules, but Ropers had held his group up in an effort to help out in any way he could with Christy's sudden problem, him having had "experience" now with just this sort of emergency. He intended walking Christy, a well-acquainted friend, through the reams of paperwork and reports that would have to be filed. Now *she* had a dead—murdered—passenger to report, and Ronny deftly held her hand through it all.

"What the hell's this world coming to?" Ropers asked Jessica, who began questioning the tearful Christy, who could tell them nothing useful.

J. T. and Jessica flashed their badges and were ushered through the yellow police tape. Ruby Inn looked like an enormous ranch turned bus stop, fields and corrals and lakes stretching out away from it at the rear. Jessica caught glimpses of horses running freely about the corrals. A part of her wanted to run screaming and free with the horses, to get as far from this case and the Phantom as humanly possible.

Out front of Ruby's, the place sported a huge welcoming sign for all the bus tour traffic, a large restaurant, rooms for rent, laundry facilities, telephones, and a gift shop.

"Another body, another message, another autopsy to tell us what we already know," complained Karl Repasi, who met them at the door.

Surprised, Jessica asked, "Karl! How did you get here so quickly?"

"I have friends in high places, remember?" he replied glumly, adding, "God, this is getting too hard, Jess, too damned hard. One smoldering body after another. Listen, please, please let me apologize for my outburst of the other day. I didn't mean half of what I said. I'm on my feet for too long and my brain stops functioning."

Jessica walked past him without another word.

"How *did* you get here, Repasi?" asked J. T., who had thought only he and Jessica, with the exception of the Vegas FBI, knew of the Ruby Inn murder scene. "Who tipped you off to this one?"

"I've been listening in on police calls since I was a child."

"Karl, you're beginning to get on my nerves as well as Jessica's," he replied.

Karl merely frowned, turned, and joined Jessica to stand amid the charred remains of the room, the dead woman's still-smoking body on the bed, the killer's now familiar scrawl on the mirror. "You need all the help you can get on this one, Jessica. Don't fight me. Let me help you. Just tell me how I can assist in bringing this madman to heel."

"How, Karl? How're you going to help me?"

"Obviously, this Charon fellow wants to tie you up with autopsy upon autopsy while he is free to go on to his next killing," Karl replied, his hands flying about. "I can give you freedom to move faster if you turn over all the autopsy work—hours of time, which the killer is using against you—to me."

"Why, Karl?" asked J. T. "So you can get your name in the papers?"

"I won't lie to you. I'm writing a book right now on my most intriguing cases for Pentium Publishing. I have a contract. A chapter detailing how I worked closely with the great Dr. Jessica Coran won't hurt the book."

"Now it begins to make sense," suggested J. T. with a cynical grin. "I thought so!"

"In fact," continued Repasi, "I was hoping you'd consent to doing an introduction for the book, Jessica. If not, perhaps you, Dr. Thorpe."

Ignoring his request, feeling him ingenuous, she replied, "I'll consider your suggestion, Karl, but at the moment, I'm busy, Doctor." She stepped up to the message on the sooty and this time cracked mirror, the surface of which looked like a roadmap with its spiderweb of crisscrossing cracks. This message, also written on greasy, fatty liquids, actually bulged outward, with sections of glass ready to peel apart and fall away. The message on the cracked mirror read:

#4 is #6—Heretics

"Pick up sticks," she muttered to herself.

"The fourth victim is a heretic?" asked Repasi, shaking his head. "Is this why she is burned far greater than those before? No, not exactly," he continued. "The room was entirely engulfed, according to the fire investigator. It went to backlash."

"Backflash, you mean?" corrected Jessica.

"Yes, backflash, flashover, creating of the room an oven of gases, which exploded inward. From there the fire spread."

"Something of a miracle the mirror only cracked and didn't explode," she said, staring into the webbed lines that streaked across the lettering to make a mosaic of her reflection. "I'm surprised the whole place didn't go up in smoke."

"Fire has a mind of its own, they say. No two fires being exactly alike, like people, they say," J. T. philosophized.

Repasi added, "The units saved came as a result of speedy work on the fire department's part, after everyone was alerted by the explosion, and the fact one of the local trucks was at Ruby's for an all-night country jamboree and barbecue at the time."

"Anyone in adjoining rooms hurt?" she asked.

He shook his head. "Just scared witless."

"I suppose they've been interviewed? Saw no one, heard nothing until the explosion?"

"All of 'em have already departed this morning, but they left statements with the local authorities. They add nothing useful."

Jessica stepped to within inches of the bed where the Whitaker woman's black-scourged body lay in the familiar crumpled, fetal position. The superheated fire had reduced her body to near dwarf size, it seemed. Maybe the bastard burned himself badly on this one, she silently prayed. "Too bad his body's not amid the rubble," she said aloud.

"Will you allow me to help, Dr. Coran?" asked Repasi.

"You'll see to it that copies of your protocols follow me?"

"I will indeed."

"Then it's a deal."

"Jess!" complained J. T.

"Karl's right, John. We need the freedom to move quickly. I can't be tied up in another autopsy, which is going to tell me nothing I don't already know, so . . . so let's get out of here."

"But Jess . . ."

Ignoring J. T.'s whining, Jessica stepped out of the crime scene and rushed to the nearby restaurant, where she plopped into a booth. J. T. chased after her and found her nursing black coffee. "You going to drink that whole pot alone?"

"Help yourself."

"You okay, Jess?" he asked, sliding into the booth.

"Stop asking that."

"Sure, sure . . . whatever you say." He poured himself a cup of black coffee, lifted the cup, chinked it against hers, and said, "Cheers."

"I'm sorry," she apologized. "This case is driving me mad."

J. T. looked up at the pretty waitress whose shadow fell across the table. "Well, hello," he said.

"May I get your breakfast order?" she asked.

"Nothing else for me," Jessica replied.

J. T. ordered two eggs over easy, hash browns, and bacon.

"You ever going to get that cholesterol down, J. T.?" Jessica said as the waitress hurried off.

Pouring himself more coffee, he asked, "What's our next move, Jess? We can't simply just wait for him to dump another body at our footsteps."

"That's exactly what he's doing, isn't it?" she asked, her eyes displaying a revelation. "He's wanting us to trail him, so he leaves a trail of bodies, but where do they ultimately lead? If we knew that, then maybe we could get a step ahead of him. Do you still have that area map you've been carrying around?''

''Got it right here,'' he replied, snatching the map from his coat pocket.

''We've got to predict his next stopover. Where he will next kill, and try like hell to stop him before he does it again.''

''But how?'' J. T. pleaded. ''How're we going to do that?''

''What if he's on one of these tour buses coming and going out of these parks, J. T.? What if he was on one the other morning, pulling out of Page at Wahweap Lodge? He may well have seen me, or you, or both of us. That's how he knew I wasn't the one on the phone back in Vegas where he called. He knew it going in; and that's how he knew to find me at Wahweap Lodge last night, to log his last call.''

''If that's the case—''

''Then he's been yanking our chains right along. It's time to turn this chase around. Let me study that map.''

· FOURTEEN ·

To a man who is afraid, everything rustles.
—SOPHOCLES

Over coffee and J. T.'s breakfast plate, they discussed tourist points on the map, of which there were too many to count. They discussed what they so far knew about the killer, each comparing the notes of the other. They discussed the new message on the mirror and how it fit with the others, J. T. displaying it on his notepad. To date, the list now read:

> #1 is #9—Traitors
> #2 is #8—Malicious Frauds
> #3 is #7—Violents
> #4 is #6—Heretics

"Now, logically speaking, his next victim will be number five, right, Jess?"

"We can't let that happen."

"Bear with me, here, Jess. If his next victim is number five, and it follows as it has been going, then we can predict part of his next message will be''—he interrupted himself to add to the list—"this. Right?''

Jessica looked down at his added line, which read:

#5 is #5

"Interesting juxtaposition, wouldn't you say, how five crosses five?" he asked.

"Yeah, but what does it mean? How does it help us to stop the bastard?"

J. T. bit his lower lip, frowning. "I don't know . . . yet. . . ."

With maps and tour bus guides laid out across the table, they continued the brainstorming session they'd begun. "J. T., you think it's just a coincidence that two of the victims were traveling on touring buses?"

"Yeah, I have to agree. It is a bit strange, but each victim, Melvin Martin and Eloise Whitaker, were using different tour bus companies."

"Still, the two buses interweaved from sight-seeing point to sight-seeing point."

J. T. considered this, sipping at his coffee. "Yeah. You saw how many buses were pulling out of the lot here this morning?"

"I saw, all right. One almost ran me down."

"Maybe the killer's that bus driver."

Jessica replied with a slight shake of the head, "More likely to be a less than remarkable passenger. Besides, come to think of it, being run over by a monster bus like that, it'd be too easy a way for me to go, so far as this guy's concerned. He wants me to suffer along with what— nine other victims?"

"You think he'll stop at nine?"

"Unless he plans to spin on nine and take it back down to one."

"I'm going to do some checking about these bus tour lines. See what I can find out about them," J. T. suggested.

"Do that. As I recall, that Pierson woman whom Chris Lorentian stayed with said Chris was in the process of— or had gotten—tickets for both of them to escape Vegas. I had assumed she meant plane tickets, but bus tickets would have done just as well."

"Hey, that's right."

"And there've been buses loading and unloading around us since . . . well, since Vegas."

"My God. If this is true, the killer took Chris Lorentian's ticket and is traveling on her reservation."

"Contact all the bus lines and run down Lorentian's itinerary, and we may know the killer's next destination. Short of that, check also for anyone with the name Charon or Nessus traveling by bus."

"That might take some time."

Jessica gritted her teeth, but looking across the room, she saw her old friend the tour guide Ronny Ropers. She scooted from the booth seat and rushed for the tour guide, asking, "Where do the buses go from here?"

Ropers, looking confused, his hands in the air, asked, "Which buses? They all go in different directions."

"What's tonight's destination for those heading north?"

"Salt Lake City for some; Pocatello, Idaho, for others; and Rock Springs, Wyoming, for others. Depends on site destinations."

"And those heading south?"

"Where we came from, Zion National Park, Wahweap Lodge, Glen Canyon country, or a straight run to Vegas. Ultimately Vegas for most, Flagstaff for others."

"Salt Lake City," she repeated while Ropers stared at her. It stood out as the largest northerly destination at the moment.

She returned to J. T. "He's headed for Salt Lake. It's a large enough city. We could lose him forever, if he suddenly decides to cut his losses and wishes to disappear, but I doubt that's his plan."

"What do we do?"

She started away, saying over her shoulder, "Follow through on your plan. Check with the bus lines. Run down that ticket."

"And what are you going to do?" he asked, chasing after.

"I'm going ahead to Salt Lake."

"Alone?"

"I'll wire Bishop to meet me there."

"I don't know, Jess. I think we ought to stick together."

"J. T., that information on what bus line he's on will be vital. It will tell us not only his next destination but also the one after that. There's no way you can get that info while traveling to Salt Lake. We need to know Lorentian's proposed itinerary and what hotels she would've been staying at, the same ones we hypothesize that *he* will be using in her stead."

"But Jess!"

She was making her way across the highway to the helicopter again. "Don't you see? That information is vital now, John. Get it! Meanwhile, I'll organize a strike force in Salt Lake, utilizing FBI headquarters there."

"Are you sure?"

Over her shoulder, she called back, saying, "I'll call you here when I'm set up there."

"But Jess . . . Jess . . ."

She had stopped listening and continued her march to the helicopter pad, determined now to be at the killer's next destination before him, glad that she had brought along an overnight bag along with her medical bag.

J. T. discovered that many of the people staying at the hotels at or near national parks such as Bryce Canyon and Zion were indeed on one bus tour or another, that on any given night at least two and perhaps four or five tour buses lodged at Ruby Inn and Lake Powell's Wahweap as well. No surprises there. He also learned that like ships at sea, there were weary-worn routes all the buses took, but that some tours included side trips that others failed to take. All of this he learned from the clique of tour guides hanging about Ruby Inn. He also learned something of the history of the inn, that it was a favorite haunt of cowboy and Western stars from Gene Autry and Roy Rogers to Audie Murphy and John Wayne.

From the bus companies he'd contacted, he had heard from only three of seven so far, and none of them listed a Chris Lorentian, a Charon, or anyone named Nessus in any of various spellings on their manifests. It had been four hours since Jessica had left, and no word. He began to worry when Warren Bishop showed up at the inn, seeking Jessica.

"Where is she?" Bishop asked J. T. where he sat before a phone in the manager's office.

"Salt Lake City."

"Why Salt Lake?"

"We believe—or rather, she believes it will be where *he* next kills."

"How does she know this?"

"She doesn't, not exactly, but bear with me."

Bishop, exhausted from what appeared lack of sleep, dropped stonelike into a chair beside J. T., who then continued, "He's a killer of opportunity. He bides his time, seeking out the weakest to prey upon, someone lonely or despondent, someone alone, and he pounces."

"I follow you so far."

"Step out to the restaurant with me for a moment."

"I'm not hungry. Get on with it, Dr. Thorpe."

"Please, come along," J. T. gently urged.

Taking a narrow passageway, they came upon the dining area. It was dinnertime, especially for the bus tour crowd staying the night at the inn. "Notice how many of these people around you here at the inn, Bishop, are just that— vulnerable one way or another?"

"They're mostly elderly people—couples, and in packs. What do you mean?"

"Women alone, women traveling with their daughters, single women, single men in search of a mate along with their adventure into the wilderness parks. Sure, there are a lot of couples, but there are also the singles. Melvin Martin was a single man traveling alone, and now this Whitaker woman, a single woman traveling alone."

"Then the killer could still be at this lodge, camouflaged among the bus tour crowds," suggested Bishop. "So, you and Jessica have concluded that he's traveling by bus, I see."

"How do you suppose he learned we—Jess, rather—was staying at Wahweap Lodge when he was *here*, killing again? He's following a bus route, and he has us marching to his drumbeat, and he knows it."

"Then he's thought this thing through thoroughly, hasn't he?"

"We believe so. As you know, he's been baiting Jessica all along. The creep was milling around in Page while we were there, just . . . just to taunt us."

"Yes, Jessica feared her path and his might cross there."

"He knew enough to telephone her there, so he either saw her there or assumed she would follow him there. . . ."

"And if he assumed . . . Well, either way, he's as shrewd as he is psychotic. I got Jessica's wire, flew out to Page only to discover you had all rushed here."

Bishop's apt description of the Phantom as a shrewd psychotic recalled Mad Matt Matisak to mind, along with a host of other satanic killers whom Jessica had helped, either directly or indirectly, to put down or behind bars, and he wondered, as Repasi had, if the Phantom might not be someone with a long-ago grudge to settle with Jessica. He suggested this to Bishop, who quickly informed him that it was unlikely, since a thorough check of all former such opponents revealed no one missing from lockup.

"But what if someone in lockup is holding the strings, telling this puppet what to do and say to terrify Jessica?"

"Maybe . . . it's a possibility, but Quantico says no. And Santiva has taken measures to stop all communiqués going out of federal asylums and federal prisons housing anyone who could conceivably hold a grudge against Jess."

"You should have seen Jessica last night after that bastard telephoned her again, Bishop. Mother wanted her to hear Eloise Whitaker's last screams.''

"Lowlife-SOB-motherfreaking-rat-bastard."

"Yeah, my sentiments exactly."

"Maybe it's possible then, at some point, he was at Wahweap Lodge in Page while you two were there," suggested Bishop, imagining it.

"I suspect our paths crossed. The killer didn't have to wait there long, just long enough for the tour guide to round everyone up, minus Melvin Martin, of course, but then a check with Martin's tour bus company turned up no one traveling as Chris Lorentian, so Melvin may not've been a part of the same tour group as the one the killer is traveling with. Actually, as it happens, Melvin was traveling in exactly the opposite direction when their paths crossed. His tour was passing through the national parks from the north down on a journey for a destination southwest—for Vegas, in fact. And the morning after Chris Lorentian was killed? The hotel parking lot in Vegas was crammed full with touring buses.''

"He made his escape from Vegas on a tour bus?" Bishop's shake of the head spoke volumes. "We had men watching the buses for anyone looking suspicious."

J. T. frowned, knowing it sounded somewhat ridiculous, but he replied, "What better way to blend in than to join a gaggle of tourists? And we never found Chris's credit cards or her purse. Besides, as the FBI profile says, this guy is so unremarkable as to be virtually invisible.''

"And using a unisex name like Chris, I suppose the tour guide would have little reason to question his sex when he went to use that ticket." Bishop sent his balled fist down on a table, the noise startling everyone in the restaurant area.

"Right," agreed J. T.

"So, supposing they were both—killer and victim— touring with the same or similar bus tour companies," suggested Bishop, warming now to the game of supposition they were playing, "they strike up a conversation, maybe have dinner together, and he slips his victim something in a drink. . . ."

"Just enough drugs to incapacitate. Then he goes up to the victim's room, concerned about the victim's pallor, which the bastard remarks upon at dinner," added J. T.

"And the rest, as they say, is smoke and history. . . ." Bishop's hard-set jaw began to quiver. "Cold, methodical bastard. Quite sure of what he wants, but I'll be damned if I know. Tell me what you know of this untapped phone call Jessica had from the creep at Wahweap Lodge."

J. T. wondered for a moment how Bishop knew the call had been untapped, but he mentally shrugged it off. There'd been no time for Jessica to place a tap on the phone. Bishop must have assumed as much.

J. T. now launched into as detailed a description of the killer's last communiqué as he could muster. He told Bishop all that Jessica had revealed to him about the phone call, and he ended with the killer's professed reason for doing people: "In order to climb from Hell himself, or so he said."

"Nifty and the freshest excuse for murder I ever heard," Bishop sarcastically replied.

J. T. nodded. "The devil made me do it."

"In your search with the bus companies . . ." began Bishop.

"Yeah?"

"Did you ask after the name she'd registered under at the Hilton?"

"My God. I'd forgotten. Chris Dunlap."

"Let's get back on the horn then."

They rushed back to the phone J. T. had left in the manager's office.

J. T. and Bishop double-teamed the effort, and they tied up the phone lines out of Ruby Inn with the help of the cache of tour guides they'd rounded up, making phone calls to all the various bus companies working the national parks routes in Arizona, Utah, Nevada, Idaho, Colorado, and Wyoming. They'd thought themselves clever by limiting themselves to the national parks tour packages in this area, since the trail of the killer appeared to be that of a tourist interested in the Grand Canyon, Glen Canyon Dam, Bryce Canyon, and the Zion area. They then narrowed their search to buses going to, through, or toward Salt Lake City, Utah, in the past twenty-four hours.

The search proved frustrating, however. The bus dispatchers they talked to were, to a person, reluctant to release information over the phone without proof of Bishop's or J. T.'s credentials. The tour guides had far better luck, their voices and tour package numbers familiar to those within a given company.

Further vexing Bishop and J. T., some of the bus company records seemed in disarray, despite their systems' computerized promises.

At one point J. T. found himself disappointed to the point of considering murder.

Finally, after two and a half hours of nonsense, someone at the other end of the line said, ''Yes, yes, sir . . . I do have a Chris Dunlap registered on our bus tour number thirteen fourteen, which is due into Salt Lake . . . ahhh, an hour and a half ago!''

J. T. had to check which bus company he was now speaking to, he'd been on the phone with so many today. It was the VisionQuest bus line. One of their buses had almost run over Jessica that morning.

''Thirteen fourteen? That's the number to identify the bus?'' he asked.

''No, no . . . that's the tour group number. Bus number is sixtyyyyy . . . seven.''

''License number?''

''Bus travels through sixteen states. Which license number do you want, sir? Arizona, Nevada plates?''

''Utah . . . Utah plates'll do.''

The voice at the other end slowly enumerated each number.

"Where is the bus now? What lodge or hotel is it at?"

"Salt Lake Hilton, downtown Salt Lake City, sir."

"Thank you, God, thank you."

"Sir, our safety record to date has been—"

"Yes, yes, sterling, I'm sure. Thanks." J. T. *finally* hung up on a call that had netted them useful information. He felt elated and grabbed the receiver back up to call Jessica, when he realized he had no way of reaching her. She'd managed to do exactly as she'd promised not to do: She was in the snake pit with this guy. She'd promised to contact J. T. here at the Ruby Inn, but so far she hadn't, and it was nearing dusk.

He turned to Bishop, who'd been on another line close to him, but found Warren had disappeared. He went in search of Bishop to find him conferring in a shadowed vestibule between the hotel and the laundry room with Dr. Karl Repasi. J. T. at first assumed that Bishop was getting Repasi's take on the Eloise Whitaker murder when suddenly he saw Bishop erupt in passion, shoving Repasi so hard the other man's weight sent him through the laundry room door, where he toppled to the floor and stayed there while Bishop pointed a daggarlike, accusatory finger and swore at Repasi some unintelligible words.

J. T. was pleased to see someone literally take Repasi to the cleaners. "All right!" J. T. said with a wide grin, feeling it served Repasi right.

Not wanting Bishop to think him a snoop, J. T. stepped back from sight and waited to catch Bishop on his return to the manager's office. When Bishop did so, there was a slight pinkish-redness about his cheeks, giving his Bill Clinton look-alike features an even more Clinton-like look, but the square-shouldered Bishop remained otherwise unruffled. J. T. brought a smile to Bishop's face when he quickly unloaded his good news, saying, "Warren, I've got the whereabouts of the impostor Chris Dunlap."

Bishop's eyes widened like those of a predator. "Let me see that." He grabbed J. T.'s notes from his hand and stared hard at the data. "I'm on the chopper to Salt Lake."

"I'm with you," J. T. replied.

"No, you've got to man a phone here and find out where Jessica is. Tell her to meet us at the Hilton, should she get in touch."

J. T. frowned and complained of being left back.

"She'll need to hear this from you," Bishop said, his large index finger on the notepad J. T. had been using.

The frown remained on J. T.'s face as he watched Bishop disappear for the waiting helicopter where Bishop got on the radio, calling out the cavalry, J. T. assumed. In a moment, Bishop was lifting off into the sun-dappled sky and blood-red-and-orange rock formations of Bryce Canyon, the helicopter speeding toward Salt Lake.

Checking with the various bus companies all this time had been annoying and frustrating, but having to sit here while Bishop raced off to become Jessica's hero was equally repulsive.

· FIFTEEN ·

Whomever is abandoned by hope, has also been abandoned by fear; this is the meaning of the word "desperate."
—ARTHUR SCHOPENHAUER

Jessica had taken a room at the Little America Hotel and Towers at 500 South Main, in the heart of the hotel district in Salt Lake City. Little America, she was told, was one of the places on the tourist visit list, and many a bus tour stopped here. Maybe she'd get lucky, she hoped. The city's oldest landmark hotels populated this area as well, and all of the touring buses coming into the city found their way to the hotel district.

Once settled into her room, Jessica made calls to local authorities and the FBI to alert them to the fact she was chasing a fugitive serial murderer on a kill spree, whom she believed to be in the area. The reaction from local authorities and the FBI was instantaneous. Undercover operatives were set up in all the major hotels, and police were placed on alert to back up the government men. This took time, but once this network had been established, Jessica got on the phone in search of J. T. and Warren Bishop. Unable to locate them immediately, she took the opportunity to contact Eriq Santiva, to bring him up to date on the case.

After she enumerated all developments and lamented the lack of progress until now, she assured Eriq that they were closer to a resolution than ever before, explaining that J. T.

was researching the bus lines. "And as soon as we have the bus line he's using, we'll know where the Phantom is staying tonight," she assured Santiva. "Then we move in on the bastard."

"Take all precautions, Jess. He sees you, he'll likely do anything to kill you. Wear a vest, hang back. Let the others do their work."

"I'll be happy to do just that."

Santiva replied, "Here, we've taken everything you've given us and put it into the hands of every medical expert and academician in the country who might have a clue, Jess."

"We've got a bit more of the puzzle pieces since the last time J. T. forwarded information, Eriq."

"Want to share?"

She thought again of the killer's messages, and how they'd looked on paper, and she remembered J. T.'s having added that #5 would be #5. She thought it a peculiar numeric anomaly for the numbers to crisscross in such a fashion. She pictured the list in her mind, trying again to make some sense of it.

"Well?" asked Santiva, becoming impatient.

"Take this down," she said, and fed the list to him, jotting it down again for herself on the hotel's stationery. It read:

#1 is #9—Traitors
#2 is #8—Malicious Frauds
#3 is #7—Violents
#4 is #6—Heretics
#5 is #5—   ?

"Someone out there's got to know where this guy's coming from—or going to with all this," she finished.

"You think?" Eriq replied.

"He said something about, I don't know, Satan's pit, dragging himself up from the pit and dragging me down into it. Something about the Devil's well. I'm paraphrasing. I wasn't exactly in any mood to memorize his every line when he surprised me the other night with Eloise Whitaker's fire assassination.''

"I can't imagine what you must be feeling about now, Jess. I'm coming out there to be with you. You need me there.''

"No, no, Eriq. Bishop's close at hand, and I've got help here on all sides from our guys in Salt Lake. They're a little stiff, Mormons as well as FBI men, but they'll do.''

"If you're sure, Jess.''

"Anything on the handwriting, the prints, anything?''

"He's wearing a pair of cheap sneakers with a Sonics logo on them.''

"Sonics logo on the bottom of the heel? Hair burned off the back of his hands and forearms. Thanks.''

"At the toe—big toe, actually. You get those shoes, we've got positive ID on that print taken at Page.''

"Anything else? What about the two aliases he's used, Charon and Nessus?''

"Sorry, but a check of VICAP files and several other listings brought up zip on the computers. Whoever he is, he's never been apprehended before as a violent offender.''

"He's too methodical to *not* be a recidivist, Eriq,'' she complained. "He's killed with fire before Chris Lorentian. I just know it. I know it in my bones.''

"If he has, he may've gone straight into the asylum, bypassing criminal conviction, in which case we have nothing on him. We're running the prints through state and local institutions for the insane now, but so far—''

"Nothing.'' Her exasperation trailed her breath. If the killer had never gone through the court system and been convicted as criminally insane, then he would not be in a facility for the criminally insane, either state or federal. "Call me when you have something.''

"Will do. Are you sure you have plenty of backup there?'' he asked.

"Salt Lake FBI branch has me on their radar. They're looking out for me; been good to me," she lied, not wishing to tell him that she had informed Salt Lake of the situation but that she had not bodily joined forces with them, preferring to remain an independent part of the coming equation. So far as Salt Lake was concerned, the fugitive was theirs if they could surround him and tie the noose.

Jessica feared nightfall, which was fast approaching. She feared he would strike again, close by, and she didn't know how to stop this shadow monster. She feared she'd be the first to know when he struck, that he would somehow know where to phone it in, like a cat with a prize to offer her, another dead body, #5 is #5.

She began to strip away her clothes, stepping into the bathroom, turning on the shower, and getting under its soothing spray. While relaxing, she thought of James Parry and a paradise thousands of miles off. After showering, she returned to the phone and dialed Jim's home. It would be midafternoon in Hawaii, and Jim might not be at home, but she needed to hear his voice, needed reassuring, needed to know that he still loved her.

"Jessica? It's you. I've been worried about you; haven't been able to get in touch. You're on a manhunt. I talked to Bishop in Vegas. He gave me a number to reach you, but you'd already left."

"Jim, I just called so you wouldn't worry, but it's nice to know you do."

"I've missed you terribly."

"Me, too. . . ."

"Tell me exactly what's going on there, every detail," he asked. "I'm given to understand that this bastard you're after has threatened you over the phone?"

"It's a bit more complicated than threats," she replied before launching into a detail-by-detail update on what had occurred since that first night in Las Vegas.

Parry, stunned at the revelations and fearful for Jessica, remained silent for a long pause after she finished speaking. "Jessica, if I know my literature, that numbering of one through nine, and the words 'heretics' 'frauds,' 'traitors'—it all sounds a bit familiar, like the nine rungs of Hell in *The Divine Comedy*."

"*The Divine Comedy*. Are you sure?"

"That's what it recalls to mind, yes."

"Of course, *The Divine Comedy,* Dante's *Inferno*," she replied. "I haven't thought of that place since . . . since I was a junior in high school, where I had to read it for Mr. Blevins's World Literature class. Jim, you're a genius. I knew there was a reason I was supposed to call you!"

"Very flattering."

"The subconcious always knows best. I called because I wanted to hear your voice, to tell you I miss you, to tell you I love you, Jim, but somehow my inner self knew that you could also help out on this horrid case."

"That's more like it. Great to know I'm needed. Still, you knew I was a lit major in college, and ancient literature was my field before I got into law enforcement, or had you forgot?"

"Obviously not," she lied. "You're brilliant as well as handsome."

"Not quite brilliant. I recently read a recap of the reasons why Dante was considered so important in man's perception of Hades, good and evil, all that in a chapter of a book called the *History of Hell,* so it's been on my mind. So, naturally, when you told me about what kind of nutcase you're dealing with . . . well, it was hardly brilliance on my part."

"So, why're you reading about Hades?"

"Believe it or not, it's required reading in my course on comparative religion and the literature of evil along with *People of the Lie*."

"You're taking a course?"

"Helps pass time. I miss you. God, I do."

"Don't beg! I miss you, too."

"And I'm worried about you. More so now than before. Please be careful there, darling."

"I'm all right. I knew this guy was killing in the name of the king of Hell, Satan, but it's all right now . . . now we know his game. Dante's *Inferno,* of course. He'd called himself at one time Charon, Nessus at another. . . ."

"Yes, the boatman who takes Dante across the River Styx to the Land of the Dead, and Nessus takes them across the river of boiling blood, guarded by the Centaurs. In fact, Nessus is one of the Centaurs."

She recalled having said to J. T. that the killer likely thought he'd be rewarded by his demons by becoming a godlike creature himself, perhaps sprouting a pair of devilish wings. She said to Jim, "Centaur, huh? This kook thinks he's a goddamned Centaur?"

"Why're you, of all people, sounding so surprised?" he asked, following with a light laugh.

"It's been a long time since I've read Dante. So this guy thinks he's a Centaur now, half man, half bull?"

"No, half man, half horse. Minotaur is the bull man."

"Got it."

"Read *Inferno* again. It could give you some insights into this creep."

"Exactly. At least now I will know something about what he's talking about. He's anxious for me to learn."

"What's that?"

"I think in all this madness, he's trying to . . . instruct me."

"So you have a monster for a teacher? Sounds like par for your course, Jess. You can beat this creep-bastard. You and I both know it."

"Thanks for the pep talk and the information. Before now, I had no point of reference when he'd make references to Hellsmouth, call himself different names."

"Don't be so hard on yourself. The guy freaked you out. Who wouldn't be?"

"Yes, Charon was the name of the guide who pointed the way for Dante and Virgil in their mythical tour of Hades," she thoughtfully replied. "Maybe we can use it against him."

"Don't take any unnecessary chances, Jess. Promise me."

She paused before saying, "Not to worry. I've got Bishop and the Salt Lake City field agents behind me. I'm surrounded by big, muscular types."

"And that's supposed to ease my mind?" His laughter washed over her.

She loved to hear him laugh, and she imagined his warm, lovely smile, and she thought of how much they had laughed together in Greece and Rome. She took a moment to tell him how much their trip had meant to her before saying, "Good-bye, James, and thanks for the help."

"Good-bye, and be careful, Jess. I love you."

"I love you, too, beyond your imagining."

She hung up, dressed, and tried again to get J. T. back at Bryce Canyon but without luck. Still the phone lines were tied up and all she could get was a busy signal. She thought of getting an operator on the line and having her break into the line, but instead she decided to locate the nearest library. With the help of the doorman, she learned it was too late for the library, that it would be closed. "Salt Lake rolls up the sidewalks at dusk, pretty much, ma'am," he apologized for his city.

"What about a bookstore?"

"Oh, yeah, there's one a half block on the southeastern corner, thataway," he said, pointing. "They may be open."

Jessica made the short walk and found the storefront shop window filled with books. Inside, she found a musty place filled with used books on wood and crate shelves. A huge orange cat lay asleep on the cash register. She finally found a dog-eared, paperback copy of Dante's *Inferno*. She

paid two dollars and twenty-five cents for the copy and
began revisiting Hades in the lobby of the hotel, and later
in her room to be near the phone so she could keep trying
to raise J. T., to let him know her whereabouts in the city.

Jessica hadn't seen or thought of Dante's strange pan-
orama of Hades since her school days, when it was required reading in her AP class. She read it anew with the
fanatical killer in mind, imagining his imaginings now.
Dante Alighieri's *Divine Comedy,* in its entirety, was enormous, but it had been his depiction of Hades that captured
the imagination of generations since its publication in
1321, and apparently their killer had been no exception.

Rivers of boiling blood, that was what the killer had
turned his victims' bodies into. The Wood of Suicides,
where the naked forms of men, women, and children dangled from thorny prongs of dead trees like so much litter
and parchment; vile creatures such as the flying Geryon,
Minotaurs, Centaurs guarding vestibules and black corridors, monsters at every turn, and those souls damned to
living out putrid lives in the land of *Dis* or Satan, inside
the body of the beast.

She read on and recalled the Furies, Medusa, and the
Harpies, all of whom peopled Satan's world, an enormous
inverted, three-dimensional mountain created when Satan
and all his followers fell to the earth. She skimmed, recalling far more than she now read. Some said the Grand
Canyon was created by Satan's fall to Earth.

Her eyes grew weary over the words, and for a time she
felt alone with the mad Phantom, alone with the Devil.
And she lay on the covered bed in her room here at the
Little America Hotel in Salt Lake City, and here she nod-
ded off with Dante's elaborate, allegorical window into
Hell on her lap.

It was six twenty-five now, a light pattering rain
having begun at the windows when the nightmare result
of her cramming metamorphosed into a garish dream that

carried her along a spiraling red river of blood without any chance of refusing. It was a river filled with muck and putrid odors so horrid they could not be swallowed. She felt herself going down into the deepest recesses of the human psyche where the demons dwelled, although some of the shadows in the room with her seemed corporeal enough to shake her from slumber. In the dark underworld, *she* saw herself staring back at *her*.

On waking, she shuddered, clawed her way to a sitting position on the made bed, and picked up the phone's receiver. She again dialed for J. T. at Ruby Inn in Bryce to inform him of the breakthrough, that the killer was working with the Dante mythos.

This time she got through. Obviously John had gotten a room at the inn, for they patched her through to his room.

"Jess, thank God, I've been worried sick about you," he almost shouted. "Where are you?"

Jessica thought she heard a voice in the background. "Are you alone?"

"Not entirely, no."

"Well, good for you. The breakfast waitress?"

"How'd you guess?"

She told him her whereabouts and updated him on the search for the killer, and as J. T. calmed, she informed him of the Dante connection. "That's wonderful news," he told her, adding, "and I have some good news, too. We located the bus he's been traveling on all this time."

She saw the noose tightening for Charon and Nessus. "Miraculous! How'd you do it?"

"Blood, sweat, tears, and a search under the registration of a Chris Dunlap. Bishop's idea."

"Bishop's there with you—good. Now tell me what you've got."

"No, Warren's probably in Salt Lake by now, Jess. You've got to get over to the Hilton. That's where Bishop will be, flushing this creep out. He's got his number now. He knows the tour number, the bus plate, and by now the creep's room number. It's just a matter of time now."

"Give me the details, J. T.!" She was shouting in excitement now. "What've you got?"

"The bus tour Chris Lorentian booked, *she* booked as Chris Dunlap, and it was on the VisionQuest bus line. The tour number is thirteen fourteen and the number of the bus is sixty-seven." He added the Utah plate numbers. "Got that?"

She jotted down the information on the hotel stationery beside the bed. "Excellent work, J. T. And you say Bishop's here in the city?"

"Yeah, he left here by helicopter some time ago."

"He must not be here yet, else he would have contacted me here through the field office."

"I don't know why he hasn't, Jess, but he's a good man. Who knows, a take-charge guy like him? Maybe he wants to handle it himself. I saw him dress down Karl Repasi for you while he was here, gave him an earful. Thought you'd like to know."

"Thanks. I've got to get over to the Hilton. See what's happening or what has happened in my absence there."

"Go lightly, Jess. Promise me you'll be careful."

"My middle name is careful. Talk to you later, J. T. I'm at this number." She gave him the number and name of the hotel she was staying at. "Now I've got to get a cab and get to the Hilton. Good-bye, J. T."

"Jess!"

"What?"

"I should be there with you."

"J. T., you've pinpointed the exact location of the killer. Something no one else has been able to do. You did great."

"Jess, be careful out there!" But she hung up on J. T.'s cautionary words.

Jessica quickly dressed, snatching on her undergarments, a pair of slacks, a pullover shirt and sneakers, and she tied her hair back with a ribbon. She grabbed up the receiver again and asked the desk to get her a cab. She found her purse, valise, and keys when the phone rang, likely the desk to let her know that a cab waited for her.

But when she lifted the receiver, she heard the faint, choking, gagging sound, followed by more evidence of someone in distress. Then he came on the line, saying, "I've found you, Dr. Coran. And I've found number five."

Jesus, her mind raced, how could he know she was here? How had he gotten her number? As if to answer her thoughts, he said, "You aren't hard to figure, Doctor. I knew you'd follow, and all I had to do was page you at the desk. They wouldn't give me your room number, but they put me through to you."

He must have randomly selected hotels around the city and taken his chances, she surmised. He wasn't supernatural. "Your time is running out, Charon or Nessus or whatever you choose to call yourself today," she informed him, summoning her strongest voice.

"Really? I thought it the other way around. Listen to this!"

"Wait! I've been reading Dante's *Inferno*."

This silenced the killer for a moment. "So, now you know where you're headed? I know where you belong, Doctor Coran."

"Everyone knows where you are now, Nessus," she threatened. Bishop and the others did know his approximate whereabouts. They knew he was somewhere in the Hilton. They were converging on his room, however, and not the room belonging to the unfortunate number five. Even so, she wondered where precisely Bishop and the others were now in relation to the killer. At any rate, she must keep the monster on the line for as long as possible. "I know where you're at right now," she coldly informed him.

"Impossible," he replied.

"You're here, in Salt Lake."

"Of course, but that comes as no surprise to either of us, does it?" He began a snorting laugh.

"You're in the Hilton here in Salt Lake, and *everyone* knows it."

This fact coming from her silenced his laughter.

"The FBI have you surrounded," she informed him as casually as the most jaded telephone operator.

"Lies become you, bitch! Listen to this, your answer."

"Wait!"

But he didn't wait any longer. He put his fifth victim to the torch, the superheated *whoosh* of the flames now as familiar as a backyard barbecue to her, while the screams of the unseen, unknown victim set a sickening snake loose to wiggle down her spine. She dropped the receiver on his maniac's laughter and left it dangling off the hook. She grabbed up her black valise and tore from the room to find a cab to race to the scene of the murder and the Phantom killer.

Jessica fumbled with the cellular phone she kept in her valise, calling 911, announcing her identity and the fact that there was a fire at the Hilton; the operator wanted more detailed information, information she didn't have. "Just get the fire trucks there, now!"

She hung up and dialed Neil Gallagher, the field agent in charge in Salt Lake City. After a series of voices and blips, she was patched through to Gallagher in the field.

"Why didn't you contact me before you zeroed in on the Hilton?"

"What are you talking about?" he asked, confused.

"Haven't you heard from Bishop?"

"Warren Bishop? Vegas? No, we haven't."

"My God. Get over to the Hilton. There's been another fire killing there. I've got fire trucks on the way."

"I've got two men posted at the Hilton, and I'm within spitting distance. I'm there!"

"On my way, too." Jessica hung up and rushed for her destination, hailing a cab and calling out as she boarded, "The Hilton, downtown Salt Lake City location."

On the short ride through the downtown district, the cab weaving to avoid jackhammers and construction block- ades, Jessica wondered again why Bishop hadn't contacted her or Gallagher, according to the other man. But why wouldn't Warren be in touch with the local FBI offices, even from the air? Why would he work around Gallagher? How many or how few people in the city knew of the killer's whereabouts while she had sat in the dark? she wondered. Warren had no doubt organized an attack force of some sort to converge on the hotel as soon as he'd arrived in the city. Had he bypassed Gallagher, knowing it was the only way to keep her in the dark about his movements? Did he really think he was sparing Jessica an ordeal? "Bastard," she muttered.

The questions continued, piling upon one another in av- alanche fashion. When would Warren's strike force strike? Why hadn't they done so earlier? What had held them back if they knew the man's room number by this time? By this time they must, she reasoned. But then why had they waited until yet another victim was sacrificed to this mad- man's unholy altar?

FBI operatives from the Salt Lake City field office, which shared jurisdiction with the Flagstaff, Arizona, field office, had encircled the downtown area, awaiting more specific information about the operation, but it was infor- mation that did not come.

Instead, three men entered the Hilton, and one among them, Chief Warren Bishop, rushed to the desk to learn what room was booked to a Chris Dunlap, a passenger on one of the bus tours. He flashed his badge and ordered up the information.

"Package like that, we just rent a block of rooms to the tour group company; they make the selections who goes into which room."

"Who do I talk to, then?"

"We can get Guy, Doris, and Maureen down here,"

said a second clerk. "They're the tour guides currently in town. They'll each have a list."

"Then get 'em down here."

Only Maureen and Doris could be found, Guy having already gone out for the nightlife. Maureen's list revealed no Chris Dunlap. Doris's list, however, did. "What do you know about this guy Dunlap?" Bishop asked the guide.

"Next to nothing. He's a cold fish, a real loner. Keeps to himself, rides the back of the bus. Wouldn't join in at all the first days of the trip, but he's thawed some lately. Getting on and off the bus, he'll help someone, you know with a hand. Everybody on the bus has tried to be civil to him, but no one's gotten to know much about him. Word is he's retired, on disability, sued someone and made a bundle, so now he just takes trips all over, spending his money. Least that's what the ladies on the bus think . . . "

"Have you seen him tonight?"

"At dinner in the hotel restaurant."

"Is he still there?"

"No, that was over an hour or so ago."

"What's his room number?"

"Five-twenty-two."

"I saw him leave with a woman from Guy's group," added the one named Maureen. "We sometimes talk about our passengers, especially the weird ones."

"Do you know what room she's in? The woman who left with Dunlap?" Bishop asked her.

"Couldn't tell you. Only Guy would know that. And Guy's not going to be found until daybreak. I don't know how that man does it, but he can even find a poker game in Salt Lake, and he plays to all hours, then—"

"Damn it." Bishop turned to the hotel clerk. "Give me the block of rooms this guy *Guy* has for the night, now!"

The clerk's fingers speedily called up this information on her computer. "Rooms six-twelve through six-fifty."

"Back me up!" he called to the other agents with him, big men who had not bothered to display their badges.

"Sixth floor! Block off all the exits. Stop anyone with a case in his hand, anyone looking the least bit suspicious! Go, now!"

As he rode the elevator up with two other men, Bishop told them to go door-to-door, knocking on every single door in the grouping. "You take the right, you take the left," he told them.

"And where will you be, Bishop?" asked one of the stone-faced men.

"Yeah," agreed the other man.

"I'll go straight to six-fifty and work my way back to you. And be careful of getting into any crossfire situation."

"You forget you're dealing with professionals, G-man."

Bishop gritted his teeth, hating every moment of this, hating Frank Lorentian, hating himself in the bargain. He looked into the eyes of the two professional hit men he'd contacted and waited for. Repasi had kept him appraised up to this point of Jessica's whereabouts, well-being, the dispensation of the autopsies, the geography of the crimes. Now it was time to erase all debts.

After this, he'd never again have any dealings with Frank Lorentian, and all Frank wanted was to see his daughter's murderer dead—no FBI involvement, no arrests, no coutroom dramatics, no loony bins or life sentences, just dead.

"You smell something?" asked one of Lorentian's thugs.

"Smoke," said the other.

"Damn it, we're too late," conceded Bishop. "But the bastard's still in the building. You two, usher everyone off this floor and sound the fire alarms. I'm going down to five-twenty-two. Send backup when you can. Got that?"

"No way," disagreed one of the hit men. "We stick together, Bishop."

As soon as the elevator doors opened, it became clear there was indeed a fire on the floor. The two gunmen looked from the smoking door just ahead to one another. "We got the bastard right here," said the taller of the two.

"Careful, he's armed and dangerous," cautioned Bishop as the two thugs moved on the door, the hallway now becoming choked with smoke and people peeping from their rooms, some now shouting and racing for the stairwells.

The hit men continued toward the door where the hot spot existed, seeing smoke rising from the bottom and sifting through each side. Suddenly the door burst open, flames bursting out at the phony agents, burning their eyes, faces, hands they'd thrown up for protection with their guns extended when suddenly they were each engulfed in a shooting flame.

People had begun to pour from the rooms, racing past Bishop and into the elevator, taking it. Others screamed and ran for other exits. Through the commotion, the flame and smoke, Bishop saw the two hit men had caught hell, their eyes fried, each man flailing like a spiked tarpon, each going to the hallway floor, scurrying to place some distance between themselves and the shadowy figure that suddenly burst from the room, wearing a gas mask, holding a butane torch with the wand out, a dark bag tucked below his arm.

Bishop raised his gun to fire but one of the hit men suddenly found his feet and stood between him and the fleeing figure on the other side of the flames. Bishop steadied his weapon and dropped to one knee, choking on the smoke. He aimed and wanted to fire but the other two men remained in his way as they fought their own frenzied battle before him. Their clothing aflame now, smoke masking the killer, the dark figure in gas mask disappeared through a door marked STAIRWELL.

Bishop smashed his gun into a glass containing a water hose. He pulled the alarm and turned the water on as furiously as he could, the hose getting away from him, spraying ceiling and floor until he got control of it and aimed the spray on Lorentian's two men, dousing them and the fire in the hallway.

Each man was hurt badly with serious burns to the face, arms, and body. Others had come up behind Bishop now, however, and they were helping their supposed comrades with words of encouragement.

"Ambulance is on its way!" Bishop assured the men he knew only as Steve and Rollo. He couldn't help but feel great pity for the two. Their faces were seared red, their eyes scorched, hair and skin falling away with the smoke that curled from them. "Hang in there, you guys," he said to their suffering screams.

Bishop dialed 911 for assistance on his cellular phone, but paramedics came rushing onto the floor even before he could get out his request. "Over here," he called out to them.

Firemen with hoses rushed past Bishop and the injured men, into the flames, beginning their battle with the room fire. Bishop knew what they would discover inside. He also knew the room number for Chris Dunlap's room in the building. Was the killer foolish enough to return there?

Bishop grabbed the elevator when it opened, carrying more FBI and police. He took the car down two flights where he glimpsed a killer, no longer wearing a gas mask but the distinct odor of smoke-choked clothes seemed to be rising off him, although the entire building now seemed permeated with smoke. The same stench had filled the carpeting and Bishop's own soggy clothes, so he could not be sure. The other man was about to dart into the room supposedly being used by Chris Dunlap this night, when Bishop leveled his gun at him.

"Hold it, right there, Mister Dunlap!"

"What?" The man jumped. "My name's not Dunlap. It's Sorensen, Thomas Sorensen."

"FBI," Bishop shouted, his gun extended at the harmless-looking little man before him. "Put your hands where I can see them."

"Me? F-BI? What's this all about? Is this a stick-up?"

"Drop the case, you fire freak, and put your hands against the back of your head, or I blow your freaking head off where you stand."

"All right, all right . . . Jesus, what's Martha going to say when I tell her about this?"

The man was unremarkable, plain, without any single outstanding characteristic. He wore a dark business suit and didn't look to be a touring tourist. He stood perhaps 5'6" or 7", weighing in around 170, the size of their suspect, small in stature, like a Lee Harvey Oswald, Bishop was thinking when suddenly the black case dropped with a bang to the floor, thundering out its weight in a clear code.

"Hands behind your fucking head, now!"

The little man gulped while lifting his hands behind his head, then he turned full around to face Bishop straight on.

"That's more like it."

"I wish you would tell me what in God's name this is all about."

"I just witnessed your coming out of a murder scene two flights up, Mr. Phantom. Charon, is it? I've been chasing you since Vegas."

"Vegas? Charon? But I've never been to Vegas, not yet. Our bus won't arrive there for another two, three days."

"Then you are on the bus tour? So, what's in the case?"

"I sell life insurance—First Continental Casualty; have since '87. One of the couples on the bus wanted to buy some security after the near accident we had today coming down the highway into Salt Lake." The man's mild manner was off-putting, and he had a ready answer for everything, and for a split second, Bishop wondered if he hadn't gotten the wrong man, and Bishop worried that if he had the wrong guy here at gunpoint, that the killer could be escaping the hotel through the underground parking lot or someplace else in the hotel. Yet this guy stood outside the door marked 522, and so it followed . . . so, he knew this must be the man posing as Chris Dunlap. Unless the desk or the stupid tour guides had gotten some number transposed.

"You're posing as Chris Dunlap, aren't you?"

"Posing? An impostor? Me? Dunlap . . . Dunlap . . . Why isn't that the unmarried, eerie fellow who sits in the back of the bus and talks to himself and no one else? Martha gets angry with me 'cause I talk too much to everyone. I'm Thomas G. Sorensen." He brought one hand down as if to offer it in a handshake, but Bishop gestured with his gun for the man to keep his hands up, and he did.

"Open the door and let's talk to Martha then," suggested Bishop who wondered now if the tour guide had gotten the room number wrong. This fellow had no red hair, and he saw no red rash along his neck as reported by the clerk in Vegas.

"Martha's not going to like this."

"Fuck Martha! Fish out your keys and do as told. Open the fucking door."

"All right, all right." The man fished into his pocket for the electronic key the size of a credit card. Unlocking the door, he was saying through it, "Martha, it's me and we have company. Are you decent, dear?"

Bishop took a step closer and when he did, the suspect raised his keys and sprayed Bishop's eyes with mace, causing Bishop to backpedal and scream. Bishop heard the gunshot, thinking his own weapon had gone off, when suddenly he felt the blood dripping down from his chest. He'd been shot by the suspect; and his head went in a dizzying spiral, and he realized only now that he was lying flat on his back, paralyzed, his life's blood draining from him.

He heard the footsteps of the Phantom as he raced away. Bishop sent up a hue and cry for help. "He's here! Somebody stop him! The murdering bastard's getting away! Damn me! Damn me to hell if I didn't let him get away!"

What few people who hadn't evacuated their rooms began to reluctantly peek from behind their doors, and the sound of a man in obvious distress convinced some to step out of their rooms while others telephoned the desk to ask for medical assistance, and still others dialed 911.

· SIXTEEN ·

The thing we run from is the thing we ran to.
—ROBERT ANTHONY

Jessica literally threw the bills at the cabbie, grabbed her valise, and raced into the Hilton, where she found FBI men had scattered in all directions, one agent taking her aside for her own safety, thinking her a civilian. "I'm FBI!" she shouted, unable to produce her badge and ID while he had her hands in his grasp. She pushed and pulled away from the man when suddenly she saw that several men were being rushed out on stretchers, two of them blackened from having fought their way from a fire, it appeared, their faces having taken the brunt of the flames.

Jessica didn't recognize the first man wheeled by but the second, even with the scarred tissue, looked familiar. She tried to place him when the elevator doors opened again and a third man was wheeled out. The form on the gurney lay still, inert, looking dead, but he had a truly familiar face. To her horror, it was Warren Bishop. He was bloody and unconscious but not fire-blackened or scarred like the other two men.

"Warren!" she called out, racing to him.

A strong-armed medic held her back.

"I'm a doctor," she informed the medic. "Let me go!"

When the agent in charge gave the medic a nod, he

released Jessica, who rushed to Warren's side. "Where are
you taking him?"

"Salt Lake Memorial, ma'am, but first we've got to get
him on life support."

"He's been badly wounded," said a tall, well-dressed
man in a suit beside her now. She turned to face Neil
Gallagher. "We got here as soon as we got your call, but
too late, I'm afraid. I don't know what the hell Bishop was
up to, but he wound up in a running gun-battle with your
fugitive, Dr. Coran. The other two injured men haven't
been thoroughly checked out as yet, but we know they're
not federals, and they have no badges or law enforcement
identification on them. They weren't carry anything to
identify them. In fact, their pockets were stuffed with
weapons, from brass knuckles to Lugers, and with
thousands in cash, but their identities remain a secret."

"What're you saying?"

"They appear to be citizens *of one sort or another.*"

She gauged his meaning. "They were hired guns?"

"They were both carrying what amounts to an arsenal."

Jessica suddenly recalled where she had seen one of the
men, and the name Rollo rolled over in tumbler fashion in
her brain. Frank Lorentian's man. What was Warren doing
in the company of Frank Lorentian's men? It had to be a
mistake, a coincidence, that Lorentian's hired assassins had
located the Phantom just at the moment Warren had. Yet
Warren had, for no accountable reason, jeopardized everything by withholding information from Gallagher and failing to locate her when he arrived in the city, as if . . . as
if he meant to see the killer executed by Lorentian's hench-
men.

These thoughts Jessica kept to herself, but she knew that
Neil Gallagher's suspicions had already been aroused.
"When . . . if Bishop recovers, he's going to have some
explaining to do," Gallagher said in her ear.

"He was following leads, like any good detective. He

didn't know he was so close to the viper when it turned on him," she said. "Simple as that."

Gallagher let it go for the moment.

The Salt Lake City Hilton, a beautiful, prestigious hotel in the heart of Salt Lake City, Utah, served as a surreal backdrop to the sudden turn of events. "Is he . . . is Bishop expected to live?"

"It's a toss-up," replied Gallagher as the medics rushed Warren away.

"What about the other two men, the burn victims?"

"Bad . . . very bad. No guarantees at this point."

"And the perpetrator? Bishop's a crack shot. Did he get him?"

"I'm afraid not."

"Damn it! You mean he's gotten away?"

"My people are scouring every inch of the hotel and surrounding area. He's believed to be afoot. We'll get the SOB."

"I've got to get to the hospital. Be there for Warren."

"He'll be in the operating room for hours. He was conscious when I found him. There's some paralysis to his left side. For you, Doctor, there's reason to stay on here, something you'll want to look at."

Jessica looked into Gallagher's sad eyes for the first time. She knew he must mean the fire room, the body, the killer's latest grim communication. "All right, show me the way."

The crime scene was a familiar one, displaying the same MO, the same cunning, and the same malicious disregard for the suffering of the victim, and in getting away this time, the killer had caused injury to three men, one of whom Jessica cared a great deal about. And settling over the entire scene lay the pervasive mystery of why Warren had attempted to take on the killer without proper backup or planning, and who the two men were who'd accompanied him if not FBI men.

Frustrated, feeling as if her hands were tied while she

was being made to watch this horror played out again and again before her, Jessica stepped into the now all too familiar, grim consequences of the killer's modus operandi, the remnants of fire and murder. In the still-smoldering, gutted death room, she found the brutalized remains of the monster's latest victim, number five.

Neil Gallagher wondered how she could be so calm as she looked down at the charred body on the bed. She could see the confusion in his eyes when she turned to examine the mirror without having been told there was anything remarkable there to see. It was painfully obvious that Gallagher's office had been given little information on the case, and she was partially to blame for this. Again, she wondered why Bishop had kept Gallagher out of it.

She pushed all these thoughts back while she studied the Phantom's latest message, scrawled in grease across the glass surface of the mirror. This one read:

#5 is #5—Wrathful & Sullen

After having a cursory look at the body, and after taking a few samples, going through the motions, Jessica pronounced the victim dead due to her burns brought about through murder. She secretly cursed Eriq Santiva and the entire FBI apparatus for not having raised anything anywhere with the fingerprint evidence. Just the same, to seal the killer's courtroom fate when he was finally caught, she asked Gallagher to get his best fingerprint technician in to search for prints on the telephone and in the written grease message. When Gallagher asked for an explanation, she explained what they knew of the messages, handing him a copy of what J. T. had given her.

Gallagher said, "Damn. I guess I've been out to lunch on this one from the get-go. Sorry, Dr. Coran."

"Not your fault, Gallagher."

"I mean, I knew this guy was on a kill spree, but none of this," he said, indicating the list of messages left at the crime scenes. "I didn't know any of this. I knew about the calls, the connection between you and the killer. Read about it in the papers, but nobody's got this."

Gallagher appeared shaken to his core. To further disturb him, she told him how the killer wrote his messages in the byproduct of the burning body: grease. Gallagher's stony face began twitching when he looked anew at the message, now knowing that it had been written in the burning fat of the victim. But in the best machismo fashion, he held himself together while she added the latest words from the killer to the list she'd kept a running tally of. It now read:

> #1 is #9—Traitors
> #2 is #8—Malicious Frauds
> #3 is #7—Violents
> #4 is #6—Heretics
> #5 is #5—Wrathful & Sullen

No longer did Jessica have to wonder what the numbers and words used by the monster meant, what drove his obsession and murderous rage; she knew now that he meant to fill the nine rungs of Hell in Dante's conception of Hades.

"I've got to get out of here. Got to be with Warren," she told Gallagher.

"Your services, your expertise, Doctor," countered Gallagher, "are needed here."

"Contact Dr. John Thorpe at Ruby Inn, Bryce, Utah. Get him up here for the autopsy. Failing that—"

"Failing that, call Dr. Karl Repasi," said Repasi, who now stood in the doorway.

"*Goddamnit,* Karl," she cursed. "You're starting to worry me. Are you and the Phantom the same man?"

Repasi laughed at the suggestion and said, "Of course not, although I can see why you might believe so, Jessica. No, Warren called me. Told me to be here as soon as I could get away from Bryce. Said you were on to something, and it appears he was right. Where is Warren?''

''Hospital, in a coma.''

''My God! How?''

Gallagher replied, ''As Dr. Coran put it earlier, Bishop took a great risk and it bit him.''

Jessica took Repasi aside. ''I think you know more about why Warren Bishop was here with two strange men than you're saying, Karl. You and Warren had an argument, a fight earlier today. What were you arguing about?''

''He was upset with me over what I'd said to you the other day, nothing more.''

''Nothing more? Nothing having to do with problems in Vegas? Nothing having to do with Frank Lorentian?''

Repasi's facial response gave him away. She had hit a nerve. She pressed her advantage. ''Lorentian got to you, didn't he, Karl? And he got to Warren as well, didn't he?''

''He's a powerful man,'' admitted Repasi.

''Powerful enough to buy himself a medical examiner and an FBI field chief?''

Repasi dropped his gaze.

''Enough said,'' she bitterly replied, storming off.

Neil Gallagher caught up with her and offered her a ride to the hospital. He started in by asking questions about Warren Bishop, how well she knew him, for how long, what sort of man he was. She pleaded for him to give her a break. ''Can we please talk about this later?'' she asked, silencing him. During the long, lonely ride over to where Warren Bishop lay in a coma, Jessica pieced all the parts together. And she felt like a fool. J. T. had warned her to be wary of Frank Lorentian, not to turn a blind eye to his threats or the reach of his power, and what had she done? She'd put the billionaire thug out of her mind and he had in fact blindsided her; he had gotten to someone she loved, and he had ruined Warren Bishop's career in the bureau as a result, managed to get two of his own men maimed for life, no doubt, and they had managed to let the beast they were all after escape once more.

She wondered how charges could be brought and made to stick against Lorentian. She wondered if Warren and the other two men would cooperate once he and they recovered. But realistically speaking, she knew that Frank Lorentian was about as untouchable an outlaw as they came, for he was an outlaw with enough money to buy anyone or anything required to float just above the law, up there with the likes of many another wealthy American baron.

The wait at the hospital was long and drawn out. Finally, Neil Gallagher approached her to say, "I'm sorry about your friend, Bishop. I hope he fully recovers."

"Why? So you can hang him out to dry?"

"No one in the operating rooms up there is going to come out of this unscathed, Dr. Coran. We will get at the truth here. Friend or not, Bishop interfered in this investigation, short-circuited a very real possibility of capturing this madman you've all chased here to Salt Lake. I have my duty, too, Doctor."

"Do your duty, then, Gallagher."

"When this is all over, I'll want a statement from you, Doctor."

"I apparently didn't know Warren as well as I thought."

"Obviously." Gallagher began pacing before her. He'd been watching her write on a notepad.

"Shouldn't you be orchestrating the manhunt for the Phantom?" she asked.

"I have my best, most trusted people on it. Believe me. We'll have him. We'll have him soon. It would help greatly if one of those three upstairs could give us something on the man we're after. And what about you, Dr. Coran? Have you been thoroughly forthcoming about what you know of this maniac who likes to fry women into oblivion?"

"Men and women, it makes no difference with this guy

so long as he has the log to burn," she replied snappishly. "I've told you all I know."

"What's that you've got there?" he asked, pointing to her notepad.

"He intends to kill a total of at least nine victims, according to our math."

"Nine? Why nine? Why not seven, like that film, or twenty or fifty or a hundred?"

"All I know is that he intends to fill up this . . . this ascending and descending"—*hole*, she wanted to say, but instead finished with—"*scale*."

"Scale? The scale you showed me earlier?"

"Which, if he's allowed to carry on, will soon look like this," she replied, handing him the hospital logo notepad she'd been working over.

Gallagher raised it to his eyes and read the newly developed listing for murder. It read:

> #1 is #9—Traitors
> #2 is #8—Malicious Frauds
> #3 is #7—Violents
> #4 is #6—Heretics
> #5 is #5—Wrathful & Sullen
> #6 is #4—?
> #7 is #3—?
> #8 is #2—?
> #9 is #1—the last victim?

"We suspect this maniac has some fixation with themes found in Dante's *Inferno*," she confessed, for giving information to Gallagher, for some reason, always felt like a confession, she thought.

"Dante's *Inferno*?" he reacted, looked up from the new list, and now he stared through Jessica, asking, "What kind of madman is this guy?"

"Some might say he is on a quest of some sort, the meaning of which only he fully comprehends. None of this means anything to the rest of us; it's all concocted in his fevered brain, and I'm sure Dante Alighieri didn't in 1321 ever expect his lurid descriptions of Hell to ever fuel a twentieth-century madman's killing lust.''

He complimented, ''Ingenious of you to figure out this much.''

''Luck and happenstance have had much to do with getting this far, but the fact remains, he's at large. There're too many holes, unanswered questions.''

''Logically, your numbers appear accurate; this is most probably accurate.'' Gallagher pressed a finger into the list. ''The man intends to kill nine victims.''

''Unless he rolls it over, goes back through the rungs to number one again after hitting nine,'' she suggested.

''All madness, complete madness.''

''We have reason to believe he's hearing voices, that he's driven, obsessed, possibly possessed, or at least he believes himself possessed.''

''Of a demon?''

''Or demons. I've sent this list along to Quantico, from where it has now gone out to the nation's leading academicians and the mental health professionals in the hope someone somewhere might recognize the thinking. Put it together with the fevered mind that has obsessed over it.''

''Yeah, I see, like they did in the Unabomber case.''

''Yeah, something like that.''

''I read something about it.''

''Read something about it? The Unabomber case, you mean?''

''No, no . . . your case, Dr. Coran.''

''Where?''

''Your earlier list, the first one you showed me. It was published in *The New York Times,* the *L.A. Times,* and every other major newspaper in the country as well as being aired on national television.''

''No one told me!''

''Sorry, I thought you knew.''

"I've been . . . out of touch. . . ."

"Thinking seems sound enough. Someone, somewhere must know this head case and his background, where he lives, right?"

"Yeah . . . we can only hope. We've also got a line of inquiry following an itinerary, a bus schedule we believe he is on. That's how I got here as quickly as I did."

"Yeah, you mentioned as much when you first informed us."

Jessica wondered how Repasi was connected to Lorentian, and she decided that Karl was hired to keep a running tab on the progress in the case, and that Warren, who had somehow become hopelessly indebted to Frank Lorentian, had succumbed to using his office for Lorentian's personal vendetta in this matter. Repasi was in the hospital, too, but he was busy downstairs with the autopsy on the latest victim, whom Jessica felt guilty over since she had not even gotten the woman's name.

"I'm going down to the morgue to see Dr. Repasi," she told Gallagher.

"I'll accompany you, Doctor."

"As you wish."

They found Repasi just finishing up. When he saw them, he said, "No surprises. Same MO down to the gasoline hot spots about face and upper torso."

Jessica needed to get away from the body and the smell of smoldering flesh adhering to the room. She felt as if she could no longer breathe. Gallagher, a sensitive man, saw her need and ushered her out almost as soon as he'd accompanied her into the morgue.

Gallagher escorted her to a hallway, and at the end of the corridor they found a balcony that overlooked the now darkened city. The warm, fresh air felt good on Jessica's skin, and it invaded her nostrils, attempting battle with the odors from the death room that had taken hold.

Gallagher now asked, "This bus itinerary—it tells you

where his next destination will be? Can we get there before him?''

''I'd hoped that for Salt Lake, but we were too late for Salt Lake.''

''Thanks to Bishop, yes.''

''I wish you wouldn't condemn Warren before he's even had a chance to . . . to defend himself.''

''All right, sorry again. I'll give him the benefit of a doubt. Meantime, where is the killer's next stop, if you don't mind sharing?''

''Wyoming. Jackson Hole, Wyoming, I believe,'' she replied. ''Can you get me there quickly?''

''As soon as you're ready to go.''

''I have to know first how Warren is doing.''

''The other side of the hospital, there's a helipad. We can take off from here together for Wyoming. It's not far by air.''

She sighed, taking in a deep breath of the clear air, and despite the humid night, a chill, made primarily of fear, wafted through her nerves as she contemplated her next encounter with this madman who'd created some sort of fantasy involving Dante's *Inferno,* Satan, nine to possibly eighteen murders, and Jessica Coran. She leaned in against the balcony, steadying herself, feeling Neil Gallagher's reassuring hand on her shoulder, hearing his whispered words.

''This must be a nightmare for you. I've only seen the one example of this madman's work. You've now seen five. Now that we know what bus he's traveling on,'' suggested Gallagher, ''we're staking it out to see if he's stupid enough to attempt another boarding tomorrow morning. Frankly, I don't hold out any hope of his doing so, but as they say, crime makes you stupid, so. . . . And frankly, Doctor, I'm a bit confused why you and the others chasing him didn't stop and board the bus before it got this far.''

''Don't you think that Warren must've given it thought? Radio the state patrol and surround the bus? Maybe get everyone inside killed? But you've got to realize, we only learned for certain that he was on that specific bus after his arrival here in Salt Lake. There was no opportunity to take him out somewhere along the road before he became a Salt Lake problem, Gallagher.''

''I see.''

''Besides, there're some thirty or so other passengers on that bus.''

''Of course. And if we didn't know before how dangerous it is to approach this lunatic, we certainly know now, don't we?''

''Yes, of course. Any attempt at an assault on the bus would have cost more lives.''

''All the same, this morning, when the bus pulls from the curb, it will do so only after a thorough check by my people. By the way, the victim of the fire was a tourist to our city, a passenger on another tour bus. Her name was Evelyn Grey.''

''We know he's crazy, but he's also cunning. It's highly unlikely he'll rejoin the tour group or follow the now known path of tour thirteen fourteen on bus sixty-seven of the VisionQuest lines. Still, he has a plan that involves killing four more people at the very least. Whether he shows up in Jackson Hole or not is anyone's guess. And as for staking out the bus, he now knows we're on to him, close on his trail. He's hardly likely to show up tomorrow morning to board that bus.''

''All the same, Quantico has asked for my full support, and as far as I'm concerned, Doctor, you people need all the help you can get. From here on out, I call the shots. Two of my men are guarding Bishop and those two questionable fellows whose faces were rearranged by your killer, possibly dying, certainly maimed for life, due to the ineptness of the investigation thus far. Now, tomorrow morning, my men will be there when tour number thirteen fourteen readies to leave the Hilton. We've interviewed the driver and the tour guide, and they know of our interest in

Mr. Dunlap, should they ever lay eyes on him again.''

"He's not a fool."

"We'll take him down, one way or another. The bus driver is being replaced by an agent, and we already have the other end covered, too."

"What do you mean?"

"At Jackson Hole. There we'll greet the bus as the owner-operators of this place he would have been staying at tonight, a place called the Wagon Wheel Motel."

"If you knew where his next destination was, why'd you bother asking me?"

"Call it a test."

"I see."

"After Bishop's performance . . . rather hard to know whom to trust."

"Sure . . . I can understand that." Jessica inwardly fumed, but she kept careful control of herself. "Refreshing to find a man with a plan," she told him, thinking his plan foolhardy and full of holes.

Still, she kept silent. "Do it." She knew that Gallagher's plans would net him nothing, that the killer wanted to be caught up with by one person alone: her. That his bread crumbs and leavings thus far had all pointed to one thing: that she be his ninth, his last victim. He was no fool. He would not return to the company of tourists on a bus with a known itinerary, not now, now that they'd come so close to catching him. If nothing else, Warren had thrown a scare into the fiend.

"Then you will join us in Wyoming, Dr. Coran?"

"Go ahead without me. I'm here until Warren regains consciousness."

Still awaiting news at Salt Lake Memorial Hospital, Jessica finally learned that Warren Bishop remained in an hours-long intensive surgery and that he wasn't expected to regain consciousness anytime soon after the operation, nor would he soon have use of his left side even if he should survive the surgery. The killer's bullet had been a spreader, a single bullet exploding from a cut jacket, creating a series of winding, twisting, tearing pellets coursing through Warren's body. He'd been wearing a Spectra vest, a technically superior vest to the Kevlar line most FBI men were still wearing, but the bullet entered at close proximity, the powder burns on his clothes telling the story, and the bullet entered just above the sternum, where the vest hadn't been completely secured by Bishop. From there, the bullet took its winding courses—up, down, around, back and forth, cutting small but deadly paths through vital organs, arteries, and veins.

While she waited, Jessica was deserted by Neil Gallagher, who'd conferred with Dr. Karl Repasi and had invited Repasi to join him in the helicopter to Jackson Hole, Wyoming. With this team away and awaiting the next strike of the cobra at the next stop on the killer's itinerary—an itinerary that may well have changed by now—Jessica at least felt some breathing space.

She remained uncertain of the killer's path now, whether he would indeed show himself in Jackson Hole, but just the same, she and Gallagher had little else to go on. An hour after Gallagher and Repasi had left her, Jessica was joined by J. T., who swept her up in his arms. They held one another for a long time, J. T. asking all in one breathless fell swoop, "How's-Bishop-doing, how're-you-Jess, 'n-what-happened?"

"Bishop's torn up on the inside like a garden soaker. If he survives, his prognosis for a full recovery isn't good." Tears filled Jessica's eyes. "Worst of it is, John, he used us, used both of us."

"Used?"

Jessica confided what little she understood and suspected of Bishop's botched attempt at ridding the world of the Phantom via Frank Lorentian's hired thugs.

"He must've been in to Lorentian big time from the get-go,'' said J. T. ''And to think, we never suspected him of a thing.''

''We may never know exactly what kind of debt he owed to Frank Lorentian, if he doesn't survive.''

''What about the other two, Lorentian's goons?''

''Second-degree burns to the face; neither man may ever see again. One of them was that guy we met at Lorentian's, his bodyguard Rollo.''

''I knew we'd be dogged by Frank Lorentian. I just knew it. But I thought it was Repasi.''

''Karl Repasi, too, was keeping tabs on us—for Warren, near as I can tell. Warren was paying Karl to keep him informed of our movements.''

''That explains a lot.'' J. T. again comforted her and said, ''I'm sorry about all this, Jess. Really I am. I know you and Bishop go back a long way.''

''I thought I knew him.''

''Don't be too hard on yourself, Jess. I didn't suspect the man of a thing, either, certainly nothing like this.''

''Meanwhile, a killer goes free. We could've had him, John! Damn Warren for that, damn him.''

Again J. T. held her, trying to absorb her pain. In a moment she pulled away, dabbing tears from her eyes with a handkerchief that appeared to have seen a great deal of use this night. It was nearing 3:00 A.M.

She stepped away from him, bent, and lifted a notepad she'd been working on before he'd arrived. ''Oh, by the way, J. T., look at this and give me your appraisal. I've had a lot of time on my hands here, and I've been reading Dante's *Inferno,* and the killer's list, all the missing pieces, you know?''

He reached out for the proffered notebook, nodding. ''Yeah, what about the missing pieces?''

''I think I know what they are, what they'll be when they come.''

J. T. gaped at her, the notepad half in his hands, half in

hers. She wanted to push it fully into his hands like a hot potato.

The notepad was filled with the information she wished to share with Thorpe, information no one else had. "Working this out is the only thing that's kept me sane in this place, waiting word on Warren," she told him. "Go ahead, check my work. What do you think? You think the killer's final list will look like this?" She tore off a sheet from the notepad she held in her hand.

J. T. stared at the long list Jessica had completed. He sat down, holding the list before him, simply whistling aloud. The notepad read:

> #1 is #9—Traitors
> #2 is #8—Malicious Frauds
> #3 is #7—Violents
> #4 is #6—Heretics
> #5 is #5—Wrathful & Sullen
> #6 is #4—Avaricious & Prodigal
> #7 is #3—Gluttonous
> #8 is #2—Lustful
> #9 is #1—(the last victim?) sent into
> Limbo . . . through the Vestibule and
> over the River Acheron

"Avaricious and Prodigal, Gluttonous and Lustful, you know the labels now from your research." J. T. scrunched up his eyes and asked, "The Vestibule? Vestibule? To where? And the River Acheron?"

"Entryway to Hell," she explained. "Hellsmouth, like Mammoth, maybe. Something he said over the phone to me once. I need to get to an atlas."

"Do you mean to tell me that this . . . all this has been some elaborate scheme simply to find a way to tell Jessica Coran to . . . to go to Hell?"

"Very funny, my friend, but I think he has more in mind than that; I believe he wants to personally send me to Hell.

Here.'' She tore off a second sheet from her notepad. ''Take a look at this, too.''

J. T. now stared at a set of concentric circles, each circle representing a level in Hades, or in the mind of the killer . . . or both. The notepaper read:

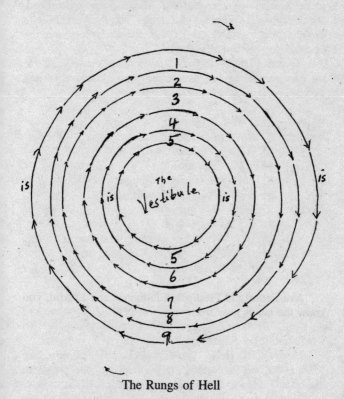

The Rungs of Hell

· SEVENTEEN ·

Lord grant me patience, and I want it right now.
                                        —ANONYMOUS

A solemn, overweight doctor in sneakers and green scrubs entered the waiting room, and Jessica leaped to her feet. The doctor explained that his portion of the operation— the intestinal tract—was finished, but that there were other complications, and that their vigil could go on for another two or three hours. "Sorry," finished the doctor, "but he was badly chewed up, internally."

"Any improvement on his prognosis, Doctor?" asked Jessica.

"I'm afraid not."

"Then it'll be hours before he's out of intensive care."

"Yes, it will. Again, I'm sorry I can't have better news for you."

Jessica knew she didn't have that kind of time, not if she wished to catch a killer, yet her heart tugged at her to be here with Warren should he recover. Should he . . . She banned her final thought.

A male nurse entered and asked if there was a Doctor Jessica Coran in the waiting room. "Telephone call at the desk for you," he announced.

Jessica looked from the nurse to J. T., a birdlike fear flitting before her mind's eye, a thought fully formed: *Who knows I'm here?*

J. T., reading her thoughts, supplied an answer: "Santiva's got to have had word by now on what's happened here. He'll want a full report."

Jessica nodded and asked the nurse to lead the way. She followed the young man to the nurses' station; he pointed to a small, enclosed office, saying, "You can take it in there."

Being alone in the room with the phone was like standing in a pit with a snake. She stared at the waiting phone where it blinked and winked up at her. Finally, she took the receiver in hand and pounced on the hold button. "Hello."

Santiva barked, "Jessica, what in hell's going on there? I thought you said this Bishop fellow was top drawer, and now I learn he's compromised an entire operation?"

"Eriq, I don't know what was going down with Warren," she lied, not wishing to discuss it now, and certainly not over the phone. "All we know for certain is that he may not make it through the night, and even if he does, he'll be paralyzed, possibly for life." She choked on the facts.

"I'm sorry to hear that. Damn it, and just when we've gotten a line on what the list is getting at, too, Jessica."

"Oh, really?"

"A Professor William Milton Jarvis, Medieval Studies Department at Georgetown University, tracked it to—"

"Really, my old alma mater? Don't tell me," she replied, spoiling his moment, "Dante's *Inferno,* right?"

"How did you know? Damn it, you're always a step ahead."

"It finally dawned on me," she half-lied, no time for detailed long-distance explanations. "And I've been reading the book since. We'll fax you our latest suspicions and an updated list as soon as possible."

"I'm coming out there to be with you," he countered.

"It's not necessary, Eriq."

"I think it is, at this juncture, absolutely necessary. I'm flying out to Salt Lake."

"Well, if you must come, make it Wyoming."

"Wyoming?"

"Jackson Hole."

"Where the president vacations?"

"One and the same. Ever been there?"

"A splendid, beautiful area, and yes, I've been there and I know how to get there from here, yes."

"There are nine rungs of Hell, Eriq, and this guy appears to be populating each with each of his victims. He's going to kill at least three, possibly four more times before he ends it, if we allow him to. Is it too damn much to hope we end it?"

"I want to be on hand, help any way I can, Jess. I'll meet you in Jackson Hole. Meanwhile, fax any new developments to the BSU; I can't sit idly by any longer, Jess. And Jess—"

"Yes?"

"I am one step ahead of you on one lead we got on this guy."

"What kind of a lead?" She remained skeptical.

"How about a name?"

"A name?"

"Feydor Dorphmann, spelled . . ." He slowed to spell the name accurately for her.

At her end, Jessica took time to write it down.

"How did you get the man's name? How accurate is this information?"

"Right on, Jess. We sent his ugly little cryptograms to all major mental health facilities in the country, as you suggested, and bingo, up comes one in San Francisco called the Lombardh Institute for the Mentally Insane, where this Dorphmann character lived for a time."

"For a time?"

"Eight years without harming a soul. Then he's released—"

"Released when?"

"Seven months ago, and not three months passed when

one of his doctors, a guy named Wetherbine, Dr. Stuart Wetherbine, is stabbed repeatedly with a knife and set aflame in an alleyway. Coincidence?''

''No one in San Francisco put those two facts together?''

''Dorphmann disappeared. He's been wanted ever since, but no one's seen him.''

Jessica thought about the time line. ''He murders his doctor three months after release, then four months pass before he goes on his kill spree? Not your usual serial killer, Eriq. Tell me, what was he in for?''

''Self-inflicted wounds—burning himself. Seems he's something of a masochist. Also delusional, something about seeing aliens behind his eyelids, that sort of thing.''

''Aliens?''

''Aliens, elves, creatures from Hell, you name it.''

''So his family committed him to the institution?''

''No, I spoke directly to the parents, both aged, in their seventies, and both didn't want anything to do with Feydor and didn't know he'd been released. I'm told they were frightened of him all their lives, something about his having burned living things—cats, dogs, you know—when he was a kid.''

''Didn't the institution notify the parents when they released the man?''

''Said they couldn't locate them. Strangely enough, they weren't under any legal obligation to notify the next of kin since this Feydor guy had actually committed himself and was of age.''

''He committed himself to eight years in a mental facility. That'll help him at trial,'' she half-joked, knowing a defense lawyer could make hay with this fact. Maybe Frank Lorentian's solution wasn't so far off the wall.

''Yeah,'' continued Santiva, ''claiming he feared he'd hurt someone if he wasn't under constant watch.''

''Damn it, this will help him at trial then. He commits himself for fear he'll harm someone, they release him, he does exactly as he feared and worse, and the defense has a hole large enough to drive a full-grown elephant through. Maybe that was Warren's concern, too, Eriq.''

''Be that as it may, we still have to catch the fiend before any defense lawyers and activists praise him.''

She smiled at this. ''Still, what do we have that ties Dorphmann irrevocably to our case? How can you be sure he's the same man who's behind these fire crimes?''

''The greaseprints . . .''

''From the mirrors?''

''*Mirror instinct*, you might say. When you figured that out, Jess, you nailed the bastard. The mental facility kept his prints on file.''

''Terrific.''

''How did you know? About the prints in the mirror grease? Who else would've given it a thought?''

''I knew instinctively because I knew this guy intentionally leaves me his crumbs. He's been testing my mettle from the beginning.''

''The important thing is the prints found a match with this guy. They match Dorphmann's medical records.''

''Bingo,'' she added. ''What about a photo of the son-ofa—''

''It's eight years old, and it's not too good. His entrance file at Lombardh, but it's being faxed to Gallagher's office, Vegas, Bozeman, Casper as we speak. It should catch up to you in a few.''

''Excellent. Now we can put a face with this pervert.''

''Too bad your eyewitness, Bishop, is under. Could give us valuable insight into what the creep looks like today.''

''Did you do a computer-aged enhancement of the photo?''

''Faxed alongside the original.''

''Dorphmann, Feydor Dorphmann,'' she repeated the name. It somehow helped tremendously to know the name of the maniac she'd been pursuing, and to know that soon she'd be able to look into his photographic eyes. It gave her a sense that he was human after all, and not at all the Antichrist, the all-powerful being he had become in the minds of his victims before their horrible deaths, and in her mind at each moment she had heard the final cries of his victims.

"Finally, we're seeing a turn in the case," Santiva said, interrupting her thoughts.

"What other good news are you hoarding, Eriq?"

"Shoeprint is this guy Dorphmann's size as well, and you were right about the photographic paper you found. From a Polaroid Instamatic. The creep is keeping an album."

Such a practice among serial killers wasn't unusual. She recalled how the vicious killer Kowona, in Hawaii, had kept such a photo album of his victims.

"We're putting the picture on the wires with a full alert, all points, concentrating heavily on your area and the area you're tracking, Jess."

"Excellent. Maybe we can now throw some fear back his way."

"I'll look for you in Jackson Hole, Jessica."

"Yes, see you there."

With the line cut, standing now with the receiver in her hand, Jessica wondered how much more she could endure. She thought of Warren Bishop, lying on the operating table, fighting for his life; she thought of the two thugs, Rollo and John Doe, agents of Lorentian, men who'd never be capable of resuming their lives as usual or their duties for Lorentian or anyone else, ever again, should they live past this night. Then it hit her, an idea that might save lives.

"Where's your hospital spokesperson?" she suddenly asked the lady sitting at a nearby desk, typing away.

"Spokesperson?"

"Who will deal with the press regarding the three men in your hospital in critical condition?"

"That would be PR, Mrs. Crighten, down the hall to your right. Can't miss it."

Jessica found Mrs. Florence Crighten on her phone, her desk in disarray. She was already dealing with the press over the FBI matter, the gunshot and burn victims in the hospital's care.

Jessica pressed the cut-off button on the woman's phone, flashing her badge as she said, "Your government needs you. We need your help, Mrs. Crighten."

Growing gracefully into middle age, Mrs. Crighten's slim waistline and ample bust spoke of a onetime party girl who'd decided a career much more productive. She'd obviously worked extremely hard to get to where she sat atop the PR pinnacle of this medical establishment. Her soft, round tones and tawny black complexion made her the perfect person to pitch news—good, bad, or indifferent.

"How can I help?"

"I want a false report sent out to the newspapers."

"What?" The woman instantly shook her head, as if Jessica had suggested something vile, something perverted. "I can't do that."

"Even if it saves lives?"

Now Mrs. Crighten's lips closed and pursed. "What kind of misinformation are we talking about? And how will it save lives?"

"Trust me, it will save lives. Two, possibly three lives, maybe more."

"Explain further."

Jessica smiled, somehow knowing that she'd come to the right woman. She felt hopeful that now she could turn the tables on the Phantom. She explained to Mrs. Crighten how the killer had been operating. She laid out before Mrs. Crighten's astonished eyes the killer's cryptograms, telling her how they'd been left, how they'd been written using the victims' own fatty secretions, after they were burned alive. She told of the phone calls, how much she personally had suffered. Finally she got around to exactly how she planned to confuse the killer.

"If three men die here tonight, then the killer has reached eight victims for his deadly charade, if he counts his shooting victim, Chief of Operations Agent Warren Bishop. That would leave only one blank space to fill in his demented, infernal game. That leaves only one more victim."

"If he takes Agent Bishop's death, and the death of the other two agents who were burned in the fire as equal, on a par with one of his burn victims," she replied. "I see. But what if he doesn't take Bishop's death as enough?"

"Then we'll have saved two lives instead of three."

"Yes, I see, but suppose he, the killer, doesn't want to count any of them?"

"He will. He's anxious for this to be over . . ."

"How do you know that?"

"We have a relationship," Jessica firmly said. "I believe—no, I *know*—how he thinks. He believes everything happens for a reason. He's quite fatalistic. He'll at the very least count the burn victims; he'll see them as reward for carrying out his . . . his duties, his responsibilities, thus—"

"Duties," muttered Mrs. Crighten, shivering where she sat, "responsibilities."

"He's quite mad."

"Of that I'm sure."

"Will you put the misinformation out there?"

"It could backfire. Family members must be alerted to the truth before it gets around. It could cost me my job."

"The FBI made you do it?"

The woman smiled and took Jessica's hands in hers. "We'll do it."

Jessica gave her a prepared statement that she had written out in longhand. It gave names for the additional two agents as Agent Thom Morganstern and Agent Raleigh Howler. To protect his office from embarrassment, Gallagher had earlier allowed hospital authorities to treat three FBI agents and not just one, but he'd left all three under heavy guard.

Finished here, Jessica said to Mrs. Crighten, "Thank you . . . thank you. . . . Now, how do I get to Salt Lake's largest TV station and newspaper office?"

Crighten called in her aide, telling the young woman to chauffeur Agent Coran to wherever she wished, when Crighten's phone rang.

Jessica and the aide were halfway out the door when Mrs. Crighten announced that the call was for Jessica. "I think it's one of your people," she cheerily said, offering the phone to Jessica. "He says he has information for you alone, Dr. Coran."

Jessica took the phone and immediately recognized the voice of the killer at the other end as he said, "Satan, disguised as a one-eyed Minotaur, carried me on one *hell* of a journey until I could see down into an endless hole where flesh and fire, like wick and candle, were one."

"Dorphmann," she let his name fall on him like a bomb, "Feydor Dorphmann, we know now who you are and why you're driven to kill."

It was as if she were whistling in a wind tunnel; the surprise seemed to have no effect on Dorphmann as he continued speaking over her. "The journey kept me always on a downward spiral, and there were rungs on either side of the belly of this place, like they were made from Satan's ribs, you see. . . ."

"Just as in Dante's *Inferno*," she suggested. "But Feydor, don't you see? If you turn yourself in now, I'll get help for you."

"Perhaps the historic Dante Alighieri in the 1300s was himself visited by Satan, because Satan wants us to praise him, you know, Dr. Coran. He wants us to never forget his presence. He must've made Dante's life a living hell like mine, turning his skin to boils and red rashes, making it impossible to live in his skin. He must've persuaded

Dante to chronicle his domain, his dark kingdom. He's very good at persuasion techniques, you know, far superior to your FBI in that regard.''

''You don't have to kill any more people, Feydor,'' she told him. ''You've killed eight now by our count.''

Jessica watched Crighten's face as it turned ashen grey with the realization that the killer was on the hospital line, her line. Feydor Dorphmann paused momentarily at her words but then continued, ''He got Dante to sing the praises of Hades. . . .''

''The two men you burned during your escape, two FBI agents, and a third you shot, Feydor. They've all died here at the hospital.''

''But those killings were incidental, not part of the bargain.''

''How do you know that? Satan works in mysterious ways, Feydor.''

''They all must die by fire, all but one—you, Doctor. . . .''

''But these men did die by fire.''

''Two of them, yes.''

''Then why not count Dr. Stuart Wetherbine, Feydor? You torched his body, remember? And he was trying to help you, remember?''

This silenced Feydor momentarily. ''Then you do know all about me. Good, Doctor . . . very good. Now you will come for me all the more.''

''What about it, Feydor? What about Wetherbine in San Francisco and the two agents you burned to death here in Salt Lake? It means you can be finished with your work, whatever contract you made with . . . with Satan that much sooner, Feydor.''

''Perhaps . . . perhaps . . .''

She prayed he was considering the possibility she held out to him.

He coldly said, ''I'll have to wait, see what *he* says about all this.''

"Feydor, every FBI agent in the territory, every cop with a gun is now going to shoot to kill, knowing you killed three of their own. The stakes have gone up, Dorphmann. We not only know who you are, Feydor, but we know your shoe size and preference, we have your fingerprints and likeness, and it will appear in every newspaper and on every television screen across this country. There's no place you can hide now."

"Don't waste your breath, Dr. Coran. I've had assurances none of that will matter once I've finished with you."

"Even if you succeed, Feydor, in killing me, number nine, there'll be no place for you to hide."

"Satan will provide. He's already removed my fingerprints and my hair, and he's working on my bone structure, my height, weight, skin color. You see, it's all part of the deal."

How do you bargain with a madman? she wondered. "Give yourself up, give yourself up to me this moment. Tell me where you are and I'll come there personally to see no harm comes to you." It was a half-truth. If he invited her, she would see to it he was put out of his misery before he could fire-kill her.

"Harm? You have no idea how much harm I've already gone through, you foolish bitch. No, I won't be giving myself up. There's still work to do. Still, I do want you to come for me."

"Where and when?" she replied instantly, challenging him.

"Soon, soon now you will know."

She knew it was hopeless, but to encourage him, she added, "Read the morning papers, Feydor, then contact me again if you don't believe me. Will you do that, Feydor?"

"I told you! I have to talk to *him*."

"Where are you now?" she pleaded. "Are you still in the city?"

He cut her off.

Jessica looked up to see Mrs. Crighten staring at her with the frozen look of a statue, shaken at hearing just one side of Jessica's conversation with the killer. "I wouldn't have your job for all the money and prestige in this life," Mrs. Crighten finally said.

Jessica turned to the aide and said, "Let's go."

As Jessica was about to leave the hospital, J. T. located her and shouted for her to wait. She'd already gotten comfortable in the car and was about to depart from the parking garage. "Mrs. Crighten told me where I could find you, Jess. You're taking on too much alone again. Let me help you," he pleaded.

"You can help by being here when Warren Bishop recovers. He's going to need a familiar face at his bedside. Will you be there, John?"

He took in a deep breath. "Mrs. Crighten told me he called you at her office. How does this fiend find you, Jess? It's uncanny. It's almost as if—"

"As if what?"

"Nothing, never mind."

"You starting to think like Repasi, that we . . . the killer and I have some sort of link?"

"No, no . . . nothing like that, Jess."

"Then what? That there's some kind of supernatural psychic link at work? What?"

"I don't know."

"He's shrewd, smart, J. T. He knows we'd be at an area hospital; he goes the rounds with the yellow pages, just like you or me. That's all."

"Where'll you be, Jess?"

"Getting the story out. Talk to Crighten about it. We're going to spread the news that the Phantom has added three more kills to his kill list."

"Hey, I get it. Fill up his list for him and maybe no one else will be hurt on your account, right?"

She gritted her teeth before replying, "You really are beginning to sound like Karl."

"I think it's a brilliant stroke, Jess."

"Only if it works. Now, let me put it into motion."

"Have you cleared it with headquarters?"

"No, no, I haven't. Something like this, the fewer who know the real story, the better."

"All the same, if you want, I'll let Santiva in on the facts."

She nodded. "Yeah, do that. And J. T., thanks again."

"Where'll you be after you finish up with the newspeople?"

"On to Jackson Hole with the others, it would appear."

"Gotcha. I'll join you there as soon as possible."

The car pulled from the lot at Jessica's request. The car pulled upward on a slanting concrete hill and out into the predawn light of Salt Lake City. "Take me to the major TV stations first," she asked Crighten's aide, who yawned and apologized, saying she was not used to such crazy hours.

Jessica finished the rounds of TV and newspaper offices in Greater Salt Lake City and then said good-bye to Crighten's aide Sue Norris when the young woman dropped her off at Gallagher's nondescript FBI branch headquarters building. With Gallagher, Repasi, and that crew long ago off to Jackson Hole, Wyoming, a beautiful western town turned tourist haven nestled in Snake River Valley, amid the foothills of the Grand Tetons, Jessica freely acquired the fax forwarded to Salt Lake City headquarters from Eriq Santiva. As promised, she had every stitch of information they had on Feydor Dorphmann forwarded to the *Salt Lake Herald*. Returning to the *Herald* editors, she orchestrated the morning headline and layout of photo and computer-enhanced photo of the killer, alongside a sidebar carrying what Jessica and J. T had composed of the killer's cryptograms and the nine rungs of Hades in Dante's *Inferno*.

In the paper account, Morganstern and Howler were listed as fire victims number six and seven and Bishop as murder victim number eight, leaving only one rung to fill. The list now appeared:

#1 is #9—Traitors	Lorentian
#2 is #8—Malicious Frauds	Flanders
#3 is #7—Violents	Martin
#4 is #6—Heretics	Whitaker
#5 is #5—Wrathful & Sullen	Grey
#6 is #4—Avaricious & Prodigal	Morganstern
#7 is #3—Gluttonous	Howler
#8 is #2—Lustful	Bishop

#9 is #1—(the last victim?) sent into Limbo . . . through the Vestibule and over the River Acheron

The city editor and crime editor at the *Salt Lake Herald* had, upon Jessica's initial visit, immediately dispatched their best reporters to the phones and the hospital for verification of Jessica's story. At the hospital, Mrs. Crighten held a press conference, detailing the kinds of wounds each of the *three* FBI agents had endured, how the doctors worked tirelessly on their behalf, but that all attempts had met with unsuccessful results in the cases of all three men. Beside Mrs. Crighten, there on the podium, doctors lamented the conditions they'd had to work under, their long faces giving credence to the ruse. Jessica watched televised news reports from the city desk editor's office. Her plan was working like a charm.

The newspapermen were ecstatic to get an exclusive from the famed Dr. Jessica Coran, but for it, Jessica bargained: They must release it to every other news wire service in the country. She wanted to be certain that Feydor Dorphmann, wherever he was, knew that she knew that he knew that she knew . . .

At the newspaper office, Jessica found huge maps of

Utah along one wall, each detailing the geographic beauty of the state, distances, and famous tourist attractions. On another wall, a similar map of Wyoming hung, and Jessica stared at the roads leading from Salt Lake City to Jackson Hole, Wyoming, and she realized for the first time in years just how close Jackson Hole was to Yellowstone National Park.

"Doing a travel and leisure piece on Wyoming," said a mild-mannered female editor who noticed Jessica's interest in the map. "You know, places to get away to that aren't too far and aren't too expensive for the middle crowd here in Salt Lake."

"I'm interested in Yellowstone," Jessica told her. "You have any detail maps of Yellowstone?"

"It's one of the major highlight of the article, and yes, I do." The woman dug into a desk and came up with a detailed map of the park itself, spreading it in lumpy and crude fashion across the papers and junk that populated the top of her desk. "It's really a breathtaking, fantastic place, almost like stepping onto another planet," said the editor.

Jessica studied the map, which brought back instant memories of a time when she had once visited Yellowstone National Park as a young assistant M.E. on vacation with a girlfriend. "Yes, I once visited Yellowstone, many years ago," Jessica told the other woman as she studied the large yellow mass, the park that formed the northwestern corner of the state of Wyoming.

"My husband and the boys loved it," the woman continued. "The Grand Canyon of the Yellowstone, that was their favorite, and the fishing, of course. Me, I became fascinated with the geysers and hot springs and mud pots."

Jessica scanned the map, her eyes gliding as if directed by a Ouija board pointer to a select few of the more than ten thousand geysers, hot springs, and boiling mud pots in the park, gasping at their resemblance to Feydor's words of earlier. There on the map, she read of the Devil's Well and Hellsmouth geysers in Lower Geyser Basin near Old Faithful and Old Faithful Lodge. A flood of memories, too disconnected and too disorganized at the moment to make any but fleeting sense to her, assaulted her senses while the editor continued to carry on about the grandeur that was Yellowstone.

"And can you imagine people coming here from the East and telling us, the Forestry Service in particular, that we need to build protective walls and fences throughout the parks? What utter nonsense. People have no idea the scale of nature out here. Why, it's enormous. Would anyone seriously entertain the thought of putting a fence around the Serengeti Plains in Tanzania or Victoria Falls or Niagara for that matter?"

Jessica only half-heard the woman. Her mind was on Dorphmann. Feydor's thinking, his quest, came into full focus. Finally, Jessica knew where he'd been headed from day one, what his final destination must be, and how he planned to kill victim number nine. "May I keep this map?"

"Ahhh, sure, sure . . . I've got enough material on the park that I don't need it any longer. I've pretty well put the story to bed."

"Whatever it cost." She dug into her purse.

"No, take it. Anything to help get this madman you're chasing. And I'm dreadfully sorry about those three brave agents."

Jessica swallowed her desire to confide any sliver of truth to the woman. "Yes, it has hit the agency hard, just as the previous five murders by this maniac have."

"Good luck on your manhunt, Dr. Coran. We all know one thing."

"And what's that?" she asked, folding the Yellowstone map back into its original shape.

"That you're the best person for the job."

"Thank you. I hope that's so."

"Well, obviously, from what you've told us, the killer certainly thinks so."

She smiled for the first time in twenty-four hours. "Yes. Yes, that certainly is so."

After the phony story was put to bed, a phone call to the hospital told her that Bishop died at 3:19 A.M. while still on the table, undergoing surgery, and that Agents Morganstern and Howler had also both died of wounds suffered in the fire. Excellent, she thought. Mrs. Crighten had played her part well.

· EIGHTEEN ·

*I do not believe in a fate that falls on men however they act;
but I do believe in a fate that falls on men unless they act.*
—G. K. CHESTERTON

An all-points bulletin stretching nationwide was put out on
Dorphmann, but Jessica knew that any resulting action
would likely only net authorities a few arrests here and
there of look-alikes, deadbeat fathers, estranged boyfriends, and the like. Dorphmann had hinted that he had
physically altered his appearance already, or rather that
Satan had done so for him. He had burned off his fingerprints, thinking this crucial to his living the life of a non-
fugitive once he'd finished the Devil's work he'd been put
to; he had shaved his head, had likely put on some weight
given the free food provided by the tour package. He might
have altered his appearance in other ways, such as changing the color of his eyes, from contact green to frame
glasses and blue eyes. There was little telling, but he obviously knew something about makeup and diversion and
escape tactics, as he'd proven in Vegas and now in Salt
Lake City.

Jessica had returned to her hotel room after leaving the
newspaper office, and now she felt badly that she couldn't
be beside Warren Bishop when he opened his eyes, but
there appeared no help for it. She had a rendezvous with
a madman, a rendezvous that was long in coming, one she
could put off no longer. She meant to put an end to Feydor

Dorphmann's maniacal kill spree so that no one else would ever suffer at his hand again.

She telephoned the hospital and got hold of John Thorpe, whose sleepy voice slurred a good morning to her. It was 9:40 A.M.

"Anything new on Bishop?" she asked.

"He's dead, or haven't you heard?" J. T. quipped.

She pleaded with J. T., "Please stay by his side, John."

"I will, for you, Jess. Meanwhile, I'll go over Repasi's findings on the Grey woman, see if he missed anything or failed to tell us anything of a vital nature we don't already know, right?"

"Clever boy."

J. T. broke the news to her that he'd gotten hold of Chief Santiva, who was en route to Jackson Hole, to report Bishop's true condition and why they had felt it necessary to plant the phony story.

"How'd he take it?" she asked.

"He thought it a long shot, but agreed we had little else to gamble on with this nutcase, so he's okay with it, Jess. He still doesn't understand what Bishop and the 'other two agents' thought they were doing. He still doesn't know about the long arm of Frank Lorentian in this matter."

"He'll know soon enough, when he touches down at Jackson Hole. Gallagher will give him an earful, no doubt."

Jessica thanked J. T., finishing with, "For all you've done, John, over the years, thanks."

"Hey, don't go getting maudlin on me, Jess. As for sitting this out with Bishop, it's no big deal. You're needed up in Wyoming, so get saddled up and get going. And don't worry about Warren. On the QT, they're calling him a fighter."

"Has his prognosis improved?" she hopefully asked.

"His condition is stable but still critical."

"Damn . . ."

"He's a tough guy. He'll weather it, and he's out of

surgery and in IC, where he's under constant watch, Jess. What kind of trouble do you suppose he was in with Frank Lorentian?''

''Most likely gambling debts. When I look honestly back on our early days together at the academy, I remember now how avid a gambler Warren always was. I'd rosily chosen to forget that aspect of his character.''

J. T. replied, ''Damn, I know it. I had a girlfriend once who'd bet on which of two apple blossoms would fall from a tree first.''

''Yeah, Warren had that shortcoming, but I had no idea it had become a driving force in his life. Maybe it contributed to his divorce. I can't say.''

Jessica felt badly that friends, coworkers, his agency, his former wife, and his kids would hear through the news media that Warren Bishop had died of a gunshot wound in the course of his duty as an FBI agent. She tried to minimize the horror of it all by pretending Bishop was, in a sense, doing decoy work in his most unusual undercover operation, most possibly his last as an FBI operative, and one he was not even aware of. She rationalized spreading the lie also in that it might save lives if Feydor Dorphmann bought into it.

''Where will you be, Jess, if he comes around?''

''I . . . I'll be at the hotel, getting some sleep,'' she lied.

''When will you be taking off for Jackson?''

''Sometime this afternoon.''

''Maybe I can join you then. Call me before you make any arrangements, okay?''

''Will do,'' she lied again, knowing now precisely where Feydor Dorphmann was directing her to go. J. T. didn't know it, but she might well have said her final goodbye to him.

Rather than racing immediately off to Jackson Hole, Wyoming, Jessica chose another course of action, or inaction, as the case turned out. She'd chosen to sit it out in

Salt Lake City for a time, hoping now that Feydor, having had time to think things through and to "talk" with his demon god, would contact her at her hotel room.

She knew that in Jackson Hole she'd have the backing of an entire army of FBI agents and local authorities, all wanting to put an end to the career of the Phantom; she knew that Eriq Santiva was flying there now. She understood that a coordinated effort to create a foolproof net to catch the killer would be instantly under way once Eriq took command there. The FBI crowd would bring to bear every known weapon in the arsenal of crime detection to apprehend the fiend responsible now for the deaths of three FBI men, the manhunt fueled with a vengeance not previously felt.

Meanwhile, an FBI hotline in D.C. was inundated with tips flooding in from every corner of the country, from people in all walks of life, from wastepaper managers to basketball players to TV evangelists who claimed divine knowledge of the messages left by the killer, to academicians whose specialty—the history of the occult and religions of the world—made them TV talk-show guests on Oprah and Rosie. Everyone had some take on the killer, each as distorted and twisted as the next.

However, not even the TV affiliates and networks, nor the newspapers buying into the exclusive coming out of the offices of the *Salt Lake Herald*, knew as much as the killer and Jessica Coran knew. But at least these more responsible sources named names and displayed photos of the killer, alongside his handwriting and his Dante's *Inferno* fetish, the nine rungs of Hades, the list of sins and victim names. They had the "story" as Jessica had fed it to them; they had the prediction that Feydor Dorphmann would kill a ninth, unknown victim to fulfill his demented contract with the Devil or devils that haunted him. . . .

She waited, armed with this knowledge; she waited this time for the killer to telephone her where she remained in

Salt Lake City. "I'm through chasing the bastard," she firmly told herself.

In fact, New York publishers were in a frenzy since the release of Jessica's story about her discovery that the killer was into Dante's *Inferno,* in a frenzy to capitalize on the moment by rereleasing *Inferno* in all of its previous lives and permutations. Since it fell into a public domain document, any publisher could bring it out under any lurid cover it liked, softbound, hardbound, mass-market, or trade-size editions.

Meanwhile, Jessica waited for his call. Waited by the phone, her notepad in hand, staring down at the list of victims, studying it, wondering if he had spoken with his twisted god to gain permission to add the FBI intruders' names to his list of victims or not.

As she waited in the silence of her hotel room for his call, she stared at the final list again, and she almost saw the final version of the list materialize before her eyes. At the bottom of the list of offenses and names, she saw her name.

"Seems suitable enough," she jested with herself. "I am suited for the Vestibule, for sure." Her rereading of *Inferno* reminded her that according to Dante's description, the Vestibule was the place for the indecisive, those who had never committed to anything, including life, so that, though they had not earned a place in Hell, neither had they earned a place in Heaven, so that they were left in a state of limbo, a state of no real death.

The Vestibule sloped down to the River Acheron, the first of three circular rivers, each of which emptied into the next, finally to flow into the frozen lake at the center of Earth, the nethermost well or pit of frigid water of Cocytus.

"Call me, you bastard," she dared the phone, but it remained silent.

She could wait no longer. She packed, called for a helicopter out of Salt Lake City's airport, and arranged for a cab to get her out to the airport. She looked again at the killer's itinerary, its final destination being Denver, Colorado, by way of South Dakota and Montana, but if he took the bait—if he read the papers and saw the reasoning, that Bishop's death, alongside those of the other two FBI agents, counted in his mad game, then he'd have only one more kill to make: her.

She put her finger on the map of Yellowstone National Park, the stop *after* Jackson Hole, Wyoming. If he killed in Jackson Hole, she decided, there would be plenty of people, Repasi included, to clean up after. If she could get ahead of the bastard, be there at Yellowstone's Old Faithful Lodge, then she might take him by surprise and end this mental case's attempt to repopulate the Inferno with innocent people who got in his way. It would end one way or another with her in Yellowstone, where the bastard had wanted her all along.

Yellowstone was the fitting place, the logical end, she realized.

It was as if the killer knew that she'd been to Yellowstone before, that he had somehow sneaked into her home in Quantico, Virginia, and rooted around in her many photo albums to know her past. It was as if Feydor Dorphmann, or his personal devil, somehow knew that she had revealed the very first murderer in her long career as a medical examiner in Yellowstone National Park.

Jessica recalled the last time she'd seen Ranger Samuel Marc Fronval and Yellowstone. She'd been on vacation with a girlfriend during her years just after college while she'd been employed as assistant to the M.E. in Baltimore. She was still taking finals at Georgetown University, completing her education in the field of forensics. She was twenty-four at the time. The memory calmed her into a near sleep in which she recalled every event as vividly as if it were the day before.

She recalled seeing the unremarkable poster of a missing young woman in the park, and how calm the park rangers

were the day her body was discovered. Not to disturb park
visitors, the rangers put up no hue and cry about the discovery; rather, they appeared more stone-faced than ever.
But Jessica had felt the menace, a bubbling excitement
below the surface at Old Faithful Lodge, just beneath the
veneer of gift shops, restaurant, lounge, and the tourist
crowd, an excitement that went unnoticed by most. But
Jessica had sensed it, had seen it in the eyes of the various
rangers and staff who daily worked at the lodge. News had
spread among them of a body found out at one of the hot
springs.

Jessica had instantly offered her services when she
learned it was a medical emergency, and since medical
assistance was some thirty miles off by air, she was en-
listed.

The helicopter she then rode in thundered through the
canyon pass, brushing over treetops, scattering nesting bald
eagles above the Shoshoni River on a breathtakingly clear,
snow-dusted morning. The pace of the helicopter and the
gorgeous scenery all around young Jessica Coran made her
gasp as much with awe as with the rollicking ride.

The pilot had said over his earphones, "We'll be there
in ten minutes. Hell of a sight."

She knew he was talking about the body and not the
Yellowstone gorge below, which she marveled over alone,
the pilot long jaded on the spectacular views. "You've
made the run earlier then? You've seen the body?" she'd
asked through the headphone set.

"I was on call when we got word from the Park Service.
The woman's been missing for three days, two nights out
here. Everybody feared the worse, you know, that she
slipped somewhere along the trail into a hot pool. You
know those suckers just sear you to death, and the body's
never found sometimes. Well, this one somehow scratched
her way out and died half a mile away in thick woods."

He banked with the curve of the canyon wall, and then
they lifted in a startling flash, rising as if yanked from

above by a godly hand. The pilot had introduced himself as Wayne Patterson, a bright-eyed, clean-shaven young fellow whose eyes lingered over Jessica. It frightened her a bit that he seemed so young and in control of her life at the moment.

The dense brown hues of the Grand Canyon of the Yellowstone here in Wyoming bordering Montana gave way to lush forests. Pine trees below created a pillowy carpet of green life swaying beneath their wake. It didn't appear there was anywhere to land.

"Just where do you intend to put this thing down?" she asked.

"There's a ranger station with a clearing just ahead. We'll have to hike back down this way to the body, Dr. Coran. Mind my asking why"—he hesitated asking whatever was on his mind—"why, ma'am, they sent you all the way out from Baltimore?"

"Presidential order," she joked. "Remember, his concern for the national parks ranks right up there with poverty and homelessness and every other big platform issue this year. Besides, I was in the area—Old Faithful Lodge."

"Oh, I get it." Her little joke had hurt his country pride.

The helicopter touched down at the remote ranger station, and Jessica, her medical bag in hand, rushed from beneath the whirring blades, sand, leaves, and twigs tornadoing about her. They got into a four-wheeled land crawler and raced to the scene. In fifteen minutes they came upon a handful of men, all standing about a prone figure in the dust, covered over with a woolen blanket.

Jessica introduced herself to the men, most of whom looked dubiously back at her, wondering about her age and sex and experience, no doubt.

One of the men, wearing the uniform of a ranger and looking like an aged John Wayne, introduced himself, saying, "I'm Sam, Samuel Fronval. In charge of this district." He then casually pointed to the heap below the blanket and sadly announced the obvious. ''She's beyond help . . . long dead.''

Jessica stepped closer. ''I'm Dr. Coran,'' she replied. ''Happened to be at the lodge. I'll have to examine her, pronounce cause of death.''

''Cause is pretty clear,'' replied another ranger, an overweight fellow who had the arms and general appearance of a white, hairless bear—and who, in fact, the other rangers called Bear.

''She never stood a chance,'' mumbled a third man. ''We figure it's that missing woman, Sarah Langley. She was hiking alone. Paid no attention to the warnings against hiking alone up in here,'' urged Bear.

''Just the same, I'll have a look.'' Jessica went to the body and pulled back the blanket. She gasped at the horrid sight of flesh that had been literally boiled from the bones. The woman had no features, the skin having sloughed away. She was so badly burned, in fact, there seemed no way she could have come so far in her state. This strange fact stood out along with something equally strange about the nude body that immediately hit her. The victim's ankles and feet, while scalded, were not in nearly as bad shape as the rest of her body. This struck her instantly as odd.

''Anyone remove her shoes? Were her clothes burned off her?''

''Maybe, can't tell. No evidence she had any clothes on, but superheated water like what she got into burns clothing into nothing,'' replied Fronval. ''I've seen it happen.''

''She didn't have no shoes on,'' said another ranger. ''I mean when we found her.''

Jessica looked again at the body, trying to make out any sign of clothing clinging to it, but there was nothing but the clothlike blotches and peels of skin remaining, whole portions moving in the invisible wind current coming off the ground.

"Well?" asked Fronval. "What's your diagnosis, Doctor?"

"Yeah, how'd she manage to get so far from the pool that killed her?" asked the pilot, equally confused.

She had to have had help, Jessica thought but kept her counsel.

"Animals musta' got at her," said Bear with a shrug. "Maybe a coyote or some grizzly come along and drug her here. There're signs she was drugged here."

Jessica and Fronval looked at the evidence the heavyset young man pointed to. Yes, the body had been dragged, but she doubted it was *drugged,* and Fronval was shaking his head, too. He near whispered to her, "If there were any bear tracks, they've been obliterated by last night's snow and destroyed by my overanxious men, but I don't think a bear got at her."

"Why not?"

"No bear marks on her."

"Gashes, you mean."

"Bear'll tear its meat into strips. Even a coyote'd leave marks where he clamped down on her, if he could even manage to drag her dead weight this far up from the springs. So, we got ourselves a bit of a Devil's Triangle mystery here, huh? What do you think, Doctor?" urged Fronval.

Jessica looked up from the corpse, the worst thing she'd seen in her young career as an M.E. student, the skin seared to molten, peeling sheets; sheaths of her skin had curled up, other portions of skin were missing, lost along the trail, revealing scorched, dehydrated veins, normally blue, turned to a white, milky hue, the blood boiled away.

With third- and fourth-degree scald burns over ninety percent of her body, she could not have survived long enough to have taken ten steps, much less arrive at this destination on her own power. There were second- and third-degree burns over the remaining ten percent of her. All her facial features and hair had been dramatically boiled away. All the soft tissues, such as the eyes, scalded into oblivion. Dental records were a necessity for a one hundred percent ID on the woman, for even if she had once had a birthmark, it, too, was gone. "If she were burned to this degree in the doorway of the best burn center in the country—" she began.

"That'd be Salt Lake City," supplied Fronval.

"—she still would have died. . . ."

"But?" asked Fronval, sensing there was more.

"But the condition in which we find her, and so far from the hot springs—where is it?"

"Closest one is a quarter mile that way." Fronval pointed with an unlit pipe, and he next supplied the name of the hot springs that had apparently killed Sarah Langley, who, from what Jessica could tell, was a young woman in her mid- to late twenties who obviously enjoyed nature and taking her nature alone in the woods. Fronval said, "She was hiking along Firehole River. She'd been seen by a couple of fishermen up that way, least that's what Brian, here, learned before we began the manhunt for her."

Jessica looked up to see which one was Brian, guessing it to be Bear. He only shook his head, suppressed eye contact, and said in response, "I figured she fell in, 'cause look, her ankles and feet didn't get it near so bad. She must've fallen in and clawed her way back outta the pool, and her feet were the only things working right. They got her away from the pool, and a large, predatory animal must've done the rest."

"We can get the body over to Mammoth Hospital. They got a long history of hot springs deaths there. They'll know what to do, all the paperwork, getting the body to her family, all that," suggested Fronval.

Jessica nodded to Fronval. "Are they equipped with a sheriff and a jail there, Mr. Fronval?"

Fronval's eyes widened. "You suspect there's more here than meets the eye, Doctor?"

"I do."

"Murder? Foul play?"

"I do."

"Can you prove it?" he asked.

"Take me to the hot springs where she *allegedly* fell in."

Bear defended, saying, "They don't always fall in. Sometimes some people jump in, confusing one pool with another, thinking it a safe sauna, you know."

"Bear's right 'bout that," said a third ranger.

Fronval agreed, saying, "Some pools are safe to swim and bask in while the one right beside it is hot enough to kill anything that dares touch it."

"So, she coulda decided to take a swim or bathe," Bear said with a shrug.

"That same place has claimed lives before. It's a tricky area on the trail," agreed Fronval, "and there're three pools there. You slip and fall in, you could be killed. We figure, well, Bear here figured, she fell into Ojo."

"Ojo?" she asked.

"Ojo Caliente."

"Spanish for hot springs," added the young pilot.

"Lower Geyser Basin," added the third ranger, whose nameplate said Fred Wingate.

"That's where that Lewis kid, six years old, fell in when he was fishing with his father back in '58. But he lived for two days afterward," supplied Bear.

Fronval supplied the rest, saying, "Yeah, the boy had third-degree burns over his entire body except for the head and neck. Died in Salt Lake. Wasn't anything could be done. Lost too much body fluids to the heat. Ojo's one of the hottest of the springs; fluctuates between a hundred ninety-eight and two-oh-two."

"But she went in headfirst—her ankles and feet weren't in the water as long as the rest of her," Jessica said. "And there's a large contusion on the left side of her head where she sustained a blow."

"Coulda happened in the fall," suggested Bear.

The other men stood nodding, imagining the possible scenarios suggested first by Fronval, next by Dr. Coran, and then by Bear.

"I'll need to examine the spot where she fell in and supposedly dragged herself out of this Ojo springs. See if her clothing is there. . . ."

"That could take days. You know how big Ojo is?" asked Bear.

"But if she fell from the trail as you theorize," replied Jessica, "then the search is considerably narrowed down, isn't it, Mr. Fronval?"

"Sure is," said Fronval. "I'll take you back that way on my four-wheeler. We'll have a look around while Bear and the others get the body over to Mammoth."

Jessica knew that the chopper was equipped to take on such cargo.

"I want to go with you, Sam," said Bear. "I'm the one found her. Feel I ought to carry through."

"No need, Bear. You go on to Mammoth with the body. Get things hopping there. Notify the family she's been located, and Fred . . . Fred, you get back to the station. We've left it unmanned long enough."

"Yes, sir," Fred immediately responded.

"You're going to need help out there at Ojo, Sam," complained Bear as Jessica stared at his gloved hands, wondering if they might not be scorched from the hot springs as well, and if they were . . . But all the men, and Jessica, were wearing gloves against the cold, frigid air.

"No, Dr. Coran and me, we'll take care over to Ojo," Fronval commanded in fatherly fashion. "You've done quite 'nough, son. I'll catch up to you in Mammoth."

Bear held them in his gaze until they disappeared in Fronval's four-wheeler.

At Ojo Caliente, a quarter mile away, Jessica and Sam Fronval searched for almost an hour before finding what to both of them appeared the place where Sarah Langley entered and most likely exited the deceptively calm hot springs where a spectral cloud of sulfur gases caressed and embraced the humans onshore. The surface water was glasslike for the most part, and while it sent up a blanket of superheated air over its wide surface, it hardly appeared to be a killer.

Fronval, using his wilderness skills, located an area where broken branches and matted grasses told him she'd tumbled from. They found not a stitch of clothing onshore, no shoes, nothing of the sort. Furthermore, there was no indication of hiking equipment strewn about, no backpack, no tent, not a trace she was hiking in this area. Only the near invisible signs Fronval pointed to evidenced her ever having passed this way.

"What do you make of it?" Fronval asked Jessica. "Did she fall in headfirst with every stitch of her gear weighing her down?"

"Could all that gear dematerialize in that cauldron of boiling water?"

"Possibly," Sam Fronval answered, drawing on his now lit pipe.

"Highly unlikely, Mr. Fronval, that nothing survived her fall."

Fronval shook his head, continuing his devil's advocate tone. "Other people may've come along, picked up anything seen as useful."

Jessica shook her head in return. Anyone watching them would think them in heated debate. "Even if she did fall from the trail along here, there would likely have been some scattering of her things here and there. And this time of year, how many other people would be along here? And everyone knowing the girl's been missing, it would've been reported."

"Besides," he said in an agreeing manner now, rubbing his chin, "the trail's much more slippery at other junctures. If she fell into the pool, why at this spot?"

"You'd know more about that than I," Jessica acknowledged. "But if she did fall in here, the natural place to've come out is right at this spot, here," she finished, pointing. "Unfortunately."

"If she did claw her way out and walk away from the fall as suggested by Brian Cressey."

"Yeah, the fellow you call Bear?"

"Nickname . . . suits him. He's strong as a bear and about as single-mindedly dumb. But if he had anything to do with the girl's death, why didn't he dispose of the body right here, same as the equipment? Leave not a trace. Wouldn't a murderer, given this great, natural opportunity to dispose completely and utterly of the body . . . wouldn't he?"

"I couldn't tell you for certain what goes on in the mind of a murderer, but we know that in an unplanned murder— that is, one in which someone loses control—the killer seldom thinks clearly or in any orderly fashion."

"I see."

"And I've read that sometimes killers hold on to the body for long periods, you know, for . . . well, indelicate purposes."

"My God," Fronval said, each word a groan.

"As for the missing equipment, I'd look into Cressey's locker, and I'd look at his hands."

Fronval's face was still twitching, still stuck on the part about keeping the body for indelicate reasons. "You really think he . . . he held onto the body to stick it to the dead girl even looking like she does now?"

"Depends on how cruel and psychotic a person he is. Just how well do you know Cressey? How long's he been a ranger?"

"Not long. Transferred in from a park, Stone Mountain, Georgia, if memory serves. Don't know much about the kid, but you're right. We gotta take a look in his boots, and we need a look below his gloves. . . ."

"I didn't like what his body language was saying back

there. I was a little afraid to call him on it, ask him to reveal his hands. He was holding a high-powered rifle.''

"I had my suspicion when he suggested maybe a grizzly got at the girl and turned up its nose to the burned flesh, but there weren't any signs of a bear kill whatsoever. It wasn't the scene of a classic carcass feeding.''

"Of course . . .'' She considered his meaning. "You're quite right, Mr. Fronval.''

"No coyotes, ravens, or magpies waiting their turn at the corpse. A bear makes a racket when he feeds, and he makes a stench and a mess of the carcass. There weren't no claw marks or teeth gashes I could see on her.''

"Perhaps the body hasn't been out in the elements as long as we suspect, sir.''

"You think she was dead when she exited Ojo Caliente, don't you, Dr. Coran?''

"It will take a full-blown autopsy to be sure, but that bruise I mentioned, the one to the temple, was considerable, since it was deep enough to show below the skin that'd sloughed away from the cranium.''

"She was dead when she exited the water. She was dead weight. All he had to do was hold her by the ankles. He likely fought with her, lost his temper, pushed her in, held her by the ankles until she was dead, pulled her out, and realized what he'd done.''

Jessica, staring into Fronval's sad eyes, bit her lip.

"But you already knew all that, didn't you, Doctor?''

She was glad he had said the words. Less argument that way.

"The search for Sarah was already on, but he didn't know what to do. It wasn't something he planned, so he had no plan for disposing of the body. Then when the search became such a big deal for everyone, he saw an opportunity to emerge as the hero who had located the body—which wasn't so tough, since he'd held on to it.

"Bastard probably kept it in a snowbank behind the

ranger station where he was putting in time alone up here.
Creepy bastard.''

''I suspect a thorough search of his sleeping quarters
will reveal that she spent some time there *after* she was
dead.''

''That would cinch it, wouldn't it? Can you be sure
there'll be trace evidence there?''

''The way she was dropping skin, yes.''

''God.'' Fronval moaned again. ''Think of it—being
held under that heat by your ankles. There was no way
she could escape his grasp or the searing heat.''

''If she had pulled herself from the water, her feet and
ankles would've been seared at least as badly as her hands,
but they weren't. As for this location, we're not going to
find any evidence without doing some archaeological dig-
ging about. It's an ideal spot for a murder, actually. No
clues left to find. You can't without doubt know where she
entered or exited the water.''

''I know it was here,'' Fronval said with conviction.

''But it wouldn't hold up in a court of law, sir. Any
other poolside in the wilderness, and we'd see indentations
in the sand, evidence or a lack of evidence of her hands
and nails having clawed her way out. But not here in all
this mineral spillover.''

The land around Ojo Caliente was constantly being re-
shaped and rebuilt, in places spongy, in other places
cracked and hard and brittle, the stuff of geyserite: a hy-
drous form of silica, a variety of opal deposited in gray
and white concretelike masses, porous, filamentous, and
scaly. Therein shown no footprints or telltale signs the
woman walked or crawled from this place, but then, too,
there were no signs of any attacker's prints, either.

''We can't prove he killed her from what we can see
here,'' she told him.

''Sonofabitch, but we've got to prove he did it; I know
it in my bones.''

''That bit of knowledge, I'm afraid, is also useless in a

court of law, Mr. Fronval. We need to bring in photographic equipment and photograph everything, even this
spot, showing the lack of any sign of struggle here. We
need pictures of the body, and we need a warrant to search
Cressey's quarters.''

"That camp belongs to the service. We don't need no
damned warrant to get in there and search.''

"But we do, sir. Else the court will throw out all the
evidence we find in the camp. It will be viewed as his
private space, his sleeping quarters, where he has a reasonable expectancy of privacy, despite the ownership question.''

"That's crazy.''

"That's the law, sir.''

"Protects the guilty and his civil liberties, huh?''

"Along with the innocent, yes.''

"Damn, I sent Bear off to Mammoth. You can bet he's
going to make tracks for the nearest safe haven.''

"Maybe not. He still wants to be a hero. Besides, we
can radio ahead to authorities there to pick him up. Our
first worry is to get a judge to give us a search warrant.''

Fronval had hold of a rifle he'd pulled from his all-
terrain vehicle. They were far enough into the wilderness
that should a bear or other wild animal attack, he could
use the weapon in the event of threat to human life. Now
they stood and began to make their way back to the all-
terrain when a gunshot rang out, striking a boulder beside
Fronval's head, sending a rock shard into his forehead and
knocking him down. Jessica looked up to see Brian Cressey smiling down at them. He raised his rifle scope again.

Jessica dove for Fronval's rifle, hearing the report of a
second shot fired by Bear and hearing Fronval groan with
the impact. Jessica brought the rifle up, shoved the bullet
into the breech, aimed, and fired, striking Bear in the solar
plexus, sending him scudding down the rocky slope toward
them, his rifle flying off in another direction.

Fronval was hit in the shoulder and his head was bleeding, but he was okay. Bear was dead. Jessica went to his inert body, his staring eyes, and she yanked away his right-hand glove to reveal serious first- and second-degree burns in a splash and splatter pattern. She next unclothed his other hand, revealing even worse burns on his left hand.

It was Jessica's first encounter with a murderer.

Jessica's fear of Feydor Dorphmann quadrupled now as she sat beside the still and silent phone in Salt Lake City.

It chilled her to know that somehow Dorphmann knew that she would follow him to Yellowstone. It felt uncanny, as though he knew of her earlier, fateful trip to the park. He knew that she had seen the bubbling cauldrons that licked Earth's crust there, like the liquid tongue of Satan, and no doubt Feydor had also been there at one time or another to look into the orifices of Hell. It was this geography that linked killer and hunter.

Yellowstone was filled with geographic anomalies, both fascinating and bizarre, some ten thousand hot springs, geysers, mud pots, and steam vents scattered over its mountainous terrain, all atop a plateau. In dramatic, exquisitely beautiful natural formations, most of the strange thermal waters were hotter than 150 degrees Fahrenheit, 66 degrees Celsius, and many reached temperatures of 185 to 205 degrees Fahrenheit, or 89 to 96 degrees Celsius. This, and the fact that water boiled at 198 degrees Fahrenheit at this altitude, made the alluring, fascinating features also quite deadly, so much so that nearby Billings, Montana's, newspaper the *Billings Gazette* routinely reported more hot springs deaths in Yellowstone than they did deaths due to grizzly bear attacks.

The worst tragedy in the area occurred on July 29, 1979, almost twenty years ago now, in midafternoon when nine-year-old Markie Hoechst of Bainbridge, Georgia, walked along the visitors' boardwalk alongside Crested Pool with her vacationing family. This awesome hot spring had several names over the years, some quite colorful, such as

Fire Basin, Circe's Boudoir, and The Devil's Well the same as Feydor Dorphmann had alluded to. Little Markie, enveloped in the billowing clouds of steam that the hot springs continually emit, lost sight of her parents. The hot vapor blew into Markie's eyes and no one knows quite what happened to her next, for she somehow got off the boardwalk and into the searing waters, which allowed her only a handful of screams before she was silenced, boiled to death in the hot spring. Despite the fact that a guardrail stood between little Markie and a searing, scalding death, she somehow managed to fall in. Some accounts claimed she tripped at the edge of the boardwalk; others said she'd climbed onto the guardrail and fell from there. At any rate, she plunged into the cauldron, where the temperature rose to more than 200 degrees Fahrenheit. Reports said the girl tried vainly to swim a handful of strokes before completely scalding to death and sinking. According to *Newsday* and *Newsweek* accounts, the final glimpse the girl's mother and father had of little Markie was seeing her rigid, manne-quinlike body and stark-white face—the mark of her pain and fear—sinking away from them and into the depths of the boiling water.

Markie's father had to be held by others, restrained from jumping in after his daughter. Her mother fainted. Later, her father stated that no one present actually saw her fall or misstep; that she had been walking along behind them, skipping along on the boardwalk, when suddenly they heard a splash. They instantly turned, only to see other tourists helplessly staring and shouting down at someone who'd fallen into the hot spring, and next horror struck: *It was little Markie.*

Her body sank from sight. Eight pounds of bone, flesh, and clothing were recovered by park rangers the following day.

Jessica wondered again at Dorphmann's suggestion that she meet him at the Devil's Well. She calculated that he'd have been eleven years of age in 1979, and she wondered if he, too, as a child, had visited the Devil's Well, and if he had become captivated by it. She wondered if others, fascinated by the eyelid of Satan in this place, might not have wanted to see what would happen if they lifted a little girl over a rail and dropped her into such a pool of super-heated water.

She wondered if a Feydor Dorphmann had been on hand that day in Yellowstone to push a foolish little girl from a guardrail that she'd climbed up onto to impress, surprise, or gain attention from her parents.

In any event, Yellowstone's geysers and hot springs re-mained from generation to generation beautiful and strange, and peripheral areas both awesome and ugly, such as the boiling pots and pits of white mud froth from which rose a sulfuric steam that covered onlookers. At dusk, all around Old Faithful Lodge, rising banshees of smoke rose and cantered off in the wind on all sides, creating the effect of an army of phantom souls released into the night. This from hundreds of hot springs and bubbling pools, some as searing as 280 degrees Fahrenheit, enough to strip an an-imal of its fur as well as its skin, should it fall in. The carcasses of buffalo, elk, deer, and other animals were rou-tinely found in this obstacle course of superheated waters bubbling up from Earth's core. And many a person had foolishly lost his life to Yellowstone's unpredictable ways, so much so that a local historian who'd chronicled the foolhardy deaths in Yellowstone published a book under the title *Death in Yellowstone*. Sales of the book in the gift shops continued to be brisk each season.

Yellowstone, of course. It appeared the perfect place for Feydor Dorphmann to end his quest.

Jessica dared tell no one of her plan. The others would find out soon enough, as soon as they tired of Jackson Hole as a staging area to catch Dorphmann.

Still no word from Dorphmann came. *The bastard*, she thought, *is going ahead as planned*. This meant a likely death in Jackson Hole, another at Yellowstone, possibly two there.

She called the desk for a cab, picked up her waiting bag and professional bag, and was halfway out the door when the phone rang. She put down her things and moved toward the phone, taking it up on the third ring.

"Yes?" she asked.

"It's time for number six."

"Wait. Didn't you see the papers? You've already killed by fire two additional victims, Feydor. You don't need to do this."

"I can't take any chances," he replied. "Those others were flukes, mistakes, not planned by *him* and me. This way, I know for sure. Number six is number four: Avaricious & Prodigal. Understood, Doctor? Now, that, that is for sure," he finished, obviously removed a gag from his sixth victim, and with a whoosh of power, ignited the gasoline already poured over her or him. Jessica could not tell from the wailing, agonized screams whether it was a man or a woman.

"There's a fire, but I fooled you again. It's not in Jackson Hole, Doctor. Your pals won't be in the right place. Only you know where I am tonight, you alone."

She realized he could be anywhere between Salt Lake City and the great Yellowstone National Park, in any of hundreds of motels and hotels along Interstate 287, the main highway of 191, or back roads spreading fingerlike from these two roads, but she said, "All right, Feydor. I'll come alone to where you want me, to Yellowstone, but you've got to promise, no one else is killed. Understood? No one else between now and then."

He hung up, the fire engulfing everything around him, no doubt, but he'd heard her promise and her request. He had heard what he wanted to hear from her. She prayed he'd go for the bargain.

Jessica left the safety of her room for the waiting cab. She'd earlier arranged for a private helicopter to take her up to Yellowstone. It was nearing 6:00 P.M. Gallagher, Santiva, and the others in Jackson Hole would remain on a long vigil until they got word of the latest fire death, Satan, God, and Feydor alone knew where.

"Salt Lake Regional Airport," she told the cabbie, who muttered something about the nice evening as his tires screeched from the curb.

Eriq Santiva and Neil Gallagher and the others now had every hotel in Jackson Hole, Wyoming, a small but bustling commercialized village, under watch. Eriq had taken time to oversee Gallagher's setup, and after approving of what the Salt Lake City bureau head had done, he began to question Jessica Coran's delay in getting to Jackson Hole.

He got on the phone to the hospital in Salt Lake City, and after several frustrating channels, John Thorpe was reached. Thorpe had earlier reached Eriq on the airplane phone, telling him of the planted newspaper coverage and the fact that all three men who'd been injured in Salt Lake City were in fact still very much alive.

Now Eriq asked, "Where's Dr. Coran at this moment?"

"She's not there in Wyoming? With you, sir?"

"No, she is not. When did she leave?"

"Well, she was planning on leaving mid- to late afternoon, but she was also supposed to contact me before she left. I'd planned, hoped to travel with her to Jackson Hole."

"I'm telling you, she is not here. She's made no contact with us here."

"I'll try to get her at the hotel. She may've overslept. She'd been going all night, sir."

"Do that, and get back to me! Meanwhile, how's Bishop doing? The other two agents?"

J. T. instantly hedged. He didn't like lying to his boss, but Jessica had asked him not to reveal the Lorentian connection to Bishop this way, over the phone. "All of the men are out of serious danger now, and Bishop is showing good signs of recovery, but all are being kept heavily sedated, sir—for the pain, you see.''

''Understood.''

J. T. hung up and tried to hail Jessica at the Little America Hotel and Towers, but he was told by the desk that she wasn't answering her phone. A stab of fear split his heart. What was she up to? he wondered, feared. Then he made out someone talking in the background there at the desk, telling the fellow on the phone that Dr. Coran had checked out and had taken a cab to the airport.

''When? When?'' J. T. pressed the man when he came back on with this information. ''When did she leave?''

''Around six, sir, six this evening.''

''Oh, all right . . . thanks.'' J. T. hung up and immediately got back to Chief Director Santiva.

''She's on her way, then. Good.''

''I believe so, sir, yes. I'll call the airport to confirm.''

''Do that.''

Again they hung up, but now J. T. wondered what was going on with Jessica. Why hadn't she called him to tell him her plans, to include him on the trip northward? Something was wrong. He felt it in the bone marrow. A quick call to Salt Lake International revealed nothing save the fact she hadn't flown out of there either on a private or a commercial plane. He asked at the hospital about any small airports in the area, and he was given several names, but the one that everyone agreed on as the best was Salt Lake Regional. A call there proved frustrating. A helicopter had taken off at six thirty-five, but as was usual with helicopter charters, no flight plan had been left with the tower. It was assumed to be a sight-seeing run, but the helicopter in question hadn't returned.

''She's not going to Jackson Hole,'' he said to himself where he sat at the useless telephone at a nurse's station outside Bishop's room. ''Damn,'' he swore. ''She's gone after him alone.'' But where? Where had she gone? Where would the showdown occur?

He rushed from the hospital to Jessica's room at the hotel.

Once at her hotel, J. T., flashing his credentials and claiming it an emergency, stepped into the room so recently vacated by Jessica Coran. She'd left the room in immaculate condition, as typical of her, but J. T. prayed for any clue as to her whereabouts. On a notepad beside the phone he found a notation she'd made, and it had a chilling effect on J. T. as he stared down at the message, which read:

#6 is #4—Avaricious & Prodigal

''Damn it,'' he muttered, knowing what the message must mean. ''He's killed again. Somewhere between here and Jackson Hole.''

''Sir?'' asked the bellman who'd unlocked the door for him.

''Nothing, never mind.'' J. T. then saw the discarded map in the wastepaper basket. He lifted out the map and unfolded it, spreading it across the bureau, instantly recognizing it for the answer he'd come in search of. ''Yellowstone. She's gone to Yellowstone.''

Another glance at the map and he saw the fine-pen circle mark around Old Faithful and the Upper Geyser Basin, with the names of the various hot springs. One in particular caught his attention and his imagination, recalling to mind what Jess had said about the one phone call from the killer in which he mentioned Hellsmouth and the Devil's Well.

J. T. raced out with the map in hand. He had to get to the airport, and fast.

· NINETEEN ·

The passions are like fire, useful in a thousand ways
and dangerous in only one, through their excess.
— CHRISTIAN NESTELL BOVEE

The helicopter pilot taking Jessica to Yellowstone had at first balked at taking her, a lone woman, into Yellowstone's wilderness area. She'd shown him her badge, explained to him that she worked for the FBI, and that she must get to Old Faithful Lodge at the greatest possible speed. He then wanted to take the time to sketch out a flight plan for the tower, and she told him it would delay them too much. It was then that she offered him twice his normal rate for a ferry to Yellowstone.

He agreed, and they began their journey together. Still, he remained skeptical of her purposes, the familiar paranoia about government types filtering in, she believed. With the rhythmic scream of the rotor blades overhead, the flume of whirring sound and vibration rocking the carriage of the chopper, they spoke to one another through the headphones.

"You got business in the park, huh? With the rangers, huh?"

"As a matter of fact, yes."

"Fronval know you're coming?"

"You know Fronval?" she asked, surprised.

"Doesn't everybody? Man's something of a legend in these parts. So, does he know you're coming?"

"Not yet, but when we're in range, I'd like to call Sam on the radio. Do you know Sam personally?"

"Sure, everybody whose ever rangered knows Sam," the pilot, who'd introduced himself as Corey Rideout, said, more curious about her now than ever.

"Oh, so you've been a ranger?"

"A lot of people in these parts go into the service. It's almost a rite of passage, you might say. But it gets tiresome after a time. It can be a lonely existence, 'specially in dead of winter at a ranger station. A man could go nuts, and some do." He looked at her again, studying her. Then he asked, "Where do you know Sam Fronval from?"

"Met him the last time I was at Yellowstone."

"Oh, so you've been to see Sam before? I get it. You're one of those Washington sanitizers, aren't you?"

"Sanitizer, me?"

"Sure, you want to sanitize the wilderness, as if it could be done! Make it safe for every little boy and girl whose parents cart them into the park in their trailers. You know it's impossible. When I was a park ranger, some years back, a tourist fella comes up to me and points at the thousand or so buffalo rooting around some hundred yards from a crowd of gawking onlookers. You know what this slicker asked me, lady? Doctor?"

"What's that, Mr. Rideout?"

"He says, 'Tell me, Ranger, these animals we're looking at, just rooting around out here . . . they couldn't be wild, right?' "

" 'They are that, sir,' I told him."

" 'No way,' he tells me. 'If they were wild, you couldn't just have them running around loose.' The man was an injury waiting to happen," Rideout finished.

Jessica laughed appreciatively.

"There're four thousand bison in the park, compared to seven hundred fifty bears, so visitors see a lot more buffalo than grizzly, but either way, many of them have only seen such animals through Disney or MGM studio releases, and they think they're as cute and mindless as, as say, Thumper and Bambi. Fools try to put their kids on the back of a buffalo to get a Kodak moment. The moment the two-thousand-pound, unpredictable, and belligerent animal erupts, they get more Kodak moments and home video funnies than they bargained for and someone dies, usually in great distress because the nearest hospital trauma center is in Bozeman. So they sue the park, and so Washington pencil-pushers hear about it's happened again, and a hue and cry goes up to make people safe from wilderness, to sanitize places like Yellowstone now that so many people visit annually.''

"I'm not here to sanitize the park," she assured Rideout.

"Then what's the big rush to get there and see Fronval? Wait a minute: You're here about the brucellosis, sure, aren't you? Now, that figures. The government sends a government doctor to Yellowstone to stamp a USDA approval on the herd, right?''

"Herd?" she asked, confused. "What herd? Heard what?"

"The park bisons. You were sent to keep the cattlemen and ranchers thinking everything's being taken care of, right?''

"Oh, I see." Jessica had heard of the unfortunate outbreak of brucellosis among the buffalo, a disease ranchers and farmers across America had done battle with for more than sixty years, and they'd nearly eradicated the nasty livestock disease, one of the reasons why milk was pasteurized. The fight against brucellosis by American stockmen, ranchers, farmers, and the USDA was no less than a miracle victory. In the meantime, another great success story had also unfolded—the story of the century of conservation effort on behalf of the American bison that once numbered fifty million and had been hunted to extinction levels in the nineteenth century. Now the breed had been rescued from its extinction-level population of six hundred remaining in 1889, the largest herd at the time a mere twenty-one, who, coincidentally, grazed and lived in Yellowstone. Yellowstone's free-ranging buffalo herd now numbered some four thousand, and Yellowstone buffalo experts boasted it was the largest free-ranging buffalo herd in the country. It was also the only herd that, throughout its history, had remained free. Today the park was proud of its herd. But now it was estimated that half of the herd was infected by brucellosis, and there was no cure short of destroying the animals.

The ranchers and cattlemen had a strong argument. For sixty years they'd fought what was commonly called undulant fever, and now it was almost nonexistent in the United States, according to the Centers for Disease Control. Only forty-six livestock herds still carried the disease, as compared to 124,000 infected herds in 1957. In a couple of years, the USDA had an excellent chance of completely eradicating the disease in all fifty states.

Yellowstone, the nation's first national park, had a history of becoming ground zero for many a fight, and now it was ground zero for this puzzling debate in which park rangers believed the buffalo and its disease posed no threat to surrounding livestock, and ranchers felt their herds and profits threatened by the infected buffalo. The media, conservationists, and cattlemen were all asking the same perplexing question: *How do you eradicate the last remnants of a disease, when it's carried by a species you want to save?*

"I guess there is more than one creature I'd like to sanitize the park of," she teased, "but I have no cure for the one, only the other."

"Nobody's got a cure for that buffalo disease. But what do you mean, two creatures you'd like to clear outta the park?"

"I'm hunting for the worst kind of animal in the woods, Mr. Rideout."

"A man? You . . . you're on a manhunt?"

"I'm with the FBI, not the U.S. Interior or the Department of Parks and Recreation."

"A manhunt. Wow, I'm part of a manhunt. Wait'll I tell Eleanor and the kids about this one. They won't believe it."

After this, Rideout burned with curiosity about her, her reason for traveling alone into Yellowstone after this killer he'd read about in the morning papers concerning him greatly. He'd worked up to what he wanted to say, and he finally said it. "Just the same, even if you are trained in such matters as detection and apprehension, Dr. Coran, someone enters a wilderness area like Yellowstone every day without the least preparation for its special dangers. I mean Yellowstone down there is more than just forty thousand elk, four thousand bison, ten thousand hot springs, and two hundred lakes. It's also full of grizzly bears that run around as freely as you or me."

"I'm tracking a more dangerous animal than grizzlies," she replied.

"Yeah, so you told me, but once you're down there in this . . . this resource, remember, it's not a zoo or an amusement park. Danger is a part of the resource."

"I know the drill, Mr. Rideout."

"You do?"

"Wilderness is impersonal."

He was mildly impressed by this, smiling. "Nature demands we pay attention, doesn't it? Whether we're putting out to sea or an overland trek."

"I know that there's good reason for why the rangers in such areas as Yellowstone preach rules."

"Good," he replied with little conviction, as if he didn't believe her just because she said so.

"Mr. Rideout, I know it's fool's play to walk amid standing burned trees from a forest fire, even one that ended years before . . . that such dead trees routinely fall on people because they come down without a sound. I know that hiking alone is deadly and again foolish. I know that wearing any sort of perfume can lure a bear faster than it can a man, and the aroma alone can turn you into his next meal, and that the bear wouldn't let a tent or a campfire stand in his way, that in fact nothing stands in the way of the most consummate eating machine nature's ever devised.''

"Good, very good," he replied, conviction taking hold now.

She added for Rideout's benefit, "Wilderness doesn't care whether you live or die, and it does not care how much you love it.''

"Spoken like someone who's been there.''

"I have. I've hunted in some of the greatest wilderness areas left us. But this is the first time I've hunted a human in one."

This was met with an appreciative silence.

The pilot had finally gotten it, Jessica thought. Rideout couldn't tell Jessica Coran anything she didn't already know about this vast wilderness below them. She knew that there were disappearances in the national parks all the time, every day, and there were *accidents* involving the beasts and natural formations, and the natural flora when some fool ingested a poisonous plant in any given park, and that most of these deaths might have been avoided if and only if what rangers called "natural curiosity, arrogance, and stupidity" in the national parks could be stopped, but everyone knew that as the impossibility of all impossibilities. Still, of late, along with fire-related deaths in and around the parks, there had been a rash of deaths this year like nothing the major parks had ever faced before. No doubt Sam Fronval had already chalked it up to the turn-of-the-century blues, that people carried their phobias and eccentricities with them into the park, and there was no way for him to get them to check their deadly peculiarities at the gate.

Congress wanted more legislation to protect people in the national parks, while the people who lived, worked, and understood the parks tried to explain—once they stopped laughing at Congress—that you couldn't put a fence around the Yellowstone gorge, the hot springs, or such wonders as the Grand Canyon. There wasn't that much fence in the world, for one; for another, any fence or sign in the wilds detracted from the very nature of nature. To develop a national park was tantamount to not having one.

Still, some people, usually people who thought of a park as something akin to Central Park in New York City, wanted the immense parks of the West to be wild as long as they weren't too wild, so wild that it might harm them personally. These people, often the first to sue a park, required a park's wilderness, yet they denied its right to exercise its wilderness character upon them.

She recalled something Fronval had said to her on the subject once. He'd often been quoted as saying the same in articles she'd seen in *National Parks,* the magazine mouthpiece for the NPCA: "Unfortunately, when people visit the national parks, they don't always leave their suicidal, masochistic, or sadistic tendencies at the park borders."

The quote certainly fit in with the manhunt she was about to propose to Fronval.

Jessica thought the argument, even the fact there was an argument of this kind, a commentary on where society was heading, that so much of society hadn't the least idea of what the wild outdoors meant, that somehow wild buffalo, bears, and cougars had been confused with movie-friendly beasts seen in Disney versions of the great outdoors. This led visitors to Yellowstone to believe they could not only feed the bears but also pet them, and that a snapshot of Junior on the back of an elk or a mountain goat was as natural an idea as a snapshot of Junior on the back of a statue. People ascribed cartoonlike, friendly characteristics to the wildest of beasts that roamed free here, but this in effect negated the very meaning of free.

She had given thought to when the outdoors was natural and when indoors in the American wilderness was unnatural. History, time, and the march of progress had turned reality inside out, and people with it.

While she and her friend Melissa Gilmore had been staying at the lodge during her first and only other visit to Yellowstone, they'd heard of an incident in which a young man, in an attempt to rescue his dog from a hot spring, had lost his life to the searing, boiling cauldron he'd dove into. Dogs in Yellowstone caused great concern to the rangers. There was good reason for the signs posted everywhere that read: DO NOT TAKE YOUR DOG ON TRAILS IN YELLOWSTONE. Dogs were never allowed off-leash in the park, and never to be taken on trails, especially trails through thermal areas. Hot springs amounted to only one reason for the ban on dogs here. Other reasons involved the fact that dogs were predatory on small animals; they chased and harassed larger animals such as moose and elk and buffalo. Dogs also attracted bears—indeed these two animal breeds hated one another. Finally, dog excrement introduced exotic plants into an ecosystem.

Disregarding all of this, the young man allowed his dog to escape his car, and the dog, panting from the heat, leaped into a hot spring of 192 degrees Fahrenheit. The young man dove in to save the yelping, helpless animal, somehow thinking himself less vulnerable to the scalding than his pet. Both man and dog died of their injuries and massive dehydration.

Another like story involved a little boy who thought the spring inviting when he purportedly shouted, "I wonder just how warm the water is" and promptly stepped off the wooden-planked path to tumble in. The boy's skeletal remains were recovered days afterward when the hot spring spat them back up, finished with the child.

Devastated, the parents sued the park in a wrongful-death action.

Jessica could see little of the majesty of Yellowstone

below her now, shrouded as it was in darkness. She and Rideout had remained silent for some time as their approach brought them nearer Old Faithful Lodge and the ranger station there. Then without warning, Rideout erupted with words that seemed to burst forth like water from a busted dike. "In your line of work, Dr. Coran, you've probably seen it all, but you ever see a man killed by a grizzly?"

"No, no . . . I can't say I have."

"I did, once. When I was rangerin'. Went out with a search party for a hiker who disappeared. I'm telling you, it looked like a chainsaw had been taken to the man. He was cut clean in two at the belt. Blood everywhere, all over the snow."

"Sounds awful."

"It was high snow season, late November, most roads into the park closed by then. Guy's name was Teller, a real smartass who wouldn't listen to any words of caution, and him wanting to be a ranger someday. Who knows? Maybe he mighta made a good ranger if he'd lived. Hiked out alone one day, like a fool."

"How old was he?"

"Oh, nineteen, maybe twenty. His entire neck was missing. Head we found later, and the torso'd been left behind, but the kid's neck was clean chewed away. Sam figured he was running when the bear caught him on the fly at the neck and just ripped away with those massive teeth."

Jessica gulped at the image while the whirring and dipping of the helicopter vibrated through her ears and down to her stomach.

"Teller's other parts were scattered and buried in so many places, we never did come back with all of him. But we found his head under a hefty mound the bear had churned up."

"Put away for later feeding," she said with a knowing nod.

"They hunted that bear down. Rangers all knew him as

Number 63, tagged the year before, but after the killing, we all began calling him Ol' Claw.''

"They put him down as a man-killer," she said matter-of-factly.

"Yeah, like it's going to teach a lesson to all the other bears—Hanna-Barbera, Jellystone Park thinking, you know. We always had to deal with that kind of mentality, sanitizers . . . but to appease the public, you know. . . .''

"Yeah, 'fraid I do in my business, too.''

He shrugged. "Sam says, 'We do what we gotta do,' but hell if I ever could understand the thinking. I mean, I just don't get it. Never did. Probably what made me a bad ranger. Whole thing was Teller's own stupid fault. The bear was only doing what come natural to bears.''

"Maybe I'll get lucky," she said. "Maybe my man will run up on a grizzly or get gored by an angry bison.''

"You can always hope. . . .''

As the chopper neared Yellowstone's fantastic cauldera filled with lodge pole pine, Jessica imagined the thousands of tourists below, settling in for the night after long treks in the park of geysers and free-roaming bison.

Despite full disclosure in the newspapers about the killer, there still remained, she could be absolutely sure, an enclave of people here in the vast wilderness of Yellowstone who had been wholly untouched by the story. Few if any down at Old Faithful Lodge would show the least alarm, she imagined.

She learned that she was right, that there would be no general alarm sounded—nor did she want one—as she explained over the radio to Samuel Marc Fronval, a descendant of French-Canadian Native Americans and the head guy among the rangers here. She knew Fronval from years past, and he'd taken her warnings in such calm stride that she wondered if he'd gone feeble, but then maybe it was the place.

It was as if this place could not be touched by such gross evil, but Fronval had to know better. Still, it was a vacation destination for hundreds of thousands annually. People came here to view the fantastic geological wonders of the infinitely varied hydrothermal features of this region, from the obsidian sand at Black Sand Geyser Basin to the vivid blue, giant eye of Morning Glory Pool in Upper Geyser Basin. People came here to marvel at the extraordinary silica that dissolved in hot water precipitates as the minerals brought from the depths of the planet cooled to create grottoes and fountains and caverns turned inside out. Algae did the rest, painting the geyserite in all the hues of the rainbow. Rainbows captured in rock, strewn about the earth.

Jessica recalled in particular the spectacular Minerva Terrace at Mammoth hot springs as an outstanding example of the variegated patterns that travertine formed as it was deposited on the surface of the cooling waters of the hot spring. The place looked like a limestone cave turned inside out. The place made the clumsiest of amateur photographers suddenly gifted.

People were indeed here to play, to party, to have fun, and not to be concerned about what went on in the world at large. The fact that there was a serial killer at work, and that he was winding his way from vacation spot to vacation spot here in the West, and that he was bent on taking people's lives by burning them to death for some hideous purpose no one would ever fully understand except for the killer himself, remained of no consequence to the typical tourist or merchant preying upon the tourist. And God forbid that Jessica's manhunt should interfere with business as usual here.

Oddly, however, Jessica's radio call to Fronval below seemed to "devil" the helicopter pilot more than anyone on the ground. Fronval had promised to put extra men on alert in and around Old Faithful Lodge, the grand hotel of the park, within shouting distance to Old Faithful, where every thirty to thirty-five minutes, the magnificent, most famous geyser of them all spouted its hot whale spray to an adoring American public.

Still, Fronval promised Jessica a full green light when she arrived by having her way cleared, pleased to be hearing from her after all these years. Fronval had kept up with her career, and she his. He remained one of Yellowstone's best loved and most respected rangers.

Coming back to Yellowstone would, under normal circumstances, have been a balm to her, a reunion for her heart and soul. The place held a spectacular appeal that no words could capture; rather, it silenced men—and even women, she jokingly thought. It was a spiritual place, a place to renew body and soul. Perhaps this was its appeal to one Feydor Dorphmann as well.

Off the left side of the helicopter now, she could see the billowing clouds rising from hot water pools, searing hot springs that welled up out of the earth's crust at temperatures of more than 180 degrees, 205 degrees in other places here. Enough boiling water to scald the entire human race, she thought.

A handful of the pools were swimmable, but every hot spring in the park remained outlawed, off-limits to everyone, since only a trained park ranger could tell the difference between a safe and a deadly pool, and even some of these so-called experts had, on occasion, become victims of the pools and their own bad or impaired judgment, ignorance, or possible suicidal thoughts.

Jessica was immediately shocked back to the present when Corey Rideout shouted, "There's a fire down there at the lodge!" Rideout pointed down toward the lodge.

Jessica stared down at the scene, certain there lay a body in the flames below, a body that the killer, in his obsession, knew only as number seven. "Damn him . . . He is here. He is here!"

· TWENTY ·

Act nothing in furious passion.
It's putting to sea in storm.
— THOMAS FULLER

Feydor knew that time was of the essence, that it was only a matter of time before they caught up to him and put an end to his—*their*—plans. He was angry with his demon god for not allowing him to count at least the two men in Salt Lake that he'd torched, the two that had died in the hospital. But there was no arguing with the supernatural being, the source of evil. That meant he must kill two more here at Yellowstone before Jessica Coran arrived.

He knew she would come. Satan had assured him that she must, and he was right. Feydor had seen the approaching helicopter. She must be aboard.

He needed one more victim. The Tolliver woman was easy. He'd flattered her in her little gift shop downstairs, bought her a box of chocolates, and had shown up at her room. He'd used the syringe on her, and while she battled, bruising him in the bargain, he'd managed to subdue her and let the drugs do the rest. Then he did her as he'd done the others.

Time was fleeting now, however, and he had no victim in mind, nothing prepared. Still, he had his tools in hand. He just needed to be smart about this thing.

He wandered the hallways, going from floor to floor, looking at room numbers, trying doors to see if anyone had foolishly left one unlocked, keeping his eyes and ears alert, watching anyone who happened in or out of a room, up or down a stairwell or corridor. He began stalking for his next victim, number eight is number two, the lustful.

He needed a soul to send to that special rung of Hades reserved for those whose minds and hearts were filled with only lust. But it was late, everyone in their beds asleep, silent. Whom might he find to fill in?

"Return to the fire," Satan said inside his head.

"Coran is here. It's not time yet to face her. You said so."

"There, staring into the fire, you will find those who lust."

It appeared the only way. "Of course, the fire."

Feydor expected to hear Dr. Stuart Wetherbine next, objecting to this final step, but Wetherbine kept silent. Wetherbine had remained silent for a long time now. Perhaps he'd been silenced by Satan.

Dorphmann knew now he must return to the seventh fire, where people would be milling about, gawking. Somewhere in the crowd, he'd find the one whose eyes shimmered with a lustful glow, the sinner he looked for. He'd have to be careful, however. Coran and others there would be searching all the faces, too, searching for him.

Jessica had instantly gotten on the radio to inform Sam Fronval of the danger overtaking his lodge. Fronval shouted back, "We know we've got a fire! We've got help on the way."

"It's got to be him, Sam! The coincidence is too much."

"We found no one at the fire but the woman who died in it, Jessica, but he did leave a message for you."

"Let me guess: Number seven is number three—gluttonous."

"Jesus, Joseph, and Jessica! How'd you know that? Never mind, I don't want to know," said Fronval. "Victim was Lorraine Tolliver, big woman who worked in the gift shop and lived at the lodge, room four twenty-two.''

"If he's true to form, Sam, he's seeking out another victim as we speak.''

"Why didn't you bring more men with you, Jessica? We can't cover the entire lodge. There are more than six hundred rooms in use here. And each wing of the lodge goes off in another direction, like the spokes of a wheel. There's the original lodge and the add-ons.''

"If he doesn't kill again tonight, he'll kill again tomorrow night.'' Jessica then told Rideout, "Get me down there.''

"Gonna scare the shit out of Henry if we set down too close to the lodge,'' complained Rideout, the chopper pilot.

Jessica frowned and asked, "Henry? Who's Henry?''

"An old buffalo who doesn't roam with the herd anymore, but hangs about the lodge. He's been there for years, but he's unpredictable. I don't want him charging my bird.''

"Get me in as close as you can, then, without setting us down on a hot spring.''

Rideout did so, and Jessica said, "Get back up in the air, and radio us if you see any other fire than the one we already know about.''

"Will do, and good luck, Dr. Coran, or should I call you The Sanitizer?'' he joked.

"Thanks,'' she called back over the noise of the rotors. "Now get back up in the air.''

Jessica was guided to the location of the fire by a ranger sent to the helicopter in order to take her directly to Samuel Fronval. Fronval stood in the hallway, smoke haloing him, as he tried in vain to disperse the crowd of curious onlookers who were in the way. Jessica pushed through the crowd, looking all about for any sign of Feydor Dorphmann, knowing full well that he'd been in similar crowds earlier, watching her every movement.

She saw a small man somewhat resembling Dorphmann, and she pointed the man out to Fronval, who immediately had his rangers grab the man in pajamas, whose shock soon translated into swear words.

Others in the crowd, seeing the detention of one of their own, and being asked by rangers in hats and carrying guns if they'd seen or heard anything unusual, began to disperse. Questioning a crowd, Jessica knew from experience, was the quickest way to break one up.

Jessica looked in on the fire room, saw the ugly message left by Dorphmann, saw the ugly remains on the bed. Firefighters were still squelching small eruptions in the room. She backed out, her face blackened from smoke. Exhausted, she leaned against the log wall, Fronval telling her he was sorry to have to see her under such conditions but welcoming her to Yellowstone just the same.

She looked into his clear, blue-ice eyes, and saw the same man in there, but outwardly he'd aged a great deal, his hair now a snowy white, his face a road map of wrinkles, every one of them no doubt earned.

"Yeah, it's good to see you again, too, Sam."

"I'm due to retire in a few months," he told her. "Damned ugly thing that's happened here on my watch."

"I'm sorry, Sam, truly I am."

"Read about what happened in Salt Lake."

She glanced down the long, narrow corridor to see a thin, emaciated man carrying a black case. The man seemed bent on following someone, his step in tune with a woman ahead of him.

"My God, it's him. It's Dorphmann, there," she said, pointing.

"Where?" asked Fronval, staring past the little man she pointed at.

"There!" She raised her gun and shouted for people to drop to the floor, and anyone remaining in the hall did so. But Dorphmann was gone. She raced, stepping over people as she did so, for the spot where he'd been.

"Are you sure of what you saw?" asked Fronval, catching up to her.

They stood at a juncture in the hallway where four separate wings spread out in four directions, any one of which Dorphmann could have stepped down. "Any doors, maids' closets along these corridors?" Jessica stared down each section of the maze.

"This way," Fronval suggested, going to a maids' closet, but it was locked.

"No way he could've ducked in here."

Out of the side of her left eye, Jessica saw a flitting shadow appear and disappear in the opposite corridor wing. "There he goes!" she shouted and gave chase, her gun raised.

Fronval stayed close behind. He knew the complicated labyrinth of the many-sided, many-added-on hotel, which had stood here since the early 1900s, a place where President Theodore Roosevelt had slept. "All the corridors eventually will lead back to the main hall," Fronval assured her from behind. "He's got to be making for an exit somewhere."

"The only other exits are where?"

"At the ends of each corridor, but there is one door midway."

"For all we know he's booked a room himself under an assumed name. He may simply have ducked into his room."

"We'll do a door-to-door search of this corridor on this floor," suggested Fronval. "It'll have to do."

A door between two sections of the hotel ahead of them creaked closed. "There!" Jessica shouted, racing after, leaving Fronval catching his breath.

Jessica, out ahead, spied a shadow racing off down the hallway on the other side of the door, still hustling with a black case in his grip. It had to be Feydor Dorphmann. She was so close that she might get a shot off if she gambled, but stopping to aim could cost her. She could again lose sight of him.

She took the gamble, stopped, and leveled the gun as the disappearing shadow turned a corner and was gone. "Damn! Damn!"

She found a stairwell, and exit sign, and a window at the end of this corridor. She heard the exit door below open and she rushed to the window to stare out into the night, hoping to see him come into view, running from the building. She prepared to blow a hole through his damned head when he did so, but no one appeared from the exit below. A noise filtered up to her. Someone pushing through yet another door, a gunshot, and silence.

She raced down the stairs and pushed through a door on yet another corridor leading to the center of the complex, and there, on the floor, lay Sam Fronval, a bullet hole seeping blood from his stomach, his walkie-talkie lying some feet away.

"Bastard run right up on me and fired. I didn't expect—"

"Save your breath, Sam!" she ordered and got on the two-way radio, calling for anyone listening, "Get those medics from room four twenty-two to ... to ... where the hell are we, Sam? Sam?"

"Main floor, corridor B, near center exit," the old ranger said, moaning now with the pain.

Jessica ripped the leather pouch from the radio and tore Fronval's belt from his pants with an effort. She wrapped the belt around the wound, shoved the leather pouch in tight against the bleeding, small-bore hole, and tightened the belt around wound and makeshift bandage as best she could, all to the complaints of Fronval, who kept saying, "I'm all right, Jessica! Get on after the bastard! Don't let him get away now! Go! Go!"

Jessica wouldn't leave until others arrived on the scene to care for Sam. She raced off in the direction the killer had taken, finding herself in the deserted, stone-silent main hall, off which stood the gift shop, the ranger information station that posted the time for the next eruption of Old Faithful, the massive dining room, a breakfast place, a lounge.

There were exits on all sides and through any number of other rooms. It was before hours, so no one was working here. Not a sound to be heard.

Jessica looked up at the mammoth heart of the old hotel, a living monument to the early interest in Yellowstone and the great white American hunter. This area was the original lodge, the workmanship magnificent, lost to the ages. And everything was on a grand, gaudy Gilded Era scale. She imagined the Rockefellers, the Vanderbilts, and the Morgans, all the powerful barons of the turn of the century meeting here, settling on prices of goods and services, enjoying themselves in a luxury not even dreamed of by others of their day. The main hall sported a wraparound second floor and elegant balcony, so huge a hundred modern-day tourists could stand upon it and watch Old Faithful blow its fifty-foot plume skyward from this observation point and never leave their seats.

Above the second-floor veranda there were rooms and more rooms and additional floors. All the walls were lined with stuffed animal heads, from bison to elk to bear, and beside these hung great, opulent oil paintings depicting scenes and events of a bygone era. Native American blankets and rugs hung everywhere.

All of it stood stark, silent. She hadn't a clue as to Feydor Dorphmann's immediate whereabouts.

Then she heard a noise, a pattering, metallic noise. It seemed to be coming from the dining area. She pushed through the closed double doors to stare in at the elegant, wood-motif dining hall, where a massive fireplace, large enough to house a small family for a portrait picture, stood at the center of the room.

Dorphmann could be hiding on the other side of the fireplace and no one could see him.

She glided into the dark room, its lodge pine interior usually inviting but currently menacing. Again, she heard noise—the sound of muffled music, pots and pans, coming from the kitchen area.

She moved slowly, cautiously, her gun extended in two hands before her.

When all had calmed at the lodge and a fire company had put out the blaze, it was predawn before anyone took a breath. Rideout had come down from the air for good and had found breakfast in the lodge kitchen where he once worked as a boy, before his ranger days. It had finally dawned on him where he'd heard Coran's name before. Old Fronval had spoken of her on occasion when telling a story of how a murder in the park had been uncovered by a young female doctor and himself.

Rideout shook his head and stared out a back window, where he could see the east wing of the lodge, scattered ghost clouds from the geysers drifting by, and through a window, he saw a sudden rush of flame in a room several hundred yards away. He instantly got on the house phone and called Fronval's office, getting some female subordinate of Sam's.

"Fire! There's another fire! He's struck again, east wing, near the end. I'm going after the bastard!" he shouted over the woman's questions.

Rideout dropped the receiver and snatched a high-powered rifle from one wall, cartridges from a drawer, and began loading the weapon when the door burst open and Jessica Coran had him in her sights, shouting, "Drop the weapon! Now!"

Corey Rideout's call had had the effect of instantly re-calling the fire trucks into action. He and Jessica now raced together for the east wing, Rideout yelling after her to wait for him as he tried to load the weapon kept at all times in the kitchen by the lodge's number one cook. Rideout had known about the legendary cook, who carried his weapon about the place whenever he felt the need.

When Jessica turned a corner of the multifaceted lodge, she saw the figure of a man rushing away from the east wing, and then her eardrums were split open by the piercing sound of a high-powered rifle. Rideout had fired from behind her, and his shell ricocheted off a brick wall, stunning the fugitive momentarily, making him drop his case. Recovering from her own reaction to the gunshot that whizzed past her, Jessica now saw the running figure drop to the ground, roll about the concrete of a vestibule, and snatch up his case. Jessica raised her gun and aimed, but Dorphmann had kept going, ducking behind the wall. She didn't have a shot.

"Are you nuts?!" she shouted at Rideout. "You might've hit me!"

"Not a chance," countered Rideout.

She momentarily wondered if she shouldn't worry about Rideout, if he could possibly be, like others before him, currently in the employ of one Frank Lorentian.

"Just be careful with that damned elephant gun, will you? Stay here and direct traffic to the fire!"

Rideout frowned and replied, "I'm not letting you go off after that maniac on your own."

"It's my job, not yours!"

She made off for the shadow man. It had to be Dorphmann. Two fires in one night. It would end his kill spree now to conclude with her, number nine, as was his intention from the start, from the very first phone call he'd made in Vegas to show her how easily he could kill Chris Lorentian, to his now eighth victim in this latest fire: #8 if #2—Lustful.

Jessica made it to the vestibule. Behind her, she heard Rideout calling out to her to wait. She shushed him, her Browning automatic at her cheek as she turned to stare down the vestibule. In the distance, disappearing into the billowing clouds of geyser smoke ahead of her, ran the fire

Phantom. Behind her, Jessica could hear the sirens and the firemen going into action, and she saw Rideout's silhouetted figure directing them, the big rifle held over his head. Confused firemen rushed now to a second and distinct fire site here this night, once again waking all the guests.

She knew what the firemen would find in the east wing; she didn't need to see it, not to know that inside the charred room, they would find the fire-blackened corpse of the Phantom's eighth victim and the message #8 is #2—Lustful.

So now Feydor had filled his quota, all save #9 is #1, all save his delivering Jessica to his god.

Ahead of her, his shoes clicked on the boardwalk that led deeper and deeper into the Upper Geyser Basin and toward Hellsmouth. It had become painfully obvious what this fiend wanted of her; for her, by her. He wanted her to be swallowed by the waters of Hell, licked to death by Satan's tongue, to enter Dante's Vestibule. He would have placed one human soul on each level of Dante's Inferno. He was ready to come full circle to #9 as #1, as all his victims shared not only the same fate but also parts of one another, shared in the traits and human frailties that had brought them to this end. That, at least, was the thinking of the madman, the force driving him. He killed only those who deserved to die, those who deserved to die by fire for the savior, Feydor Dorphmann—Moses and messenger to Satan.

And Feydor was so anxious to see an end to it, even as anxious as she was to see an end to it.

He expected great rewards, she realized.

Behind her, the second fire raged out of control. In front of her, Feydor awaited her, Hell awaited her, Satan awaited her. Somehow, Feydor Dorphmann had gotten it into his head that Satan required Jessica Coran's soul as a crowning achievement in a string of murders. It still all added up to dementia.

· TWENTY-ONE ·

He maketh the deep to boil like a pot.
                                    —JOB 41:31

John Thorpe had wasted no time in contacting Eriq Santiva at Jackson Hole to inform him that Agent Jessica Coran had deciphered the final mystery of Feydor Dorphmann's strange and bizarre odyssey. Santiva and Gallagher were far closer to Yellowstone than Thorpe was. They could intervene far more effectively and speedily. They had an army of FBI agents under their command.

Santiva and Gallagher now raced toward Old Faithful Lodge, knowing that it was Jessica Coran's new destination and that she was close on the heels of the madman Dorphmann. When their helicopter approached the lodge, they could see the evidence of a new blaze below them, the activity of firefighters, confirming J. T.'s suspicion. Nearby Jackson Hole had been quiet, a decoy jumping-off point for Dorphmann's kill spree. The near capture in Salt Lake City had spooked him and he had changed his plans, or so it appeared.

On the ground at Old Faithful Lodge, the evidence of Dorphmann's presence could hardly be denied: two fires, one under control, one being battled as they landed. And somewhere in all the confusion was Jessica Coran.

Behind them, in radio contact, Dr. John Thorpe followed

in another helicopter. Over the radio, he was told the situation.

He blared out to Santiva, "We've gotta find her! Help her!"

"We're doing everything possible," replied Santiva. "Over and out."

Gallagher and Santiva leaped from the helicopter even before it touched earth, the powerful wind from the rotor blades dispersing the smoke, steam, and haze surrounding them, blinding them. They'd been in radio contact with Sam Fronval's people and had gotten word of Fronval's having been attacked, that he was rushed off to a nearby hospital, and word had it that Agent Coran had disappeared out into the Upper Geyser Basin springs along the visitor boardwalk that snaked inward for several miles along a honeycomb of hot springs.

Daylight had yet to break. Taking a helicopter over the basin might prove futile, but Eriq hailed J. T., who was still up in the air, to do so. They watched as the Salt Lake City police chopper carrying Thorpe turned up its powerful searchlights. Nose down, it zeroed in on the Upper Geyser Basin to begin visual pursuit. Santiva and Gallagher then raced for the boardwalk, which went in two directions where it forked in a huge circle around Old Faithful. "You take that way, I'll go north," Santiva told Gallagher. Both directions were obscured by ground clouds that swelled up from the hot springs here.

"Leave it to Jessica Coran to get into this kind of quicksand," bitched Eriq Santiva.

Before Jessica Coran stretched a lunar and Mars mix of landscape that must appeal to Dante or any aficionado of his Inferno, for here in the vast region of the Upper Geyser Basin of Yellowstone, encircling the wondering gaze of the frail human form, were Hell's venting ports, the lifeblood of Hades itself, touching God's morning breeze to singe His breath and turn it to sulfuric clouds. These clouds joined as they rose, moving across the land like the mightiest of ghosts heavenward, while still trailing an attachment for the dark underworld from which they came in the form of silicified rock.

As Jessica raced after the killer, her nostrils and eyes assaulted by the sulfuric acid, the stifling air all around her, she panted with running and swallowing the horrid stench that now enveloped her. The thermal clouds, at once beautiful, fantastic, alluring, captivating, and dangerous, now hid a killer who had enticed her this way, leading her to this time and place all the way from Las Vegas, Nevada, that first night when she heard the dying pleas of Chris Lorentian.

The killer had gotten off the footpath, or else he had stopped stone still somewhere in the sulfuric mist ahead of her. She felt dangerously close to the hot springs, which could be as hot as 180 to 200 degrees Fahrenheit. All around her she heard the gurgle and burp, the sputter and swallow of the superheated minerals here, as if they called out a chorus to the aeons-old *danse macabre* between good and evil here. She could no longer hear Dorphmann's corporeal steps on the boardwalk. Where the hell was he?

Jessica cautiously continued her pursuit. ''I'm here, Feydor!'' she shouted, her anger rising. ''For the first time you have to face a lucid victim, someone with her senses intact. You cowardly bastard!'' She hoped insults might instigate a mistake on his part. She listened for any sound.

Nothing.

''Feydor! Feydor Dorphmann! It ends here!'' she shouted.

''Yes! Agreed!'' he shouted back and her gun went instinctively to the direction from which his voice came. She fired twice into the mist, his form hidden in the steam clouds ahead of her.

''You stand before the Vestibule, the mouth of Satan and the River Acheron,'' he shouted, and again her gun went up and fired at the sound, this time in another direction.

"Number nine is number one, *you*, Jessica Coran." Again she fired, this time three shots. She had two left in the Browning.

"Sonofabitch," she muttered, trying to hold her gun firmly on him, or what appeared ahead as possibly him, possibly a tourist who had gotten between them. She prepared to put a bullet through his brain, his heart, whatever it took, should he make one move toward her.

"Number nine is number one in Dante's *Inferno*, isn't it, Dorphmann," she replied. "That would be Limbo, now, wouldn't it?" she asked. "Satan has asked you to send me there, and that's the reason for this entire deadly charade, isn't it? Isn't it?"

The dark figure ahead of her spoke. "Yes, I knew that you would finally understand . . . Wetherbine never fully believed, but you . . . you do, don't you? You know the power of the Dark One."

"I understand this much, mister: If there's going to be a ninth fire for a soul to be placed in Limbo, it'll be your damned soul and not mine."

A thick, choking cloud of sulfuric mist suddenly divided them, Feydor's form disappearing before her eyes. She fired where his heart had been, but she heard no result, no thud, no outcry. She'd missed.

She leaped into the cloud that had engulfed him, running along the boardwalk in an area without railings now when suddenly she felt someone grab hold of her ankle and snatch her feet from beneath her. She held tightly to her gun even as she fell from the boardwalk and onto the spongy, cracked earth that made up the lip of the hot springs called Hellsmouth. She fought to get to her feet, fearing to stand and take a step, fearing the ground beneath her not solid enough to hold her, but it held. Then she saw him, standing over her, a pair of ragged sneakers at her eye level.

"Go ahead then," he said, "shoot me. . . . Kill me if—"

"If, hell!" she declared. "No ifs!" She raised the gun, but he had already aimed and fired from a Mace container, which she saw at the last moment before snatching her eyes away from the direct shower to her face. Jessica felt him wrench the gun from her grasp the instant she protected her eyes. His unearthly laughter followed.

She clambered to her feet and backed from him, in an attempt to avoid the brunt of the pepper gas he continued to taunt her with. She now backed frightfully close to the hot pool behind her, almost losing her balance, while her gleeful attacker followed with an attempt to shove her into the bubbling cauldron of the white sulfur and winking blue pit. She realized only now that he'd been under the boardwalk, like some ogre in a child's nursery rhyme.

She felt her foot slip and go under the scalding water, and instinctively she went to her knees to gain a foothold before the hot spring behind her, but she feared losing control as she clawed to stay on solid ground, fighting madly to regain her balance, just as he rushed her, kicking out at her, still laughing maniacally.

She dodged his first blow by rolling to one side. Screaming his victory, in hot pursuit and sure of victory, he charged, but Jessica brought up a board from below the boardwalk—left there for years, for this moment, for her to grab hold of—and she brought it against his charging temple. Both the board and Dorphmann fell into the pool, him up to his thighs, screaming with the pain of it, dropping to his waist in his frenzied fight to return to solid ground; the board was seared to boiling like a large hot dog, and then it sank below the superheated water.

He attacked with renewed vigor, although his legs and lower trunk must be tearing at him, burned as they were, smoke coming off his clothing. Unarmed, not wearing a second gun as was her usual habit, because she'd earlier insisted J. T. take it, she attacked him with a molten rock that had solidified here.

This creature was trying to send her to Hell via the hot springs beside them. The rock hit him solidly at the already fried kneecap, sending him dazed, reeling back, struggling anew for his footing, his lower extremities still seething and sending up a small cloud of smoke. Feydor Dorphmann now screamed in frustrated anger as well as pain.

"Get thee behind me, Satan!" she shouted the familiar biblical epitaph just as he lost his battle with equilibrium and his footing. He toppled for the second time into the hottest of the hot springs here.

She struggled now to get a hand out to him, to help him save himself, searching frantically for something at hand to assist, but there was nothing, no trees or branches nearby.

She tried desperately to pull him out, but he appeared rigid, as if rigor mortis had prematurely set in, his eyes still alive, still staring back at her. But he remained unable to move, dead in the water—shock and rapid dehydration, she guessed. He was next pulled under by the heavy, hot saliva of Hell, and she somewhat gratefully watched him go, thinking him the most grateful of the grateful dead now . . .

Taking a deep breath and regretting it, for she'd filled her lungs with the sulfur fumes free-floating here, Jessica fell back against the earth at the edge of Hell, and relaxed her guard now, panting, catching her breath. Her breathing was just returning to normal when suddenly the scalding waters beside her erupted and Dorphmann's hand reached from Hell to take hold of her, his body surging upward, taking hold of her ankle, desperately attempting to drag her down with him, using his body weight against her.

Jessica kicked wildly out at him again and again, ramming her heels into him until both her shoes fell away and turned to searing, inert balls of boiling gruel before her eyes as Dorphmann continued to struggle to bring her into Hellsmouth with him.

His face emerged in a mask of madness and sloughing

skin, portions of his face peeling away with the weight of the superheated waters that had infiltrated every pore and the spaces between his cells, turning him into a gelatinous creature.

Jessica pulled away and his palms came away with her while his bone remained with him.

She pulled farther and farther away, gasping and crying as she did so, frightened beyond all reason, seeing him rise now in some superhuman way from Satan's belly until he crawled on all fours from the pool, flopping onto the ground beside her, still desperately trying to pull her back in and down with him, a look of deepest pleading on his seared features, his white-red boiled skin falling away, tumbling with his eyebrows from his brow, his eyes now two red, unseeing oranges.

He was blind, his eyes having been boiled away. His skin sloughed off in a pasty, gelatinous material, exposing bone in places; what seemed an entire foot slipped off and, like a mackerel, slithered back into the nearby, bubbling pool, claimed by it.

It was too late for medical assistance for Dorphmann. He died in a blinding, searing, white-hot liquid heat that had become a part of him. Jessica kicked out again and again to release the frozen, solidified hold on her ankle, and when the monster's hand came off, the rest of him slid down into the pool. There, his clothing and skin finally consumed by Hellsmouth, the flesh became fishy and it wobbled and flopped from his every bone, his face a mask of pain so intense that a frozen rictus smile would forever remain.

He's dead . . . He's got to be dead now, she assured herself. Dead of dehydration and the burns suffered over one hundred percent of his evil body and brain. Only silicified bone and teeth would remain, if anything of him at all could be salvaged from Hellsmouth.

He still blindly reached out to her again and moaned in

a sepulchral voice, "I didn't want to do it. He made me do it. . . . Now he's got me. . . ."

Jessica passed out as the dead man slipped away from her, back into the cauldron.

When she opened her eyes, Jessica found a crowd of onlookers staring and shouting at the scene, some calling for medical assistance.

Jessica found that her own burns frightened some of the onlookers. Dirt and tears stained her face. Her blouse ripped, her skirt torn, her shoes missing, she was lifted onto the boardwalk by Rideout and some of Fronval's rangers. Rangers with salves and clean gauze bandages began to wrap both her ankles and her hands where she had been scalded either by Hellsmouth's waters or Dorphmann's touch. She heard the words "second-degree burns" and "third-degree burns," but she felt no pain.

From the other side of the crowd, she heard J. T.'s voice and that of Eriq Santiva, each calling out her name, terrified of what they would find when the crowd parted around her. The cavalry had arrived just a bit late, but all the same, she was pleased to know that J. T. and Eriq were nearby.

J. T. fell to his knees over her, his hands feeling for any broken bones, his questions coming at her in rapid succession. "Are you hurt? Where does it hurt? How bad are the burns? Get those bandages around her wrists, hands, ankles before any infection can set in."

Santiva, equally concerned, now held her head in his lap, looking down over Jessica, asking if she were all right.

"I'm fine. A few aches and pains, but I'll survive. For some reason, I don't feel the burns."

"That's because you're in shock!" J. T. shouted at her, chastising her. "You fool, you bloody fool. You might've gotten yourself killed. You might be at the bottom of that searing hot pool right now."

Neil Gallagher now knelt over her, shaking his head. "I have to agree with Dr. Thorpe on that score, Coran. And Dorphmann, the Phantom? What's happened to him? Has he escaped into the park? Shouldn't we be launching a manhunt, Santiva?'' he asked.

Jessica realized only now that no one besides her had actually seen the horror of Feydor Dorphmann's end, that no one else had witnessed the death. She imagined Karl Repasi's smug and debunking attitude now: With no body, who was to say if Dorphmann had actually been killed here or not? She was the only person alive to see him removed from this world. If nothing of Dorphmann were ever retrieved from Hellsmouth, there would always remain an element of doubt on the part of others. She alone would know the truth, that the monster had been relegated to another, more scorching environment.

Jessica's mouth had gaped open with her thoughts.

"Well, Dr. Coran?" pushed Gallagher.

"Let her be," snapped Thorpe.

Jessica said, "Someone here must've seen what happened to Dorphmann!"

"He's resting comfortably in Hellsmouth," pronounced Corey Rideout over Santiva's and Gallagher's considerable shoulders. "Isn't that right, Dr. Coran?"

Karl Repasi came into Jessica's line of vision, and she heard him ask, "Is that right, Dr. Coran?"

Jessica's eyes lit up, and she reached out with her half-bandaged right hand, the bandage like a spectral gauze peeling from a mummy, laden as it was now with the sulfur-filled, phantasm-like breezes here. She pointed to Rideout, asking, "Then you saw him die?"

Everyone turned to Rideout for an answer. He'd been ahead of the other men with his high-powered rifle, in search of the killer and first to hear Jessica's distressed cries, and first to find Jessica here. It had been Rideout who had lifted her onto the boardwalk with the help of other rangers.

"Well?" asked Santiva, "Did you see the man drown in that?" He pointed to the boiling, steaming water alongside the boardwalk.

Rideout had their attention, including Jessica's. His answer must corroborate her story. It meant at least a second witness to the man's final demise, that she would not be alone in that judgment, as she had been alone all along with the man's evil phone calls.

"Well, no, I didn't exactly *see* him go down, no . . . but I sure heard his screams, screams straight outta Hell. All the rangers and savages with me—park employees, I mean—they all heard him, too, didn't you, boys?"

A wave of agreement went up among the rangers and park employees, known in Yellowstone parlance as savages.

"He tried to drag me into Hell with him," she explained. "Had some idea that an exchange would be made, that his soul would be set free for mine. It was some supernatural message he'd received from the ruler of Hades himself."

"Satan himself wanted a go at you, heh, Dr. Coran?" asked Repasi. "That should play big in the press."

"Shut up, Karl!" shouted J. T., losing control. "One more word from you and I'll knock your lights out."

Repasi ignored J. T., continuing with, "You must admit, Jessica, your ahhh . . . *relationship* with this fiend is big news. The *National Enquirer*'s gotten hold of it."

"And how much did they pay you for it, Karl?" snapped Santiva.

"Damn you, Repasi," J. T. exploded, gaining his feet and shoving the other man away from Jessica. "Go chew on somebody else's bones." When J. T. returned to Jessica, continuing to minister to her medical needs, he said to her, "Karl's rantings can't be taken any more seriously than those of that madman Dorphmann."

Repasi called out, "I never meant to imply for one moment that Jessica was the root cause either of this man's obsession or the god-awful acts he has committed in the name of that obsession."

"Well, thank you for that," replied Jessica, but she

didn't believe Karl was here in the interest of mending fences.

Gallagher quickly agreed with Repasi's last words. "Dr. Repasi is absolutely correct, Dr. Coran. Listen to him."

"Thank you, gentlemen," she replied. "Whatever the truth, we may never know, not completely. All the same, I'm just glad that we've been able to put an end to this madness."

"But did we?" asked Repasi. "Or did Dorphmann end it?"

"Either way, it's over," Jessica countered. "Thank God."

"Whose god, yours or Dorphmann's?"

"Goddamn you, Repasi," said J. T. "I mean, it! Shut up!"

Around them, the park was coming awake, into the light of a new dawn. There was a softness to the light as it filtered in among the steam pools here, like a scene filmed through a filter, Jessica thought.

"Dorphmann was a raving lunatic, a madman," muttered Santiva. "No doubt his god was also a lunatic."

"A lunatic god," muttered Repasi. "Very good, Agent Santiva."

Eriq ignored Repasi and spoke directly to Jessica. "We'll have the pool dredged now that light is coming on. We'll recover the body."

"Maybe the skeletal remains, the bone and teeth," she replied, "but nothing else."

J. T. quickly added, "We have the bastard's dental records. We'll ID him."

"Problem is, sometimes these pools don't give back anything of a person who's fallen victim to 'em," said Rideout. "We might get lucky, maybe in a few days, what little remains of the man might rise to the surface, maybe not."

"Just hafta wait and see's all," added one of the rangers standing by.

"How's Sam Fronval?" asked Jess.

"Hold still, Jess," complained J. T. as he continued bandaging her hands. "Both your hands are badly scalded. It's going to be a while before you wield a scalpel again."

"How bad, J. T.? How bad is Fronval?"

The ranger in charge replied, "Sam's a tough ol' bird. From what everyone could tell, he's going to be all right. The medics took him on down to Mammoth, to the hospital there. He was sittin' up and cursin' when they hauled his ornery ass off."

This made for an eruption of laughter from all those who knew Sam.

"I'm more worried about your burns, Jess," J. T. told her.

Jessica considered her injuries. "I don't feel any pain. How bad off can I be?"

"You will," he replied.

Her eyes implored him for the truth.

"Don't worry. Like I said, it'll take some time, but you'll heal. Your ankles and feet aren't quite so badly burned. You must have had quite a struggle with that maniac. I can't believe you got so close!" He was angry with her. "Can't believe you let him get his hands on you. Damn you, Jess." J. T. was near to tears, and to combat them, he finished off the bandages about her feet and ankles, shouting orders to the rangers to get a stretcher out to them and to have an ambulance waiting, that he wanted Dr. Coran transported to the nearest burn facility.

"That'd be Mammoth hospital, over to Mammoth," said Rideout. "We don't need to wait for assistance. I'll take her in my bird."

Jessica felt herself being lifted in the hands of her pallbearers, but these pallbearers were carrying her away from the death that Dorphmann and his Devil had planned for her, Gallagher, Repasi, J. T., Santiva, and Rideout, all fussing for the privilege to help her away from the grave. She closed her eyes, exhaustion settling in over her, and she blacked out.

· EPILOGUE ·

Fire is an event, not an element.
—STEPHEN PYNE

Later, at Old Faithful Lodge, the team recuperated, sitting out on the massive deck, drinks in hand, watching from comfortable knotty pine chairs the eruption of Old Faithful every half hour or so. Everyone was pleased that the Phantom had finally been put down, and a twenty-four-hour watch had been placed on Hellsmouth in the hope that something of Feydor Dorphmann might return to the cauldron's surface.

Jessica remained in Mammoth for now, her injuries being attended to by people who knew a great deal more about rehabilitating burned tissue than J. T. or Repasi or anyone else on the deck here. The bus that Feydor Dorphmann had been using for the greater part of his trek to his wished-for freedom from his demon had arrived, bus 67, carrying its cargo of sight-seeing passengers and Doris, the tour guide. J. T. recognized the VisionQuest bus as soon as it pulled up at midday. Had Dorphmann not been interfered with in Salt Lake City, if J. T. hadn't run down the bus and tour group that one Chris Dunlap had attached himself to, if Dorphmann hadn't had the run-in with Warren Bishop, the fiend might well have remained on this schedule, today's schedule. Feydor Dorphmann would be arriving this moment at Old Faithful Lodge, awaiting Jessica's arrival in a less agitated state of mind, far more prepared to face her and put an end to his fevered brain one way or another.

J. T. considered this possibility. What might Dorphmann have done differently had he the luxury of time? The night Dorphmann had arrived here, he believed he must kill two more sinners for his crusade or puzzle before facing down Jessica Coran. Dorphmann had hastily done just that, killing two more innocent bystanders, hurrying his showdown with Jessica.

Again J. T. wondered how differently things might have worked out if Feydor Dorphmann were just now getting down from bus 67, which J. T. stood staring down at now from the deck overlooking the front entry to Old Faithful Lodge. He imagined the monster among the meek travelers now searching impatiently for their bags.

J. T. found himself vacating his position above the bus to stand at the side of the bus tour director. She didn't know who or what he was until he flashed his FBI credentials and asked if he might have a word with her.

"I could use a drink," the heavily made-up lady with the name tag of Doris replied.

J. T. waltzed her into the lounge, which was, at this hour, nearly empty.

"How can I help you?"

"I thought you'd like to know that Dorphmann, the man you knew as Dunlap, was killed here by an FBI agent early this morning out at one of the hot springs."

Doris's mouth hung open for a moment, and after a deep breath, she said, "That's good news."

"You don't sound convinced of that."

She was understandably shaken. She told J. T., "I knew from day one he was a sad man. Lonely, I figured, like . . . well, like so many. But he warmed a bit the last few days he was with us. Ask anyone on the bus. I mean, he seemed such a . . . a nice man. . . ."

"Really?"

"I mean after we got the ice to break with him. I mean he was always helping others on and off the bus with a smile, bought little presents in the gift shops not for himself or his family—guess he had no family—but for people on board the bus, strangers to him. Couldn't get him to join in on the sing-alongs, but Chris, Mr. Dunlap . . . Dorphmann, always offered a kind word to me about my voice. Said I was a fine entertainer, that I could play Caesar's Palace in Vegas if given a chance."

"I see."

"I just can't believe it—that he'd kill anyone, and in so brutal a fashion as they say. Are you writing a book, too?" she asked.

"Ma'am?"

"In Jackson Hole I met another medical man, an M.E. like yourself. Said he was writing a book in which this case would figure prominently."

"Oh, yeah. . . . That'd be Dr. Repasi."

"Yes, that's him. So, are you?"

"Writing a book on the case? No, not me."

J. T. thanked the woman, paid for their drinks, and said good-bye. He momentarily wondered how Karl Repasi intended to portray him in the book, if he'd be mentioned at all; then he wondered how Karl meant to portray Jessica, and he wondered if anything remained of the teeth in libel laws. Then he promptly forgot about Repasi and his damned book.

Several days had passed and Jessica had returned to the lodge, where she was the guest of the FBI. Santiva had told Jessica to take off as many days as she felt necessary, while he, J. T., Gallagher, Repasi, Rideout, and everyone else returned to their normal lives. Jessica was left to wonder what exactly "normal life" meant. She feared she would never know the feeling of a *steady* existence. She feared for her friend Warren Bishop, whose wounds had thankfully healed to the point where he was talking of leaving the hospital in Salt Lake City but the moment he did so, the FBI brass wanted to see him. He was up on charges of selling his position and influence, his connection with Frank Lorentian in this affair now public information. She worried for Warren, knowing that if he had any future with the bureau at all, it would be a dim one, three steps back.

At the hospital in Mammoth Springs, Jessica had received telegrams, flowers, and cards from well-wishers, friends, relatives, colleagues, and strangers. With hands heavily bandaged, she had a nurse open them all for her. One enormous flower arrangement had been waiting for her in her room, brought in moments before she'd come up from the ER. The arrangement's size and beauty, twenty-four mixed-colored roses, had her believing that it must be from James. A nurse read the card to her, saying, " 'Thank you for sending that murdering pervert straight to Hell.' Signed 'Frank.' And there's a . . . a sizable check made out to you, Dr. Coran.''

"Check? Let me see that.'' She looked at the amount. It was a stunning one-hundred-thousand-dollar check. She hoped that Frank Lorentian had finally found some closure in the horrid death of his daughter. Obviously, his answer to everything in life was wrapped in green. In the meantime, he had bought and paid for one FBI agent who'd subcontracted out to a once-reputable medical examiner already. And Karl Repasi planned an early retirement on royalties from a book that promised the unvarnished truth in the Phantom case. Enough was enough, Jessica concluded, and asked the nurse, "Would you please give these flowers out among all the other nurses on the floor? And make arrangements for me to see whoever's in charge of accepting donations for your burn center? I'll be wanting to make a sizable donation.''

That'd been a week before, and now Jessica was back on her feet, so to speak, with the help of a pair of crutches she hated. Jessica now hobbled from the lodge on crutches she was tiring of. She breathed in the fresh air of this morning, the sun bright in a cartoon-blue sky set off by milk-white clouds whipped up only in Wyoming. It took her considerably more time to get out to the hot pools on crutches than the last time she'd been here, but she made her way out to Hellsmouth, and now she stood over the bubbling repository and stared down at the spot where she and Dorphmann had combated for life. Nothing, not so much as a finger bone belonging to Dorphmann had been given up by the monster hot pool. The hot-pool watch for signs of Dorphmann's remains had eased off somewhat by now, most rangers and staffers of the opinion that Hellsmouth wasn't in the mood to return any fragment of its catch.

Clouds of sulfur, white and shapeless, rose up to greet Jessica, taunting her with their silent, unending parade from out of the depths of this place. She agreed with the rangers: Nothing of Feydor Dorphmann would ever be found here, and what little of him that might be coughed up would quickly be covered over by layers of silicified mud and rock, in which case the only way to recover his skull or teeth or bones would be to launch a bizarre archaeological dig here. Not likely, she conceded. Not at the expense of time and money and energy required to cover the entire lip of the searing hot pool that stretched away from her in an irregular circle with roughly a hundred-yard diameter.

Alone now for the first time since Feydor Dorphmann had attempted to drag her into the Inferno with him, Jessica stared deep and long into the blistering, watery abyss that had claimed Dorphmann. With the sun at her back, Jessica's shadow rippling atop the pool, this place didn't look as frightening and fearful as it had in the dark. She could see the pretty blue eye of the burning cauldron; she could see into the winding depths of the pool, the epicenter that appeared to reach down into Dante's Inferno, to the River Styx, the City of Dis, where suicides wandered the Forest

of the Dead. She imagined the hot spring as the liquid eye
of Satan himself, ever glancing upward into the world of
man, ever anxious to make of man a monster after his own
failed angel's heart. She saw the allure of the pool here
beneath the sun, God's eye.

Somehow no one else, no matter how close, not J. T.,
not Eriq, not even Jim Parry would ever completely understand what had happened here between her and this man
she had never known before his first contact with her. The
others did, however, understand her need to be alone for
a while, that she needed time and space and aloneness,
something only mystics, seers, and old wise men in Hawaii
and a few other places on the globe understood. Still, J. T.
and the others, and even James, who'd called on hearing
of her hospital stay, understood and respected her privacy.

She needed peace. She needed to sort out things.

She needed to face her own devils and hopefully come
away a better, more enabled person and not the shattered
creature that Feydor Dorphmann had become.

She leaned a little toward the pool and spit into it.
"Damn you!" she shouted into the pool. "Damn you,
Dorphmann, and all your kind!"

A large, gaseous bubble arose in response, sending a
flume of sulfuric acid skyward and near Jessica's face.

"Tit for tat, heh?" she asked the natural formation,
which seemed to mock her.

Overhead she heard the wild, free cry of an eagle, and
she looked upward to see it disappear into the sun. Still
leaning on her crutches, she felt one of them give way as
it slid off the boardwalk, almost sending her over the side.
She regained her balance, gasping and kneeling before the
fiery pool.

She felt weak, helpless before the enormity of the evil
she felt dwelling here, spouting its venom into the atmosphere. She had only destroyed a man who'd been touched
by this evil via birth, the brain, the DNA perhaps. She
hadn't begun to destroy the evil itself. She knew it would

return with a vengeance, a vengeance directed at her, again and again.

"Pardon me, miss," came a voice to her left, "but suicide is no answer to anything."

She'd gone to her knees, attempting to retrieve the lost crutch. She looked up at an elderly man in jogging fatigues offering her a hand.

"No, you misunderstand," she told him. "I . . . I just dropped my crutch." Her hands, wrists, and feet had healed well, as she'd been told by the Mammoth doctors, but the bandages made her look like the leftover result of a previous suicide attempt. It was not surprising that the old man thought so, too.

"Of course," the man replied, "how clumsy of me to suggest—"

"Could you reach my crutch?"

The man obliged, actually stepping off the boardwalk to retrieve the crutch. "Be careful," she pleaded.

"There's something odd here," he said.

"What's that?"

"Something down here, below the walkway."

Jessica leaned in and stared below the walk to see a discarded black case, Dorphmann's case, the case he'd been carrying that night. Why had no one else found it?

"Can you reach it?" Jessica asked the stranger.

He used the crutch to lift the case handle and inch it from below the walk, under which all manner of strange green growth flourished atop the lunarlike surface of the silicified earth here. In a moment, both crutch and briefcase clattered noisily onto the boardwalk. "What's in it?" asked the curious jogger now.

Jessica itched to open the case. It had to be Dorphmann's legacy. Who else might have left it at this exact spot?

"Quickly, open it," said the stranger as he climbed back onto the boardwalk.

Her fingers held over the clasps. *Maybe there is a reason*

why I'm here, she thought, conversing with herself. *Why the killer brought me to this place, and perhaps I just found it.*

"Open it up!" insisted the man, a gleaming curiosity filling his green eyes, his white beard showing his agitation as it bobbed.

Dorphmann was no fool. He had led her from the start, as if she had a ring in her nose and he a rope. If he put the case here for her to discover after his death . . .

The old man grabbed the case, saying, "It's mine. I found it. Whatever's inside belongs to me."

"Damn it, mister, it's evidence in a crime that occurred here. I'll have to confiscate the case, sir. And I don't want it opened until it can be checked out by a bomb squad."

"Bomb squad, fiddle-faddle. That's ridiculous. A crime scene, out here?" He threw out his arms, one with the case dangling from it, to indicate where they were, and he laughed.

"Careful with that thing, please! I'm the FBI woman who stopped Feydor Dorphmann at this very spot. Surely you've heard the story if you're staying at the lodge?"

"No, I've heard no such thing." He was clutching the case close to him now. His eyes and his body language told her that he didn't believe a word she'd said. He began examining the case, ignoring her. She'd come out in a pullover and jeans, and she'd left her gun and credentials in her room.

"Be careful with that thing. It's full of explosive materials. Butane, gasoline, who knows what else? Dorphmann may've rigged it to go off in the event—"

But the man had begun to step away from her, backing off, and Jessica had grabbed up her two crutches, trying to keep pace, imploring him the whole time when he cut her off.

"If you're FBI, I'm the King of Wales."

"But I am!"

"Where's your badge, then? Your gun? Show me some proof."

"I'm on vacation. I left all that in my room, but, but—"

He turned and jogged off with the case, going toward the lodge. Jessica futilely tried to keep pace. She saw him disappear into a sulfur cloud and turn a corner along the boardwalk ahead.

"Please!" she shouted when suddenly she heard and saw evidence of a fireball explosion ahead of her. The old man now came running mindlessly, wildly back at her, engulfed in flames, his hands outstretched, his head and entire body captured in its own holocaust, his screams like those of Dorphmann before him. Jessica realized that his cotton jogging suit continued to fuel the blaze that the briefcase-triggered bomb had begun. She saw that his left hand was completely gone, his right dangling by a thread of tissue.

A few feet before her now, Jessica attempted to tackle him, bring him down, and do what she could to smother the flames, knowing she had little hope of doing so. She could easily find her own clothing on fire. But just as she threw herself at the flaming figure, he went soaring off the boardwalk and into the spongy, moving earth alongside Hellsmouth pool.

Jessica knew that but for the grace of God, the writhing figure on the edge of the hot pool might well be her. Now the blazing, tortured man rolled into the now inviting, enticing pool in a vain attempt to end the pain of fire. Once more, she was witness to the searing, blistering tongue of Satan as it licked up the flaming figure of the man who'd only stopped in an attempt to help out Jessica Coran.

It was as if Satan, bent on destroying her, like a bad shot, managed to hit everyone around her instead.

The wails and flames and shouts brought other joggers and walkers along the boardwalk racing toward the scene as Jessica cautiously climbed down from the boardwalk, discarding one crutch, using the second as a futile lifeline to the stranger who'd first befriended her and then suspected her of lying. The man miraculously found the crutch and the strength to hold on by wrapping an arm through it, his hands being useless. By now, others along the boardwalk, alerted to the incident, were beside Jessica, and they helped heave the dying man crawling from the pit.

There was little left to save.

His feet slipped away from him like melted paint from a canvas, leaving only bone. Jessica knew that it was a matter of how long he'd suffer at this point. He had third- and fourth-degree burns over a hundred percent of his body, the jogging suit gone, the skin tattered, peeling away like soggy mattress pieces, sodden and useless.

All around her, Jessica heard park personnel and rangers yelling in a bucket-line fashion all the way back to the lodge that someone had fallen into Hellsmouth, that air transport to Mammoth or Bozeman was immediately needed.

A sudden last breath expired from the man in a cloud of heat, and then he, too, expired, a blessing, an end to what must be absolute hell, she thought.

Jessica now called up to the closest ranger and shouted, "Forget the rush. There's no hope for this man. He's gone. See if anyone recognizes his features, so we can identify him, notify any kin."

"That was a brave thing you did, Dr. Coran, pulling him back in like that," said one young ranger. "I never seen anything so gutsy before in my life."

Jessica was helped back to the walk, her crutches handed over to her, onlookers blocking her view of the steaming corpse, what remained of the old man who'd taken her place out there in Hellsmouth.

Now a kid ranger called for assistance over his handheld radio, telling headquarters, "We got another dead body out at Hellsmouth, and there's been some sort of explosion. Best get out here, sir." Through the confusion of noise, Jessica heard a young woman who worked at the lodge say that she thought the dead man was a Mr. Harmon, who'd only come in on a bus the day before.

Jessica found her feet, her bandaged wrists and ankles dirty and sodden now. She next struggled along the walkway with her crutches to the area where the flaming man had come from. She located bits and pieces of canister, briefcase, and flesh remaining in and around a bench where he'd obviously stopped to tear open the case. Debris littered the area on and off the walkway here where the man, consumed by his greed, had snatched open the case to reveal its contents, only to be met with a chemical bomb that spewed forth butane and gasoline and flame over him.

Unfortunately, it was not over in an instant for the elderly gentleman.

Jessica would have to live with this ninth and final death in the Dorphmann case, just as she had to live with the deaths of eight others destroyed by Feydor Dorphmann's mania as prerequisites to *her* death. Even in death, Dorphmann had reached out a final time, only to miss her once again. Still, he had not failed to fill the ninth level in his personal inferno with the death trap he'd set for her.

All along the way, Dorphmann had known her steps, and so he still did. He'd somehow known, in the event of his death, that she'd return to this place; and he had somehow known she would discover his final calling card.

She cautioned herself, however, saying aloud, "I dropped my crutch, which led to the discovery of the case. Nothing supernatural in that." But why had she dropped her crutch over the side at exactly the spot where the killer had left the firebomb? *Because that was the place I wanted to see again,* she cautioned herself. *That's all there is to it.*

More rangers from the Lodge began arriving, some instantly recognizing her, some keeping their distance. She saw Sam Fronval, who'd made a remarkable recovery, rushing out to her, his arms outstretched to take her in.

Sam had returned to finish out his final tenure before retirement, and to turn over his headquarters to veteran ranger Charlie Venable, a man of Native American parentage whom Jessica remembered from her first visit to Yellowstone.

Venable stood alongside them where Sam held Jessica and her crutches in an enormous one-armed bear hug, his left arm and shoulder in a harness. Venable, his ranger hat covering his brow, looked squarely into Jessica's eyes and gave a little gasp, as if he saw something dark and sinister in her. Seeing her return his stare, Venable gathered in the scattered debris about them with equal awe. Then he looked beyond Jessica, as did Sam, to take in the body still lying on the crusted earth between Hellsmouth's bubbling waters and the boardwalk path, some twenty yards from where they now stood.

Out of breath, Jessica nonetheless found voice to say, "Sam, we need to throw up a barricade around this debris and call in a bomb expert."

"What in God's name've you got yourself into now, Dr. Coran?" asked Charlie Venable with a little shake of the head.

"Moments ago, I was almost killed by a dead man, Mr. Venable, Sam. That's what's up. Buy me a cup of coffee at the lodge and I'll tell you all about it."

Fronval smiled and said, "Sounds like a plan. Take care of things here, Charlie, will you? Jessica and me, we have some catching up to do."

"Please wait for a bomb squad to get here," Jessica cautioned Venable. "I'd like to recover as much of the incendiary device as possible to reconstruct the attempt on my life from a dead man."

"Yes, ma'am, of course," replied Venable, a heartylooking, weatherblown man whose wild shock of hair waved in the wind here. Jessica and Fronval, each with wounds given them by Feydor Dorphmann, walked into the mist and away to the lodge, Jessica's crutches tapping out an anthem.

Venable turned and stared at the debris, seeing parts of it off in the distance, far from the safety of the boardwalk. They also had the old man's body to recover. It seemed to Venable, as it did to the other rangers, that the solemnity and peace of the park had been destroyed since the moment of Coran's arrival here, and it appeared that loss would continue until she left for good. No one would be more pleased to see her leave than Venable, just as he'd be pleased to see the last of old Sam.

The park was entering a new era, and new leadership was required, so far as Venable was concerned. Sam knew his feelings on the matter. There was no hiding anything from a man like Fronval. For now Charlie would take Sam's orders to oversee the men and the mess left by Coran here, but soon Charlie would be overseeing *his* men and calling the shots.

Jessica wanted to cast aside her crutches, wanted to make her way back to the lodge on her own two feet, but she still couldn't bring her full weight down on the burned feet and ankles, still in cumbersome bandages. It wasn't the first time she'd been left scarred by a killer; she prayed it would be the last.

"You'll have to pardon my savages, Jessica," he told her, apologizing for the stares and the underlying fear his rangers displayed of her. "They don't know how to behave before a living legend."

Jessica laughed at this. "Then Sam, how can they possibly ever behave properly around you?"

He laughed in return. "They don't! Let's go find that coffee, Jess. Then maybe you'll be up for a hunt?"

"On these crutches, sure!" she complained.

Sam laughed even harder and said, "You on crutches will do better than most *men* I know on two good legs."

COUNTERPARTS

GONZALO LIRA

A NOVEL

PUTNAM